How Do I Love Thee?

NANCY MOSER

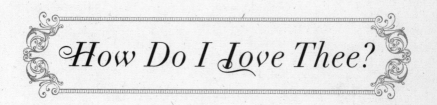

How Do I Love Thee?

A Novel

BETHANYHOUSE
MINNEAPOLIS, MINNESOTA

Published by Bethany House Publishers
11400 Hampshire Avenue South
Bloomington, Minnesota 55438

Bethany House Publishers is a division of
Baker Publishing Group, Grand Rapids, Michigan.

Printed in the United States of America

Library of Congress Cataloging-in-Publication Data

Moser, Nancy.
    How do I love thee? / Nancy Moser.
        p.   cm.
    ISBN 978-0-7642-0501-9 (pbk.)
    1. Browning, Elizabeth Barrett, 1806–1861—Fiction.   2. Browning, Robert, 1812–1889—Fiction.   I. Title.
    PS3563.O88417H69   2009
    813'.54—dc22

                                                          2009005413

NANCY MOSER is the bestselling author of twenty novels, including *Just Jane,* the Christy Award–winning *Time Lottery,* and the SISTER CIRCLE series coauthored with Campus Crusade co-founder Vonette Bright.

Nancy has been married thirty-three years. She and her husband have three grown children and live in the Midwest. She loves history, has traveled extensively in Europe, and has performed in various theaters, symphonies, and choirs.

ONE

⌇

"I will die soon."

My brother Edward leaned to an elbow on the company side of my bed. "Oh posh, Ba. You've been dying for years and you are still with us."

He was right. Although I had celebrated a childhood of good health, the journey through my teen years, my twenties, and now my thirties had been greatly spent in a position of recline. And decline.

Bro popped a grape into his mouth and sighed. "No one can die here, Ba. Torquay is the happiest place in southern England. The sea will not allow such talk. So I must insist you desist." The grape met its demise and another was plucked as Bro's next victim.

I pulled my shawl closer, leaned back against the pillows, and gazed out the window at the sea sparkling in the May sunshine. We had come here in 1838, and though our initial intent was to stay only one winter here, we had spent nearly two years away from our family's home in London, partaking of the salt air that was supposed to make me well. The situation had transpired due to an ultimatum from Dr. Chambers. He had informed Papa that if I were kept in London—with its soot and fog and unhealthy air—he would not be held responsible for the consequences. And so Papa had relented.

But unfortunately, in requiring such attention, two of my siblings had to accompany me: Henrietta as my helper and Edward as our chaperon. Other family came and went, and at times there was more family here than in London. I knew the situation was the subject of much tension back home—which was unfortunate—but I was not in charge. Papa was. It was regrettable that propriety forced three of us to be pulled from the family home, but in truth, neither of the others seemed to mind as much as I.

Henrietta—who, unlike me, found books and learning a bore—always discovered friends and society no matter where she was planted. And Bro . . . he was quite willing to lounge with me at Torquay if it prevented his being sent to our family's plantation in Jamaica, where he would be forced to do more than paint a few watercolors and see to his poor sister's happiness. As the Barrett heir, much was desired from Bro, although, alas, much was not expected. Bro took no interest in and had little aptitude towards carrying on the family business. It was as though he were waiting for Papa to *make* him interested and able. I loved him dearly, but I knew he was not distinguished among men. His heart was too tender for energy.

When Papa had made murmurings that it was time for Bro to leave Torquay and take on some business responsibility, I, in a rare moment of assertiveness, had insisted he be left with me. To gain my own way, I had even sobbed, begging that Bro be allowed to stay. On his part, Bro, as a true alter ego, had declared that he loved me better than anyone and he would not leave me till I was well. But Papa . . . I never forgot Papa's reply: *"I consider it very wrong of you to exact such a thing, Ba."* I mourned his harsh words, but my desire—yea, my need—for Bro's company allowed my shame only a short visit and was far outweighed by my delight in his presence.

And all had worked out well. Our brother Charles—Stormie—had gone to Jamaica in Bro's stead. So for now, we had received a reprieve.

Jamaica . . . the thought of that awful place forced me to pull my eyes away from the calming view of the sea. For my most recent decline had been caused by the news that our brother Sam had died of fever there not three months previous—dead for two months before we even received word. Funny Sam, six years younger than I, boisterous and witty, though admittedly, a bit too fond of drink.

Bro sat upright and pointed at me, making his finger dance an accusatory spiral. "And what is this? Sorrow in my sister's eyes? I will not have it."

I adjusted the cuff of my mourning dress. "I was thinking of Sam."

He used the moment to state his case. "Do you see why I do not wish to go to Jamaica? If Sam succumbed to its temptations, I most surely would—"

Temptations? I had only heard talk of fever. "What temptations?"

I watched regret and panic play upon my favourite brother's face. "I misspoke. Sam died of fever. That is all—"

"Apparently that is not all. As the eldest I demand to know the truth." My bluster was for show. I did not really want to hear the details. I was well aware of the peculiarities of my eight brothers and two sisters and loved them dearly, but in response to my familiarity with their characters, I oft preferred to turn a blind eye to their lesser qualities.

In turn, Bro, who knew *me* too well, gave me only partial disclosure. "Papa has warned us boys of the lures that dwell in Jamaica. So far from home, with great responsibilities and no family close to offer support and guidance . . ." He sighed with great drama—as was his way. "Sam was . . . Sam."

"Ah." I would let it remain at that. I pulled a volume of Balzac's *Le Père Goriot* close. "I do long for the day when we can all be together again under one roof. Although I may have found benefit in Torquay at one time, now I am too weak to bear being away. I find it dreadful. Dreadful," I repeated. "I am crushed, trodden down, and death nips at me from afar, but also from far too near." I sat upright to gain Bro's full attention. "What is there to recommend this place when my own doctor has died here?"

Bro looked confused. "Dr. Barry died months ago."

"Which makes his death from fever acceptable?"

"It happens, Ba."

"He was the only doctor I liked as a person. Back in London, Dr.

Chambers may be the doctor of the queen dowager, but I do not much like him. Nor others with fewer credentials. Only Dr. Barry was amiable enough for me to call *friend*."

Bro offered an incredulous look. "But was not Dr. Barry the doctor who scoffed at your habit of not rising until noon? Did he not command you to get up at an earlier hour and force you outside in the afternoon?"

"Yes," I admitted. "And I hold to my feelings that rising at such an early hour is barbaric, and the fresh air made me fit for nothing."

"After ten days he declared you better."

Of this I could offer dispute. "He declared my lungs better, yet I felt far worse. I was in such lowness of spirits that I could have cried all day were there no exertion in crying." I thought of Dr. Barry's greatest sin against me. "He *was* aggravating in that he forbade me from deep study. As a result I was forced to bind my Plato to appear as a novel so he would not ban it from my room. And as for writing my poetry, he claimed the toil of it was too much of a strain. Toil? Writing is my life. It is not toil. And he cannot stop me."

"No. Now he cannot."

Bro could be so . . . so . . . concise. But I would not let him enjoy the victory. I had a point to make. "As I said, Dr. Barry moved me, and now that he has died, his passing grieves me."

Bro crossed his arms and gave me a look of smugness.

I feigned ignorance, though I felt my cheeks grow warm. "Why do you look at me so?"

"This doctor, whom you fought at every ford, moves you, and is mourned by you?"

"In spite of our disparate views, he was the most amiable doctor I have ever employed." I thought of another point. "And for him to die when he had a wife who was with child . . ."

" 'Tis a tragedy, I do not dispute that," Bro said. "But it should not cause you to fear for your own demise . . . all this talk about death nipping at you."

He did not understand. The actual deaths of Sam and Dr. Barry reinforced the shortness of life. I thought of another example to add to my argument. "Then there is the death of Mrs. Hemans, a poetess like me—though of far further renown—dead at the age of forty-one. I am already four and thirty. The longest years do not seem available to writers of poetry."

Bro stood and set the plate of grapes aside with a roughness that caused many to fall upon the carpet. "Enough, Ba! Enough. Papa may have encouraged your grievous state with his lofty compliments of your 'humble submission' and 'pious resignation,' but I, for one, have had more than enough."

I was shocked by his outburst. During Papa's month-long visit after Sam's death, he had indeed applauded my bearing during my time of grief. I had never considered my behaviour as anything but appropriate and correct.

Bro was not through with me. "Do you not realize that others in this family grieve too? That perhaps they are in need of Papa's comfort as much as you?"

He had never spoken to me like this. "Of course, I—"

"Is not Henrietta's grief equal—if not superior—to your own? Were not she and Sam as close as you and I are?"

I felt my heart rumble in my chest. Conflict did not agree with me, especially if I was proved in the wrong. "I never thought—"

"No, you did not." Bro retrieved the grapes that had rolled to the edge of his shoes. He tossed them onto the plate. "We all loved our brother. We all grieve him. You do not have the exclusive privilege regarding that state."

Oh dear. I extended my hand towards his, sorely ashamed. Although I wished to blame my behaviour on the years of illness that had made me accustomed to close attention and measured words, I knew I should not fall back upon such excuses to the detriment of true, compassionate character. "I am sorry," I said.

With a small shake of his head, he came to my side of the bed, took my hand, and brought it to his lips. "And you are forgiven, now and always.

You know that, Ba. As you have forgiven me a thousand faults, I can forgive your few."

My heart calmed, though I took selfish pleasure in knowing that he *had* required of me more cause for forgiveness than I him. Although I loved him more dearly than all the others, he was not a perfect man. Far from it. There was a wildness in Bro, a carelessness that often tried me and made me wonder why it was that I loved him best. Our connection was proof that love is blind and often comes unbidden and without conscious reason.

As was his nature, Bro allowed the moment to be fully repaired and returned to his place on the other side of my bed. His countenance left his vexation behind and took on its more usual display of good humour and mischievousness.

"Would you like to hear some gossip?" he asked.

"Of course." I was glad to leave our dissension behind. "About whom?"

"About me."

I laughed. "One does not usually gossip about oneself; in fact, I am not even certain it is possible."

"It is when it concerns romance."

I tossed my book aside, needing full room to hear the next. "You are in love?"

He shrugged and brought one bent leg fully onto the bed. "Perhaps."

"What's her name?"

He wagged a finger at me. "I will not say. As yet."

"That's not fair," I said. "You cannot tease—"

"I always tease."

Bro took great pleasure in teasing me. But though I knew him to have an active social life, I had never heard of a romance.

"Do you wish to marry her?" I asked.

His smile faded. "My wishes will have little to do with the outcome."

My own smile faded. "But Papa would surely wish for the Barrett line to continue, and you *are* the oldest son. The 'crown of his house.'"

"At thirty-three, nearly too old. At this age Papa had already been married thirteen years and had eight children—or was it nine?" He wiped some dust off his shoe with the edge of his sleeve. "I will never understand why he forbids any of us to marry."

"He does not expressly forbid it," I offered, for I was always the one to defend our father from all slights against his character. And yet . . . I knew my comment was a weak offering.

"Oh no, there is no written decree," Bro said, "though there might as well be."

I nodded my acquiescence. Ever since our mother had died when I was twenty-two—a complete surprise to us all—Papa had grown zealous in his desire for purity and chastity in his children. Although it was in conflict with his own choice to marry for love and the happy marriage that had ensued, his stand on the subject was a fortification that none of us children had been brave enough to breach. "Papa merely wishes to keep us from sin," I reminded Bro.

He stood once again and made his way to the window. "Marriage is a sacred trust. There is no sin in it, not if the couple loves one another."

I had never heard him speak of such emotions. "So you do love her?"

He gazed out to sea. "Perhaps. Perhaps I could. If there was hope for a satisfactory end."

I thought of another complication regarding any of us ever marrying. "Is money . . . ?"

Bro turned to face me. "Of course money is at issue. I have no means for financial stability without Papa's intervention, and we both know that will not be forthcoming."

It was an insurmountable truth, at least for the near future. Some of my brothers were making their own ways financially—George was a lawyer, and the other boys were in various stages of their higher education with great hopes of gainful employment lying at their feet. Yet Bro had never excelled in school or in business. The benefit of his staying with me in Torquay had been mine. It had not done his future any good. Was it my fault that Bro was not financially stable?

Then I thought of a way I might be able to make amends. "I could help you," I said. "My inheritance from Grandmother Moulton's estate, and some from our uncle's. . . . Although I have to be cautious, I do have some means."

He raised an eyebrow, making me remember what might be a point of acrimony between us.

"Forgive me for bringing that up," I said. "That Uncle would single me out, out of all the nieces and nephews . . ." I smoothed the throw that covered my legs. "I do not know why he did such a thing, nor why he set me up to receive income from one of his merchant ships."

"Stop worrying, Ba. You cannot help being the most loved. We do not condemn you for it."

He could not think of it in such a way. "I was not the most loved. The most needy, perhaps . . ."

He tucked the throw around my feet, showing once again how blessed I was to receive the abiding care of my family. "How much *do* you receive?" he asked. "I am merely curious."

I could have feigned ignorance, for I did not like to admit I had interest in financial details — I certainly had no talent with numbers — but this was Bro asking. From him I withheld no secrets. "Generally I receive two hundred pounds from the ship annually, and Papa has invested the four thousand from Grandmother's inher—"

"Four thousand?"

The guilt tightened in my chest. "I have had to pay for my own care here in Torquay. There are many expenses beyond the room and food. The doctor and medicinal bills are extensive, over two hundred pounds. In addition I must pay for Crow's lodging. I do not know how I would survive without her daily care." Elizabeth Crow was a godsend, the first maid with whom I felt a strong connection. She had a talent for taking charge. Even though she was eleven years my junior, she was a powerful and comforting presence in my life, one that I could not do without.

Bro stroked his chin, thinking. "I am not certain what I will do regarding matrimony," he said. "I appreciate your offer of money, but . . . it is too soon to commit, either to the money or to the woman."

I hated to admit feeling more than a little relief, for I was not certain how I would have procured the funds without Papa finding out. "When you know," I said, "remember I am here to help you. I will admit that the benefit of income is the freedom it bestows of not having to think about it."

Bro reached across the bed and squeezed my foot. "Thank you, Ba. For offering."

"You are quite welcome." With a sigh I realized I was weary of such heavy subjects. "Now," I said, "to lighten the day, tell me the gossip about Queen Victoria's wedding. I so missed being in London to see the celebration."

Bro gave me a chastening look. "You? Go to the celebration? Any event where crowds are present?"

I conceded. "I do not dislike crowds per se, but have no use for any individual contact with strangers. I am not comfortable with chitchat. Stormie and Papa feel the same way."

"Stormie does not feel comfortable because of his stutter."

And my reason? I did not take time to analyze my foibles. "My dis-ease with society and strangers does nothing to abate my desire for news of them. Come. Do tell."

Bro did not disappoint, and our afternoon was relegated to frivolous chatter, a fitting antidote for our more serious discussions, which had offered no resolution or satisfaction.

I was in a foul mood.

Although Bro's visits usually brought me joy or diversion, his visit on this day proved to be less than amiable. It was as though we were not on the same page, nor even living within the same book—a certain fallacy, since his life and mine had always been intertwined, two beings separated by a few scant months and destined to be soul mates forever.

15

And perhaps it was the weather. July was unbearable, still and hot, and even though it was but morning, the sea breeze was not strong enough to reach me with any degree of relief on Beacon Terrace. And yet from my sofa I felt *in* the sea. I could not see a yard of vulgar earth except where the undulating hills on the opposite side of the lovely bay bound the clearness of its waters. Whenever the steam packet left it or entered, my bed was shaken with the vibrations. An amiable setting, and yet . . . the stifling heat.

Or perhaps it was the story in a London newspaper that added to my mood. I admitted to the sin of gossip and often asked God to forgive me for it. But since I was so secluded, and since news and conversation in Torquay were incredibly mundane, I prayed the Almighty would allow me this one diversion.

Lately, however, the diversion had angered me. The newspapers were full of scandal. Lady Flora Hastings was a lady-in-waiting to the queen, and apparently, this particular unmarried lady was accused of being with child by Sir John Conroy, a man the queen detested because — it was intimated — he was the lover of the queen's mother. Apparently, the rumours commenced when Lady Flora began to grow larger. The papers were full of the continuing scandal, and the news that she had been forced to submit to a medical examination to prove her innocence. . . . If such limited measures as her self-declared blamelessness did not suffice to save her reputation . . . If I had been she, I would have shown the full boil of my temper. For the queen to ostracize her in spite of the proof that she was a virgin was untenable.

The newest paper in my possession reported that she had recently died of a liver tumor, which had caused her symptoms. She, only thirty-three and innocent, yet forever scorned without cause. How could people be so cruel?

It was into this mood of heat, anger, and disgust that Bro had come. He sprawled upon a chair, linking a leg over its arm. "I am bored."

"If you wish to be stimulated, read this." I extended the newspaper to him.

He refused it with a flip of his hand. "I have no wish to know what other people are doing, what merriment they are having in my absence."

"It is not merriment," I said, pointing to the article. "Lady Flora has died."

My declaration received a mere raising of his eyebrow. "That is one way to escape a scandal."

"But she was innocent and the queen never acknowledged—"

"At least she had a chance to experience some excitement."

That he could relegate Lady Flora's tragedy to a pleasurable stimulation . . . "You are shallow, brother."

"Of course I am. How can I be otherwise, embedded here in this tedious place?"

Embedded. With me confined to my bed. Did his use of this specific word indicate the degree of his enmity for the situation I had caused by being ill?

"You may leave if you wish," I said, flipping a hand at him, as he had flipped his at me. "Go back to London! I will be fine without—"

His feet found the floor and his voice adopted a patronizing tone. "But I cannot leave, my dear sister. For you are in need of a chaperon, and I am the designated lackey." He rose and bowed low with great exaggeration. "Your wish, and Papa's command."

My guilt increased, as did my anger. "You may leave," I said. "For as you know, I have no real use for you here. Since I do not leave my room, what need have I of your services? And as for lackeys, I find they annoy more than amuse."

He froze, and though his face did not reveal a change in emotion, I could see an alteration in his eyes. I had hurt him.

Suddenly, he was all movement, taking his hat, striding to the door. "Since my presence offends, I will be off."

"No! Bro!" I tossed the throw aside to stand, but it wound about my feet and I could not be free of it. "Don't go!" I called after him.

I heard his feet upon the stairs and the slam of the door.

Crow appeared in the doorway. "Miss Elizabeth?"

I rushed to the window and watched him bolt down the street, causing many a person on holiday to move out of his path. Never had I felt so helpless, never had I detested the lack of health that held my body hostage. A fleeting image appeared of the child Elizabeth, running through the fields of the family estate at Hope End, with Bro running beside me. Carefree. Laughing. Inseparable. Well.

I felt Crow's hand upon my arm. "You must get back in bed. You know upsets of emotions do your health no good."

Nothing did my health good.

Suddenly, the truth of that statement took me by the shoulders and gave me a shake. If nothing did my health good—in this place so far from home, which was causing Bro and Henrietta absence from *their* home— then I need not stay a moment longer. I could not stay.

I allowed Crow to help me back to bed, but when she began fussing with the covers, I said, "Please get me my writing desk. I have a letter to write."

In spite of the heat, she tucked the throw around my feet. "There will be no letters, miss. You must rest."

Although I rarely went against her wishes, in this . . . "I will rest later. I must write a letter to Papa. At once."

She eyed me a moment, then nodded and fetched my desk. Although I was proud to call myself an author, I prayed I would find the right words that would convince our father to bring us home.

～❦～

I heard the front door open, then feet upon the stairs. Good. Bro was coming back to me. I would have a chance to make amends. Earlier, in the afternoon, Crow had posted my letter to Papa. It was a good letter, persuasive and respectful. Papa did not condone disrespect, and I would not consider wearing that sin. I was excited to tell Bro that soon, very soon, we would all be going home.

The steps on the stair stopped, yet Bro did not enter. "Come in, brother. I am not asleep. I long to—"

The door opened and Henrietta came in.

"Oh. I thought it was Bro," I said. I looked at the darkness descending upon the day. "Surely he has returned."

Henrietta put her fingers to her lips and shook her head. Then she forced a smile. "I am certain he will come at any moment."

"I do wonder where he has been all day."

"The *Belle Sauvage* is a good yacht. It has won prizes at regattas."

It was an odd statement. "Yacht? Why do you speak of yachts?" I asked.

"Bro went sailing." She looked to the window. "But it is a fine day for such a thing. A fine day. Such a sea could harm no one."

"Harm?"

"No, no, surely not harm. The yacht is simply overdue. There are rumours . . ." She shook her head against them.

I too looked to the window. The darkness no longer signified the inevitable visit of my brother, ready to make amends and spend a pleasant evening in each other's company. With him not yet home, and with Henrietta's anxiety apparent . . .

She gave an exaggerated sigh. "While we wait I will ask Crow to get us some tea and scones. Yes, yes, Bro does love scones."

She escaped the room. I was glad to see her go, for her nervousness only intensified the fear that had begun to gnaw at me.

Alone in my room, I managed to get out of bed and stood shakily at the window. *Why are you so late, brother? Come home to me. Don't tease me so viciously. I am sorry about our quarrel this morning. Please don't test me so.*

I watched the sun sink into the sea, and with its passing, so went my heart.

And my hope.

❦

Henrietta dozed on the bed nearby. Crow lay sprawled in the chair, her head lolled back, allowing soft snores to escape.

I could not sleep.

I could not think.

I could only feel.

Too much.

And yet not enough. For if my emotions were of any use, then surely my desperate desire for Bro to return to me safely would wield some power. And if my emotions were powerless, then I had to turn to the source of true power.

I prayed, although my petitions held no structure, no noun, no verb, no adjective. My talent in using these structures of grammar was rendered worthless by my fear.

My prayers to the Almighty came forth in moans that words could not express.

⁂

The morning dawned. As mornings do. And yet on that day, I, who found hope in sunshine and blue skies, accosted them with annoyance. For how could the sun raise itself in the sky and the clouds stay hidden so the day could be deemed fully fair, when my brother had still not returned?

Suddenly, Henrietta awakened and sat upright. "Uh." She saw me. "It is day."

"So it is."

"He is not back."

Her declaration did not deserve a response. If Bro had returned, the house would be alight with celebration, not alight with verification of his absence.

As yet. As yet. I vowed to keep my faith. If only for my sister's sake.

"I will get breakfast," Crow said. She slipped out of the room.

Henrietta moved to the window, stretching her arms above her head. She gazed at the sea that I had grown to know by heart. Her shoulders lowered as the facts of the day came into focus. She turned to me. "Should we send word to Papa?"

I was torn. The thought of Papa rushing towards us from London gave comfort, and yet, the thought of Papa, broken with an anguish I wished no one to bear unnecessarily . . .

"Not yet," I said.

Hopefully, not ever.

❦

Near night on the second day, Henrietta burst into my room. Her eyes widened and she pressed a hand upon her chest. Her breathing was rapid and short.

"What?" I demanded.

Her gaze moved to the window.

"Henrietta!"

She rushed to my bedside, pushing me back in order to sit beside me. She took my hand, an act that made me wish to snatch my hand away, not wanting to hear the news that surely accompanied such an action.

Her hands were cold. "There seems to have been an accident."

I pulled away from her touch. My head began to shake with a compulsion all its own.

"A boat," she said, "was seen wrecked after an unexpected storm in Tor Bay."

I glanced out the window at the bay that looked far too innocent for such an accusation. "But yesterday was fair."

"There was a squall," Henrietta said. "Though short in duration and not fierce by any measure."

I put a hand to my forehead, trying to comprehend. "Who says it was Bro's boat?"

My sister shook her head. "At half past three, a yachtsman spotted a boat similar in description go down four miles to the east of Teignmouth."

A witness. A saviour. "Then certainly he saved them."

"He set sail for it, but by the four or five minutes it took to get there, he only saw the point of her mast."

An odd smile pulled my lips, reacting to the sheer inconceivable nature of this conversation. "But Bro is an excellent swimmer. And his friends . . . even if the boat went down, they would be there, treading water."

"There was no one."

"Then another boat picked them up first. Or Bro . . . he swam to shore and any minute now will come traipsing into this house, soggy wet and exhausted from the experience."

Henrietta's head hung low against her chest. She had already given up. I, however, would not do so.

I pushed against her shoulder, forcing her off my bed. "Do not sit there and mourn. He is alive! He has to be." I thumped a fist against my chest. "I would know if he were dead."

She stood a step away, her hands finding comfort in each other. "It is true they have not found any . . ."

I finished the statement, needing to bring it to full view. "Bodies. They have not found any bodies."

"No."

"Then there is no death to mourn. Now go and be useful. You have many friends in this place. Go find them and have them arrange search parties. If they balk, tell them I will pay whatever it costs. We must have full news. When Bro returns we must be able to prove to him the extent of our devotion. And faith. We must express our faith in God's mercy." I suddenly wished Papa and my other sister, Arabella, were here. They were the pious ones. Of all of us Barretts, they knew best how to pray.

In the meantime, I held out my hand and pulled Henrietta back to the bed. I clasped both her hands, and together we bowed our heads.

Once we had implored our Father in heaven, I took out paper and pen to send word to our earthly father, who was unknowing and unprepared for the news that must now be shared.

A burden shared is a burden halved?

I was not so certain, for my burden was the greatest of all. I had quarreled with my brother. I had sent him away.

I was to blame.

Two

Papa came to the rescue, as did my sister Arabel.

Together we waited for news of Bro's rescue.

And waited.

And waited.

Days.

Weeks.

Papa sent out search parties and offered a reward for information. We spoke with optimism of Bro's good swimming ability, and the thought that someone might have picked him up in their boat . . . perhaps he was hurt and unable to declare his name so word could be sent to us.

We tried to cling to these hopes, but soon they were dashed. The *Belle* was found on its side, and the body of Captain Clarke washed up. . . . He still wore a jaunty flower in his buttonhole. The image haunted me, the incongruity of the flower, now sodden and spoiled, an incomprehensible reminder of the joyful intent of that day upon the water.

Captain Clarke found. But where were the other three men—the pilot, my brother's friend Charles Vannek, and Bro?

The days poured one upon the other, blending together like milk poured into milk. We all slept poorly, awoke with questions upon our lips, and spent the days doing . . . something. All actions were blurred, done by rote, and quickly forgotten.

Today, as other days, Arabel and Henrietta sat with me in my room, needlework in their hands but Bro upon their minds. I, however, could do nothing of use. As one day slipped upon the next, I found myself sinking deeper, deeper within the abyss. I could not sleep unaided and relied upon the dear opium that had been my companion against physical discomforts since I was fifteen. Dreams took over my mind with nothing but broken, hideous shadows and ghastly lights to mark them.

And yet . . . although the condition of my physical being was usually the star of my life's production, while waiting for Bro it became but a secondary player. My mind, my spirit, my very soul vied for attention and support.

But none was forthcoming.

And none was deserved. For it was my fault Bro was missing. If I had not begged Papa to allow him to stay in Torquay with me; if I had not been ill in the first place, forcing my siblings to accompany me to this place; and if he and I had not exchanged peevish words on that Saturday, sending Bro away to find diversion elsewhere . . .

He would be sitting with us now, amusing us with some exploit among the locals.

Henrietta broke through the tumult of my guilt with a sigh. "Ah me." It had become her mantra. As was her repeated observation: "The seas were calm that day. It was just a freakish squall."

Freakish or not, that one squall, set apart from days and days of fair weather, had captured my brother's fate. . . . It did not seem possible.

Or right.

"God protect him," Arabel said. This was *her* mantra, and I was more than willing to allow her to repeat it often and pray for all of us. I gladly relinquished my prayers—which had obviously proven ineffectual—into the care of Arabel and Papa. Surely God would hear them above us all.

I did not respond to either sister, rather closed my eyes—not to sleep, nor to pray, but to travel into the cache of my memories. Although they had always existed, I had suffered no need to visit them until recently, when I'd begun to pull them out one by one, finding ease in *their* place and time far more than the dis-ease within the present. They were vivid in displaying their wares. I found memories of childish schemes Bro and I had hatched against the duo of Henrietta and Sam, and races we had run when he let me win—or not. I heard his voice singing songs to me, foolish made-up ditties about my pony, Moses, or the nasty way our baby brothers could smell, or even my tiny feet. Then came the memories regarding his love of parties . . . one time he and his friends had attended a soiree for the very foolish purpose of inhaling laughing gas.

Laughing. Yes, yes, Bro could always make me laugh. I could hear him even now . . . but crying too. For Bro was always the adytum of all my secrets and plans. Who would I confide in now, if—

Suddenly, the tread of boots upon the stairs made my eyes shoot open. *Bro? Is that—?*

But it was only Papa who appeared in the doorway, and for a brief moment, I saw him to be an older version of the one who was missing from our clan; our family that had already lost one brother and one tiny sister when she was but four, as well as our mother.

I blinked the image away and shut the lid on my memory cache for later opening. "Anything?" I asked.

He shook his head and entered the room, walking between my sisters and my bed, heading towards the window where he had spent endless hours these past weeks, gazing out to sea, searching, pondering, praying.

And then . . . his back straightened and he took a step closer, touching the sill.

"What is it?" I asked, sitting full upright.

"A man is coming up the street. Running . . ."

"Is it Bro?" I asked.

Henrietta and Arabel rushed to the window. I was slower in coming but had to see—

"It's not Bro," Papa said before I could even fully stand. "I see now it is but a young lad."

Henrietta put her hands on his arm, trying to see around him. "But he *is* running towards our house. Perhaps there is news?"

"I'll get the door." Arabel hurried down the stairs. Papa and Henrietta headed after her.

There was a knock below and my heart tumbled within my chest. "Crow!" My maid appeared at a run. "Help me downstairs. Now. I must—"

I heard the front door open, then voices. I had to get downstairs! I had to hear!

Crow put her able hands on my arm and about my waist. "Easy, Miss Elizabeth. You have not been downstairs in months."

"But I must. I must be there."

My body rebelled at my request for full movement, yet I could not give in to it. Not this time. I reached the top of the stairs in time to see my sisters fall into each other's arms. And then . . . and then their wails sped up the stairs and stabbed me in the heart.

The implications wove around me like greedy ropes, tightening, strangling, binding. *No. No. No. No.*

Needing more support than Crow could provide, more support than any human being could give, I gripped the baluster. "Papa?" I said.

He interrupted his conversation with the young man who stood in the entry beyond my sisters, his cap in his hands. Papa looked up at me, said a few words to the boy, and let him out the door.

And then he came towards me, one foot upon the stair, and then another, his own hand seeking guidance from the railing. He did not gaze at me, nor at the air between us, but kept his eyes downcast. I heard his breathing, far beyond what was demanded by the physical effort.

"Miss, oh, dear miss," Crow whispered in my ear. She pulled me a step back, allowing Papa room upon the landing.

He took over my support, placing his hands upon my upper arms. His grip was firm, as though trying to transfer the strength I would need. . . .

"What?" I managed, but only a whisper. "What news?"

"Your brother has been found washed up upon —"
I heard no more. Could bear no more.
I collapsed.

⧉

I looked at my pen, glaring at me from across the room. Daring me, taunting me. *Pick me up. Use me and I will set you free from your misery.*

Over two months had passed since Bro's body — and that of the pilot's — had washed up in nearby Babbacombe Bay. His friend Charles had never been found.

Two days later, we had buried Bro at Torre Church. Two months later, I still suffered. And two years from now? I could not imagine my condition would be altered.

Ever since the sea had greedily taken my brother from me, I had been unable to write either poetry or letters. That task which was so innate to my very being became elusive. How could I return to that commission which was so essential to my life, that normally flowed so easily, when Bro had experienced feelings beyond those we had ever shared: fear, panic, desperation, and the ultimate pain?

Yet also the ultimate release of death. I tried to loose myself from the bondage of the heavy, cold chains which had entered into my soul, by thinking, not of the moments before my brother's death, but the moment directly after, when all arduous feelings were dispelled with the singular sight of our Saviour, come to greet him and welcome him into paradise.

Although I knew Papa desperately needed to be back in London to attend to business, he remained with my sisters and me. He was our rock.

I owed him . . . too much. For I had caused his heir to die. He would not speak of it at all; would not let me voice my guilt. Bro gone, the second son, Sam, gone. The third son, Charles — Stormie — was . . . a nervous young man, shy, with an unfortunate stammer. George was a stuffy sort with too little sense of humour for my taste. Of the younger boys, Henry annoyed me with his stubborn, selfish will, and Alfred did not often fall or rise into enthusiasm. I could not condone such apathy. One must embrace life within the confines of the lot bestowed. To be apathetic . . .

The seventh and eighth sons, Septimus and Octavius—Sette and Occy—were still boys at ages sixteen and seventeen, and would always be boys to me. They were a sweet and enjoyable pair, always able to elicit a smile from those around them. But they were not near ready or able to take on the position of heir. Nor would the dictates of society allow such a thing.

Papa deserved a perfect child. Someone who would give him the respect, the interest, and the sense of his duty fulfilled that would allay his grief, his sense of hopelessness, and his aborted dreams. In spite of our shortcomings, Papa loved us all, and yet . . . my other siblings were immersed in their own concerns; and even attempted to push Papa to the edge of their lives—as much as was possible. No one loved him as I did. And so, since the love of my life was now gone, I vowed to love Papa with a greater love, a love that could look past his censorious ways. He was a good man. Considering my sin, he deserved all that I could give him.

He deserved to not have to worry about me.

Inspired by his sacrifice to stay with me during our grief and determined to strengthen my faith through witness of his own, I felt the responsibility—ready or not—to take up my pen again and write.

Not poetry, for my mind was still too muddled. But perhaps a letter?

That settled, I tapped a finger against my lips. To whom should I write?

Before Bro's death I had been in correspondence with many elderly gentlemen scholars, and had been immersed in a stimulating exchange with the editor and critic Richard Henry Horne. He was incredibly witty and frank, and enticed me with gossip and news. He had made my separation from the literary society of London bearable.

Yet I did not feel it proper to offer my first letter after so long a silence to any of these gentlemen, for the fact being they were . . . men.

I immediately thought of the women in my life, and my thoughts flew to one special woman who deserved the honour of my first intention.

Mary Russell Mitford was my best friend and a fellow author. I, who was not easily befriended and who did not easily befriend, had been introduced to this woman over three years past. Nearly twice my age, never married, devoted to her invalid father, Miss Mitford had achieved success with *Our Village*, a series of essays on country life first published in *Lady's Magazine* twenty years previous. Papa admired her work—which was not an easily earned compliment. He said the essays reminded him of our little world back in Hope End. A lifetime ago . . .

I sat back on my sofa and closed my eyes, once again letting memories wrap around me like a warm blanket. In hindsight, I was appalled at my reluctance to meet her. Papa's cousin John Kenyon, an affable gentleman who knew everyone worth knowing, had been forced to urge me for months towards a meeting with Miss Mitford. My disinclination had stemmed from nerves regarding such direct contact—I so preferred the physical distance provided by letters. Cousin John became peeved at me, telling me I caused him to feel like a king beseeching a beggar to take a dukedom. He had deemed me foolish, a blemish I deserved yet found difficult to clear from my character.

I had finally succumbed to his gentle but persistent pressure and agreed to meet Miss Mitford at London's Diorama and Zoological Gardens. At that time in my life's journey I still ventured into public on occasion, but the anticipation caused me immeasurable worry. Yet it was not the visit into nature that caused me consternation but the contact with this stranger. What would we say to each other? Would she like me? What recourse would I have if it did not go well?

As usual, my worries had made me ill. My heart beat with an alarming rhythm, and I paced my room all morning. Adding to my disquiet was anger—at myself. How could I feel at ease discussing all manner of intellectual subjects with scholars (albeit through letters far more than in person), yet spin myself into a web of anxiety at the thought of meeting a revered spinster woman who by all accounts was amusing, kind, and had interest in meeting *me*?

Yet upon meeting her . . . I was made ashamed of my fears. I was delighted to discover that like me, Miss Mitford did not partake of womanly chatter, but spoke of life and books and interesting literary figures she had met. The very evening before our meeting she had been introduced to the young poet Robert Browning, and the very next night was going to a dinner at Cousin John's home—to which I had also been invited—at which Robert Wordsworth would be in attendance. I had been fighting my fear regarding this dinner for weeks, looking for excuses not to go, yet knowing that the chance to meet this famous writer would prove irresistible, even amid my debilitating shyness.

During our meeting, as Miss Mitford and I walked among the chimpanzees and giraffes, I found myself sharing my life story with her, completely unbidden and unplanned. My childhood at Hope End, my mother's death, the idiosyncrasies of my family, my health, and my hopes and dreams of literary greatness fell into the fresh air between us and were nourished by her kind interest.

Burgeoned by the success of the day, the next night I did attend the dinner at Cousin John's with Bro and with Miss Mitford also in attendance. I sat right next to Wordsworth, nearly fainting from the very thought of his proximity. And yet . . . he did not impress me as I had imagined he would. He was an old man, his eyes lacked fire, and his countenance was void of the animation I had expected of such a great man who had written words that sparked my very soul. It was rather disconcerting to have my image of him dashed.

Another literary genius in attendance, who proved to be of far more interest, was Walter Savage Landor. He was opinionated, impetuous, high-spirited, and entertained Bro and me with witty epigrams. I enjoyed his presence as much as his work. His recently published *Pentameron* possessed some pages that were too delicious to turn over. On the way home, elated by the evening, I realized I had never walked in the skies before;

and perhaps never would again when so many stars were out. I continued to live on those memories. . . .

Memories.

Suddenly, the memory of that special night faded, and another memory intruded. The words I had shared with Bro returned. *I will die soon.* The impulsive remark elicited great regret. Who was I to say such a thing? Who was I to complain about my lot? I was alive, and though I was not well, I needed to accept the benefit of my condition and go forth—for Bro's sake, and for his honour.

Yet my heart was not in it. Each breath required effort, each thought was pulled from my mind with force, and each daily task was attended to by rote and with little recognition or feeling. I went . . . on.

What little energy I owned was used to mask my inner desolation from others who did not need to add worry for me to their burdens. I held my complaints in check and created a façade that carefully separated my serene appearance from the turmoil and angst which lay within.

How I longed to fully *be* what I pretended to be. Although I doubted it was possible, I was determined to try.

But who was I? Was I what people thought of me? Or someone altogether different?

Although I wished to think otherwise, to most people I was "the invalid," the middle-aged spinster who lay abed all day, rarely venturing out-of-doors. Added to that, I was the sister-in-mourning, a woman to be pitied. When people walked past this house, did they whisper such things to one another? "See that house there? The woman who lives there never comes out. Her brother drowned last year and she blames herself."

I looked towards the window, as if the parties in question were on the street outside. The people of Torquay had no reason to think any more of me. And beyond that . . . what *more* was there? Of me?

I let the pen and paper renew its invitation.

First and foremost, I was a writer. *That* was my calling, my destiny, my mission. The undefined illnesses that plagued my body did not define me. My mind, my thoughts, my feelings, my creativity . . . those were the things that determined who I was to myself and to the world. Those were the things that I had shoved aside after Bro's death, and even before. I needed to regain the stimulation of intellectual discussion, the passion of thought, the exhilaration of imagination. . . . My book *The Seraphim and Other Poems* had been published in 1838, shortly before I moved to Torquay. I had been absent from London during the time when it had received its first response, its acclaim, however small. I had been set apart from its reality. Removed. Ostracized by circumstances beyond my control.

But no more.

I must reclaim the life I had once lived.

How?

I had to renew the correspondences which had previously brought me great joy and purpose. It was true that since becoming an adult I had not possessed a normal connection with anyone. The usual chatter of society bored me, and I was ill at ease in crowds. Only through letters was I able to sustain meaningful discourse with others of like mind. In most cases, they were men. Much older men. Men of learning and literature, such as Sir Uvedale Price and Hugh Stuart Boyd, both elderly scholars who miraculously treated me as a peer, far from equal, but a contemporary who was willing to learn. They gave my writing genuine criticism—which I encouraged. Although a good poet is one of God's singers, it did not mean improvements could not, and should not, be achieved. If I only accepted accolades—whether the work be worthy or no—then I would be cheating the Almighty and revealing the sin of pride. Although I *could* be proud, I was not a cheater. I was also not a versifier as so many women were. I did not casually jot down stray verses that ambled through my thoughts. True poetry was sacred. It owned a dignity and sense of purpose, and as such, I strove to embrace those same traits as my own.

A few months earlier, in the midst of my mourning, I remembered Martin Luther had stated that a person's entire life was a task set by God. The idea planted then now moved me towards action. I would try to please God, and please myself and others in the process.

Towards that end, I rang the bell, calling Crow to my side. "The pen, Crow, if you please? And paper and ink."

Her smile was verification that it *was* time. "Anything else, Miss Elizabeth?"

"No. Thank you."

She left the room, and I took up my pen to write to Mary.

And yet . . . my hand trembled. I set the pen aside and flexed my fingers, willing them to remember their duty to bring thought to paper. I grasped the pen again and willed my hand to obey.

It acquiesced, though tentative and not without a flutter to the script: *Dearest Mary . . .*

It was a beginning.

⤙⋄⤚

Three months had passed since I had renewed my correspondence with Mary Mitford. I looked forward to her letters above all others, above even those of Papa, who had returned to London in December, leaving Arabella here in Torquay with Henrietta and me. Miss Mitford's letters gave each day a new purpose as we discussed our work and families and . . . life. But there was more than her letters which brought me anticipation. Mary was sending me a very special present, one I had objected to most vociferously and ineffectually because of its value.

A dog.

He was due to arrive at any time and caused me to rise from my pillows on more than one occasion when I heard a cart stop out front.

As it did now. Crow, who was putting some clothes away in the bureau, glanced at me. "It's just a dog, miss, which, if I be honest, I'm not too keen on getting. Dogs are dirty and smelly."

She was right—they could be. But they could also be pleasant companions. "It's good you've only been with me here in Torquay, Crow, for back in London, Henry has a bloodhound and a mastiff, and Occy has a terrier. Myrtle is the ugliest dog in all Christendom." I did not mention that at one time I had tamed a squirrel and had been owner to multiple rabbits, a hen, and a poodle named Havannah, as well as my pony, Moses.

"If that many dogs be there, then I be glad I'm here," she said, pushing the drawer shut.

"This is not just any dog, mind you," I said. "He is the son of a champion spaniel, one Miss Mitford could have sold for twenty guineas. I know she needs the money and yet she is sending him to me."

Crow looked skeptical. "A spaniel. How big is—?"

I heard a bark outside and my heart leapt. "He's here!" There was a knock on the door. "Help me up!"

Crow helped me into the hallway. And then I saw him. A rambunctious six-month-old golden cocker spaniel. Henrietta bent down to meet him and he put his paws upon her knees, his tail wagging madly. How I wished I could have run down the stairs to greet him properly.

Crow held my arm, then looked up at me. "You look flushed, miss."

"If so, it is his fault," I said. "Come here, my little Flush. Come see me."

The dog heard my voice and, after a moment's hesitation, lumbered up the stairway. I knelt to greet him and for my effort received a thousand wet kisses.

It was love at first sight.

⚜

I looked at the envelope, stunned. I had not received a letter from Richard Horne since soon after Bro died. Now, ten months later . . .

I broke the seal, eager to reconnect with my peer. I absorbed the words and quickly realized how much I had missed his witty dialogue. But then my reading stopped. I held my breath and read the last phrase again: *I wondered if you were up to a collaboration? A drama where the hero would suffer persecution from the hauntings of his soul.*

"Yes, yes," I said, surprising even myself. For I had always prided myself on working alone, letting no one else take credit—or blame—for my work. And yet, the theme was so timely as to be irresistible. And close to home. For in the past year I had certainly felt many hauntings of the soul. Now I could write about such things from true experience. The play could be about real situations, with real men and women talking aloud to each other, exploring real emotions. Joy and grief, a child, and perhaps a wedding . . .

I felt an inner stirring that made my blood flow fresh and vibrant through my body. It had been too long since I had felt such invigoration. Ideas vied for attention, each wanting a part in the project.

I lay back upon the sofa, pressing the letter to my chest. Dear, dear Richard. I knew he was making the offer half out of kindness and the wish to amuse my mind. But I did not object to his charity and found, if anything, it endeared me to him. He had written as if I were well, and that was exactly what I needed. I was tired of being the invalid. The worst had not happened — I had not died.

I repeated the phrase to myself, as if to cement it to the moment: *I had not died, and was not going to die.* Although I had once wished not to live, now . . . the faculty of living had emerged from under the crushing foot of grief. The poetical part of me had sprung to life again, and I felt it growing as freshly and strongly as if it had already been watered for many days.

I found the bell to call Crow but put it down before it made its announcement. No. I would not call her to retrieve my writing utensils for me. I looked to Flush, lying at my feet. "No, Flush. I will do it myself. And even better . . ."

And so I set the letter from Richard aside with the careful diligence of setting aside a sacred relic, then got out of bed. I moved delicately across the room to my desk. I pulled out the chair and sat. It was far less substantial than my bed or sofa, yet there was something enticing about sitting well up, forcing my back to be the support God had intended.

I pulled out paper and pen and let the thoughts flow.

And felt once more, finally, alive.

The boat tossed in a windswept sea. The rain assaulted my face, a thousand pinpricks forcing my eyes shut, compelling my arms as ineffectual shields. Although all instincts implored me to shudder in the stern, taking shelter in my rain-soaked cape, I stood at the bow, determined to be stalwart and brave, determined to be the first to see him bobbing in the water, waving to me.

"Come save me, Ba. Come. Come!"

A bolt of lightning joined with thunder, compelling me . . .

I shot upright.

In my bed.

Eyes open wide.

Wounds open wider.

I pressed a hand against my chest, willing my heart to calm, my lungs to stop their turbulent gasps.

I tried to press nightmare and night into separate corners, choosing the darkness of the latter over the blackness of the former.

But even in the true moment of *now*, I felt guilt as a cape that offered no protection. It was a smothering confinement, a prison for my sin.

My bedchamber lit up in a flash of light, God's lamp illuminating my transgression. *See it? See? You cannot escape!*

Thunder rumbled its affirmation, and rain pelted against the windows as the wind wailed: conspiratorial jurors in the trial against me.

I could not endure their condemnation. I huddled amid the covers of my bed, making myself as small as I could manage.

Making myself as small as my worth decreed.

⁓⋆⁓

I was surprised to awaken the next morning to sunlight streaming in my window, to a new day dawned. To time continuing forwards. Surely the storm would have claimed me as a sacrifice in exchange for Bro's death.

But I was alive.

A horrible error that would one day demand correction.

⁓⋆⁓

"You do mope so, Ba."

Henrietta stood at my bureau, rummaging for a scarf she often borrowed since I had no use for it, never venturing out-of-doors.

"I do not mope." I knew my defence was weak, if not false in its entirety. The continuing nightmares pulled me away from the hope of writing a play with Richard Horne and shrouded me with daily doom.

The scarf retrieved, my sister closed the drawer. "Then come outside with me. It is a lovely day."

Lovely was a measurement I could not fathom. For my nightmare refused to let me think otherwise. Always present, tormenting me with its closeness, was its author: the sea. Its proximity was a battlement that held me captive, tormenting me with every nip of the ocean breeze, the stench of the salt air, and the thunder of the waves breaking upon the shore. And the people of Torquay, daring to make their living in its wake . . . and those visitors on holiday, parading past my window, having the audacity to laugh and chatter about nothing of importance. Henrietta was one of *them*, and to venture out with her would be to surrender to the enemy.

"You go along," I said. "I have another letter to write to Papa."

She rolled her eyes. "He is not going to let you go home. Not until Dr. Scully declares you well. Coming with me on my outing will help prove your case with him. Playing the part of the invalid will not aid your cause."

"I am not playing a part."

She shrugged and headed to the door. "Have a morose day, Ba."

I sucked in a breath in order to reply, but she was gone too soon to be the recipient of my anger.

Let her mock me. Let this place mock me.

Although I persisted in my quest to be allowed to go home to London, I could not help but feel that being stranded here was a suitable purgatory. I resisted calling it hell, because in hell there was no hope. And hope was what sustained me and kept me striving for heaven.

I pulled out paper and pen for yet another plea towards that end.

Getting home to London would be my heaven. My release.

If I ever got there.

❦

In spite of my best intentions to remain despondent and punished, my nightmare eventually receded into a dark pocket, hidden and only remembered when I accidentally reached in and touched it, immediately withdrawing, recoiling from the memory of my trial upon the waters.

I gave thanks to God for His respite and interminable mercy; to Flush, who loved me without restraint; and to Richard Horne, who trusted me completely and utterly by persisting towards our partnership. Through their determined intervention the despondent portion of my character took a much-needed rest, and the poet within me attempted once again to grow fresh and strong, a seedling responding to nurturing care.

While I was not physically stronger, my mental and emotional capacities had improved. Although I was loath to admit it, Henrietta had been right. If I was ever to be deemed healthy enough to travel home, I had to make an effort to at least assume such an appearance.

I had come to Torquay to improve my health, yet despite my assurances I was better—and would be better still, safely ensconced in the Barrett home—our family doctor, Dr. Chambers, worked against me, continuing to warn Papa of the sure state of my health if I spent any time in foggy, sooty London. As such, Papa saw no advantage to bringing me home, not when I was still in such a weakened state. I appealed to him on all fronts, though I did not want to press with as much alacrity as I had when I had pushed and prodded to make him let Bro stay here with me. The outcome of my pressure, then . . . I would not insist on my way again. Ever. Poor Papa's biases were sacred. I would never again stir them with even a breath.

But that did not mean I was averse to laying out my case plainly and with determination. If he understood that the sea, the maddening sea, which at one time had given me such pleasure, was now torture to me . . . The very sound of it, the smell of it, the sight of it—even in its most tranquil moments—elicited a pain as great as any discomfort sourced from within my physique.

Plus there *were* things I could do back in London to help the family. Some of my brothers needed additional guidance. That I also needed *them* would be a point later made if necessary.

Beyond sending letters directly to Papa, I elicited the help of my brother George to plead my case. If I were at home perhaps I could help my brother Henry settle down. He had great dreams of being in the military — which was not an objectionable occupation but for the fact that Henry saw only the gain and the glory, and refused to acknowledge the hard life and true dangers involved. He had always been impulsive and a bit selfish. When he'd been on his grand tour, he'd purposely run off by himself in Switzerland, causing no small amount of worry.

Stormie would also benefit from my help. After Bro's death he had returned from Jamaica, but had changed much. He barely stirred from his room. Did he feel guilty for not being present when Bro died? Would anything have changed if he had been here? Surely I could appease his distress, for only I was guilty.

My other brothers needed me less — Alfred was doing well studying art, and Sette and Occy . . . I missed them so. Sette and his desire to be historical, logical, and oratorical, and Occy's obsession with Dickens' Mr. Pickwick, and his talent at judging the weather. If only he had been here the day Bro had died . . . would *he* have foreseen the freakish squall?

But most of all, I did not long for any *one* of my siblings, rather for the set of them. Alone they were unique and precious, but as a collection of eight they were an entity that gave me strength.

Henrietta popped her head in the door of my room, interrupting my thoughts of home. "I am going out," she said, tying her bonnet under her chin.

"Again?" I asked. There was condemnation in my voice. I did not know how she could traipse about this seaside city which had taken the life of our brother. "I can't understand your craving for excitement, sister. Mine is for repose."

"And I do not understand your fear of stimulation. I have errands, Ba. Errands and people to see."

It was as though nothing had happened to Bro at all, and her cavalier attitude enraged me.

When I did not answer her, she sighed heavily. "So you wish me to sit in this prison you have created for yourself, and moan or say little? You are *not* the instigator of lively conversation of late, Elizabeth."

She was right. When we fell back on *only us* we were found hard and dry.

She tucked her hair beneath her bonnet. "And I am not up to your reading me dreadful poetry from that Browning man." She caused herself to shudder.

"It is not dreadful," I said, defending the *Bells and Pomegranates* series I'd been reading. "Although it is a bit hard to understand."

She expelled a puff of air. "I, for one, do not enjoy reading anything that requires a dictionary."

No, she would not. And I could not argue that Robert Browning's poetry required work. It had taken me three readings to access its full glory and see its genius.

Henrietta opened her drawstring purse to search inside. "Arabel is gone too, off helping those children."

"Those children" attended a school nearby and benefited greatly from Arabel's philanthropy. I was quite certain Henrietta would have had trouble even spelling the word, much less understanding its meaning.

"I will not be gone long," she said, ready to leave. Then she stopped and turned back to me. "Oh. A letter came from Papa—for you."

The "for you" included a hint of bitterness that was justified. And yet Henrietta frustrated me anew. "Why did you not bring it to me?" I asked. "You know I'm trying to get us home."

She shrugged—a common answer. Then she thought more of it and answered fully. "Have you ever considered that perhaps I do not wish to go home?"

I was shocked. "But I thought . . ."

"You think only of yourself, Ba." She looked towards the hallway leading to the door below. "I enjoy it here in Torquay. I have friends here.

And the beauty of this place versus dark and grimy London . . . I would miss the sea."

I was once again stunned by the differences between us. "The sea that took our brother's life."

"The sea, which acts according to its nature, came into contact with our brother, who acted according to his. If there be any fault, it is with — "

"No!" I would not let her say it. For if Bro acted in any way impetuously, it was I who was to blame for spurring him towards that action.

Henrietta's face softened. "Oh dear. I apologize. I know how sensitive you are, how vulnerable."

How guilty.

"I will fetch the letter for you now, before I go out." She made her escape from the awkwardness of the moment — another Henrietta trait I had come to expect.

I pulled Flush's head close and let him lick my cheek. "She will get us the letter," I reassured him. A few moments later she returned, letter in hand. I greedily read through the contents looking for the magic words *You may come home now, Ba.*

I came away from the reading confused. Papa was still uncertain regarding our return. It seemed Dr. Scully, my doctor here in Torquay, had told Papa that although he would not forbid me to go home, no trip could be taken any later than the tenth of September.

I stared at the words. "But it is already August the fourth. A mere month to arrange our journey?" As I reread the page a question arose. Why September tenth? Why that date in particular?

I did some calculations. The tenth was a Friday. It was not a holiday. And as far as I had ascertained in all my time in Torquay, the world did not change on this day. And the weather . . . September was far too early to worry about snow or sleet. I saw no reason or logic for the time limit.

Yet reason or logic aside, I knew Papa would elevate Dr. Scully's proclamation to law. I felt like a prisoner who had been given a date of release, but whose joy was unfairly burdened with conditions bordering on impossible.

If only we could discuss it in person. The exchange of letters was excruciatingly slow and time was running out.

Yet what alternative did I have but to send a message accepting the offer and pleading with Papa to facilitate our departure before the ominous September the tenth.

As I took up my pen to create my petition I added a plea to our heavenly Father. Surely He would allow us to go home.

⁓⁕⁓

Calm, Ba. You must stay calm.

Finally, we were leaving Torquay. After my letter earlier in the month, Papa had relented. I saw no reason for his decision, as the words I had chosen in my argument were no more persuasive than any others I had used over the past fifteen months, and so, I gave credit to God for changing my father's mind.

The question upon everyone's mind—especially my own—was whether I was well enough for the journey, which was expected to take a week or more. Over two hundred miles of travel. Four women and a dog, unaccompanied by male escort other than the driver. Papa had ordered a carriage specially altered, allowing me to recline, but I knew there would be much to bear, much to dread. Yet I had to remain strong. I had wanted this, begged for it. If I suffered, it was my own fault.

Crow tucked a blanket around me as the driver finished tying our trunks. "There you be. All snug." She gave me the pointed look she often utilized, lowering her head, her eyes intense. "You all right, miss?"

I hugged Flush closely, finding comfort in his warmth. "I have to be, don't I?" I whispered.

Crow glanced at Henrietta and Arabel as they settled on the facing seat of the carriage and whispered back to me. "I will help you through this. I will. There will be no turning back, not with me here."

I squeezed her hand, taking succor in her presence—and her strength. God had been very wise and merciful when he had brought Elizabeth

Crow into my life. And now it had come to this, two Elizabeths, united by determination.

I had the feeling this was not the last time we would be so joined.

❧

I reminded myself to breathe.

The carriage was moving. We were off to London. Soon, very soon, I would be ensconced in our Wimpole Street home, a part of the family again, no longer separated by endless miles.

Henrietta looked out the window and sighed. "Oh, how I will miss this place," she said.

Again, the differences in our opinions astounded me. But I did not argue with her. I, for one, was glad to be finally away from this place that had taken the life of our brother and that had not granted me the full health that had been promised.

"Look out the window, Ba," Henrietta said. "Most likely it is the last time we will ever see this vista of the sea."

I shook my head and leaned it against Flush. To further express my view, I closed my eyes.

Thankfully, she turned her attention to Arabel, and together my two sisters recounted the good times they had experienced in Torquay.

In defence, I forced myself to remember Bro and *our* good times long before this awful place had come between us . . . until sleep came and blessedly took me into its arms.

❧

"Ba, contain yourself," Henrietta said. "Papa would never forgive us if you expired before you got out of the carriage."

She was right, of course, and I closed my eyes and forced my breathing to abandon its rapid rhythm. I was less successful with the beat of my heart but hoped that agitation resulting from such a happy occasion would not prove detrimental. I wanted to show Papa that his decision to let us come home was made wisely. For even though the eleven-day trip had been exhausting, pushing me beyond many levels of comfort and its opposite, I had persevered. We were home!

The carriage passed Portman Square, and I looked upon the trees and gated gardens in front of Montagu House knowing that in just a few blocks . . .

I hoped Papa and the boys would be at home. We had sent word after our last stop that we would be arriving today, but such messages were only partially reliable, as there was little to stop the messenger from lagging along, or never delivering our message at all.

But if they weren't home . . . I had allowed my imagination a pleasant succession of circumstances to cover this possibility. We would get fully settled, and if there was time, we would have the cook put up a grand tea and be waiting in the drawing room when the men of our family arrived. Upon seeing their surprise, I would rise to my feet as casually as my weakness allowed and simply say, "Tea, Papa?" We would fall into each other's arms, and the three years of my absence would dissipate with our laughter.

The carriage turned from Wigmore Street onto Wimpole. The familiarity of our neighbourhood warmed me as no blanket ever could.

I suddenly wondered if I looked too pale. "Do I look well?" I asked.

Arabel reached over and took my hand. "You look fine, Ba."

"Fine as you ever look," Henrietta said. "Though you could pinch your cheeks a bit."

I did as she suggested, causing Flush to nip at my hands' unaccustomed busyness.

"Whoa!" we heard the driver shout.

The carriage came to a stop. Henrietta exited the door nearly before the driver had a chance to unfurl the steps, and Arabel right after. How I wished I had their energy and health. I would have fought them for the privilege of being first into the house.

"Help me, Crow. Please help me." Together we pulled the blankets away, causing Flush to tumble to the floor of the carriage. He exited the door and I was about to call him back—would even my dog enter our home before I did?—when I heard Papa's voice.

"Well, well. You must be Flush."

I cried out with such joy I felt my heart would burst. "Papa!"

He appeared at the carriage door, tall and handsome but for the weak chin of all Barretts. But even that one flaw mattered not a bit. His face was alight with joy. "My dearest Ba."

He held out his hand to me. Suddenly my awkwardness fell away, and I easily moved to the door of the carriage and let him wrap his able hands about my waist and lift me to the ground as if I weighed nothing.

My arms found his neck and I clung to him, there on the street, my ear to his chest. "Oh, Papa, I am so glad to finally be home."

He kissed the top of my head and whispered for my ears alone, "Your absence has pained me more than any other."

I relished being his favourite and, as such, vowed to never make him worry again.

He gently pushed me back and threaded my hand through the crook of his arm. "Come now. Come inside and greet your brothers."

I was home. Here I would be content. And here I would stay.

Forever.

THREE

Crow adjusted the hooks on the back of my dress, finishing my toilette for the morning. Flush nipped at the black hem, wishing for me to settle so he could follow suit.

"The sofa or the bed today, miss?"

I quickly made an inventory of my ailments and chose the bed. She helped me to it, adjusting a myriad of pillows to use as backing for my throne.

"Anything else, miss?" she asked.

"Just my desk and pen. Thank you."

Crow retrieved them for me and left the room. I opened to yesterday's page and began to make my list: *malaise in morning, slight convulsive twitches of the muscles, a general irritability of the chest. Treatment: draught of opium.*

I closed my eyes and let my thoughts settle upon this morning's symptoms. My head did not hurt. And my chest? I took in, then released a few breaths, gauging its condition.

Nothing.

Nothing?

How could that be? I always had symptoms to report.

When I opened my eyes I noticed the window box that my brother

Alfred had made and planted for me. "Every sanctum needs flowers," he had said as he pressed the scarlet runners, golden nasturtiums, ivy, and blue morning glories into the soil.

Their beauty was vibrant. The very sight made me happy.

And yet . . . the blooms of the morning glory—alive for but a single day—were already beginning to fade and list towards their afternoon's demise.

Am I at risk of fading into my own demise? Am I rushing toward the afternoon of my life?

A sudden anger welled within me and I sat upright. What kind of foreign thoughts were these?

Yet I felt compelled to answer them.

I had been home five months. Spring was fast approaching, a time of renewal and fresh beginnings. I had been established in this lovely third-story room with family all around me. Cousin Kenyon often visited with literary gossip and new books for me to read. I was just about to bloom. I could not fade into the afternoon, into an early death.

I looked at the notebook before me and saw it with fresh eyes. Pages and pages of daily notations of symptoms and ailments. Years' worth. A catalogue of misery and despair. An enumeration of hopelessness.

Suddenly, the sight of it and the very the touch of it filled me with disgust. Was this all that I was? All I had to look forward to?

I tossed it across the room, where it bounced off my bureau and fell with pages open to the floor. "Take that!" I declared. "I want no more of you."

I took a few breaths—which came with surprising ease—and buoyed by my new resolve, I smiled. Yes, yes, this was better. To some extent there *was* a choice to be made, and perhaps—just perhaps—I had made the wrong one for too long.

Needing a witness to my new resolve I took the bell that sat upon my bedside table and rang for Crow.

She appeared immediately. "Yes, miss?"

"Help me up," I said.

She looked confused.

"I wish to go downstairs with the others."

Her head shook no. "You do not go down."

"I do. Today I do." I swung my legs over the side of the bed and held out my arm for her. She took it and helped me to stand. I wobbled.

"Miss, you need to lie down. You are too weak."

She was right. My legs had grown apathetic to their intended use. I sat back upon the bed. Perhaps I could not descend downstairs as yet, but that did not mean I could not implement changes that would make me stronger.

Once she had me settled again, I took hold of her arm and said, "I need you to help me get better."

"That is what I always try to do, Miss Elizabeth."

"I know, and I appreciate all you do for me. But . . ." How to put it into words? "It is nearly spring. The world will soon be coming alive again. I wish to be a part of that."

She patted my hand and smiled. "An admirable goal."

"I want you to help me do that. Help me get strong again. Help me find the right combination of rest, warmth, and healthful foods. And no more doctors." I was surprised most with this declaration. "I am sick to death of doctors."

She laughed. "The whole of the profession will despair at your declaration. As will their bank accounts."

Indeed. How many pounds had been spent on their opinions? Yet had any of their lofty views and prescriptions cured me?

My resolve fed upon itself, gaining strength. It was time I cured myself.

At the exertion required to make such a choice I found I was hungry. I thought of my usual coffee and scone. What would give my recovery fullest benefit?

The foods God created, the foods that came from the ground . . . those had to be the most wholesome.

"Do we have any fruit about?"

"You do not like fruit."

"I will learn to like it," I said. "And fresh vegetables."

"Fresh vegetables are hard on your digestion."

"Raw vegetables. But surely cooked . . . the rest of the family eats them. I need to eat more than soups, gruel, bread, and mash. I will eat mutton. And roast beef—which is Flush's preference." Upon hearing his name, the dog looked up at me and I scratched under his chin.

Crow's eyebrows rose. "It is Flush's preference that his bread be buttered thick and plentiful. Would you like that too?"

The thought of it was not appetizing, but I said, "Perhaps."

Crow placed her hands upon her hips. "And who will bear the brunt of the consequences such foods will surely elicit?"

She was right. Being on the third floor, any . . . regurgitations that might transpire would force Crow to carry the ill-matter down four flights of stairs to the basement. I did not need to add to her burden. I had been too much burden already.

She must have seen my consternation, for she said, "We shall start slowly, miss. Small changes taken gradually. Surely those will bring you good health."

Whatever it took. I was determined.

Occy entered my sanctum and fell upon the company side of my bed in a way that immediately propelled my thoughts back to Bro. That I could have such thoughts and not grow instantly morose was progress. I had been home six months to this day and continued my quest to be content.

"So," he said, tugging on Flush's tail as the dog lay beside me. "Henrietta is all atwitter. You are letting her go to one of Cousin Kenyon's literary soirees in your place?" He added the final condemnation. "Again?"

"She enjoys them."

"You would enjoy them too. You come downstairs to socialize with us, so why not go out and be among your peers? You are the writer.

Henrietta cares nothing for books but that they can offer her a place to set a glass or potted plant."

I had to smile. "And you? Have you come to appreciate books for their content?"

"I am eighteen now."

I did not respond to his non-answer but continued to smile. It was true he was no longer a boy. When I had departed for Torquay, I had left Sette and Occy as children and came home to find them fully grown.

"I am not a scholar like you are, Ba, but I do find diversion in a book—once in a while."

Once in a great while was more the truth. Yet I did not expect Occy to embrace reading as much as I. He was a vibrant young man who had a charm that could take him far—or cause him trouble. Again, I thought of Bro. If only Bro had used his charm to succeed in a vocation. One of my greatest regrets for him was that he had been so aimless and without purpose. A sense of purpose was vital to moving from day to day. To day. I had been unable to spur Bro towards a sense of calling, but it was not too late for Occy. "When I was your age—"

Occy interrupted. "When you were my age, I was born."

I was taken aback. Yes, indeed, I had been eighteen when my youngest brother was born. In so many ways he could have been my own, for our mother died when he was barely four and I assumed many of her responsibilities.

He left Flush's tail alone. "I missed you," he said simply.

"I missed you too. I missed you all. I missed home."

"Don't ever go away again, all right?"

I was moved by his request and reached for his hand. "I have no intent to ever leave. I'm trying very hard to be well so I can stay here."

He nodded once, then said, "At least you'll never marry."

Again, I was taken aback.

He saw my surprise and rushed to explain. "There's Papa's general opposition to the institution—that I will never understand. But beyond that, you are . . . I mean, your age . . . I . . ." He snapped his mouth shut. He got off the bed and picked up a book. "Aeschylus? Who's he?"

He'd mispronounced it. "It's Es-ka-luss. He's a Greek playwright."

He set the book down and looked at me through thick lashes. "I apologize for the comment about your age. You are not that old."

"But too old to marry." I did not add the obvious, *at thirty-six too old to start having children.*

He lounged on my sofa, lifting one knee and placing the other foot upon it. "Did you ever wish to marry? I mean . . . were you ever in love?"

They were good questions. "I did want to marry — in theory," I said. "As a child I assumed I would marry. Yet as I got older and saw how our mother suffered . . ."

"Mother suffered?"

I should not have brought it up. It was not something a man — young or old — could ever understand. "Nothing. I overspoke. She loved her life."

He pivoted on the sofa and let his feet find the floor. "Was it because of me? I was the youngest. Was I too much for her? I was so little I don't remember anything except the smell of honeysuckle."

I nodded at the memory. Mother had often used a toilet water scented by that flower. "You did not make her suffer, Occy. She loved you. She loved every one of us. But . . ." I hesitated, but decided to say it. He was eighteen. He was not completely ignorant. "She had twelve children in eighteen years and all but one lived. Mother's body was spent. Weak. Her entire life was given in service to others — especially Papa. Yet he was rarely there. He had our flamboyant house built at Hope End, then was off in London most of the time."

"He had to make a living to support us. And the estate. Nearly five hundred acres, Ba. That is commendable."

Guilt nipped at me. "Yes, it was. And of course Papa did his best, but Mother, with all those children . . . she was completely worn out. And isolated."

"Isolated? At Hope End? There were thirteen of us. It was a heavenly place, built like a Turkish castle, with minarets and ponds and grottos and horses and fields to run in. I remember green, lots and lots of green."

"Too much green. The foliage was so dense that it seemed to be a wall keeping us in. A prison."

He looked shocked.

I waved a hand, needing to explain. "As a child I loved the place as much as you. I did not see the walls. Our total seclusion in our own little world, built especially for us by dear Papa. He built it, set us up inside his creation, and then left us to fend for ourselves." Was I being too harsh? To talk of Papa this way . . . And yet, the only time I allowed myself dissention in regard to Papa was when I thought of Mother. Occy had a right to know her as more than the memory of honeysuckle. "As I grew older, I saw the effect of our isolation on Mother. She wanted adults to talk to. She wanted friends. She wanted to see her family up north. But Papa was determined to keep us—" I tried to think of a proper word—"contained."

"As we are contained here in London?"

He spoke a truth I could not address—as yet.

I returned the discussion to our mother and tried to think of better times. "I remember one special occasion when Papa took Mother and me to Paris. I was only nine and felt very special to have been singled out, as Bro, Henrietta, and Sam were left at home." I did not mention that our sister Mary had died the year before, nor that as an adult I had recognized our trip as an escape for Mother's grief. Occy had never known Mary. She was never mentioned—except in my heart. "In crossing the Channel to Calais, I did not get seasick at all. Papa did not fare as well. And then a Frenchman came and carried all of us through the water to the pier." I smiled at the memory. "Papa did not like that one bit. I think it made him feel unmanly."

"I can imagine."

I leaned my head back, letting the memories rush in. "Mother was at her finest in France, for she knew the language and had to take charge since Papa knew not a word. She and I went to the Louvre and spent hours looking. . . . I don't remember any one thing, just the joy of being with her alone, and of seeing her so happy."

"I want to go to Paris. Papa said perhaps I could. Henry got to go on a grand tour."

"You should go. Absolutely," I said. "Although I do remember it to be a filthy place. But that was in 1815, right after the Napoleonic wars. Perhaps it is cleaner now."

"I can't imagine Papa in another country like that."

"I don't think he ever returned. He has never felt at ease in society of any sort."

"Why not?"

It was a good question I had not pondered in years. Then I thought of a possible answer. "Papa was moved here from Jamaica when he was twelve and put in school at Harrow. But there was some incident with another student where Papa burned his toast and was beaten so severely for it that—"

"For burnt toast?"

It was as absurd as it sounded, but I remembered Mother trying to explain the incident to me. "The other boy was expelled, but Papa was pulled out of school by his mother, and though he was accepted at Cambridge for college, he never attended."

"*He* didn't have to go to school, but I—?"

I leaned forwards, offering a deep confidence. "The lack of education did not serve Papa well, Occy. Honestly, with the wealth of the Jamaican plantations, his mother did not see the need. The Barretts were *the* richest plantation owners on the island."

"But we have money now," Occy said. "Perhaps there is no need for me to attend—"

I shook my head adamantly. "Papa works very hard to take care of us now, but back then we were quite rich."

"What changed?"

"The slaves in Jamaica rebelled and much of our plantation was destroyed."

"Slavery is a horrible institution," Occy said. "It is good it has been abolished."

"It is detestable," I said. "But at the time, it was vital to our family's livelihood. Without the income from Jamaica, and with money needed to rebuild there . . ."

"That is why Papa sold Hope End, yes?"

In an instant I decided it was not necessary for my brother to know that Hope End was seized to pay debts. Even I had not known of this until much after the fact. Papa always kept our finances close to the chest. To answer his question, I said simply, "Yes."

"I do not remember it much," he said.

I shared his grief in this. As the eldest, I had benefited from many happy years there, but Occy, being the youngest — eighteen years younger than I . . . I tried to remember what we were talking about before the conversation turned to the perniciousness of financial necessities. "Ah. Paris. The lovely trip I took with Mother and Papa. Even after we returned, Mother kept the memory of it going. She hired a French governess and encouraged me to write her notes in French — even when we were in the same house. I remember her saying to me in French, 'Un jour de travail dur vaut mieux que deux de repos.'"

Occy looked at me blankly.

"One day of hard work is worth two of idleness."

He made a face. "Oh."

"Cheer up, little brother. When you find your true calling, hard work will be a joy. You are so lucky to be a man."

"Because I *have* to work, because I am expected to work?"

"Because you *can* work. I used to tease Bro because I longed to do scholarly work and was not allowed, and he, who could have embraced it, had no interest." I shrugged. Such inequities were timeless and would never change.

"But you have attained much, Ba. Your books, your writing . . . you are having the same chances as a man."

"I am having chances, yes. But I do not put my name on any of my work—Papa forbids it. Not that I yearn for fame, but . . . it saddens me that it reaches the world anonymously."

"Perhaps as a woman that is best?"

"Perhaps." I hated that my pride longed to see my name upon a cover. Perhaps this was God's way of keeping me humble? There was some compensation that I *was* known in literary circles, if not to the public. "At least our parents never believed the common misconception that girls' minds were inferior to boys'. I learned Greek with Bro when Mother taught us at home and did better at it than he did. But then . . ." The memory of Bro waving from a carriage as he left me behind to attend school brought old hurts to the surface.

"But then?"

"But then he was sent to school and I was left behind. I, who loved learning, was left behind."

"And he, who cared little for learning, was given the chance."

I took a new breath in order to answer. "Yes."

"But you still learned plenty, Ba." He pointed to the book by Aeschylus and the shelves of books beyond.

"But I could have learned more. If I'd been a man, and if I'd been well."

Occy leaned back on the sofa, his arm behind his head. "Do you think they loved each other?"

"Mother and Papa?"

He nodded.

What did I know of love? An invalid spinster who had never been kissed and who would never *be* kissed. Had my parents loved each other? My mother had been an excellent wife: dutiful, subservient, intensely loyal to my father. And Papa . . . had he been a good husband?

When I thought about the father of my youth, I pictured him smiling, watching our various plays and productions, reading my feeble attempts at writing, crowning me the Poet Laureate of Hope End, even though I was only nine or ten. He supported us in so many ways. Supported Mother?

I also remembered finding him hunched over his desk, his face serious, his brow pulled in concern. Having holdings in Jamaica, half a world away, holdings that had been dependent upon slavery, yet hating the institution and not knowing how else to run our plantations. . . . When slavery had been abolished nine years ago, our setbacks forced the sale of Hope End. But through it all, Papa provided for us to the best of his abilities. After all this, and after Mother's death, he had drawn us all close, keeping our family tightly knit amid the upheaval and uncertainty.

Too tightly knit?

Knowing the foibles and weaknesses of my siblings and me, I could not consider the gift of more freedom as being a good thing, or wise. Together, we Barretts became strong, each providing some needed aspect of a rightful whole.

"I lost you," Occy said, waving his hand at me.

Indeed, he had. And I still had to answer his initial question, in spite of the incompleteness of my knowledge. I tried to think of appropriate words to define our parents' love: respect, appreciation . . . neither of those were quite right. "I believe they did love each other, in the way that the two of them created a family and were united in that purpose."

"But were they *in* love with each other?"

I smiled. Although I sat upon the outer border of the possibilities of love, Occy was perched at its beginning. "I . . . I don't think so. I never witnessed any passion, any yearning, one for the other." I shook the thought away. "But what do I know of such things? Love is an equation I have not ciphered. Perhaps such a love only exists in novels."

"I hope it exists," Occy said.

"Do you have someone in mind?" I teased.

To his credit, he reddened. "No. Not yet. But I will."

"You will? You know such a thing?"

"I want to know such a thing."

Such innocence and hope. Had I ever experienced those feelings? If so, the memory was too dim to relight.

⌘

Crow stood at the window and fanned herself against the stifling summer heat. Then she put down her fan and tried—for the umpteenth time—to open my window farther than its frame would allow. Perspiration made stray hairs cling to her face. "A person could expire from lack of air," she said.

"Papa should be pleased," I said. "He so enjoys the heat."

"Not this heat," Crow said. "Although he pretends it has no effect on him, this afternoon I heard him tell your sister his tea was too hot."

I laughed. "Not a sigh against the sun, only against the tea? It is great criticism indeed."

"You take after him," she said. "Still a throw upon your feet? If propriety permitted, I would rid myself of my petticoats, chemise, and—" She stopped her list before it became more risqué. "I would make myself comfortable, that's all."

I was proud to say I took after Papa in this tolerance of heat. It was the cold that plagued us the most. My one concession to Crow's complaint was to keep my door open, allowing air to move freely from one level of our home to another. In actuality all windows were open, with only the front door closed against the busyness and publicity of the street.

Hearing voices below, she moved to the hall. "Mr. Kenyon and Miss Mitford are here."

A double blessing. "Go greet them and ask them up. And get tea and biscuits for us, and cream cheese for Flush. I've promised it to him all afternoon."

She shook her head. "You spoil that boy."

So be it. Whom else did I have to spoil?

Within minutes my room was alive with visitors. Cousin John kissed one cheek and Mary, the other. "Welcome," I said. "Sit, sit."

They were just settled in when Crow returned with the cream cheese in a bowl and a shaker of salt. "The tea is coming," she said, handing me a spoon.

I sprinkled the bowl with salt and began to stir it into the cream cheese that was Flush's favourite.

"What *are* you doing?" John asked.

"I am the only one who knows how much salt is just enough."

"I am not inquiring about the salt, but the cream cheese. For a dog?"

Crow interrupted. "That dog gets whatever he wants. Cream cheese, sugared milk in a purple bowl, macaroons . . ."

"The last, only on holidays," I said.

Mary rolled her eyes. "*I* do not get macaroons on holidays."

I knew I deserved their censure. I spoiled Flush greatly, and knew it stemmed from guilt for taking him away from the green fields he would have had at Mary's home at Three Mile Cross, and virtually locking him away with me in my dark city room. And so I indulged him shamelessly. Or with a modicum of shame. I had made Flush into quite a dainty fellow. Papa scolded me and often said, "No dog in the world could be of his own accord and instinct so like a woman."

"He looks like you," Cousin said.

"I beg your pardon?"

John made a downward motion along either side of his face. "The dog's long ears framing his face, and your long curls framing yours."

"And you both have sad, soulful eyes," Mary said.

Before I could take true offence, or acquiesce to the truth in their statements, Flush anticipated his cream cheese by hurling his front paws onto the bedside table from whence I worked. The pages I had been writing upon, along with a perfume bottle, crashed to the floor. The perfume seeped over the pages, causing the ink to run.

"Bad dog!" Crow yelled, scrambling for a towel.

Flush retreated under the sofa and looked so absolutely mournful that I nearly didn't mind the damage to my work, caring only for the damage to his sensitive nature.

John carefully handed me the pages, along with a handkerchief. "You dab them. I don't want to be responsible for making them worse and destroying the work of the ages."

A heady floral fragrance wafted over me and I looked upon the words elongated by the liquid. They looked as if they were crying. . . .

"Perhaps Flush is a good editor," I said, letting the pages dry by the air. "Perhaps this work is best lost, best never read."

Crow mopped the last of the floor. "You should not let him off so easily. This is not the first item damaged, the first glass broken. He is not a puppy anymore. He should know better."

I did not argue but placed the plate of cream cheese under the sofa and shielded his sup from prying eyes by sitting above him and spreading my skirts. I would lure him into my company after he had been properly fed and calmed.

Cousin John and Mary returned to their seats in front of the dormant fireplace. John crossed his legs. "Now. To the question which has brought me here this afternoon. What's this about Charles Dilke wanting you to write for him?"

So they had heard. News traveled fast in London. "He wishes for me to be a reviewer for *The Athenaeum*."

"Review other people's work?"

Oh dear. I knew it sounded presumptuous. Me, who was fairly new to the literary world, comment on other writers' work?

Mary answered for me, for she knew of the arrangement. "Our Ba suggested a series of sketches on the Greek poets of the early Christian centuries."

I added the next to solidify my qualifications. "I have read them all, you know. And am reading them again to bring them fresh to mind."

"I do not doubt your scholarship, Ba."

I was not so certain. "I doubt it. I am half afraid it's conceited of me to let myself be lifted up to this . . . this bad eminence of criticism. After all, who am I?"

"I did not mean to make you doubt yourself," Cousin said. "As far as your credentials, you are as well-read as any and more analytical than most. If this is what the editor wants, why *not* you?"

I knew he was being kind, but also sensed a sincerity that helped me accept his compliment.

"So . . . ?" he asked. "You have accepted?"

"I have already turned in one offering. I will say going from being languid and without purpose to writing to the clock and being busy upon busy is quite a change."

Mary's toes skimmed the carpet. She was as petite as I and no more ample in girth. Cousin John often teased that we were two tiny dolls, Mary the middle-aged mother and me the daughter. That my curls were dark and Mary's light brown did not dissuade him from his teasing. To him we were a pair. And perhaps we were, for we were both spinsters. Both highly devoted to our fathers. Both writers.

Mary spoke to John. "I have commended Ba for her project, and yet I worry she is wasting her talent. She is so meticulous of each point and quotation that I fear I do not read *her* in the reviews, but an interchangeable scholar who offers each fact with scrupulous care."

Cousin raised an eyebrow. "Overscrupulous perhaps?"

"Perhaps," Mary said.

I lifted a hand to stop their dialogue. "Pardon me, but I am present—in the room. You should not discuss my flaws so fearlessly."

"Would you prefer we speak of them behind your back?"

"I prefer you not speak of them at all—or even acknowledge their existence. An 'interchangeable scholar'? I have no wish to own that title in any aspect of my life."

John clapped. "Bravo, Ba! There is the feisty girl I love."

He still thought of me as a child. "Woman, cousin."

"Authoress," Mary added. "What new creative piece are you working on, Ba?"

I was glad the discussion had moved away from my shortcomings. It was true that I did not wish to be known as a reviewer but as a poet, the creator of my own work. "Since my last book of poems came out four years ago, I have been compiling work for another compilation. Yet I would like there to be a significant, longer piece as the foundation—perhaps six or seven hundred lines."

"Since you have the classics freshly planted in your mind, perhaps a classical theme?" John suggested.

"Father wishes for a religious theme."

"And you?" Mary asked.

"I was thinking of something Napoleonic."

"Something short and repressive?" John said with a smile.

"Something long and powerful."

He nodded his approval. "Why do you not begin, then?"

"I have already told Mr. Dilke I would start a survey of English poets next."

"Ah me," Mary said.

"I have promised him as much."

"You should have promised him less," she said. "Your own work must take precedence."

"The reviews are my own work now."

"They are a rehashing of other writers' work."

I was hesitant to tell them this next but felt compelled to do so. "In truth, I am currently without a publisher. Moxon—who as you know is the publisher of Keats, Shelley, Tennyson, Wordsworth, Browning, *and* me—has recently deemed me noncommercial. Although he respects my work, he has told my brother, told George, that he can't afford to publish me."

"Perhaps he can be persuaded?" Mary said.

I shook my head. When Bro used to act as my intermediary, he hedged his words to me, softening the harshness of rejection. But George—being good and true, honest and kind, but a little over-grave and reasonable—told me exactly what was said. Although I appreciated knowing the truth and the whole truth, sometimes I missed Bro's protection. "I will put off trying again for a year or so and spend my time improving the quality of my offerings."

"None of us are beyond improvement," John said.

"I do have good news, though," I said. I would wait for them to ask.

"Oh, do tell," Mary said.

"Cornelius Mathew, an editor in New York City, is interested in my work. He has deigned himself to be my trustee for the further extension of my reputation in America."

"Bravo!" John said.

Mary shook her head. "Just like Jesus. His hometown spurned Him, and He only gained followers elsewhere."

I did not feel comfortable with the comparison. "Many people are better known beyond the boundaries of their home ground." I nodded once for emphasis. "I like Americans. From what I've heard, they are kind and courteous."

Out of the blue, Mary changed the tone of the conversation. "Caroline Norton was just ranked first in a list of the top ten British poetesses."

My breath stopped. "Who created this list?" I hoped for some obscure publication.

"*The Quarterly Review.* I believe Hartley Coleridge assembled it."

John pursed his lips and nodded. "Admirable."

I waved my hands. "Admirable? She is a machine, churning out four volumes of poetry in this year alone."

"Poetry that is selling well," John said. "Or so I've heard."

"She is so young," Mary said. Then she looked at me. "Two years younger than you, isn't that right?"

"Are you trying to make me feel bad?" I asked.

Mary extended a quieting hand. "I am trying to make you focus on your own creations."

I knew she meant well, and I too enjoyed the creative process more than the reviews I was doing for Mr. Dilke. And yet it was still frustrating to hear of the success of Mrs. Norton. She was not a good person.

As if reading my thoughts, John said, "She has had a hard life, Ba. A marriage that was . . ." He leaned close and lowered his voice. "It is said her husband beat her so that she was forced to leave him. He refuses to allow her a divorce. That is why she writes so prolifically, to earn her own money."

I had not heard that. All I knew was that a few years previous she had partaken of an adulterous affair with Lord Melbourne, who had been prime minister at the time.

Mary pointed at my face. "I know what you are thinking. But Mrs. Norton was just friends with Lord Melbourne. You must remember the facts correctly, Ba. Her husband tried to blackmail him, demanding fourteen hundred pounds, but Melbourne would not bite. There was no proof though the accusation nearly brought down the government. Her cad of a husband continues to keep her from seeing their three sons."

My envy faded to compassion. "That is unconscionable. A mother needs to see her children."

Mary shrugged. "So you see, her commercial success is necessary for her very survival."

Guilt assaulted me, for though I would have enjoyed monetary success, it was not a necessity for my subsistence. "God does provide. Mrs. Norton obviously needs success far more than I do. I apologize for the sin of envy. And pettiness."

"You are hereby forgiven," John said. "Really, Ba, you are allowed such feelings, especially among friends."

I was glad he had exonerated me. And yet, especially among friends . . . should I not show my best self?

"Do you wish to know who causes me to envy?" John asked.

"Who?" Mary asked.

"Charles Dickens. In only six years he has produced six novels and is now in New York City, giving lectures and attending a ball in which three thousand of the highest society turned out to see him. Three thousand," he repeated. "At London readings we are lucky to gather a handful."

"I enjoy his stories," I said. "Though I find his women characters to be rather passive. I far prefer Frederika Bremer—even more than Jane Austen."

"Whyever would you say that?" Mary said.

I had never been forced to defend Bremer and so was not sure . . . I felt Flush nudge at my skirt, and pulled the fabric aside to allow him exit from his retreat. He took a seat at my feet, signaling all was forgiven. "I think I like Bremer because Serena, the character in *The Neighbours*, is so completely self-sacrificing. Her refusal to marry because it would mean leaving the grandparents who had raised her . . . the serenity, the sweetness, the undertone of Christian music in her choice . . . it's a poignant example of Christian sacrifice."

"Ill-conceived sacrifice," John said. He cleared his throat. " 'Therefore shall a man leave his father and his mother, and shall cleave unto his wife: and they shall be one flesh.' " His voice took on a polite but slightly condescending tone. "Children are supposed to leave their families and create new ones."

Mary put her hands on her hips. "You are speaking to two spinster women, Mr. Kenyon. You will get no takers to your argument. That both Ba and I have chosen to remain loyal to our fathers—"

"Loyalty does not require being caged. Though, Ba, as your identity comes out, your readers are fascinated with the notion that you are a nightingale, kept hidden from the world in your Wimpole Street cage."

"My readers need to concentrate on the worth of my work, not the details of my personal life." Just as my anger began its rise, Arabel appeared at the doorway. "Hello, Miss Mitford, Cousin John." Her eyes strayed to Flush. "Would you enjoy a walk, young man? Shall we escape this stifling heat to find the fresh air in Regent's Park?"

Flush sprang to his feet, his wagging tail his answer.

John stood. "It is incredibly warm up here. Perhaps we should all join you."

Arabel glanced in my direction. "I could get your wheelchair, Ba."

"No, no, you go. I am fine here." I pushed myself to standing. "In fact, if I could presume on Miss Mitford, I should like to retire to my bed."

"We will wait for *you* to join us, Miss Mitford?" John said.

She looked at me, asking permission. I answered for her, "Yes, by all means wait for her. We will be just a moment."

As they left, Mary took my arm and helped me into bed. "You have made great strides, Ba," she said in my ear as she adjusted a pillow behind me. "Venturing out-of-doors for an outing would be the next step."

A step I was still unable — or unwilling — to take. "I must not strain myself," I said, falling back to my usual excuses. "I know the results of becoming overtaxed."

"You know best," Mary said. "I suppose."

I was not certain she was right, but only certain I could not go out. I just couldn't. It was as though there were a wall erected at the front door, prohibiting me from egress.

Mary kissed my forehead and descended to the foyer, her voice adding to that of Arabel and John. Then the door clicked shut and I heard Flush's excited barks fading. Fading into the distance.

Crow returned with a tray of tea and scones. "They have left."

"To seek the cooler air outside."

"Would you like to go with them?"

Like? Yes, I would like to go with them. But could I? I shook my head and waved her away, to leave me.

John had accused me of being caged. Was I? I looked across the room at the dove I kept caged there, the dove I had nurtured when it was but an egg. Its mother gone, I had warmed its shell, rolling it over and over in my fingers until the bird had broken free.

No longer free. For I had rewarded its birth by placing it in a cage for my own enjoyment. Its soft *coo-coo* was a lullaby that often accompanied my descent into sleep.

I looked to the window, open as an invitation to the summer breezes. What I should have done was stride across the room, fling open the dove's cage, and carry him to the windowsill where he could fly away, soaring into the freedom of the sky.

I waited a moment. Then two. My body did not respond but lay fixed. Rebellious.

Or was I giving it undue blame? For I *was* better — better than I had been in years. I could have gone for a walk in Regent's Park with my sister and friends, or at least been taken for a walk in my wheelchair. That I had decided not to do so, when able . . .

"Am I a recluse?" I asked the air.

As if in answer to my question, I heard feet upon the stairs. Heavy feet. A man's feet.

Father's feet.

I sat upright, prepared to greet him. He knocked on the doorjamb.

"Come in, Papa."

He stepped inside and greeted me with a smile I knew was mine alone. "Ba. How are you?" His smile left him and he came to my bedside. He put a hand upon my forehead. "You are flushed. Are you feeling unwell?"

For once, I, who always enjoyed his kind attention, wanted none of it. I took his hand and removed it. "I am fine, Papa. Just fine."

He sat on the edge of the bed, his countenance heavy with concern. "You say the words, but I do not believe them."

I sighed. He could always read me too well. "It is not a physical ailment that plagues me, but one of the spirit."

When he looked even more worried, I hastened to explain. "Why do I not go out, Papa? The day is fine and Cousin John and Miss Mitford and Arabel asked me to go, and yet I chose to stay. Here. Alone in my room. Even Flush has gone."

"You do not need people as others do, dear Ba. You have your books and the companionship of your creativity. And we, your family, are here for you."

"But is that enough?"

He looked away, his face pensive. Then he looked upon me once more. "I have been reading the Roman poets. One such man, Juvenal, said this: 'One path alone leads to a life of peace: The path of virtue.' There is no one more virtuous than you, daughter. You are pure of heart and noble of thought. Let those attributes calm your discontent."

I knew he needed a nod of acquiescence, and so I gave him one. He kissed my forehead and left me.

Alone.

Alone with my virtues and noble thoughts, neither of which — if they were in attendance at all — were good company.

❦

I heard a commotion in the foyer below. Crow came running up the stairs and burst into my room. "You have a delivery!"

"What is it?"

"From Mr. Kenyon," she said. "It's a . . . you'll see."

I barely had time to get out of bed. Since a stranger was coming, I stood by the window and listened to heavy footsteps coming closer. . . .

A few minutes later, a workman appeared at my door, carrying a small table. Upon seeing me, he blushed, set it down, removed his cap, and said, "Mornin', miss." He donned his cap again and dug a note from the pocket of his dirty jacket. " 'Ere's a note I's supposed to give you."

Crow was the intermediary. On the outside of the envelope was simply *Ba*. Inside . . . *Accept this addition to your sanctum. The rails along the top of the table should prevent canine paws from causing further damage.*

I laughed and looked at the table with new eyes. The oval top was ringed with two rows of metal barrier, spanning three inches in height. "Over here," I said, wanting it next to the sofa.

Crow quickly moved the current table out of the way, and the man placed its far-superior replacement in its stead. I gave the man a coin and he left us.

"Well, well," Crow said. "What a novel idea."

Flush sniffed the table suspiciously. *He* may not have approved, but I thought the piece delightful.

"Did Mr. Kenyon have it specially made?" Crow asked.

"I would not be surprised."

I was so lucky to have friends who looked after all my needs.

FOUR

Crow pressed towels along the edge of the window and sill, trying—with little success—to curtail the bitter draft that relentlessly strove to gain access. Outside, snowflakes danced in a celebratory tribute to their season.

I huddled beneath covers while sitting on my sofa, my heaviest winter shawl insufficient against the cold. The fire in the fireplace roared, trying its best to soothe me.

Flush suddenly rose from his place beside the sofa and barked.

"Someone must be here," Crow said. She went into the hall and looked down the stairs. "It sounds like Miss Mitford. Shall I fetch her up?"

"Yes, yes, please," I said.

I heard Mary's slow ascent and her puffing upon taking the three flights from the foyer to my chamber. She hated our stairs, being far more used to the wide, open expanse of her home in Reading, where homes were not required to be built *up*.

"Catch your breath, Mary, and get warm by the fire."

But upon seeing her face, I knew it was not the trek up the stairs nor the cold that was causing her discomfort. I rose from the sofa to go to her. "Mary . . ."

68

She fell into my arms. "My father. He has died."

Beyond the initial shock, my first response was mentally expressed in two words: *Finally died.*

I was ashamed at my reaction and with Crow's help, removed Mary's cloak and led her to the sofa, where we sat side by side. "Were you with him?" I asked.

She nodded and retrieved a handkerchief to blow her nose. "He succumbed peacefully."

In spite of proper decorum for such situations, a small laugh escaped. "*That* is a change."

I was relieved when she returned my smile. "He *was* a difficult man."

"Demanding."

"Stubborn."

"Reckless." I hastened to add, "With money."

She agreed with a nod. "My money."

I ran a hand across her back. "You supported him for so many years."

"Money ran through his fingers. He'd always been that way. When I was a child he spent Mother's inheritance, and then even my lottery winnings."

I had forgotten about that. When Mary was ten she had won twenty thousand pounds, which her father had spent with great speed and abandon. His penchant for spending often ended him in debtors' prison, where he was repeatedly rescued by his loyal, hardworking daughter.

Mary gripped the handkerchief in her fist. "I wanted to be the greatest English poetess of all time, yet my poems have never sold. How ironic that my prose, *The Village*, which I was forced to write to pay the bills, found success. And now I am alone. So alone." She fell into my arms once again.

"You are not alone, Mary. You have many, many friends, most of all me. And this house. You must come and stay here."

She shook her head vigorously. "Your father would never allow it. When I visit he barely nods and always appears stern, as if I am an intruder."

I hurried to defend him, for she was not the first to misunderstand Papa's reticence. "He is merely shy and feels intimidated by those he admires, those with high intellect and wit. He doubts his ability to host, not in your ability to be a suitable guest. He is really very kind and caring and . . ." I thought of a point that would be his best defence. "He has been praying for your father during his illness. I did not ask him to. He did so out of his own mind, and quite from the heart. He was the one who suggested we send your father gifts to cheer him."

"The chocolates from Jamaica. Father loved those."

I nodded earnestly. "That was Papa's doing. And the oysters. And the grapes."

Suddenly she sat erect. "Why did I never marry?" She gave me a pointed look. "Why did *you* never marry?"

Her question took me by surprise. "I . . ."

"Why did love pass us by?"

I had never thought of it in this manner. "Perhaps it was we who did the passing."

Her eyebrow rose. "You received offers?"

Although the question was innocent, I felt myself blush. "No, there was never anyone—anyone that was . . ."

I had piqued her interest. "Was . . . ?"

I chose the first word that came to mind, even though it was insufficient. "Feasible."

"Love and feasibility do not belong in the same sentence."

"They do when they describe a young woman falling in love with an elderly man; a middle-aged blind man, four years older than Papa."

She scooted away from me, as if to study me better. "Who?"

"You do not know him. Hugh Boyd."

"Hugh Stuart Boyd, the Greek scholar?"

I was pleased she did know of him. "When I was but twenty-one and we still lived at Hope End, he was staying in nearby Malvern and sent me a letter, saying he admired my writing in *An Essay on Mind.* It was utterly unexpected; he was a complete stranger."

"How exciting."

I nodded. "Through extended correspondence I discovered we were of like mind. He was so learned, so well read, and was also a poet. I wanted him to teach me." I hurried to clarify. "By letter. Although he wanted to meet me, I made excuses — feeble though they were — as to why I could not meet him."

"You prefer to test a friendship on paper first, do you not?"

"I confess, that *is* the case."

"But you did meet him?"

I gave her a chastising look. "You get ahead of the story."

She held up a hand, yielding.

"Our correspondence eventually moved beyond a scholarly discussion to a more personal vein. He was fascinated with our family and life at Hope End, and . . . and he saw through the excuse of my bad health, the weather, my lack of transportation, and . . . such . . . as barriers to our meeting. I finally had to tell him that Papa would never approve. Papa had told me that, whatever gratification and improvement I might receive from a personal intercourse with Mr. Boyd, as a female — a young female — I could not visit him without overstepping the established observances of society."

"Oh posh," Mary said.

I allowed myself a moment to access the fuller truth. "Actually, although Papa did object, the main obstacle to our first meeting was my fear."

"Ah," Mary said.

Suddenly, I realized how many years had passed from then to now. I had started being reclusive fifteen years ago? Or even longer? Or had I always been this way? I let myself remember those last years of my youth, when my health had caused me to change so drastically. . . .

Yet with those memories came a few that were unflattering. . . . "I remember feeling quite well more often than I let on. I would tell Papa otherwise to suit my whim. I knew he did not like society much, and so

I played into that—at will—knowing that he would not force me to do what brought *him* discomfort."

Mary smiled and pretended to chastise, "Ba! I am shocked."

So was I, in retrospect. Yet at the time . . . "Mr. Boyd deemed my excuses ridiculous. And as far as propriety? He was blind, a married man, and had a daughter as old as I."

"At the risk of jumping ahead . . . you *did* meet him?"

"Finally. I had been walking with my sisters on the street and—"

"So you *were* well?"

"Well enough. I did get out occasionally to visit an aunt and Grand-mother Moulton, who rented a cottage close by. And on one of these occasions, I spotted Mr. and Mrs. Boyd, walking. Although I had never seen them, Henrietta knew who they were and suggested we go say hello, but I could not, just could not, and slipped into a shop without greeting them."

"Ba, that was rude. That was your chance."

"I know that now. I knew it then, but I have always been low on courage." And yet . . . I remembered otherwise. "Actually, soon after that incident I showed great courage, perhaps one of the few times I have ever done so."

"What happened?"

"On that day, Mrs. Boyd had recognized my sisters, realized I was their companion, and told her husband of my slight. He wrote me a scathing letter pointing out that if I were well enough to visit others, I should have been well enough to visit him, a respectable, married man. But no matter, they were leaving the area soon, and so that, quite simply, was that."

"He had a point."

"He did. But his letter wounded me so, I went to Papa and showed it to him, and asked him to give me good reason why I could not call on the Boyds."

"And he . . . ?"

"He had no good excuse since I *was* well enough, and the situation was respectable enough, so—"

"He admitted he was wrong?"

A laugh escaped. "No, no. That would never happen. Has never happened. Ever. But he did say, 'Do as you like,' which I considered a victory. And so I did. As I liked."

"Bravo!" Mary offered soft applause.

The full memory spurred me to urge her to stop. "I was too nervous to go alone, so I asked Bro to accompany me, and Henrietta and Arabel agreed to go in the little carriage as far as a friend's home. But on the way down the Wyche—a very steep hill—the pony's trot turned into a panicked gallop, and though Bro warned everyone, 'Don't touch the reins!', I instinctively did just that, and the carriage overturned."

"Were you hurt?"

"Henrietta hurt her ankle and my hat was torn, and we were all dirty from the road, but no serious injuries. And luckily another carriage came along and took Henrietta off to our friend's home. Bro ran after the pony, but I was so scared, I would not let him connect the animal back to the carriage, so Bro took the shaft and pulled Arabel and me as if he were the pony."

"What a sight that must have been!"

I held up a finger, for the story was not finished. "In such a state we came upon Mr. and Mrs. Boyd, and I was so rattled because I was dirty and torn and—"

"Did you not say he was blind?"

I remembered others in my family presenting that same point, yet at the time, his blindness didn't matter. "This was the first time I had ever been in such close proximity, and . . . I made a fool of myself and rambled on about how our visit would obviously have to be cancelled."

"What did he say?"

"Not a word. His wife was very gracious, but he, he said nothing." I could still see him, his face paler and more amiable than I had imagined. "This man who instructed me, argued with me, critiqued my work with such power and compassion, had a gentle countenance, but had eyes quenched and deadened."

"As you said, he was blind."

I shook my head. "I knew that, but during our correspondence, I had forgotten or set it aside, for his words and thoughts were full of sight and insight."

Mary nodded, and I knew she understood.

"I realized then upon seeing him on his wife's arm . . . for a man of his nature to be completely dependent . . . all my excuses not to meet him had been silly. And so, I arranged another meeting, and another, and another, and soon I was reading Greek to him. I became of use to him as he was to me, and . . ."

"You fell in love with him."

I pinched a button on my bodice, unwilling to meet her eyes. "It was the happiest summer of my life."

"But . . . but he was married."

I looked up, needing her to see the sincerity of my expression. "Nothing untoward happened whatsoever. It was the first love of a young girl. He did not reciprocate." I sighed, remembering another folly. "To my shame I even kept a diary that focused on my . . . intense feelings for him."

"Did he know your feelings?"

"Not directly, though he had to have known. Sensed. Are not the senses of the blind more keenly set on instinct and subtleties the rest of us miss? And yet I never expressed my love to him. I relegated all my feelings to that awful diary."

"Awful?"

"The emotions were unseemly and tortured. Obsessed. Eventually, they disgusted me. I felt so intensely, and dissected each word said between us, each meeting . . . I thought I was above such feminine frivolity, and finding I was not . . . I could make myself nearly hysterical trying to find justification to my feelings, and I was always questioning his. Did he really care for me?"

"Did he?"

"Not in the way of romance. As a student, as a comrade, as a protégé. He was a gentleman, and yet . . . sometimes he could be very cold."

"Perhaps he sensed your feelings and his distance was his way of try-ing to quell them."

I nodded. "I did not realize that then, but I do now. I forced him to be cold."

"I am sorry you had to go through that."

"I am not sorry. I was deluded. I acted childishly. I believed him to be the perfect friend."

"No one is—"

"Not even him." I took a deep breath to rid myself of the first part of the story and get to the end. "In truth he was rather self-centered, and . . . even indifferent. I have a tender nature; I am easily swayed by emotion."

"You are a poet," Mary said. "And a woman."

"A wiser woman now." I remembered her original question. "So no, there have been no offers. No one true love."

"I am not a pretty woman, but you, Ba. Why did you not have suitors?"

"I was ill and . . . life was complicated."

"Your father complicated things."

"No, not just . . ." I could not finish it, for she knew the truth of it.

She nodded, reinforcing her statement. "For their differing rea-sons our fathers became the men in our lives, and insisted on being the only men."

Up until this moment, our fathers, being who they were, had been a solidifying factor in our friendship. Yet previously we had spoken of them with full respect. I did not like the vein of our current conversation.

She put a hand on mine. "Admit it, Ba. If not for our fathers' posses-sive natures, and perhaps our own loyal temperaments, you and I would be married with a passel of children between us."

"But I was sick and—"

"Perhaps a loving husband would have made you well."

I was stunned. "Surely you are not implying that the care I received from my father, from my family, was inadequate?"

"A father's love is adequate, Ba. To get by. To sustain. But what of romance? Finding a soul mate? The one person who can be . . ." Mary dabbed the corner of the handkerchief to her eyes. "Have we missed much, Ba? Missed too much?"

I was uncomfortable with our discussion and rose to walk to the window. I scraped at the frost with a fingernail so I could see the chimneys and rooftops before me. I imagined the families in the buildings . . . husbands, wives, and children. "What good does it do to have regrets?" I asked myself as much as Mary.

"None," she said plainly. She moved back upon the sofa, causing her legs to dangle from its edge. With her small size and soft features she looked like a child—a middle-aged child. "Though I do regret not having children, don't you?"

To that I had a definite answer. "I do." I patted the side of my skirt and Flush immediately came and licked my hand. "Children and animals are the soft spots of my heart."

"You could still have children, Ba."

I laughed. "I am thirty-six." I turned to her and smiled. "I will let you go first."

"At fifty-five . . . God would need to produce a mighty miracle."

Even at thirty-six, a miracle would be necessary. Especially since there was no beau in my life, had never been a beau, and would never be a beau. This was my lot. When I first grew ill as a young woman, I never dreamed twenty years would pass me by.

Suddenly, Mary's face crumpled, and she began to sob anew. "Oh dear Father . . . I will miss him so."

Fathers. And daughters. The complexities of the connection were not easily understood—nor maneuvered.

⁓⁂⁓

Mary was allowed to stay with us, and after an evening spent reading to each other, was comfortably ensconced in a small bedroom. There had been many tears throughout the day and she was in much need of sleep.

I too could have used sleep, but I could not succumb—as yet. There was a nightly ritual which must—

I heard a tap upon my door. I looked up from my reading and glanced at the clock on the mantel. It was two minutes until nine, which meant . . .

"Come in, Papa."

The door opened and he entered, his Bible under his arm. I rose and moved to my place by the sofa. He took my hand and helped me to my knees before kneeling at my side. He groaned a bit at the effort, but I knew it would be the last complaint I would hear.

Without preamble he set the Bible on the cushion in front of us and opened it to his choice of passage for the evening. "I will read tonight from the Psalms. Chapter sixty-two, verses five through eight." He cleared his throat. " 'My soul, wait thou only upon God; for my expectation is from him. He only is my rock and my salvation: he is my defence; I shall not be moved. In God is my salvation and my glory: the rock of my strength, and my refuge, is in God. Trust in him at all times; ye people, pour out your heart before him: God is a refuge for us.' "

It was not like Papa to read verses of comfort from the Psalms, for his verse choices were prone to passages that offered moral lessons he wanted me to apply to my life. But today's verses . . .

I risked a glance in his direction. Was he moved by Mary's loss? Was he seeking comfort for his own mortality? Was he thinking of how I would feel when he passed on?

He did not acknowledge my gaze and reverently closed the book, placed one hand upon it, bowed his head, and began to pray aloud. I liked that he did not pray out of a book, but simply, in a flow of words from his heart.

I was mesmerized by his mellow baritone, the warmth of his body so close to mine, the strength of his presence. And once again I was moved by the fact that each evening he chose me—and me alone—as a partner in his prayers. What would I ever do without him?

I felt new tears sting as I remembered Mary's loss. Of all his children,

I loved Papa best. I alone heard the fountain within the rock and I alone struggled towards him through the stones of the rock.

And though it was not *done* I unclasped my hands and slipped one of them around Papa's arm. His only acknowledgment was a slight pause between one word and the next. But he did not tell me to remove it.

And so . . . we prayed. And I added a silent prayer of my own, giving God thanks for the blessing of my father.

FIVE

I put the most recent copy of *The Athenaeum* down with disgust. "They are completely unfair, for he is a genius."

"Who is a genius?" Papa asked. He had brought the periodical to me and sat at the fire, reading the daily newspaper.

"Robert Browning," I said. "He just opened a play, *A Blot in the 'Scutcheon.'*"

Papa made a face. "I do not think the title appealing."

"Appealing or no, I am certain it did not deserve the review it received." I lifted the copy to read aloud. "'If to pain and perplex were the end and aim of tragedy, Mr. Browning's poetic melodrama would be worthy of admiration, for it is a very puzzling and unpleasant piece of business. The acts and feelings of the characters are abhorrent.'" I set the page upon my lap. "He does not deserve such a scathing assessment."

"Perhaps he does. You have not seen the play."

"I do not need to see it to know that its contents cannot be this detestable. Although I never saw him in my life, do not know him even by correspondence, the truth is — and the world should know the truth — it is easier to find a more faultless writer than a poet of equal genius."

"But unfortunately genius does not always incur success."

He spoke the truth. "So which do you suggest poets pursue, Papa? Faultless writing hoping for the good review, or genius?"

"Genius for genius' sake may find only a small audience. It depends on the goal: reaching the masses or grasping genius for the sake of the challenge." He lowered his paper. "Which do you aspire to, Ba?"

It was a good question. I had not had any book published since 1838, the year Bro and I moved to Torquay. . . . "I wish to have my work appreciated."

"By whom? Other poets or the woman or man reading in their drawing room on a cold evening?"

"Both," I said.

" 'Tis not always possible," Papa said.

Unfortunately, I knew *that* to also be true.

⌘

Cousin John rose, his head shaking in frustration. "But I do not wish to have one of your sisters at my dinner party. It is you who would benefit from being there with Wordsworth, you who would add to the discussion. He has asked to come visit you twice, you know. And Robert Browning read some of your work in *The Athenaeum* and also wanted to come and—"

I felt panic rise. "But—"

John held up a hand. "I told them it was not possible." He looked at me over his glasses. "Although it should be."

I knew him to be right. To have these literary notables wish to see *me* and yet be unable to summon the strength of body, and mind, and emotions . . . In many ways I might as well have been in a wilderness, or a hermitage, or a convent, or a prison, as in my room. Yet knowing the condition of my setting and being able to escape from it . . . I could do no more than acknowledge the one and grieve the impossibility of the other.

John sighed. "But back to the dinner party at hand. As dear as your sisters are, they do not possess the breadth of knowledge that entices dynamic conversation."

I did not know what to say. I appreciated his compliment—without being unkind to Henrietta and Arabel. He was generous to continue his invitations. I was sorely tempted and, moreover, desired to go in so many ways. And yet . . . it was impossible. Although there was no physical lock keeping me at home, there was a lock that was just as formidable as iron, keeping me from venturing *out*. The lock was invisible, untouchable, and unexplainable to those who carried on normal lives beyond the walls of our home. They could not understand how I could ever be content. And so I had stopped trying to explain it. For I knew if I complained of my lot to Cousin John he would vehemently come to my defence and incite a royal ranting regarding the unfairness and unfathomable nature of my home imprisonment. He may have been Papa's cousin, but that did not mean the two men agreed—about much. If I had given John leave, he would have fought for my freedom with slashing words and cutting arguments.

That I, a suffering damsel, did not wish to be saved by his gallant actions . . .

John paced back and forth, becoming agitated. I needed to calm him. "I assure you, this home that you take to be a gaol is a place teeming with arts and literature. I am not oblivious to the world." I thought of an example and spotted the basket next to the sofa. "I read the latest magazines. I have read every issue of *Punch* since it came out two years ago."

"I shall get you a commendation from the queen."

He mocked me. But speaking of the queen . . . "In the six years she's been on the throne, Her Majesty has had a tremendous effect on the arts. I approve of the step away from its past brazen nature, into art revealing a more respectable theme. Even I have been affected. Have you not noticed that my poems contain a more optimistic tone?"

"They are still consumed with death and dying."

I raised a finger to make a point. "But within the death is a shred of hope, and the existence of good amid the evil. I have a new volume coming out at the beginning of next year. In it, you will see."

He did not respond but plucked a dead leaf from a philodendron and tucked it into his pocket. "I've asked you to hear Mendelssohn play, and asked you to go to the theatre with me, Ba. You would so enjoy—"

"I do enjoy such things, cousin—in my own way. I am well informed as to the best plays in town, even though Papa forbids both theatre and opera from our experience. I know their story lines, their successes, and their failures. For instance, I know that William Charles Macready is making strides toward supporting new English drama. I heard he produced and starred in Robert Browning's play *Stafford*, and Lord Bulwer-Lytton's *Lady of Lyons* and *Richelieu*. And I know the difference in styles between the actors Kemble and Kean." I thought of something else that might repress his worries. "What do you think of the new invention, the daguerreotype?"

"The . . . ?" He looked confused for but a moment, then nodded. "Nothing will ever take the place of a painted portrait."

My brothers shared this view. "I agree that a painting has the advantage of color and style, but think of a man sitting down in the sun and having his facsimile appear as he is at that moment; a slice of time captured for all eternity."

"They have to be kept under glass; they are very delicate."

"Is not a painting delicate and hung in safekeeping on a wall?"

He put on his grumbled look. " 'Tis not the same."

"Exactly!" I said. "What also excites me is that the artist attempts with the visual what I attempt to do with words: stop time, create a moment, and celebrate the process."

He studied me, and I could tell he was forming an opinion. "These daguerreotypes cannot be reproduced. How have you seen—?"

"That I have not seen does not mean I cannot appreciate."

He nodded, but his lifted eyebrow revealed his belief that he had won the argument.

No. I would make him concede the point that I was attuned to the world, even here, separate from it. I thought of something else that might sway him. "Did you know that I correspond regularly with Benjamin Haydon?"

"The artist?"

I nodded. "Mary arranged for Arabel and Sette to visit his studio where they saw his portrait of Wordsworth. They were so delighted with it, and told Mr. Haydon how much I would enjoy seeing it, that he had it sent here in a cab, for my personal viewing."

John's eyebrows rose. "He sent the portrait here?"

Finally, I had impressed him. "We have been corresponding ever since."

"You've met him, then?"

"No, no. He calls me his 'invisible friend,' but his letters are delightful. You know I prefer correspondence to actual encounter." A tidbit came to mind that would entice him. "Did you know he once was smitten with Caroline Norton?" I did not delve deeper into the gossip I had heard from the artist but secretly enjoyed hearing anything about this poetic rival whose success surpassed my own.

To my disappointment he did not bite but moved to the window and pulled the sheer curtain aside. "There, Ba. Out there are people, teeming with life and emotions, just waiting for you to join them. You say Arabel and Sette went out, and I know Henrietta dines all round, and—"

"Without a chaperon," I added.

John gasped dramatically, putting his hand to his chest, then staggering backwards against the wall. "Oh no! The hussy!"

I looked downward to hide my smile. "It is not proper."

"Henrietta is not a child," John said. "Or even a young woman."

He was right. My sister was thirty-four. Yet there was still the question of the propriety of her actions. There were consequences to being out in London by herself. Dangers from without—and within. If Papa ever found out . . .

John took a seat and crossed his legs. "You need to follow the example of your siblings, Ba. I admire them for their independence. And Henry too."

Showing any admiration regarding my foolhardy brother was unthinkable. "You condone my brother's going against our father's wishes, simply disappearing to Dover after he had been told not to go?"

"It was his twenty-fourth birthday, Ba. Doesn't a young man have a right to celebrate with his friends?" John said.

"But Papa told him no; told him it was nonsense."

"It was not nonsense to Henry." John put his feet to the floor and leaned forwards. "If you are so against your siblings' acts of scandalous freedom, why don't you tattle on them?"

He had made a point I found hard to counter. "I just . . . I cannot do that."

"Why not?" John asked. "If your father is justified regarding his restrictions, and you agree with him in all ways, then why don't you act on his behalf and be warden to this Wimpole Street gaol?"

"This is not a gaol," I said. "Our home is sacred, our home is a loving place, our home is run on—"

"Blind loyalty?"

I felt my heart palpitating yet I could not let Papa's character be disparaged. "You know Papa allows us to go out, he allows friendships and amusements."

"Allows. That is the key word which elicits deeper inquiry," John said.

"Papa simply *suggests* it is not necessary to venture far beyond our own family for satisfaction. We *are* enough. If only my siblings would realize that it would be far better for all of us." I did not tell him how pained I was when they caused Papa to chastise them. How I detested the sound of loud voices and conflict.

John lounged in the chair once again. "I hear George and Stormie are leaving on a grand tour. Apparently, they feel this house is *not* enough."

"That is different," I said. "And if I were strong and free, I should be running myself all over the world. I should be in Paris and Italy. I should be longest in Germany, in the Alps and the Pyrenees and—"

John's face revealed his shock. I realized the duplicity of my comments and felt myself blush.

His surprise changed to smugness. "So . . . it appears Wimpole Street is not enough for even you, the ever-loyal daughter and keeper of the familial flame."

"There is no betrayal in desiring to see the world, the wonders of God's nature, the cities that gave birth to great civilizations, the architecture of—"

John sprang to his feet. "Then let us go. Now."

"Go?"

"London is the birth city of a great civilization. There is plenty of architecture and parks and rivers to inaugurate your world journeys." He moved to the doorway of my room. "Crow? Fetch Miss Elizabeth her wheelchair and wrap. We are venturing out, into the autumn bliss."

Crow appeared at the door, her countenance confused. "Miss?"

"No, no," I said. I looked at John imploringly. "Please, cousin. Stop. I don't feel well and—"

His eyes found mine. Then he sighed, his head shaking with frustrated acknowledgement. "High talk comes cheap, Ba."

I raised my chin. "I am allowed dreams, am I not?"

He offered a barely discernable shrug and checked his pocket watch. "I must go. My dinner party, you know." He gathered his hat and walking stick, and came to the bedside to kiss me on the forehead. "Forgive me for being so frank with you, Ba, and for causing upset. I only want what is best for you."

And so, with a rustle of busyness, he left me. Alone with my dreams.

My unattainable, unreachable dreams?

Suddenly, the weight of them pressed upon me and threatened me with suffocation. I needed air. I needed release. I needed . . .

"Crow!"

She appeared at the doorway again. "He's gone," she said, as if that were the reason for my calling.

"I wish to go out."

"Out?" She repeated the word as though it were foreign. She looked over her shoulder, then said, "Are you going to Mr. Kenyon's dinner party?"

I diverted an answer with action, pushing myself to standing beside the sofa. Flush, who'd been asleep in the sunlight, aroused and came to my side. Could I go to the dinner party?

Crow hurried to my armoire and opened its doors. "I don't think you have a thing to wear. But maybe you could borrow an evening dress from Miss Arabel or Miss Hen—"

The image of fussing over dresses and hair and jewelry quickly overwhelmed me. It had been so long since I had attended an occasion that I had no basis for the process. Besides, I had worn only black since Bro's death. . . .

I looked at the sofa longingly. It called to me: *Sit with me. Recline. Relax in my gentle comfort. Do not venture into the bustle and noise of the world. Stay here with me.*

But Flush, awakened from his nap, scampered towards the door of my room, then back in, then towards the door. He needed to go out.

Out.

"Flush needs a walk."

She glanced in his direction. "I will take him. Hopefully, he will do his business quickly so I can get back here to help you get ready to—"

"No, *we* will take him," I said.

"We?"

"I am not going to the dinner party because I am taking Flush for his walk."

"Walk?"

She took the word too literally. No, I did not walk much, even within the house. "We are taking him *out*," I said. "Get my wrap and the wheelchair. We both wish to take a jaunt to Regent's Park." I suffered immediate second thoughts. "Is Father at home?"

"No, Miss Elizabeth. He is still at work."

I nodded tightly, my mind reeling. Should I still risk it? What if Papa came home early?

Crow took the decision out of my hands. "I'll get the chair put out, then come back for you."

She was already on the stairs when I offered a weak, "I'll be here."
And soon there.

May God help me.

⁓❦⁓

The noise assailed me first. Although I regularly heard the clatter of the street through open windows, it was far removed. To be out, to be in the midst of it, to have it swarm and pulse around me . . .

I was afraid.

I knew it was ridiculous, but I could not help it. I wanted to grab Flush into my lap and cling to him as if our combined strength could make us safe from . . . from whatever it was that was so frightening.

It was immediately obvious Flush did not share my fears, for he trotted beside the wheelchair as if this were his domain and he were a prince on parade.

And his subjects responded with adulation. A fruit seller bent low and called him by name, "Come 'ere, Flush, me boy. Come get yerself a berry." Crow turned the wheelchair towards the man, allowing Flush access to the treat—and a pat to the head and a scratch behind the ears.

The man stood and doffed his cap. "Afternoon, miss, Miss Barrett, I assume?"

"Yes," I said, a bit baffled he knew it was me.

He must have seen my perplexity, for he added, "We alls around 'ere know Flush, but it's an honour to meet his famous mistress."

Famous? Me?

Crow took over. "We have to be going now, Will'am. I'll want a few plums on our way back."

He nodded and stepped aside, allowing us to continue our journey towards the park. When we were but a few steps away, Crow leaned close and said, "Last year his daughter married the butcher's son."

"That's nice," I said.

"He's just found out there's going to be a baby soon. So proud was he, he nearly gave away the contents of his cart the day he found out he was to be a grandfather."

Grandfather. And grandchild. What a blessing.

Then a thought struck me as mightily as if a hand had struck my cheek: Papa would never receive the pleasure of being a grandfather. If none of his children married, then—

Suddenly, a man rushed towards us, and before I had time to focus upon his nearness, he snatched Flush into his arms and ran, pulling Flush's leash right out of my hands.

"Flush!"

"Thief! Thief!" Crow screamed.

People's heads whipped in our direction, then up and down the street.

"That way!" I said. "He took my dog and ran that way!"

William, the fruit tender, caught up with us, gathering men and boys along the way. "That way, men. Go fetch Miss Barrett her dog."

Following his direction, they made haste down the street. William stopped beside us. "I am sorry for that, miss. Dog-pinchin's have become far too common of late."

At first I thought he was joking. "Dog-pinchin's?"

"There's an organized band of thieves 'oo call themselves The Fancy. They make a good living from the habit."

"They sell the dogs?" I asked.

William shook his head. "They ransom them."

"We won't pay a farthing," Crow said.

"Oh yes we will!" I countered.

William looked at Crow. "It is the only way to ever see the mutts ag'in. In fact, you best get home so's to get the ransom note."

"But how will they know where to send—"

"They most likely recognized you, Miss Barrett."

"But I don't go out—"

He waved a hand at the neighbourhood around us. "We alls know where you live. We alls know your work and your—" he glanced at me, sitting there in the wheelchair, and then away—"your situation."

Cousin John had intimated that people of London knew about my personal life, but I thought he was exaggerating towards the cause of getting me to socialize. To know that a fruit vendor, and even dog thieves, knew about me was disconcerting.

"You best go home and await the demand," William repeated.

"Yes, yes," I said. "Crow, take us home. Quickly."

As we hurried away, William called after us, "I'll keep the boys on it, miss. We'll do what we can to get our Flush back."

Our Flush?

My Flush. My dearest companion. Taken because I had been fool enough to venture away from the safety of our home.

⁓❦⁓

I heard the voices of my brothers as they came through the front door and raced up the stairs to my room. Sette entered first with Henry and Alfred at his heels.

Sette was out of breath. "We've posted the flyers as you asked, Ba. Everyone in a ten-block area knows about Flush."

"But it's been a full day," I said. "How can there be no sign of him?"

Henry fell into the chair nearest the fireplace and dabbed at his forehead with his handkerchief. "As we suspected, this is not some random thievery. We heard that the organized dog banditti make four thousand pounds a year from their evil trade."

Four thousand? It was an income that would make most men far satisfied.

Henrietta came to the door of my room. "Papa says it is dinner and you are all to come down at once."

"Good," Henry said, rising from the chair. "I'm famished."

"How can you eat, when dear Flush—"

"I will not expire for a dog, sister."

I took offence. "If it were your Catiline who had been stolen, I am certain you would be without appetite."

"If those ruffians had tried to steal my mastiff, she would have bitten their hands off."

I did not doubt it. I disliked my brother's dog and kept Flush away from her.

They left me and I heard the faint rumblings of the family gathering three floors below in the dining room. Crow stood in the hall, peering over the railing. "Would you like me to fetch you up a plate?" she asked.

"No, nothing," I said. "I will not eat until Flush is safely—"

A heavy knock on the front door sped up the stairs to my ears. I held my breath. Was it the thieves?

I heard a voice in the foyer.

I motioned Crow close, wanting her to help me up. Together we hurried to the landing to listen.

"Give him back to us," Alfred said to the visitor.

"Well, you see, I can't do that," a man said. "I woulda worked with you, but since you had the cheek to post bills, advertising the . . . the situation . . . I just don't know."

"You expected us to stand by and—"

It was my idea to display the flyers. If my action hurt Flush . . .

"Well, perhaps we can come to some sort of arrangement."

"How much?" Alfred asked.

"Five guineas should do it."

"I don't have it."

"But I am sure somebody in this grand house does."

Suddenly, I heard my father's voice. "Sir, you are a rascal. I should not give you any money for your crime, but will give you two guineas. If you do not accept my terms, then you shall be given into the charge of the police."

"Well, sir, then I bid you adieu. And you can bid your dog adieu too."

"Out!" Papa said. "Get out of this house!"

I heard the door slam shut and would have hurled myself down the stairs if I'd been able. "They can't let him go," I said to Crow. "They can't!"

From below I heard my father's voice, muffled by his proximity in the dining room. "Do not tell your sister of this. We should not upset her."

I stepped back in my room and leaned against the door. "Not upset me? As if the thievery itself was not cause for upset enough?"

Crow tried to lead me to my bed, but I remained firm. "Help me downstairs. I must make them pay the money."

"You can't do that," Crow said. "You know you can't. Your father . . ."

She was right. If I were to burst into the dining room and demand my father make the ridiculous payment . . . All that I was, all that I tried so hard to be, would be lost.

I let Crow get me back to bed. "What am I to do?" I asked her.

"I don't know, miss. But we'll think of something."

⁘

I thought of something. The idea came to me in the middle of the night, interrupting my fitful sleep.

I would get Papa to pay the two guineas that he had offered, and unbeknownst to him, I would pay the other three out of my own pocket. If I was careful, he would never find out. I would send one of my brothers to do the deed, and by the time Papa got home from work Flush would be returned and all would be right with the world.

Henry would be the best one to ask. He was accustomed to taking risks and was known to rebel against Papa. He would probably find satisfaction in the subterfuge.

It was hard for me to not wake Henry in the midnight and tell him of my plan. I forced myself to wait until the dawn began its ascent and I heard movement in the house.

I quietly summoned Crow, for no one ever expected me to be up before noon. She was surprised by my call, and I caught her in her nightdress. "Miss?"

"Go summon Henry. Ask him to come here. Quietly."

Her face asked why, but she did not wait for an answer.

I pulled my dressing gown about me and sat in a chair to wait for him.

He came to the door, buttoning his shirt, his hair disheveled. "What is it, Ba? I was asleep and have no reason to wake so early—"

I motioned him close with the crook of a finger. "I have a proposition for you," I said. "It involves much danger and intrigue." Some danger and some intrigue.

His face lost its sleepy softness and gained an awakened edge. "What is it?"

I told him my plan and he nodded his approval. "You surprise me, Ba."

"I surprise me too," I said. "Let's just say my despair has overcome my sense of obedience."

"I applaud the cause and hope it is the first of many acts of courage to come."

"It is my only act," I said, "and it is accomplished for the sake of poor Flush, who is probably suffering horribly at the hands of those hooligans." I motioned him away. "Now go. You must ask Papa for his two guineas before he leaves for work."

Once he had gone, Crow asked, "Do you think it will work?"

"It has to."

⁓⁂⁓

I could not read. I could not write letters. I could not sleep. My ears were those of a deer in the forest, keen to all sound.

Although Crow and my sisters had tried to lure me downstairs to be closer for Henry's return from the dog thief, I could not bring myself to do it. Now, above all other times, I needed the comfort of my room.

And yet, all around me were reminders of my Flush. His pillow on the floor, placed where it could be warmed by the sun for his afternoon nap. His bowl of water near the fireplace, his favourite knotted stocking that he loved to play tug with, and a bone from the beef roast that had been enjoyed by all the evening before he was taken.

He is just a dog.

I shook such traitorous thoughts away. Although they toyed with logic, they also toyed with my very soul. Flush was more than a dog to me, he was *mine*. In this household, in the midst of this family, we belonged to each other, and loved each other unconditionally, ignoring our imperfections as inconsequential, and taking our strengths and attributes to a higher level simply *because*.

I had heard Henrietta whisper to Arabel, "If this does not turn out . . . we *will* get her another dog," and it had taken all my self-restraint not to verbally attack her cold illogic. How I wished to march to her chair, stand over her, and say, "Could *you* be replaced with another woman off the street? Could Arabel? Could I?" But I did not say the words aloud. I knew my love for Flush was unique. That my sister did not know such a love was her loss.

I looked at the mantel clock. Henry had been gone over three hours, and Papa would be home from work any minute. I didn't want to have to explain—

I heard the front door open and held my breath, waiting to hear Papa's usual "I'm home, family" or Henry—

The sound of feet scampering up the stairs pulled me out of my bed as though yanked by a leash. Flush ran into my skirts and I knelt down to take him into my arms. He licked my face, and I buried my nose into his fur. Henry and my sisters found us very much in celebration—which I left in order to embrace my brother.

"How can I ever thank you?"

He put a hand on the cheek that I had kissed—too seldom. "You can take care to not let it happen again, for next time I will not go after him."

All entered my room and sat. Without any prodding Flush jumped upon my lap and snuggled on the cushion of my skirt. "Was it so horrible?" I asked.

"I never want to venture into such a neighbourhood again. I, who like adventure, have hereby realized there is a limit." He shuddered. "The conditions those people live in, the filth. The atmosphere of ever-present danger."

I pulled Flush's head to my chest. "I cannot abide the thought of the horrors my Flush has experienced these past two days."

"He seems well enough," Henrietta said.

Arabel wrinkled her nose. "Though he is a bit more . . . fragrant."

I allowed myself to inhale the scent of him. She was right. I had been so enraptured with his return, I had not noticed. I looked for Crow and saw the edge of her skirt as she slunk into the hall, out of sight.

"Crow?" I asked.

She stepped into the doorway with a sigh. "A bath for Prince Flush, yes, yes, I'll see to it. Come, boy."

Although I hated to let him out of my sight, I let him go.

"The thief did not ask for more than the two guineas?" Henrietta asked.

I gave Henry a quick glance. We had decided not to share the details of our arrangement to lessen the chance that Papa—

We all heard the front door open once more. "I'm home, fam—" Then, "Well, well, young Flush. Glad to have you home."

"He's going to be washed, Mr. Barrett," Crow said.

"Ah. So. Fresh and new."

Henrietta and Arabel went down to greet him as he ascended the stairs.

"Ah, daughters. I see Flush has returned. So the ransom was paid?"

I held my breath. Henrietta answered. "Two sovereigns, I believe— but I really know very little about it."

"Hmm," Papa said. "Two sovereigns and I dare say three besides."

Henry and I gasped and looked one to the other. "He knows?" I whispered.

Henry held up a hand, proclaiming his innocence. "I said nothing. He can't know."

But he could. Papa knew everything.

When I heard his feet upon the final stairs, my entire body tightened. He would chastise me for going against his wishes, for ignoring his proclamation to the thief that we would pay no more than two guineas. I had never, ever knowingly disobeyed him. That I had done such a thing *and* asked my brother to conspire with me was a horrible offence against everything I held dear between us.

And yet . . . because of my action, Flush was returned. Surely that counted for something.

As Papa gained the last few steps, I steeled myself towards that defence. Yes, I was sorry for taking matters into my own hands, but surely he could understand the importance of the risk and celebrate with me the happy result.

As soon as he entered the opened door, his eyes scanned the room. "Henry."

"Father." Henry stood. "If you'll excuse me?"

As Henry passed, Papa put a hand upon his arm. "Do we have you to thank for Flush's return?"

He cast a furtive glance over Papa's shoulder towards me. Then he met our father's eyes. "Yes."

There was a moment between them, a precarious slice of time perched upon a fence post, wavering left, then right . . .

Finally Papa nodded once, clapped Henry on the arm, and said, "Well done."

Henry wisely did not wait for more but escaped down the stairs in double time.

Papa turned his eyes upon me. Would I receive the same grace? Or would he ask about the source of the extra "three besides," which could only have come from me?

He approached the foot of the sofa and I moved my legs to the side to allow him space to sit. He put a hand upon my knee and I held my breath.

But then . . . he smiled. "You have had a hard few days, my dear puss."

He had not called me that in years. It was a childhood endearment that was mine alone.

I managed a nod, a hand upon his, and a weak smile. "But now all is well."

"All turned out well," he said. "Somehow." There was an extra emphasis on the last word that told me he knew, he *knew*. . . .

But before I could react, could fall into his arms with weeping apologies, he stood to leave. "I must change. It has been a long day. I will be up later for our prayers." He paused at the door and gave me a pointed look. "We must come before God and confess our transgressions and thank Him for His mercies."

Indeed.

Six

I heard a disturbance above, from the roof. Sette? Screaming?

I remembered seeing my brother and his fencing tutor traversing past my room to the open space of the roof to go practice—

Fencing.

Swords.

The scream gained horrific meaning.

I tossed my writing aside, jumped from the sofa, ran into the hallway towards the small door leading—

Sette appeared with the tutor close behind. He had a handkerchief pressed to his eye. It was scarlet with blood.

"Sette!" I stepped to the side. "In here. Lie down!"

"He was not wearing a mask, even though I repeatedly reminded him," explained the tutor. "He slipped and the sword—"

"I feel faint," Sette said, stumbling against the frame of the door.

I took one side of him and the tutor took the other. Together we led him to my bed. I gathered a clean towel, wet it in the basin, and exchanged it for the handkerchief. The gash was not large, but so near the eye as to cause me to wince at the implications.

There was commotion on the stairs, shouting and many footsteps. Henry came in first, took one look, and said, "I'll send for a surgeon."

Yes, yes, and quickly too.

The room filled with my brothers and sisters, and I willingly let them take command. I slunk into the background, hoping Sette's eyesight would be saved. And even beyond that . . . only a minuscule measure higher and the stroke would have been instantaneously mortal.

I wished Papa were home.

"You will be fine, I think," Alfred said, handing the now bloodied towel to Henrietta for changing.

But would he? We Barretts were known to die with little warning. Would Sette join the others who had gone before? Mother, Sam, Bro, and even our little sister Mary, when I was but a child myself.

Arabel saw me tucked away in the corner between curtain and wall. The pity on her face marked her move from Sette's aid to my own. "Ba, you are too pale. Sit or we will have you to nurse too."

She was right. This drama was not about me, and I had no right to draw their care. I sat in the chair farthest from the bed and gripped its arms, willing it to give me the strength I sorely needed for this moment.

And then I prayed. And prayed.

~ ❦ ~

God heard my prayers and answered them. Sette's injury had indeed been cause for fear, but the cut would heal, and the black and blue around his eye gave him much fodder for conversation. Although Papa chastised him for not wearing the fencing mask, and though Sette promised he had learned his lesson, I was not so sure. Sette was still one of my favourites, but he was more boy than man, and embraced the attitude of invincibility that so often fooled the young.

I was not so easily deceived. I knew death lurked around every corner, just waiting for us to lower our guard.

And so, as Sette spent the evening in the drawing room, regaling his close call with an alarming sense of bravado, I took to my bed, hugging the pillow upon which he had laid his head, thanking God for His mercy, and begging Him to erect a dome of protection around my family. They must be kept safe. I could not live without them. They were everything to me.

This is what I get for being too happy. . . .

I knew I shouldn't feel this way, yet the repetition of crises at various points in my life—just as I was on the verge of crawling out of my dour hole—was undeniable. My prayers of *Why, God, why?* received no response. I knew the Almighty could and would do what He wished, when He wished to do it. Yet, pragmatic woman that I was, I wished to know His reasons.

Actually, I longed for more than that. I wished God would listen to my advice and adjust His will to match mine.

I did not share this desire with Papa, for I knew he would be on God's side and I would receive a discourse on accepting authority, both temporal and divine. The line between heavenly Father and my earthly parent often became blurred, for I was beholden to both. Subject to both.

And so as Sette quickly moved past his brush with death, I sat with it placed firmly in my lap, vying for room with Flush. Death was an indefatigable threat, and on its opposite, life was tenuous, dangerous, and unpredictable. I was repeatedly torn between the desire to emerge and engage versus my instinct to withdraw and reject all that was not safe and planned and under my control.

There was little enough of that.

And yet . . . as I heard laughter and conversation rise up the stair shaft into my room, I despaired of ever being like the rest of them.

I kissed Flush on the head and pulled him ever closer. Somehow, somewhere . . . could I find the joy that eluded me? I needed to become resolved to look at the brightest side as long as there was any life left within me.

"But where is that brightest side?" I asked aloud.

At that moment Flush bounded out of my arms as though launched to some canine purpose. He was not graceful about it and caused a sheaf of papers to scatter on the floor.

"Crow—"

I stopped my calling, for Crow had taken the evening off. It was up to me to clean up the mess.

And so with a grumble on my lips and a groan to my limbs, I got to the floor and gathered pages thrown here and there, pages of my newest attempts at poetry. As I put them one upon the other, my eyes glanced across a few of the words: *I think we are too ready with complaint in this fair world of God's....*

My hands stopped all motion, and so too my heart stopped its beating. These words . . . they were mine, an observation, a chastisement.

A confession?

I read the words again, reconnecting with each one, reclaiming them as my own. And I read further, until the final word finished the full thought.

> I think we are too ready with complaint
> In this fair world of God's. Had we no hope
> Indeed beyond the zenith and the slope
> Of yon grey blank of sky, we might grow faint
> To muse upon eternity's constraint
> Round our aspirant souls; but since the scope
> Must widen early, is it well to droop,
> For a few days consumed in loss and taint?
> O pusillanimous Heart, be comforted
> And, like a cheerful traveler, take the road,
> Singing beside the hedge. What if the bread
> Be bitter in thine inn, and thou unshod
> To meet the flints? At least it may be said
> "Because the way is short, I thank thee, God."

Tears found my cheeks. The poem expressed my soul and challenged me to set aside my complaints and be cheerful. Life *was* difficult, but we had a choice as to how to make the journey. Would complaint be our companion? Or joy?

"Take your own lesson, Ba," I said to the room.

Flush, unused to having me on his level, came to my side with tail wagging. I used him as the audience to my decision. "This work, boy, this work . . . all my earthly futurity as an individual lies in poetry. In other respects the game is up. But poetry lingers. It is like a will to be written."

It was a will, but also took an act of will. And so . . . I gathered it up, and returned to my calling.

My legacy.

And the complaints that disgraced my character? They had to stop.

God deserved better.

My best.

Such as it was.

⁓❦⁓

I looked at the engravings of fellow writers, set before me across the mantel.

"Is this agreeable?" Cousin John adjusted the last two so they would fit.

"Very," I said. "They are a gathering of the finest literary minds."

He stepped back, joining me in assessing the effect. "Your likeness also appears in the book, yes?"

"Oh no," I said, perusing the engravings of Dickens, Smith, Talfourd, Wordsworth, Carlyle, Tennyson, Browning, Jameson, and Martineau that Richard Henry Horne had given me after their use was complete within his book, *A New Spirit of the Age.* "Richard asked for my portrait, but I could not do such a thing." My gaze returned to one portrait in particular. I moved to the mantel to study it better. I turned back to John. "Is this a good likeness?"

"Browning? Yes. I suppose it is."

I nodded and returned it to its place among the others. It was in profile, with a nose somewhat large, a sensitive mouth, and long hair. I found myself wishing that his neck were not covered with beard. I longed to see the true jawline. Did it possess the strength that I found within his written word?

John perused a copy of the book, just released. "I will say it is pleasing that women are allowed in this study of the leading literaries of the day."

"Hence, the *New* in the title," I explained. "Mr. Horne wished to distinguish this work from that of Hazlitt in 1825 in which only men were noted."

"You worked so hard to help Horne compile the writings." He closed the cover. "Yet I see no acknowledgement?"

There was an explanation for that. "Whatever I sent to him, he added to, so there is little that is mine alone. I have not read the final version as yet, but am sure he did my suggestions justice. And so I am willing to let him take credit for the editing. He is a dear friend."

"I have not met him. What is he like?" John asked, taking a seat. "In person."

I felt myself blush. "Oh, I have not met him either—although he has tried with great persistence." I thought of the time I *had* agreed to meet him, only to have him send word that he could not come, an act which had caused me to clap my hands for joy when I felt the danger of his society to be passed.

"But you speak of him as if . . . I know you have worked with him for many years."

"Ah, the power of the letter," I said. "In words he proves himself to be a cultured and gracious gentleman."

"Perhaps in words . . ."

Innuendo was evident. "You said you did not know him, cousin."

"But I have heard—" he glanced at me, then away, then back—"I heard he proposed to two women in two days—each possessing a fortune, which no doubt increased his interest."

I was shocked. This was not the man who had revealed himself to me in our correspondence. "Perhaps it is just gossip?"

John cocked his head. "Can the truth still be labeled gossip?"

The truth was . . . the truth and could not be veiled. "*If* what you say is true," I said, "then I declare his baldheartedness ten times over worse than his baldheadedness."

John laughed. "An apt take on the situation, dear Ba."

I returned to my sofa, patted my lap, and Flush took his place. I was through discussing Mr. Horne. To change the subject I pointed at the portraits. "I was thinking of having a few of these framed for my wall. They are such nice likenesses."

"I can guess which one," John said.

Oh dear. I had not wished for my interest in one of the writers to be so obvious. "A *few of these*," I repeated. "In right hero worship," I added. "Perhaps Tennyson because he is a poet on the rise. He makes me thrill sometimes to the end of my fingers, as only a truly great poet can." I perused the others, giving commentary. "Wordsworth, for certain, Carlyle . . . and Harriet Martineau because she is the profoundest woman thinker in England."

I felt, rather than saw, John smiling.

"And . . . ?"

I might as well just say it. "Probably Browning because of his height and depth of thought. In his *Paracelsus* I saw sudden repressed gushings of tenderness. He is a poet in the holy sense. "

"Um-hmm." He looked far too smug. "For him to have written *Paracelsus* on the one hand and the child's *Pied Piper of Hamelin* . . . 'tis quite a contrast, and hardly holy. I have heard Miss Mitford state that it was too bad Browning had missed his true calling of being an engineer or a merchant's clerk."

The words *were* Mary's, and they stung. "She and I disagree, and she peeves me greatly when she says such things."

"I am certain Robert would be honoured to have such an avid defender. Perhaps I should bring him by. Or one of the others?"

In spite of myself, my heart leapt. "Who?"

"You choose," he said with a grin.

I hid my blush by burying my cheek against the top of Flush's head. He anticipated the attention and turned his face to greet me with a lick. "I could perhaps meet Mrs. Jameson." I felt John's eyes upon me, and willed myself to appear unaffected. "Do you know her?" I asked.

"Of course," John said.

With those two words, I felt the heat of my face dissipate. "I do admire her work. Eleven books to her name, from analyses of Shakespeare's women to art and travel books. I especially enjoyed her *Pictures of the Social Life of Germany*."

"You know why she has traveled so much, do you not?" John asked.

I had heard many rumours but wished to hear his version. "Not really."

"Her father painted court miniatures and made sure Anna learned Persian, French, Italian, and Spanish."

"Persian?"

"By the age of seven."

"Truly a precocious child."

"As was someone else I know."

I accepted his compliment. "The languages would certainly have come to good use in her travels. Did she go with her father?"

John shook his head. "She became a governess at age sixteen and traveled with the family. She is a great observer."

I used this moment to bring up the rumours regarding her marriage. "I heard at first that she rejected her husband, and that after they became betrothed, he, in revenge, rejected her at the altar."

"Not true," he said.

I found myself disappointed, for the story read like a scene in a novel. "But she is *Mrs.* Jameson."

"She is. Though her husband is not here. He has a position in Canada."

"Why is she not with him?"

"Their marriage is not . . . amiable."

"Oh," I said. And suddenly, my inappropriate pleasure in the gossip turned to sympathy. "I am sorry for her."

"It is what it is." His face brightened. "But I know she would enjoy meeting you. She is aware of your work."

That such a woman would know of me. Suddenly, the idea of receiving her opinions . . . "Perhaps she could write to me?"

"She would much rather meet you. Do you remember that I wanted you to meet her two years ago, but you sent your sisters instead?"

"But through them I gained knowledge of her — in her whole anatomy. You know how talented I am at living vicariously."

"Perhaps you should try living directly?"

It was an old argument and I shook my head adamantly. "A letter, cousin. Could you request a letter?"

He sighed with his usual frustration. "I will suggest it."

I was satisfied. To acquire another correspondent gave me great joy. I may not have had face-to-face friends, but my friends of the pen . . .

I would hold such relationships against any others.

⤝⋆⤞

I stared at my copy of *A New Spirit of the Age*, certain I must have read the line wrongly.

I reread a comment I recognized as originally my own but found that Richard had completely changed its meaning by the addition of the word *not*. I had said I admired a work, and Richard had made me say the opposite. How could he?

This was not the first edit that was misappropriated. On an earlier page I found that my description of Mrs. Shelley's work had been ascribed to Mrs. Trollope.

It was one thing to edit a word here and there, but to change my meaning was . . . was unconscionable.

I scratched Flush fiercely behind the ears. "No wonder the book is being disparaged so. Surely others have found the discrepancies and the sheer falsehoods . . ."

Suddenly I feared what Mr. Horne had written about me. I had thought it too pretentious and prideful to seek the passage first thing, but now . . .

I found the page regarding my own literary contributions. I was horrified to see that Richard had paired my name with Caroline Norton — my nemesis!

I read part of the pairing aloud. " 'One is all womanhood; the other all wings.' " I knew very well which was which, and resented that it implied I was not womanly.

I read further and found more distress. *In spite of poor health and being shut up in one room for six or seven years as an invalid—often spending several weeks in the dark—she is deeply conscious of the loss of external nature's beauty. Her work too often contains an energetic morbidity on the subject of death, together with a certain predilection for terrors. And yet, she is like an inspired priestess whose individuality is cast upwards in the divine afflatus, and dissolved and carried off in the recipient breath of angelic ministrants.*

"What?" I pressed a hand against my chest, trying to calm the sudden palpitations. Richard had made me out to be a freak, owning macabre tendencies while holding myself up to be some ethereal seraph.

I slapped the book closed and tossed it across the room. "How dare he!"

Crow rushed in to check on the commotion.

"Go!" I yelled, which of course did not send her running but caused her to withdraw with a shrug. I did not have tantrums often, but when I did, Crow knew it was best to leave me alone with them.

With one hand pressed to my chest, the other found my head — which had begun to ache. This morning had started well, with my feeling in reasonable health, but now, because of Richard Horne's duplicity . . .

What should I do?

What could I do? There was no way to defend myself—especially since the essence of how Richard had defined my personal life was based on truth. I could not publicly defend myself without going public, and that, I could never do. I now saw the lack of my name on the cover as a blessing.

But the pairing of my work with Caroline Norton's, that hurt me more than the exaggeration of my situation.

And that . . . that I could do something about.

If I had wanted to get a new book published before, now . . . I was determined to make the world see that Elizabeth Barrett and Caroline Norton were not in any way similar.

Weakened from the emotional upheaval, I did not feel well enough to get up and gather my work. I rang the bell for Crow.

She entered my room and said, "It is safe now, I assume?"

I ignored her comment. "My work. Please bring it to me."

She shook her head. "Not after that outburst. I know you, Miss Elizabeth, and I know that at such times what you need is—"

"My work," I said again. "If you please."

The strength in my words—however applied—was enough to get her to gather my pages.

In spite of my fragile state, I took up my writing where I had left it off.

Richard Henry Horne would not get the better of me.

Just let him try.

∼✥∽

"You are what?"

Crow stood before me and raised her chin defiantly. "Married, miss. Since the thirtieth of last December."

"But it is nearly April."

"I . . . we . . ." Crow faltered. "My William thought it best to keep things as they were as long as possible."

Things "as they were" was having Crow minister to me, and her new husband, William Treherne, hold the position of our butler.

" 'Tis not like we—the both of us—have not been loyal, miss. I've been with you five years, since before you went to Torquay. And William, he's been with the family since Hope End, starting out as a tenant farmer before coming to work for you as a stable boy. We are loyal, miss. You know that."

I knew that. Most of our servants were loyal. Minny Robinson had started out as Arabel's nurse and was now our housekeeper, meaning she had worked within our family for over twenty-five years. Although I would miss my maid—for Crow had become much more to me than that—what soured me the most was the deceit involved, for deception was a wicked transgression worthy of the highest disdain.

"And . . ." Crow shifted to her other foot. "You might as well know that I am with child."

My mind reeled with the implications and I felt a headache coming on. "And you married in secret? Do you realize what people will infer?"

Crow blushed. "Let them infer all they will. William and I are legally wed, and . . . and we've done our jobs well all these months, being man and wife yet not truly living, not staying . . ." Her blush deepened.

I tried to think of a time I had seen them together where they might have given some indication . . . I could think of no such time. As far as my eyes had seen, they had been discreet. Actually, I could be certain that no Barrett had suspected anything, or I would have heard of it.

She continued. "We know you don't approve, so we are both giving our notice. We're going to start a bakery shop."

A laugh escaped. "You are not a cook and neither is William."

She shuffled her shoulders. "We knows enough, and we can learn the rest. With a baby on the way, we need to 'ave our own business. We stayed as long as we could." She put her hands over her midsection.

"Has my father . . . ? Has William given his notice too?"

"Aye, miss. Today. He'll be leaving straightaway to get the shop set."

"And you?"

"I can stay a few weeks, to help you find a replacement."

I shook my head, stalling until I thought of some argument against that which was already accomplished. I soon thought of something. "He is not good enough for you."

"Ah me, do not say such a thing."

"He is honest and good in a common way, but he is not remarkable."

"Neither am I, miss."

"*Au contraire*, dear Crow," I said, taking her hands in mine. "You are the essence of all things good. You manage me with infinite wisdom and kindness, and you carry me — in all ways." I thought of the times Crow had actually lifted me wholly and carried me. "You are my keeper, sheltering me from any and all who would harm me."

"No one wants to harm you, miss," she said.

"Upset me, then," I countered. "You keep the world away and are due great credit towards creating my lovely sanctum here."

"I merely want you to be happy," she said.

With those words, without warning, even from within my own being, I hurled myself towards her, encasing her in my arms. "What will I do without you? You are more than a maid to me. We have sat in this very room and read aloud together. I have lent you some of my prized volumes."

She gently, but determinedly, pushed me towards standing alone. "You are dear to me too, miss, as dear as a sister, and I have enjoyed our times together through sickness and . . ."

She could not say *health* because in the five years she had been at my side, I had never been truly well.

"Sickness and hard times," she finally said. "When your brother died I was saddened as if he were my own."

This time, it was I who put some distance between us. "And so . . . knowing the loss I have suffered, you cannot leave me. I will not allow it."

She gave me one of her looks that was stemmed with patience yet edged with condescension. "William and I 'ave a new life now, miss, and with the baby . . ."

I knew I should be happy for them, for wasn't it every woman's dream to have a family and a home of her own?

Not every woman . . .

Yet even with my inner acknowledgement the pettiness leached out.

"Fine," I said. "You leave. Abandon me to fend for myself while you . . . you . . . go and . . . bake something."

There was that look again, but this time, a smile was added. She patted her abdomen and said, "Yes'm, I guess I'll learn how to deal with two types of buns in the oven."

Her wit and use of words had been another endearing attribute. I could not withhold a smile. With difficulty I forced it away and shook a finger at her. "You have angered me, Crow. You know that, don't you?"

She clasped her hands in front of her apron. "I know that," she said with a nod.

"You have saddened me beyond words." Tears threatened, which was, after all, a right response to having one's world torn apart.

"I know that too," she said. Her eyes glistened as well.

We stood there, looking upon each other a good moment. Then, both needing release, she held out her arms to me, and I went to her, and let her take care of me — one more time.

⁓⁘⁓

Henrietta helped me with my hair, curling the ringlets around her finger and setting them as a frame about my face. "There," she said, taking a step back. "You are lovely."

"I am never lovely," I said. "But I suppose I am presentable to a *maid*."

I hated the disdain in which I had pronounced the last word. For I prided myself on treating servants well. It was my mother's doing; she had set the tone for us. That some people of society taught their children not to talk to servants . . . it was an atrocity both in morals and instincts.

Henrietta did not comment on my faux pas. She knew how stressed I was about the changeover from Crow to this new maid she had interviewed and hired. Her name was Elizabeth Wilson. She had been referred to us by a Barrett cousin and was from Northumberland. Supposedly she was gentle-voiced and of a bright and kind countenance.

It did not matter. That she was not Crow outplayed any of her supposed attributes.

There was a knock on the door below. Henrietta jumped to her feet. "That must be her." She pointed a finger at me. "You will behave, won't you, Ba?"

I could only give her a shrug.

As she left me I allowed myself one last thought of Crow, who was now leading her own life, away from me. Although she had vexed me horribly by getting married — in secret besides — I had given her a large sum as a wedding present. And I had done her the favour of not telling Papa about her condition.

In thanks, I was the unwitting victim of collusion. My family and Crow decided I should not know which day was her final day, so as not to send me to bed weeping at the mere thought of it. And so, one day she simply did not come back. I expressed my dismay to all who would listen, but in truth, I welcomed their intervention. In a life full of *lasts* I had embraced a method of self-preservation: I did best if I did not allow myself to acknowledge the *last* of anything until after the fact. For some reason, then, it was easier to accept. It was a game I played with myself, for I knew what I was doing when I refused my thoughts to think beyond the moment, to enter that bastion where the *last* designation resided. And yet, by not allowing them full access to wallow in that label, I gained enough strength to get through, to carry on into the time beyond the *last*.

I heard two sets of feet upon the stairs. I braced myself for disappointment, not that the looks of a maid had anything to do with her true dispensation. Crow had given every appearance of gentleness, and yet had come to assert a great authority over me, like a parent to a child. At age thirty-eight I knew this was an odd arrangement — especially when it was preferred by the one subjugated — but I did not require or request a maid who slunk into the shadows as if fearful I would bite.

Henrietta led the woman into my room. "Well now. Here we are. Ba, Elizabeth, I would like you to meet Elizabeth Wilson. Wilson, my sister, Elizabeth Barrett."

Wilson did a little bob for a curtsy and blushed. "Two Elizabeths," she said, adding, "Miss."

Yes. Well. I decided not to mention that Crow's first name had been Elizabeth too.

On a whim, I pointed to the window and said, "Would you please close that?"

Wilson did—after bumping a shin on the edge of the sofa and nearly knocking a bluebird figurine to the floor. The window closed and she turned towards me, her face begging for affirmation.

I did not give it to her. For the window had been a test. It was a warm day in May and the breeze was necessary on this, the top floor of the house. Crow would have given me a look, shook her head, and said, "You will *not* have that window closed, Miss Elizabeth. I will not have you expiring from lack of air."

That Wilson had acquiesced to my request was understandable and yet . . . I did not want acquiescence. I wanted . . .

What did I want?

"May I leave you now?" Henrietta asked. "I have some shopping to do."

"Yes, yes," I said. "Thank you. We shall be fine."

Wilson's expression looked as though the thought of being left alone with me would be anything but fine. Her face took on the expression of a child left with a stern headmistress or a demanding stepmother.

"We shall be fine," I repeated for her benefit.

She quickly nodded. "I will do my best, mistress. But I am afraid it is nobody equal to Miss Crow."

Mrs. Treherne now.

It was a true enough statement, but her humility made me take pity. "We will learn this together, Wilson."

"I *am* willing to learn, mistress."

Good. "Then the first thing you can do is open the window."

She looked confused.

I tried to explain. "You must learn what is best for me, Wilson, even when I proceed otherwise."

She looked even more confused.

I tried to explain. "If left to my own devices I will take too much morphine, go to bed far too late, and talk as long as I like, none of which are to my ultimate advantage."

It took her a moment, but I saw recognition in her eyes. Yes, yes, although I was a grown woman, old enough to be Wilson's mother, in action I was a disobedient child who needed scolding on occasion, reminders of right action when I proceeded otherwise, and stern direction when appropriate.

"Oh," she said with a nod.

I could not tell whether she disapproved of my weaknesses — as I certainly disapproved of them — but she seemed willing to accept them, and address them.

Perhaps she would work out after all. If we both behaved.

SEVEN

I held them in my hands. It had been six years since I had experienced such a thrill. I traced my fingers along the simple title of the two volumes, which was set in gold against the dark green covers: *Poems.* "They are beautiful," I whispered.

"They are long overdue." It had been Cousin John Kenyon who'd brought me the first box of my newest publication. Without his influence and his prodding Edward Moxon, the publisher, I knew the books would never have become a reality. After all, just two years previous hadn't Mr. Moxon declared my work "uncommercial"? The only thing that had changed between then and now was having John as my champion—and becoming a better writer. For this work *was* superior to my last, *The Seraphim.* It was fuller, freer, and stronger, and worth three times over.

Opening the front cover and spotting the dedication, I immediately regretted not dedicating the volumes to my dear cousin. Instead I had given the dedication—once again—to Papa. An odd thought skittered across my mind regarding my motive for penning the lengthy bit of adoration. Had I hoped to gain something through my choice? A special blessing? A paternal dispensation?

John interrupted my musings. "Now, to get it out to the masses," he said. "I assume you wish to send copies to Wordsworth, Landor, Carlyle, Miss Martineau . . ."

"Do you think I should?"

"Of course. Word of mouth is essential. And I will make sure the proper reviewers read it."

I shuddered at the thought, for although I longed for critical intercourse and took critique well, I also knew that I had no real inkling of whether or not the work was good—in other people's eyes. And after Moxon had taken yet another chance on me . . . it had to be moderately successful, for his sake. And for my own. For if there ever was to be another book . . .

Would there be another book? I *worked* at poetry—it was not for me a reverie, but art. Writing was my life, and until my body succumbed I would allow my mind full release and expression. God willing.

Of course, being able to show Papa some sizable royalties would also be a thrill. To show him that I too could contribute to our family's sustenance would be nearly as exciting as holding the books.

John took his usual seat by the fireplace. "Of course we could implement a marketing strategy like your friend Mr. Horne did with his *Orion*. We could instruct Mr. Moxon to sell the book for only a farthing—with no change given."

I took up the well-known anecdote where he left off. "And no one will be allowed more than two copies."

"And if anyone does not say the title correctly, they will be denied purchase and sent away empty-handed."

Although we laughed at the details, the astonishing point remained: Richard's ploy had worked. The illusion that a reader might not get a copy had enticed sales and *Orion* was a success. On that success Richard had ventured to publish his *New Spirit* tome—which had *not* enjoyed success at all, either critically or financially.

"So," John said, with a dangle of his foot. "Are you fulfilled?"

It was an odd choice of words. "Because of this book?"

"You *are* a writer. An author. Surely there is no higher achievement."

I measured the weight of the books again. They were heavy. With words. With thoughts. With droplets of my life, pooled together into this stream of one page leading to the next. Would readers feel refreshed by my offering, or would they drown in it and snap the pages shut for want of air?

And yet . . . I reluctantly possessed an inkling that this might be my final offering to the world. My health, my life, my creative power . . . although I dabbled with the notion of additional publications, I did not distinctly imagine any future accomplishments and attainments. What was now was accessible. Even in my mind's eye, in my heart's beat, I did not clearly foresee *more*. Although I tried not to dwell on it or even verbalize it, I knew that what stood as a barrier between now and *more*, was death.

"Ba?"

"Yes. Sorry, cousin."

"Are you pleased?"

"It is something," I said.

"It is more than most women achieve."

I did not argue with him, and yet what most women achieved — the love of a husband, the joy of children — these would never be mine. Were these volumes my surrogate family? My proxy for flesh and blood progeny?

The complexities of the issue threatened to taint the moment, and so I left John's statement of achievement as it was and responded with a simple nod.

I heard Wilson come bounding up the stairs — only she came in such a fashion. She burst into the room out of breath and thrust a note in front of me.

"This just came from next door. Their butler is waiting for an answer."

Next door? Although we knew the family, we did not *know* them. Why would they send us a message? Me, a message?

Flush sniffed at the envelope, reminding me that the note was mine to read. I pulled out the card: *I am visiting next door. May I come by to meet you in person? Yours, Mrs. Anna Jameson.*

I gasped.

"Who's it from?" Wilson asked.

"An acquaintance. A fellow writer. She wants to stop by."

"Stop by?" Wilson repeated my words with full disdain. "No one stops by the Barretts'."

She had learned well. Although some of my siblings did not mind such casual practices, Papa and I found such actions objectionable. And yet my desire to meet this woman who was the very genius of literary criticism . . .

"What excuse should I give?" Wilson asked.

Even to my maid it was not a question of yes or no, but a question of how to decline the offer. I retrieved my pen and wrote a reply on the back of the card. *How very nice to hear from you, Mrs. Jameson. But alas, if only I had heard from you at the hour of five instead of six, I would ask you to step in, but, unfortunately, a visit is not now possible.*

I considered adding *perhaps another time* but I did not want to be put in this situation again. And so I added my close and slipped it back in the envelope. "Take this," I told Wilson.

I held my breath in order to hear her exchange with the neighbour's butler. Then the door closed.

And *that* was that.

I was relieved.

And disgusted at my own cowardice.

◈

I read the note, just handed to me by Wilson. *Dear Miss Barrett, once again I find myself next door. I would so love to meet you. I can come at any hour. Fondly, Anna Jameson.*

Wilson anticipated my needs and brought me a pen. "She is nothing if not persistent," she said.

Nothing if not crafty. For, by the way she had worded the note, there was no way out. *Any hour . . .*

It seemed she knew me even before meeting me. For the truth was, I did want to meet her but was too fainthearted to say, "Yes, come!" But upon knowing that I would have to allow her a visit or appear ungrateful, my heart almost broke itself into pieces with bumping.

And so . . . I wrote a quick note before what measly courage I had could dissipate: *I look forward to your visit. Perhaps at two?* I handed the envelope to Wilson.

"I suppose she'll come again and again until you finally let her."

"I told her to come at two."

Wilson's mouth gaped. "Two? Today?"

"An hour from now." Oddly, I enjoyed shocking her. In recent years I had grown far too predictable and had lost the ability to shock anyone. "Now go. Get the message on its way, then come help me get ready."

The short time it took Wilson to parlay the message was time enough for my body to rebel. The beat of my heart combined with a shortness of breath, causing me to feel faint.

"Stop it!" I commanded.

I hesitated a moment to see if my words had any power over my anatomy. There *was* a lessening of panic, though it was far from an eradication. I swung my feet to the floor and forced myself to take several deep breaths as fuel to my determination.

I would do this. I would.

⁓⁂⁓

I did it.

After seeing Mrs. Jameson—Anna—out, Wilson returned to my room to find me standing at the fire, basking in its glow.

"Enough, miss. You needs to get to bed again and—"

I turned towards her. "I think not."

Her brow tightened. "But you talked and talked, and you know how such exertion tires you."

"Tired me," I corrected. And though I was as surprised as she regarding my new resolve, I continued. "I found the visit quite stimulating."

"But so much stimulation—"

"Will not do me harm."

Wilson lifted an eyebrow, questioning what we both knew to be a falsehood.

Or was it merely a misconception? Just because I had previously reacted thus and so, did that mean I was preordained to always react in such a manner? To shrink and grow pale in the spirit? One point that remained constant was that after such a meeting took place, I had a hard time recalling why I had been so anxious about it. Such had been the way when I had met Mary Mitford. I'd worked myself into a tizzy over the very thought of such a meeting, when it had led to a friendship that had lasted for years.

Now I had two female friends who had broken the Wimpole Street barrier and could come to call. They were far different from each other. Mary was petite and plump, with a vibrancy and openness that enticed many a confidence. And now Anna . . . she had a certain indecision of exterior. She had very pale red hair, no eyebrows, and thin lips with no colour at all. Both women had a strength of mind that inspired me. And though Mary was eighteen years my senior and Anna twelve, they were my peers. We were three women united by a passion for the written word.

Wilson stood across from me. I had left her confused. Over the past seven months she had come to know my ways, my schedule, and my preferences. And now . . .

I was throwing a stick into the spoke of our finely tuned carriage, and the very act of it . . .

I felt fortified—and ambitious. "Are my sisters downstairs?"

She blinked. "Yes."

"Then help me descend. I wish to join them."

"Join them?"

"They are in the drawing room, yes?"

"I believe so."

"It is my drawing room too, is it not?"

"Well, yes, Miss Elizabeth, but—"

"Then help me."

⁓❦⁓

A mantra of *I can do this, I can do this* was alternating with *Why am I doing this? Why am I doing this?*

Even as Wilson helped me traverse the mountain of stairs to join my sisters below, it took all my will and determination to not halt the process and request to be brought back to my room. By the tentativeness that I felt in Wilson's assistance, I knew she expected a change of heart at any moment and had prepared herself to about-face and retreat.

Perhaps this tentativeness on her part fueled my resolve. Between the repetition of my inner mantra, I turned my thoughts to what would surely transpire upon my success. I would enter the drawing room and all eyes would turn to me.

Exclamations of "Ba!" would sprinkle the room and my sisters would rise and come to my aid, leading me to a chair by the hearth, gaining me a coverlet to drape across my lap, one sister calling to the butler to order a pot of strong coffee because it was my favourite.

As we rounded the final landing Flush ran ahead, and for once I wished to scold him, for he would surely steal my thunder and dilute—

But then I heard my sister's voice race up the stairwell. "No, I won't! You are not being fair!"

I audibly gasped, yet the sound seemed once removed, as a sound heard through a window.

Wilson whispered in my ear, "Perhaps we should go back upstairs, miss—"

I shook my head. Although I preferred not to be embroiled in my sisters' squabbles, my visit with Mrs. Jameson had given me new courage and I was not about to let a tiff about a bonnet or a dinner menu terminate my victory and resolve.

"Come," I told Wilson. "Let me finish this. As the eldest, perhaps I can help."

I knew this last to be bravado. No one in the house needed me to settle their differences or even to offer an opinion. In my upper room I had created a world set apart. I had defined the rules and marked the boundaries. For me to impose upon *this* conversation could be likened to Henrietta coming into my sanctum and insisting I get up and dance a jig.

And yet, I could visit their world as they often visited mine. And perhaps by my very entrance I could help dispel the tension—

I spotted Arabel, backing into the outer margin of the room, her skirt finding escape into the passage that stood between us. By her manner I knew this wasn't her argument, so who—?

"You will obey me, daughter! I demand it!"

My heart leapt to my throat. Papa? Papa was home?

"I am not your slave!" Henrietta shouted. "This is not Jamaica. This is—"

Suddenly, I heard a slap, and then . . . a thud; the ringing of knees upon the floor. I saw Arabel recoil, one hand to her mouth, one to her chest.

And then, Henrietta's wail rose and I saw Stormie and Henry on either side of her, carrying her flailing and fighting into the space just a few steps below me.

They looked up, and Papa appeared in the doorway and looked right at me, his face florid and twisted and foreign. And then—

I fainted.

⤞⤝

A soft murmuring reached my consciousness, words said so softly as to nearly express a constant hum. Occasional words found fruition: *God, Father, help* . . .

My other senses stirred and I felt the embrace of my mattress, tasted a parched mouth, and smelled the musk of my Flush close by. Sensing my return to him, he licked my hand and gently bit my little finger as if to encourage me towards full wakefulness.

The last of my senses demanded release and I opened my eyes.

As I had ascertained, even in my groggy state, I had been returned to my room. Which brother had climbed the many stairs with me as his burden? Or had Papa—

I stopped the thought as a memory demanded attention. *"You will obey me, daughter! I demand it!"*

I shuddered as I heard—as though freshly created—the awful slap, the thud, and my sister's wails.

Arabel was suddenly at my side, her Bible clutched to her chest. "We thought you dead," she said.

I attempted to push myself to sitting, and managed, with her assistance. She adjusted the pillows as my support. Then she headed towards the door. "I will get—"

"No!" I called her back. "I must know what happened."

"You fainted."

"No, no. Between Henrietta and Papa. Whatever could cause such an awful contest between them?"

Arabel glanced towards the door, then back at me. "Henrietta has a suitor."

It was the first I had heard of it. "Who?"

"Our second cousin, Surtees Cook."

I had never met him and must have looked perplexed because Arabel moved to explain. "We share a great-grandfather."

"Are they engaged?" I asked.

"Henrietta would like them to be." Arabel shrugged. "But Mr. Cook's financial condition will not make him easily accepted."

"He is poor?"

"His mother is widowed but has connections, yet he is but an army lieutenant." She hastened to add, "But apparently he is writing a novel. I believe it is entitled *Johnny Cheerful*. He hopes to be made rich by it. I heard Henrietta tell him when the time came, you would offer your advice."

"I will do no such thing!"

"Why not?"

"Because he . . . because Papa does not approve of him."

Instead of arguing with me—which would have been beyond her character—Arabel sighed. "He will never approve. And though he has allowed Mr. Cook to dine with us—he being a relation—he will never allow marriage."

I knew her last statement was all-inclusive. It was not just the groom potential of Surtees Cook that was in question; the ban against marriage was absolute. At age thirty-eight, I had long ago accepted that dictum as law, but Henrietta, a few years younger, still grasped on to hope.

She must have really been in love for her to risk Papa's wrath—a wrath I had never, ever witnessed. Although on no occasion had I been the recipient of Papa's anger, I had heard him chastise my siblings on occasion, his stern words standing without emotion or fury. But today . . . what had Henrietta done to elicit such rage?

Arabel set her Bible down and tucked my covers between bed frame and mattress. "Although Papa will never approve of Mr. Cook, his wrath today was provoked by Henrietta's secrecy." She stopped her tucking. "She has been having Mr. Cook come to lunch while Papa is at work."

Ah. As the uncontested head of our Wimpole Street household, Papa would never condone covert actions behind his back. That I had brought Mrs. Jameson into the house without his knowledge . . .

A tightening in my midsection told me I would never take such a risk again. To do so was usurping his position. Although I had meant no disrespect I *had* crossed the line of a good daughter's deference.

We both looked towards the door when we heard feet upon the stairs. Was Papa coming to check on my condition?

Instead Henrietta, Stormie, and Henry came into view. Upon seeing me sitting upright, Henrietta rushed to my side and flung her arms about me. "I was so worried. That you are well . . ." She stood back to see me. "I never would have forgiven myself if you had suffered true damage."

"Ah, she's well enough," Henry said. "It was just the drama of it that overtook her." He leaned against the doorjamb. "You did put on quite a show, Hen."

He looked to Stormie, who nodded and smiled, but without the satisfied malice. "Papa . . . wwwwaassss . . . mmmmad."

Henrietta sat on the side of my bed and took my hand. "I made it worse. I argued. I shouldn't have argued."

"It is not allowed," Henry said. There was bitterness in his voice, and a note of finality. We all knew it was the truth. I abided by Papa's pronouncements out of love and respect, but I feared some of my siblings did so for more mercurial reasons. Other than George, none of them earned enough income to subsist on their own.

"Where is Papa?" I asked. For it was his concern I desired the most.

"He is about," Arabel said.

"Has he come to see me?"

The look they exchanged spoke in more layers than Arabel's simple no. She hurried to add, "Not yet."

Had he found out about Mrs. Jameson? And had that one impulsive act put me into the same league as Henrietta's deception? I quickly thought of an excuse. I could tell Papa that Mrs. Jameson's note had not allowed a refusal. Surely he would understand—

There was a communal cessation of breath, then an instant check in all movement, as we heard Papa's feet upon the stairs.

Henry leaned towards the room. "Glad you are better, Ba." He hurried out the door with Stormie at his heels. I heard the door to the roof click open, then shut.

They had made their escape, leaving behind the one who needed escape the most. To her credit, Henrietta remained seated at my side, though a twitch to her hand told me she had considered otherwise.

Papa's massive presence filled the doorway, and the three women of the household waited to gauge his mood and motive.

His eyes quickly scanned the room, falling twice upon me—at first and at last. "I see you are awake."

It was not quite an apt term for coming out of a dead faint, yet all I could say was yes.

"Good." He nodded once. "Well, then. Good night." With that, he turned to leave.

Henrietta made to rise. "But, Papa—"

I grabbed her arm and pulled her to silence. Arabel added her own shake of the head. *Not now.*

None of us moved until Papa's footfalls faded into the silence of the house. Only then did we breathe.

"Will he ever forgive me?" Henrietta said.

"Of course he will," Arabel said. "The Bible insists on forgiveness."

Henrietta shook her head. "But does Papa?"

They proceeded to ask after my needs and I assured them Wilson would take care of me. Then they kissed me good-night and departed.

Only after the solitude of my room was retaken did I realize that Papa had not stayed to pray with me.

He had never missed an evening. It was our special time together.

Yet tonight...had he deemed me so undeserving that he was repulsed by my very presence? Was he so disgusted with Henrietta's sin that he now lumped me as one with her? Had I forever lost his favour?

I gazed at my Bible on the table near the sofa where we always knelt. I could pray alone. I often did so, but had never attempted these final prayers of the day without my father's influence.

I could kneel down without him. And yet, somehow the idea of bypassing one father to speak with another . . .

I remained where I was, across the room from our holy place.

I had never felt so alone.

And unworthy.

EIGHT

I should not care for praise.

But I did.

The Bible says that *Pride goeth before destruction, and an haughty spirit before a fall*, and because I do not wish to fall, I tried to keep my pride in check lest I demand divine repercussions.

"Do you need more paste, Miss Elizabeth?" Wilson asked me.

For the briefest moment I mistook her word *paste* for *praise*. I did not need more of either. "No, thank you. I am nearly through with my scrapbook." I looked to Cousin John, who had brought me the various periodicals to peruse, then cut, then paste into my scrapbook of book reviews. "Yes?"

He lifted the much shortened pile in his lap. "Yes."

I held out my hand for the next on the pile. John opened a copy of *The Athenaeum*. "Here is a good one. The tough-minded H. R. Chorley says, 'Were the blemishes of her style tenfold more numerous than they are, we should still revere this poetess as one of the noblest of her sex.'"

I put a dramatic hand to my chest. "Blemishes? He finds blemishes?"

"There are a few, I would think," John said.

"More than a few," I admitted. "I wrote too much of the book in a rush when the publisher wanted the two volumes to be of equal length. In my quest, I resurrected *Lady Geraldine's Courtship* from its standing as a work in progress and bounded off nineteen pages in one day."

John handed me the Chorley review and I began to cut around it. He moved on to the next publication. "I do like this one from the *Metropolitan Magazine*," he said. He adjusted his spectacles to read. " 'Miss Elizabeth Barrett seems to us one bright particular star, shining from a firmament of her own. She deserves to be esteemed and admired at once and throughout future generations.' "

I didn't know what to say to such acclaim. Although it pleased me (more than it should have) it also left me embarrassed, for although I believed my *Poems* to be good work, it was not this good. Speaking of . . . I thought of a magazine that habitually took pleasure in abusing my work. "What of *The British Quarterly Review*?"

John placed his hands upon the stack. "Are you certain you wish to hear it?"

Ah. So their abuse continued. "Fair is fair," I said. "I cannot accept the good without acknowledging the bad."

He pulled the bottom periodical from his stack—proof he had been protecting me. He cleared his throat and read. " 'We object to Miss Barrett's fantastic images and phrases and find much of what she has written unintelligible. Whether this stems from her lack of knowledge on the subject in question or to her thoughts being too sublime and grand to be spoken out in clear, connected phrase we do not know.' " He looked up to gauge my reaction. "You are not weeping. . . ."

"One does not weep over the truth. I do write about things unknown to me in real life." I spread my hands to encompass the room. "This room is my life. Only my work takes me beyond these walls. That a reader occasionally finds error when comparing my prose to reality is acceptable, and nearly expected." I tapped a finger to my head and then my heart. "I write from a world that exists in places that are indeed grand and sublime."

John applauded. "Bravo, Ba. That is the right attitude."

I did not deserve his applause, for the attitude was what it was, and was not contrived for his benefit. But—to my shame—I returned the discussion of reviews to the positive. I turned back a few pages in my scrapbook, then put my hand in the page to mark it, deciding to summarize instead of quote. "I did receive a letter from the painter Dante Rossetti that said he and his brother reveled with profuse delight in my work. He wrote that they have read many of the poems half a hundred times over and could recite them from memory."

"Perhaps you should instruct them to give public recitals. Your sales would surely benefit." He pointed to the sheaf of paper on my desk. "There. Write them a note now."

I batted his finger away. "I will do no such thing." I nodded at the reviews still left in his lap. "Is there one from *The Westminster Review* in your stack?" I asked the question with trepidation, for it was one of *the* most influential quarterlies.

"There could be," he said.

His lack of effusion spoke volumes about their response. "Out with it," I said.

He pulled it out and opened its pages. " 'The work in *Poems* lacks humour and wants for the ease of colloquial expression, which is surely caused by . . .' " He paused to look at me. "Are you certain you wish for me to continue?"

"Of course," I said, although I was not certain at all.

" '. . . which is surely caused by Miss Barrett's prolonged isolation. She has lived too much in the world of books, which in turn, has become a handicap to her art.' "

Although this review was similar to the other for which I had found no fault, there was something about this one's presentation that made my heart race with anger. "I . . . I . . ."

"You did say as much yourself," John said.

He was correct, and yet the manner in which the reviewer had identified the truth reminded me what the public thought of my personal life. I was the odd recluse, a scholarly priestess held prisoner in her castle turret, handicapped by her situation. I was a woman to be pitied.

"I have upset you," John said.

It was not his fault, and my reaction was beyond that which was required, or correct. "If they wish to know the truth, cousin, I would as a poet exchange some of this lumbering, ponderous, helpless knowledge of books for some experience of life and man."

He perked to higher attention. "You *have* been feeling better these past months. Perhaps it is time to venture out and—"

I shook my head adamantly, my fear of life and man out *there*, away from *here*, overwhelming even my deepest desire to experience it.

Wilson saved the moment by bringing me the post. The letter on top distracted my inner keening. "Oh my," I said. "It is from Mr. Robert Browning."

John slapped a hand upon his thigh. "Well, well. Has the chap finally gained the nerve to contact you?"

"Have you been goading him to—"

"Me? Never." I knew by his grin such an exchange had taken place. "Open it, Ba. See what the man has to say."

I was not sure I wished to read the letter with him present, but since my cousin *was* the connection between Mr. Browning and me, I submitted. I read the first line in silence: *I love your verses with all my heart, dear Miss Barrett. . . .*

"What does he say?"

I was not exactly certain. I was not used to effusive praise that went beyond polite convention. In fact, it frightened me with its implied passion while it enticed me to read more.

But I could not read on with an audience. "It appears he has read my book and enjoyed it." I felt my face flush. "Quite a lot."

"Excellent! I sent a copy round to his sister, Sarianna, because I knew him to be in Italy. He must be back. She must have given it to him."

"You sent a copy . . . ?"

"You quoted him within one of your stanzas in *Lady Geraldine*, did you not? What was the line? Something about a pomegranate?"

I knew the line by heart. It was when Geraldine listed the books she delighted having read to her. " 'Or at times a modern volume, Words-worth's solemn-thoughted idyl, Howitt's ballad-verse, or Tennyson's enchanted reverie, or from Browning some "Pomegranate," which, if cut deep down the middle, shows a heart within, blood-tinctured, of a veined humanity.' "

"Obviously you have cut dear Robert deep down the middle."

My blush deepened and I tried to hide it by lowering my head and letting my ringlets act as cover.

"What else does he say?"

There was much more to the letter which was written in a flowing cursive I found most amiable to the eye. I often shared letters with my cousin. Yet there was something about this letter . . . I could not read it in John's company. With an attempt at apathy I set the letter aside, putting it within a drawer of my desk. "I will read it later."

Suddenly, John rose. "I will allow *later* to be immediate." He came to my side and kissed my cheek. "Enjoy his words, dear Ba," he said, and shut the door with a gentle click.

The room was mine once more and lay completely still as if awaiting my next move. Even Flush lay unmoving at my feet. The moment lingered, hesitant to move on to the next. More surprisingly, I found that I too sat paused, caught in time, unsure what *should* transpire, what *could* transpire, and moreover, what *would* transpire next.

I was hesitant to allow my eyes to move too far, and felt the constraint of sight marked only by the placement of my neck and head. My eyes could move left, then right, up, then down, but were limited by this odd need to remain without motion, to remain *here*, right now. Still.

Expectant?

My brain did not abide by my body's constraint. New thoughts were swift lightning, streaking through my mind's sky with a fierce power that defied previous experience. I could not capture any thought nor predict the next, any more than I could capture or predict lightning in a stormy sky. Although all this happened within my own consciousness, it was as though I were merely an onlooker, once removed, with no say, no power, no control.

I shivered—from excitement or trepidation?

The physical movement, small though it was, was enough for a cognizant thought to gain entry. Yet the intrusive thought seemed a statement made by a third party rather than one that originated within my own realm.

All is different now, it said.

The pragmatism of my nature intruded to ask *In what way?*

But instead of giving me an answer from within, I found my hand breaking free of the frozen moment and moving of its own accord to the drawer in my desk where I had placed . . .

My fingers touched the letter, and oddly, I had the distinct feeling that the letter touched my fingers in return—the softest graze, a kiss, barely there, and too soon gone.

Ridiculous, I thought. It was but a letter. My life was replete with letters. Why did this one seem different?

With a shake of my head I forced logic into the moment—and immediately regretted its entry. I mentally recanted, longing to regain that sweet breath of reverie that had been held with such exquisite delicacy.

But it was gone and I could do nothing but mourn its passing. Would I ever experience such a moment again?

The clock on the mantel relentlessly announced the passing of more moments, leading to more, and more.

Whatever slice of the sublime had occurred was now gone from this reality. But it would never be fully gone from my memory. Although I would be hard-pressed to ably recount it, I knew I would never truly forget the awe of its pleasure. It was as though I had been allowed to glimpse the face of the Almighty. I knew someday I would feel that way again. Even now, I longed for it and anticipated it as I had never awaited anything before.

I looked at the letter from Robert Browning. It looked no different than other letters I received from other correspondents, from other . . .

men. Although its opening line had filled my need for praise, I had received others just as complimentary, and from poets I admired with equal intensity as I admired Mr. Browning.

But something was indeed different. There was only one way to determine what that was. . . .

This is no off-hand complimentary letter that I shall write, whatever else, no prompt matter-of-course recognition of your genius and there a graceful and natural end of the thing: since the day last week when I first read your poems, I quite laugh to remember how I have been turning and turning again in my mind what I should be able to tell you of their effect upon me, for in the first flush of delight I thought I would this once get out of my habit of purely passive enjoyment, when I do really enjoy, and thoroughly justify my admiration—perhaps even, as a loyal fellow-craftsman should try and find fault and do you some little good to be proud of hereafter! But nothing comes of it all, so into me has it gone, and part of me has it become, this great living poetry of yours.

I stopped and let his words linger like a comforting shawl against the cold of January. That he had attempted to give criticism—which would have been welcome indeed from a poet such as he—but had been moved beyond a cutting apart to a welcoming in . . . There was no greater compliment than to know that my work had touched someone, had accessed an inner place, and had sparked emotion.

Wanting, needing more, I read on:

I can give a reason for my faith in one and another excellence, the fresh strange music, the affluent language, the exquisite pathos and true new brave thought—but in this addressing myself to you, your own self, and for the first time, my feeling rises altogether. I do, as I say, love these books with all my heart—and I love you too. Do you know

I was once not very far from seeing—really seeing you? Mr. Kenyon said to me one morning, 'Would you like to see Miss Barrett?' Then he went to announce me, then he returned. You were too unwell. And now it is years ago, and I feel as at some untoward passage in my travels, as if I had been close, so close, to some world's wonder in chapel or crypt, only a screen to push and I might have entered, but there was some slight, so it now seems, slight and just-sufficient bar to admission, and the half-opened door shut, and I went home my thousand of miles, and the sight was never to be! Well, these Poems were to be—and this true thankful joy and pride with which I feel myself.

Yours ever faithfully,
Robert Browning

He had come to visit me?

When?

He said 'years ago' . . .

I tried to remember the occasion but could find only the vaguest of memories, of Cousin John telling me that Browning wanted to meet me. As had Wordsworth, and the critic Chorley, and Richard Horne, and, and . . .

I could have grown a large head at such kind attention and the interest of my peers but for the utter terror spurred by the very thought of such meetings. To think of Mr. Browning, standing outside this very house, waiting for John to return with an invitation.

"I sent him away."

My words cut through the silence with their surprising accusation. I answered with a silent response: *I send everyone away.*

But . . . what if Robert Browning would appear on this very day? If Cousin John rapped upon my door and said, *"Mr. Browning is downstairs and he would like to see you,"* would I let him in? Or would this dreaded, awful, annoying fear of meeting another face-to-face once again grab control and forbid my yearning for connection its chance?

This letter, and its intimate glimpse into the heart and mind of Mr. Browning, was an extension of his hand towards mine, a gesture of introduction, an . . . opening of the door between us. Upon this recognition, I knew a decision was being placed before me: Should I push my door ajar and let the *idea* of a meeting gain a breath of new air?

My heart pounded as the reckless thought took root. Before it was snuffed out by habit or convention, I drew a piece of stationery close and began my reply: *Thank you, dear Mr. Browning, from the bottom of my heart. You meant to give me pleasure by your letter—and even if the object had not been answered, I ought still to thank you. But it is thoroughly answered. Such a letter from such a hand!*

I sat back, looking at the words. Were they too forward?

Keep it about the writing.

Yes, yes. That was the proper direction.

Boldly, I left the opening paragraph as it was, then wrote that I would appreciate any comments or criticisms he had to offer. Poet to poet. Professional to professional.

But then, before I thought enough to stop my pen, I found my words addressing our near-meeting:

> Is it indeed true that I was so near to the pleasure and honour of making your acquaintance? And can it be true that you look back upon the lost opportunity with any regret? But, you know, if you had entered the "crypt," you might have caught cold, or been tired to death, and wished yourself "a thousand miles off," which would have been worse than traveling them. It is not my interest however to put such thoughts in your head about its being "all for the best," and I would rather hope (as I do) that what I lost by one chance I may recover by some future one. Winters shut me up as they do dormouses' eyes: in the spring, we shall see. I am so much better that I seem turning round to the outward world again.

I sat back, stunned at my admission, stunned at my suggestion that we *could* meet, and might meet in the spring. *We shall see.*

Indeed.

Although the words within my letter had come from my hand (and thus from my mind and heart), to see *I seem turning round to the outward world again* in blackened ink, ascribed to be real, addressed to this man I had never met . . . .

Was I ready to venture into the world again after a half lifetime away? My hand told me so.

And yet I knew too well the gulf between intent and action, logic and achievement. I could want to be like others from morning to night, yet until I actually took steps to succeed . . . it was like talking to the wind.

When *was* the last time I had smelled the fresh air? Touched a tree's leaf? Heard the laughter of children playing hoops or tag? When was the last time I had felt cobblestones under my slippered feet, or felt the sun upon my face?

My memories sped in the reverse, settling upon the outing in my wheelchair when Flush was stolen. September. Of what year?

1843. It was newly 1845. Sixteen months had passed since I had been out of my room and into the world.

But remember what happened last time. Flush was stolen. If you go out again . . .

No, Flush's abduction was the excuse, not the reason for my self-imposed hermitage. The truth? Nothing since then had been strong enough to propel me *out*. Still to answer was why had this letter shined a light upon my darkness. Why had this letter ignited in me a desire for something different?

I did not know, and was a little uncertain I wanted a true answer. For I enjoyed the sensation and was content — for now — to live in the presence of this moment and leave the future its . . . grand possibilities?

I laughed at the very thought of it.

～❀～

Time had passed. I was not certain how much time, but the light in my room had changed from white to amber. And still I held the letter in my hand — my response to Robert Browning.

The pluck I had shown earlier had left me, and doubt had taken its place. Perhaps it was not wise to respond to Mr. Browning at all.

And yet . . . I corresponded with many male scholars and literary figures. I had never felt the slightest trepidation writing to other authors, painters, or intellectuals. Why was I hesitating to send this simple response to Mr. Browning?

My gaze fell upon his portrait on the wall, then quickly sought the others I had placed there: Wordsworth, Carlyle, Martineau. And suddenly, I knew—I just knew—that the only portrait I had truly wished to display was Mr. Browning's. Had I displayed the other portraits to disguise my true desire to have Robert's delightful countenance on display?

Robert?

I shook my head against the impropriety, the audacity . . .

"Mr. Browning," I said aloud, in an attempt to make amends.

"Excuse me, miss?"

Wilson was watering the ivy in the window box. I had forgotten she was there. I looked down at the letter in my hands. My own cursive reiterated the name I had just expressed: *Mr. Browning*.

Wilson nodded at the letter. "Do you wish for me to give that to Miss Henrietta to post?"

That was my usual way. Since my sister went out on errands daily, I always gave her my letters.

Wilson craned her neck to see the addressee. Upon seeing it, she glanced at the portrait on the wall. "Oh."

Oh, what? I held the letter close to my breast and felt myself blush.

This was absurd. It was just a simple letter. To a colleague.

But then Wilson nodded in a knowing manner and whispered, "Don't worry 'bout a thing, Miss Elizabeth." She made a locking motion at her mouth, then held out her hand.

Surprised into action, I relinquished the letter into her charge.

She slipped it into the pocket of her dress and headed for the stairs. Then she stopped and returned to me. "Do you wants me to check the return mail every day to see if . . ." She nodded towards the portrait again.

I was suddenly appalled and nearly snatched the letter back. Intrigue was not for me. It was utterly against my character.

Perhaps seeing the panic in my face, Wilson said, "Never mind," and hurried down the stairs.

But what she'd said lingered. Return post? It *was* my desire that Mr. Browning respond to *my* letter.

And then you will respond to him. And then he . . .

What was I doing? What had begun?

By the fitful beating of my heart I knew that something had been set in motion. Something out of the ordinary, something remarkable. Something exhilarating and . . . and . . .

Life changing.

I pressed my hands to my head, both encouraging its fervent shaking *no-no-no* and rebelling against its negativity.

Why couldn't I change? Why couldn't this one letter be the beginning of something . . . something . . .

New.

At the word's arrival into my consciousness, I froze.

New? What was *new*? The word itself—though simple in design—was foreign to me, to my very thinking. I did not deal with anything *new* but wallowed in the tried-and-true, that which existed now and had always *been*. *New* involved change, and I did not change, my life did not change, my family did not change. We existed on the plane of what was, what is, and never ventured in thought or action into what was yet to be.

What was new?

The image of Wilson, bustling through the snowy streets of London, my letter to Robert Browning clutched in her mittened hand . . .

Run faster!

I gasped at the thought. What was happening to me? What was so different about this letter compared to all the hundreds I had written before?

I closed my eyes and let my mind try to encircle the emotions that seemed scattered like naughty sheep on a hillside. Deliberately I drew them close until there seemed some semblance of containment. Once I had them within my influence, once they were gathered, I looked into their faces and recognized a commonality in their gaze.

Expectation.

The very thought of it, the very novelty of the sensation . . .

Was the most thrilling experience I'd ever had.

⁓⁂⁓

I bustled about my room, touching this, adjusting that, picking up one book only to discard it for another. Poor Flush followed behind me like a desperate puppy wanting to be released from a maze.

Wilson came in the room with a stack of clean clothing to be put away. She placed the stack on the bureau, opened a drawer, but then stopped in her chore. "Pardon me for saying, but what's wrong with you, Miss Elizabeth?"

I forced myself to stand in place. "Wrong? Nothing is wrong."

Wilson showed her unbelief with a shake of her head. "For two days you've been out of bed more than in, have touched upon every single item in this room, have gone to the window, then the door more times than all counted in the time I have known you, and seem . . ." She studied me a moment. "Agitated."

I could not deny any of her observations. But instead of agitation I defined my condition as excited and hopeful—far more gainful conditions.

Wilson placed the clothing in the bureau. "Would you like a dose of your elixir? You know how it quiets your mind and calms your pulse."

I shook my head vehemently. Although the thought of taking my dear opium was tempting, I did not dare. For what would happen if a letter from Robert came while I was so eased in spirit? Whether my true condition was agitation or expectation I could not risk being less than fully . . . me.

She looked confused, but then, with a shutting of the drawer, I saw her eyes brighten with understanding. "You're waiting, aren't you? For a letter from *him*."

Although I knew I should deny such a thing and chastise Wilson for being so familiar . . . I needed a confidante, a conspirator. If my current state was one I would repeat with every waiting, for every letter, then I could not uphold the ruse of an excuse. And so, I told the truth—or rather, acknowledged the truth she had suspected.

"Yes," I said simply. "I await his reply."

Her face beamed with utter joy, and I knew I had made the right decision to bring her into the secret. She took a step closer and lowered her voice. "Do you want me to go check to see if the post has arrived?"

Suddenly, I imagined Wilson entering the drawing room with great stealth and stealing from the table any letter from Robert. She would slip it into her pocket and race up the stairs on tiptoe.

It was not that I objected to her intent or even her methods, but I feared if she was caught in the act, she would be hard-pressed to explain herself. And when one of my family insisted she relinquish the letter she had taken, they would see the sender's name and their suspicions would soar. As it was, Mr. Robert Browning was simply another colleague, a literary correspondent. To draw attention to his letters would be to risk . . .

Everything.

But what exactly was this *everything* at risk?

Shaken by my own question, I needed to be alone. "Don't make a special trip to check the mail," I told Wilson. I put a hand on her shoulder and led her to the door. "I do not wish to illicit suspicion with too much eagerness."

"Oh, I see," she said. "I understand. I do. But I knows how to be discreet, Miss Elizabeth. You can count on me for that."

"I will surely do so," I said. "Now go about your business as if nothing is astir."

She gave me a nod and a wink and left me alone—a much needed condition.

I shut the door behind her and let the question return to me. What exactly was this *everything* at risk? What did it matter if my family knew I was corresponding with Robert?

Because it's different with him.

These five words caused me to lean my back against the door as if keeping the world away. At bay. Within these walls I would wait for him, and upon his entrance — through the lines of his letters — I could create a different world from any I had ever known.

Flush let out a bark, most likely reacting to my odd stance and to his sense of the foreign emotions that seeped from my every pore.

I went to him, finding his neck with my fingers. "It's fine, boy. All is fine. And good. I am fine." And would be good when Robert's letter arrived.

If it arrives.

I swung round towards the door, needing to run down the stairs myself to check the stack of mail. It had been two days since I had sent my response to him. When in receipt of his first letter, I had posted mine the next day. Perhaps he had been disgusted by my words, or bored enough to decide that further correspondence was unappealing.

My expectancy fell into despair and I returned to my bed. It welcomed me as an old friend, as if saying, *"Foolish woman. I knew you'd return to me. Do not again be gone so long, for I alone care for you and offer true comfort."*

Oddly, instead of jumping onto the bed — as was his habit — Flush stood beside it and peered at me, his tail low, his eyes uncertain. In spite of his earlier confusion, did he prefer his recent mistress who moved about the room, who rendered expectation rather than surrender?

I too preferred that persona, and yet, as doubt sat upon my heart, I found no energy to choose it over the tedium of my standard.

Not until a letter came.

If a letter came.

I turned onto my side and burrowed my face into the pillow. It had to come. He had to answer. . . .

⤞⤝

My mind swam with thoughts of Robert Browning. My heart beat a new rhythm of anticipation of his letter, and yet, as I suffered through the horrible interim between the uncertainty of *now* and the pleasure of *then*, I realized I knew ridiculously little about this man who spurred such newfound emotion.

What I knew of him I knew from his poetry—which, considering his talent, was plenty, and yet, not enough. I knew his mind and had seen glimpses into his heart, but I wanted to know of his life. Of the man, Robert Browning, not just the poet.

Towards that end, I concocted a plan. Earlier in the week, Mary Mitford had told me she was coming to visit on this very afternoon. Mary would know the details I longed to hear. But I could not seem too obvious. Even though Mary was my dearest friend, I was not ready to relinquish the privacy of my feelings to her—or anyone. That Wilson knew the base of them was enough. So far she had proven herself discreet, and she would have to continue to do so if she wished to retain her position.

Since when had discretion been a requirement for my employ?

Since now. Since Robert.

But back to my visit with Mary. How could I glean information without her suspecting the core of my interest?

I patted my answer: the copy of Robert's *Paracelsus* in my lap. If I were reading Robert's book when she arrived, then it would be natural for me to turn the discussion in his direction. Mary and I had long ago discussed it, and though she was not as resolute an admirer as I was—though sometimes I too wished his work were clearer, more concise—the discussion, in whatever form, would serve my purpose. Since the issue of passion was so on my mind, perhaps I could bring up the obvious passion within his work. He was such a master of . . . clenched longing. It verily burned though the metallic fissures of the language.

I looked at the clock. Three o'clock. Mary owned the virtue of promptness.

As if in response, I heard commotion from below. And feet upon the stairs.

I opened the book, found it upside down, rearranged it, and pretended to read. I could not actually accomplish such a feat, as my eyes were suddenly incapable of clear focus. My heart raced with an unfamiliar surge. This was not one of my attacks, this was different. This was . . . exhilarating.

Wilson accompanied Mary to my door, then left us.

My friend entered with a sweep of agitation. "The train was delayed, and cold, and crowded. Although I like living in Berkshire, the logistics of traveling to town can be trying."

"I admire your bravery," I said. "I would never dare ride in one of those locomotives."

"You don't ride in the locomotive, Ba, but in a car meant for humans. Though as it does not contain the proper facilities to . . . to make oneself fully comfortable, I do not advise it. But the speed . . . we travel twenty miles in but an hour."

Mary removed her cloak and draped it over a chair near the fire. Then she took her usual place in a chair near my bed. "Enough of that. I am here." As I'd hoped, she lifted the book on my lap to see its cover. "Browning?"

"He is a genius."

Mary shrugged. "Maybe a genius to some, but I find his work uneven. Although *Paracelsus* had some success, his subsequent *Sordello* was disastrous. The damage to his reputation still lingers five years later." Her eyes sparkled with mischief. "Did you ever hear what our dear Tennyson said about it?"

I knew, but had handily ostracized the mean-spoken words from my mind.

Mary took my silence as curiosity. "He said that the only lines in *Sordello* he understood were the first and last—and both of them lies." Spurred by the gossip, she rose and went to the bookshelf where she found my copy. She opened it and read the first line, " 'Who will, may hear Sordello's story told.' " She flipped to the end of the book. " 'Who would, has heard Sordello's story told.' " She snapped the covers shut with a *thwack*. " 'Who will' or 'would' indeed. It is unintelligible. Completely and absolutely."

This was not going well. Although I had also seen the flaws of the obscure nature of *Sordello*, I did not begrudge an artist the courage of taking a risk. If only I would be so brave.

But now that the subject of Robert had been breached, I continued with my plan. "I've heard he lives with his parents?"

Mary nodded. "So he does. Thirty-two and still living at—" She must have remembered she was talking to a Barrett of similar condition because she stopped her disparagement. "I will say he is as devoted to his parents as you are to your father."

I was glad to hear it. "And his siblings? Do they live at home too?"

"A sister. Just one. Sarianna."

"What a beautiful name."

"She is a beautiful girl. I often see them at parties. I am not certain she has traveled the continent, but her brother has enjoyed the privilege."

I felt my usual twinge of envy. "To spend Christmas in Italy. What a stunning situation."

Mary's eyebrow rose. "He was in Italy for Christmas?"

Oh dear. I had said too much. I hurried to cover my knowledge. "I believe Cousin John told me as much."

Mary showed no undue interest. "He *is* very learned in Greek. I've heard his parents' library has hundreds of volumes and he has read them all."

My heart flipped, for nothing could make him of more interest to me.

"His father, though not rich, has subsidized all his publications," Mary said. "I do believe he is urging his son to achieve a parcel of his own dreams."

"The father is a poet also?"

"I would guess. Though he is mainly a caricaturist of some talent."

Mary brushed at a bit of damp on the hem of her dress. "Actually his family and yours have some history in common."

This sort of information was better than I had imagined. "Of what sort?"

"There is the West Indies connection. His father was in Jamaica but had no interest in the business there, nor its mode of application. He returned to England, much to his family's dismay, and had to turn to clerking at a bank to provide for them."

I nodded. "I do not begrudge him his decision, but rather, understand it. Although my family has had ties—still has ties—to that place, slavery is deplorable. By his action, the elder Mr. Browning showed courage and a noble character." I wanted to turn the discussion back to his son. "I assume his son shares those attributes."

"Other than Robert's lack of a real profession, I can think of nothing definite against him," she said.

"He does not have employment?" I found this to be a concern, though I was not certain why.

"Oh no. As far as I am aware he has never had real employment. His parents adore him and fully support his poetry and plays, even when they would be wise to tell him to give it up and get a real profession."

"He cannot give it up!"

Mary's eyebrow again lifted upwards. "You show keen interest in—"

I waved a hand at her concern, hoping the gesture quelled her interest. "As a fellow poet I despair of anyone with literary aspirations and talent, as Mr. Browning most certain possesses, being forced into mundane employment rather than allowed the freedom of time and inspiration."

"Men have to work, Ba. They have families to support."

I was taken aback. "But you said Robert lived with his parents."

She assessed me with a level gaze. "No, I believe you said that. And though it is true, I . . ." She sat on the edge of her chair. "You show more than the interest of a peer, Ba. Is there something you wish to tell me?"

I nearly looked towards the desk, where Robert's letter was stored—but did not. I wished I were a more dramatic sort like Henrietta. My acting ability had never been fully tested, yet I had no choice but to test it now. "You know how I love gossip, and as much time as Cousin John spends here, he is a bad influence on me."

Her gaze did not falter. "That is all, then?"

I attempted to laugh at the absurdity of her question. "I assure you I have never met Mr. Browning, nor do I have any intention—" With a start I realized this final statement was not exactly true. Yet, unable to linger in my realization, I changed direction. "I have never been romantically inclined, you know that, Mary. My passion is expressed through my work and within my own spirit."

Mary looked to her lap and I could tell she was looking inwards. "You and I have talked about this before, Ba, about love, about our lot to never experience the love of a husband."

"And we came to the determination that it was all right. We have both accepted it as God's will. And as such, I cannot say I have regrets. I have been made this way and you your way, and our lives play out accordingly."

She shook her head, but it was a movement of appreciation. "Your inner strength amid your physical weakness continues to amaze me."

And suddenly, I knew she was wrong. Although my inner strength *had* been a constant in a life focused on adapting to my illnesses, now, with the reception of Robert's letter—and my reply—everything had changed. I was not certain how exactly, but I could feel that a portion of my being had shifted from the known to the unknown, from the hazy towards the clear, from mere warmth to a heat . . .

I shook the thought away. I was not a woman of heat, of ardour, or romantic fervor. As I had told Mary, my passion was reserved for things other than a flesh-and-blood man. In fact, what did I really know of flesh-and-blood men? Although I had six brothers within the confines of Wimpole Street, I did not see much difference between them and my sisters and I—except that they, as men, held power, while we, as women, held none. And yet . . . alone in my room, I was a far step removed from their lives. Had any of them ever loved a woman? Felt the kind of passion that was—and ever would be—absent from my own life?

"Ba? You have left me well alone here," Mary said.

"So sorry." To make amends I changed the subject from Robert. "Tell me what you have been doing."

But as she told me the goings-on of her life, I found my thoughts returning to the man who had invaded mine.

Where *was* his letter?

⚬⚬⚬

The light through my window was dimming with the quick coming of the winter dark. There had been no letter. Although my visit with Mary had distracted me, it had not erased the deep ache for Robert's words. His thoughts. The precious allotment that would feed me until—

I heard someone coming up the stairs. Running? No one ran in this house.

Except . . .

Flush sensed the difference in the gait too, for he lifted his head from my lap and looked towards the door.

Wilson burst through it. In her hand she waved . . .

"A letter?"

"A letter!" She brought it to me. "Miss Henrietta had not gone through the post as she usually does, but as I was passing the drawing room, she called me in and gave this to me, to give to you, and—" she drew in an extra breath—"I brought it to you as fast as I could."

Although I longed to rip open the seal, although Wilson knew of my interest, I restrained myself for the sake of decorum—and the risk that my eagerness might cause her to want to stay in the hopes of hearing details. "Your effort is much appreciated," I said as calmly as I could. "That will be all."

Her face fell and I could see her thinking, *all?* But being the good maid she was, she gave a little curtsy and said, "Yes, miss."

I felt sorry for her and nearly called her back. But the lure of reading Robert's words in solitude overrode any urge to satisfy her curiosity.

I let my legs dangle over the bed, broke the seal, and leaned towards the lamp for better reading: *Dear Miss Barrett, I just shall say, in as few words as I can, that you make me very happy and that, now the beginning is over, I daresay I shall do better . . .*

I let my thrill in knowing that I had made *him* happy enrich my journey through his missive. He wrote of my work, of our common work, sharing details that solidified our connection. When he succinctly captured the essence of our art, I read the lines twice, as if taking two delicious sips of clear water. *For an instructed eye loves to see where the brush has dipped twice in a lustrous colour, has lain insistingly along a favourite outline, dwelt lovingly in a grand shadow. For these "too muches" are so many helps to making out the real painter's picture, as he had it in his brain.*

I felt the same way about our art, the same deliciousness in sensing not only the result, but the process of the artist.

But then, in his next line, I nearly panicked as he spoke of signing off. . . . *Night is drawing on and I go out—yet cannot, quiet at conscience, till I repeat (to myself, for I never said it to you, I think) that your poetry must be, cannot but be, infinitely more to me than mine to you—for you do what I always wanted, hoped to do, and only seem now likely to do for the first time. You speak out, you. I only make men and women speak—give truth broken into prismatic hues, and fear the pure white light, even if it is in me. But I am going to try, so it will be no small comfort to have your company just now. You will nevermore, I hope, talk of "the honor of my acquaintance," but I will joyfully wait for the delight of your friendship, and the Spring, and my Chapel-sight after all.*

I started at the last phrase. Chapel-sight? I had heard that before. . . .

I went to the drawer in my desk, where I had faithfully kept his first letter. My eyes scanned the page, and then . . .

I found it. The passage in question. Robert had been describing how he and Cousin John had come for a visit—a visit that had never transpired. *Then he went to announce me, then he returned. You were too unwell. And now it is years ago, and I feel as at some untoward passage in my travels, as if I had been close, so close, to some world's wonder in chapel or crypt, only a screen to push and I might have entered. . . .*

I pulled in a sudden breath. Chapel-sight. The meanderings of my imagination found reality. He did wish to see me. To come face-to-face with my person.

No!

In spite of any inappropriate thought otherwise, I could not let it happen. Except for a chosen few, I did not *see* people, and never anyone of the male persuasion who was so . . . so . . .

Young.

My head shook in short bursts, confirming my heart. No, no, never would I consent to meet him. But I did not wish to lose this precious correspondent-camaraderie we had already established.

And so, even though the hour was late, I pulled out paper and pen, ready to tell him what must be the boundaries of our relationship. And yet . . . I feared if I said it so plainly, he would take offence and write me nevermore.

Instead, I did what I did best. I ignored the hint of a meeting and responded solely as a writer to a writer. I requested — as I had requested my other correspondents — that he give a true opinion of my work, that he teach me how to be a better poet.

If life provided me more . . .

I could not think about *that*, yet my cowardice did nothing to dispel the possibility of experiences beyond my control.

The rush of fear — and excitement — overpowered me.

NINE

Spring!

I stood at the opened window and peered out. Wilson had implored me to open the window wide, yet I had instructed her to open it but a little. Yet even though little, I could smell the difference in the air, the newness of it.

The winter was over and I had just escaped with my life. I might thank it for coming at all. Spring—until this spring—had never caused such elation in me. But for the end to the cold and the menace of the wind, it was always just another passing, as inevitable as night into day. But this year, seeing it—reading of its arrival through Robert's eyes . . .

Had changed mine.

I returned to the stack of his letters to find one penned a week ago. Once again—one time out of many—I let his response to the season become mine. *Wednesday morning—spring! Real warm spring, dear Miss Barrett, and the birds know it; and in spring I shall see you, surely see you. For when did I once fail to get whatever I had set my heart upon?*

My heart skipped at his last, and in its own defence returned to his glory of spring.

Without success. For though I could find pleasure in his mention of birds and warmth, and acknowledged my own relief in the disappearance of the east wind to mar their music, the intent that I so handily skipped over demanded attention.

I shall see you, surely see you.

The very thought of it sent me mentally staggering back, back, away from such a thought. Such a reality. My response was rife with alarm and angst. Two days ago I had reacted with panic and had written to Robert of my odd desire to lean completely out the window, escaping this prison with my life. It was a disturbing and unfamiliar desire of my soul to leap over the threshold of my world into another.

I had alarmed him by my talk. I held his subsequent letter and read the last line: *And pray you not to "lean out of the window" when my own foot is only on the stair. Do wait a little for yours ever, RB.*

I glanced at the window again. The air had changed from cold to fresh. The pigeons cooed upon the rooftop instead of lying huddled against the wind. And though I never *leaned* out the window, I often stood at the edge of it and—

Why did I never lean out the window? Was the act too bold? Too frightening? Too courageous?

Yes.

But also—since Robert—something more.

The words began to flow within my mind and I hurried to my desk to get them down.

Wednesday, 5 March 1845

I did not mean to strike a "tragic chord," indeed I did not! Sometimes one's melancholy will be uppermost and sometimes one's mirth—the world goes round, you know, and I suppose that in that letter of mine the melancholy took the turn. As to "escaping with my life," it was just a phrase. At least it did not signify more than that the sense of mortality and discomfort of it is peculiarly strong with me when east winds are blowing and waters freezing. For the rest, I am essentially better, and have been for several winters—and I feel as if it were intended for me to live and not die, and I am reconciled to the feeling.

I let my scribbling stop and allowed myself to fully comprehend my last words. Although odd, they were an essential—and surprising—truth. In the past two months, while corresponding with Robert (for he was decisively "Robert" to me now, at least within my own thoughts), I had turned a page of my own book of life. No more did I feel as though *now* was finite, or the future was a shadow that could never be caught. There was something beyond this room that perhaps *could* be mine.

I returned to my letter:

> You are not to think—whatever I may have written or implied—that I lean either to the philosophy or affectation which beholds the world through darkness instead of light and speaks of it wailingly. Now, may God forbid that it should be so with me. I am not despondent by nature—and after a courage of bitter mental discipline and long bodily seclusion, I come out with two learnt lessons (as I sometimes say and oftener feel): the wisdom of cheerfulness and the duty of social intercourse. Anguish has instructed me in joy, and solitude in society. It has been a wholesome and not unnatural reaction. And altogether, I may say that the earth looks the brighter to me in proportion to my own deprivations: the laburnum trees and rose trees are plucked up by the roots, but the sunshine is in their places, and the root of the sunshine is above the storms. What we call Life is a condition of the soul. And the soul must improve in happiness and wisdom, except by its own fault. These tears in our eyes, these faintings of the flesh, will not hinder such improvement!

I stopped writing, and once again sat in amazement at how I could write to him in a captured moment, without looking up, without even noticing my pen moving from paper to inkwell and back again.

I was done talking about me. It was time to address Robert's view of life. I had the feeling — nearly a knowing — that he had not experienced any true sorrow, any trial that could push one to the edge of living or the need to escape. With only joy and contentment encircling him, how could he ever understand my journey and the situation that had placed me where I was? As I was?

Suddenly, a thought: Should I tell him about Bro? Should I share with him the wrench of my heart and my very soul? And should I speak of this illness which had plagued me for —

Tomorrow was my birthday! Tomorrow I would be thirty-nine. Nearly old. Nearly done.

No. That was my old resignation. Things had changed.

Yet Robert was six years younger, still young — in years and attitude. Although he had seen more of the world by being out amongst it, in a way, I felt as if I had experienced my fair (or unfair?) share from within. Robert had seen and enjoyed the heady experience, like a little boy visiting a favourite place. He saw no shadows, no clouds. To him the world was bright and good.

I had lived within the shadows, with clouds hung low over this room which was my world. During our correspondence I had grown interested in his world, but I was still uncertain how he would react to mine.

I shall see you, surely see you.

In spite of my grand musings, the idea of his coming to my room still tore me with fright. I was safe within the letters, he *there* and me *here*. I had to encourage him to leave things as they were.

I do like to hear testimonies like yours, to happiness, and I feel it is to be a testimony of a higher sort than the obvious one. Still, it is obvious too that you have been spared up to this time, the great natural afflictions against which we are nearly all called, sooner or later, to struggle and wrestle — or your step would not be "on the stair" quite so lightly. And so we turn to you, dear Mr. Browning, for comfort and gentle spiriting! Remember that as you owe your unscathed joy to

God, you should pay it back to this world. And I thank you for some of it already.

I reread the words, hoping he would gain appreciation of my view, and not take the words as chastisement. He could not help that he had not suffered, and I did not wish suffering upon him. The innocent joy he found in life was infectious. *That* is what I needed for him to know.

How kind you are! How kindly and gently you speak to me! Some things you say are very touching, and some surprising, and although I am aware that you unconsciously exaggerate what I can be to you, yet it is delightful to be broad awake and think of you as my friend.

May God bless you.

Faithfully yours,
Elizabeth B. Barrett

"There," I said aloud.

Flush looked up at me, as if waiting to hear more.

That was enough. For now.

But what still needed doing . . .

I pushed my chair back from the desk and stood. My eyes gazed at the opened window, that opening that separated my here and the rest, there.

It was time to breach the barrier, to do what I told Robert I felt compelled to do.

I stood in front of the window, and with arms unused to physicality beyond the pen, with effort and much puffing, I slid the window high within its frame. And then . . .

Then I placed my hands just so upon the sill, my fingers the first to pass into strange territory. Encouraged that they did not retreat and suffered no repercussions, I urged my head and shoulders forwards, past the boundary, into the new frontier.

My heart and lungs reacted to the effort—and the drama—but did not rebel. And so I stood there, hands on the sill, torso thrust forward into the world outside, and breathed deep.

I looked right, then left. The rooftops of our neighbours greeted me, and I noticed another window down the way. Was someone in that room now? Was their window opened or closed? If I spoke loudly I could call to them.

But no. I was not ready for that.

And yet the lace of their curtain found release and fluttered its silent hello.

I laughed, and felt a place within grow larger.

Unused to my presence, a pigeon fluttered in agitation but soon settled and strutted its head in greeting. I heard a baby crying from some other window, but found only delight in its pure evidence of life.

The breeze — which had full permission to enter my room, flew around my face and entered freely into the folds and crevasses of my dress. I shivered, but not from any cold. My lungs, jealous of the attention, drew the breeze deep, and only with reluctance let it free again. The smell! It was new and fresh and clear and held every promise of the rebirth of the season.

All this wrapped around me and made me fully know that this small act of leaning through the window was a good thing, an accomplishment as heady and meaningful as any poem penned or letter created. It was a beginning.

I lifted my face to the sun and let its warmth and light caress me with its favour.

∽∗∾

I sat before my dressing table while Wilson unrolled the rags from my hair. She was quite expert at forming the curls into right ringlets about my head.

"Oh dear," she said, her fingers squeezing a lock of hair. "This one is still damp. The curl will surely fall."

I had some reading to do and did not wish to prolong my morning toilet. "Can you not just sweep it under, beneath the pinning. Or perhaps—"

Suddenly a burst of laughter rushed up the stairs to our ears. One guffaw was unfamiliar.

"Do we have a guest for luncheon?" I asked, although it was truly none of my business, as I never joined the family at meals.

"It's just Mr. Cook."

Just Mr. Cook? Her tone implied his presence was a normal occurrence. Although I was aware of his visits at dinner on occasion—when Papa was home—I did not know he still came during the day in Papa's absence.

"Does my father know about this?" I asked.

I watched Wilson's expression in the mirror as she set the ringlets right. "Oh no," she said. "Or I wouldn't think so." She noticed my eyes upon her and met their reflection. "I don't think he is aware of the continued intensity between your sister and . . . To him Mr. Cook is but a cousin, on visit."

"You imply he *is* more than that? Even after the horrible argument Henrietta had with Papa?"

"Oh yes." She tucked the offending curl beneath the rest and secured it with a pin. "You should see them together—they see no one but each other."

The thought that all this was going on unbeknownst to me, while I was in the house, the eldest sibling, the keeper of Papa's honour . . .

I put a hand on Wilson's primping. "Please tell Miss Henrietta I wish to see her at once."

"But your hair—"

"At once." I had a sudden flush of fear that the both of them would appear in my presence. "Alone."

She left to convey my message and I finished my hair as best I could. Hair did not matter right now. The propriety and reputation of our family prevailed over all trivialities.

I heard footsteps upon the stair and stood. Although I was not used to wielding authority of any kind, I did know from observation that the one in power did best to stand. Although neither I nor my sister possessed height as an attribute, I would ask her to—

She entered my room. "Yes, Ba? What do you want? I have a guest."

"Have a seat, please."

"I don't have time for a seat. As I said I have a—"

"Guest. So I heard. A man, here, when Papa is gone."

Henrietta rushed to my side, her voice low. "Don't tell him, Ba. Papa has met Surtees; he approves of him."

"As a suitor?"

She pulled away. "Papa's view on such things is ridiculous. How can he expect none of us to marry? It is all right for you, but for—" Her eyes flashed with recognition of her slight, but she quickly recovered. "I only mean that you have chosen not to pursue love. You are fulfilled within your work. But I have no such work. I only want a husband and children and a home of my own and—"

"You plan marriage, then?"

"Perhaps. One day." She flounced down upon the chair. "There are the stirrings of love, and the natural progression is towards a union. But the only way to know for certain is to spend time together, to see if our attraction expands to a knowledge and respect. . . ."

I watched her countenance beam and found the change in her striking and disconcerting. Had she truly found love? Was this what love looked like to an observer? So obvious? So gleeful? So emphatic?

"I do see a marked change in you."

She was at my side again. But this time she knelt down, pulling my hand to her chest. "Oh, Ba. I am changed. And when he puts his hands about my waist, and when he kisses—"

"He's kissed you?"

She was across the room in a second. "Alfred is our chaperone. He accompanies me to chapel, to Regent's Park, to skating."

"Skating? It is spring. This has been going on all winter? Even after Papa got after you and yelled—"

"Mr. Cook is an expert skater."

"That is not the issue."

The petulant look—a common condition of my sister's countenance—returned. "The issue is . . . we love each other, and true love like ours will not be denied."

"Papa will deny it. Has denied it."

"Then we will deny him."

This time it was I who went to her side, my hands on hers, imploring. "You cannot do such a thing. The repercussions would be—"

"Would be what?"

I had rarely thought of it in such tangible terms. "He would disown you."

"I would not need him. I would have Surtees, and we would have our own home, our own family, our own life."

No, no, no, no. "You cannot leave our family."

"Even the Bible says, 'Therefore shall a man leave his father and his mother, and shall cleave unto his wife: and they shall be one flesh.' And though he may like to think otherwise, the Bible has authority over even Papa."

Cousin John had quoted this verse. To me. I mentally completed the next verse . . . *And they were both naked, the man and his wife, and were not ashamed.* I could not repeat the verse to my sister. We Barretts did not speak of such things. But perhaps . . . was this latter part of the passage the key to Papa's attitude against marriage?

I retreated to a practical issue. "What does Mr. Cook do? Can he support you?"

Henrietta straightened to her full height. "He is an officer in the army."

Ah. Yes. I remembered now. Arabel had told me he was a lieutenant— a poor lieutenant, with a widowed mother to consider.

Their union would never work. How I wished I had never heard their laughter and summoned her.

"If only you would meet him," she said.

"No!"

She was taken aback. "Whyever not? You have seemed more well of late. Perhaps if you came down for lunch one of these days and visited with—"

"I could never do such a thing, condone such a thing, not behind Papa's back."

"But surely in this, Ba, you could. You have no idea the depth of the feeling, the passion we feel for one another."

I felt my cheeks grow red. No, I did not. I had long ago set aside such childish possibilities. I did not need nor desire passionate love. To commune with another on a higher level, as I communed with Robert . . .

Henrietta flipped her hands at me and walked out the door. "Oh, why do I bother? You, of all people, will never understand."

This time she did not retract the slight.

Surprisingly, the statement stung, more than it should have. But amid the sting was something I was rare to feel.

Regret.

And dismay.

Where was the woman who had so boldly leaned out the window into the world? My reaction to Henrietta's romance showed that old habits, old bastions of believing, were hard to set aside. I should have reveled in my sister's happiness.

And yet . . . to encourage her would be to go against Papa's dictum. It did not matter whether I agreed with it or not, he was our father. He loved us. He wanted what was best for us. And if that meant never to marry, then—

A sudden catch in my chest hinted at an alien feeling of rebellion that started an argument within.

But why doesn't Papa want us to marry? Where is the logic?

Papa knew best. He always had. What other father in the world would continue to care for all his children well into their adulthood? The financial sacrifices to keep us all together—

Hidden away.

We were not hidden. We could go out.

But do you?

I was not the issue. My siblings went out.

Only to Papa-approved venues.

Henrietta sneaked away....

She'll get caught, and then what?

I remembered when Papa had screamed so loudly at Henrietta and had slapped her, sending her to her knees. The memory still upset me. I did not wish for such a scene again.

For her sake? Or yours?

I noticed the novel I had been reading, staring at me from my bedside table. It was a book by Stendhal called *Le Rouge et le Noir—The Red and the Black*. It was a tragic tale set in France during trying political times. Since I had finished it, it had ridden me like an incubus. It was a book to be read at all risks. What interested me the most was how Stendhal—unlike any other novelist I had read—lingered in the minds and hearts of the characters, letting us know what they felt and thought. Mind and heart... it was a place where I was most at home. But beyond the style which so enraptured me was a story of people held captive by the rules of those in power, suffering the need to play a role in order to receive the support of those they loved.

Just like you are held captive. Just as you play a role and suffer.

"I do not suffer!"

There is hypocrisy in pretending to be virtuous.

I answered my own accusation. "I do not pretend—"

But Papa does.

Appalled by such disloyalty, I grabbed the book and marched it across the room to the farthest bookshelf, where I placed it on the bottom of a stack of five.

There.

To counter the thoughts ignited by the book—and my discourse with my sister—I chose another book off the shelf. *Pilgrim's Progress.* One of Papa's favourites. We had spent many hours discussing its virtues.

I retreated to the sofa, waited until Flush fit himself into his place by my side, and dove into the safety of its pages.

～❦～

As I read the newspaper I became more and more enraged. I slapped a hand against the offensive words. "This is not fair. Moreover, it is unchristian."

Sette looked up from his perusal of my bookshelves for something "diverting." "Whatever are you talking about?"

Occy rolled a ball across the room, sending Flush after it. "The price of crinolines rising, Ba?"

I took offence. I cared little for fashion. That was Henrietta's department. "I speak of the Corn Laws."

"What *are* you talking about?" Occy asked.

Without warning, Papa entered the room. "What's this I hear? My Ba mentioning Corn Laws?"

Finally an ally. I held out the paper for his review. "The tariff on English corn must be repealed so the price can lower and poor families can afford bread."

Sette yawned and arched his back. "As long as we can afford bread, I do not see that it matters."

Papa glared at him. "Such elitist attitudes are not worthy of a Barrett," he said. "And you only afford bread because I buy it for you."

"Sorry, Papa." Sette reddened and went back to his book search.

I was heartened that Papa supported my empathy for the poor. Mother had always encouraged charity work, and though I had been unable to physically go out among them as Arabel often did, I could offer moral support and . . .

Perhaps something more.

"What if I offered a poem in the opposition's support?" I asked.

The room turned silent. Then Occy and Sette looked at each other and burst out laughing. "A woman's verses? Think of the impertinence of it," Occy said.

Sette let his voice rise an octave. "Oh, dearest corn, how wrongly you have been priced! Without repeal our bread cannot be sliced."

I was horrified by their laughter and derision. " 'Tis a serious subject. If the poor spend their meager wages on bread, then they have no money left for luxuries like clothing, and the demand for clothing falls. With too much clothing on the market, the price must surely fall in order to entice people to buy, and subsequently the wages of the clothing workers will also fall, creating more poor."

Sette grabbed a book to his chest and gasped. "Oh my! What shall we do?"

"We should think of someone beyond ourselves," I cried. "Life exists beyond these walls."

"How would you know?" Occy said.

Once again, the room silenced. Then Occy ran to my side. "I'm sorry, Ba. I didn't mean . . ."

Papa cleared his throat, then finally spoke. "Your compassion is admirable, Ba."

I nodded victoriously at my brothers.

"But . . ." He stroked his chin, thinking. "I do not consider it wise for you to be included among the dissenters. It is not proper for a woman to be involved in political work."

I did not know what to say. As a learned woman was I not permitted to have opinions? To share those opinions? To try to change the cruelties of the world for the better? I thought of an example of a time when I had helped through verse. "Two years ago I wrote 'Cry of the Children' about child labour conditions. And other writers added their pen to the horror, so much so that Parliament enacted a new law, and Fleet Prison was closed."

Papa's look was condescending. "I believe Mr. Dickens' stories were the ones deemed instrumental in provoking the changes."

He was right. I immediately regretted mentioning my paltry offering. But my pride proved stronger than my regret and I added, "In America,

Edgar Allen Poe gave my poem on the children effusive praise. He even dedicated a book to me."

Sette snickered. "From what I've read of Poe, I am not certain that was a compliment."

Papa took a step towards the door and motioned to the boys that it was time to leave. "We are all proud of your poems, Ba, but keep your subjects set on dead Greeks and seraphims and leave the issues of society to men."

I was deflated. It was as though my body had been pierced and all life-giving air had been released.

I heard my brothers scramble down the stairs while Papa paused one last moment for a final offering. "You must be careful of your reputation, Ba. Poe giving you a dedication, and then there was the time when your name was mentioned in a magazine near that of George Sand. Any connection with that abandoned woman can cause irretrievable harm."

I was struck dumb. Although I did not agree with the way some other poets lived, or even some of their work, that did not mean we could not appreciate one another's efforts.

"I assume this will be the end of your inclination towards involvement in the Corn Laws?" Papa said.

I nodded, but only because I wished for him to leave. When he had done so, when I was alone from the appalling masculine rampancy to which I had been afflicted . . .

How dare they demean me so? Demean the power of my work? They did not need to remind me that I was but a woman and had no power, no rights, no standing.

I should write it in spite of them . . . to spite them.

I knew I would do no such thing. I would not vex Papa for the world.

But as I heard the dulled sounds of my family going on with their day below, I felt a vacancy and silence which struck me as freshly as ever and with equal despair. The men of my family did not care to hear my views, indeed did not even believe I deserved any. My sisters may have been content to live within these feminine restrictions, but I was not. Not completely.

Wilson came to the door with a letter. "It's from him," she whispered.

Another man.

When I did not take the letter right away, she pulled it back. "Do you not wish to read it?"

I shook my hesitation away. At this moment Robert was the only man I wished to hear from. I took the letter and plunged into his words with hope of comfort and affirmation. I quickly received both: *Pray tell me, too, of your present doings and projects, and never write yourself "grateful" to me, who am grateful, very grateful to you, for none of your words but I take in earnest.*

I stopped reading and felt the sting of tears. This man—this one man among all men—cared what I did each day, what I thought, what I dreamed. This man would not laugh at me but with me, would not disparage but lift me up, would not ignore me but offer appreciation.

And I . . . I would return the favour.

❧

I waited patiently as the doctor counted my pulse while looking at his pocket watch. When he was through, he dropped my wrist and shook his head. "It is too fast, Miss Barrett, far above your usual rate. Have you been exerting yourself?"

I was surprised to feel myself blush. I hastened to give him an answer that would satisfy. "I can assure you I have made no physical exertions. As is the rule, I am here all days, finding my worth in solitude and reading."

He looked unconvinced. "Perhaps you have been writing? Perhaps that is what has taxed you so?"

Writing poetry? No. I could honestly assure him that the upheaval of my body was not caused by the strains of creation. But, of course, I had been writing . . . Had my correspondence with Robert been the cause of my racing heart?

I could not tell him that, and so I merely said, "I have not been working."

"Then I do not know why you are feeling so poorly." He looked down at me, stroking his whiskers. "Knowing your history, there must be something that is causing you agitation." He opened his bag and removed two bottles of medicine.

Suddenly, the thought of his prescribing more than my usual draught of opium did not appeal. "I will be fine, Dr. Chambers."

He gave me a second glance. "*Fine* is not a word I have heard from you."

He was right. I generally welcomed doctor visits and encouraged additional medicines. In fact, it was I who usually had Papa request the doctor come. This was the first time in recent weeks that it had been Papa who made the call in spite of my protests. *You are not yourself, Ba. There is an agitation with you lately, a stirring that surely must be caused by a nerve disorder of some sort.*

He was wrong. The doctor was wrong. Although I had felt weakened, and had first blamed it upon the blustery winds, I had come to see in the past days that the wind that stirred my nerves into unrest was not external, nor something that was shared by anyone else. The winds of agitation blew from within and were flamed by a few words in Robert's last letter to me: *You think that I "unconsciously exaggerate what you are to me" ... I never yet mistook my own feelings, one for another. Do you think I shall see you in two months, three months? I may travel perhaps. ...*

In the week since I had received the letter I had suffered every range of emotion. I was elated and humbled by his feelings for me, astounded by his confidence in them, agitated by his mention of a meeting, and horrified at the thought of his traveling to some far-off land. Not that letters could not span the miles between here and there, but to have him close, but a short distance in New Cross ...

The chance of it made the idea of a meeting more judicious. If I did not agree to meet him before he left for months and months—with all chance of meeting evaporating within the distance that separated us—could I live with myself?

And so, as usually happened when I worried, my body rebelled, weakened, and progressed into the chest congestion that was always waiting in the wings of my life for its chance to make an entrance.

But in order to even fathom the idea of a meeting, I had to be well. This time, of all times in my invalid life, I could not linger in the sickbed, content to be ill—and nearly encouraged to be so—because I had no better use of my time.

If Robert might leave . . .

The doctor left the draughts on the bedside and closed his doctor's bag. "Are you still taking the opiate?"

"For sleep," I said. "I do not seem able to be without it."

"There is no need to try," he said. "Use it as often as you like. And these too," he went on, pointing at the new bottles to add to my collection. "Twice a day, one teaspoon each."

I did not ask what the new elixirs would do for me. "To make me better" was the goal, and I could be assured by the depth of Dr. Chambers' skill that they would not make me worse.

The doctor headed to the door. "I am glad your father called me. He said you were not in favour of a visit, but we all know that he and I have your best interests in mind."

"I do know that," I said. And I did not lie in my agreement. But what neither of them understood—what I was still trying to comprehend—was that I no longer wished to be ill. Although I did not know how to be well, I wished to try it. For only in wellness was there any future.

My future.

Never would I have thought I would entertain such a word. Robert was to blame, or to thank, depending on how that word played out for good or naught. But the very chance of it turning for the better . . .

After the doctor left, I retrieved my lap desk from beneath the covers. I had not responded to Robert's letter as yet but was in the midst of it when the doctor had come. The writing was taking time, due to the condition of my agitation and my subsequent weakness, but more so because of the content that I was determined to include. If . . . if . . . Robert and I were to move forwards in our friendship, if we were to actually meet, I had to indulge his many requests for information about *me*.

But what to say and what to omit? The composition had been slow in coming, had taken many drafts, but was close to completion. I read it through, knowing it was far from perfect but hoping I would deem it good enough to post.

> Whenever I delay to write to you, dear Mr. Browning, it is not, be sure, that I take my "own good time" but submit to my own bad time. It was kind of you to wish to know how I was, and not unkind of me to suspend my answer to your question—for indeed I have not been very well, nor have had much heart for saying so. This implacable weather! this east wind that seems to blow through the sun and moon! who can be well in such a wind? Yet for me, I should not grumble. There has been nothing very bad the matter with me, as there used to be—I only grow weaker than usual, and learn my lesson of being mortal, in a corner . . . but all this must end! April is coming. There will be both a May and a June if we live to see such things, and perhaps, after all, we may.

Although I had been forthcoming about my weakness, I was not ready to give him the true explanation that the very thought of *him* was the cause. Best to blame it on the weather. I read on, delving into our proposed meeting and the discomfort it caused:

> And as to seeing you besides, I observe that you distrust me, and that perhaps you penetrate my morbidity and guess how, when the moment comes to see a living human face to which I am not accustomed, I shrink and grow pale in the spirit. Do you? You are learned in human nature, and you know the consequences of leading such a secluded life as mine—notwithstanding all my fine philosophy about social

duties and the like. I will indeed see you when the warm weather has revived me a little and put the earth "to rights" again so as to make pleasures of that sort possible. For if you think that I shall not like to see you, you are wrong (for all your learning). But I shall be afraid of you at first—though I am not, in writing thus. You are Paracelsus, and I am a recluse, with nerves that have been broken on the rack and now hang loosely, quivering at a step and a breath.

I quivered now as I read it. To tell him—in writing—that we would meet . . . it made me glance at the vials Dr. Chambers had left for me.

But no. The decision must not be celebrated or endured with elixirs, but in full mind and heart. And Robert must know my full mind and heart. And past:

> What you say of society draws me on to many comparative thoughts of your life and mine. You seem to have drunken of the cup of life full, with the sun shining on it. I have lived only inwardly; or with sorrow for a strong emotion. Before this seclusion of my illness, I was secluded still, and there are few of the youngest women in the world who have not seen more, heard more, known more of society than I, who am scarcely to be called young now. I grew up in the country—had no social opportunities, had my heart in books and poetry, and my experience in reveries. My sympathies drooped towards the ground like an untrained honeysuckle—and but for one person, in my own house—but of this I cannot speak.

Although I wished to share my past with him—and that past most certainly included Bro as a key player—I was still not ready to tell him full measure. Not of that which continued to pull at my very being. But I could talk to him about Hope End.

> It was a lonely life, growing green like the grass around it. Books and dreams were what I lived in—and domestic life

seemed to buzz gently around, like the bees about the grass.
And so time passed, and passed—and afterwards, when my
illness came and I seemed to stand at the edge of the world
with all done, and no prospect (as appeared at one time) of
ever passing the threshold of one room again; I turned to
thinking with some bitterness (after the greatest sorrow of
my life had given me room and time to breathe) that I had
stood blind in this temple I was about to leave—that I had
seen no human nature, that my brothers and sisters of the
earth were names to me, that I had beheld no great mountain
or river, nothing in fact. I was as a man dying who had not
read Shakespeare, and it was too late! Do you understand?
I have had much of the inner life, and from the habit of
self-consciousness and self-analysis, I make great guesses at
human nature in the main. But how willingly I would as a
poet exchange some of this lumbering, ponderous, helpless
knowledge of books for some experience of life and man,
for some . . .

I did not wish for him to think of me as a complainer. I moved to
explain:

But grumbling is a vile thing. We should all thank God
for our measures of life, and think them enough for each of
us. I write so that you may not mistake what I wrote before in
relation to society, although you do not see from my point of
view; and that you may understand what I mean fully when
I say that I have lived all my chief joys, and indeed nearly all
emotions that go warmly by that name and relate to myself
personally, in poetry and in poetry alone.

Like to write? Of course, of course I do. I seem to live
while I write—it is life for me. Why, what is to live? Not to
eat and drink and breathe, but to feel the life down all the
fibres of being, passionately and joyfully. And thus, one lives
in composition surely—not always—but when the wheel goes
round and the procession is uninterrupted. Is it not so with

you? Oh—it must be so. For the rest, there will be necessarily a reaction; and, in my own particular case, whenever I see a poem of mine in print, or even smoothly transcribed, the reaction is most painful. The pleasure, the sense of power without which I could not write a line, is gone in a moment; and nothing remains but disappointment and humiliation. I never wrote a poem which you could not persuade me to tear to pieces if you took me at the right moment! I have a seasonable humility, I do assure you.

I smiled at the words, but more than that, at the freedom I experienced by sharing them with this man—this one man of all men—who might understand.

How delightful to talk about oneself; but as you "tempted me and I did eat," I entreat your longsuffering of my sin, and ah! if you would but sin back so in turn! You and I seem to meet in a mild contrarious harmony . . . as in the "si no, si no" of an Italian duet. I want to see more of men, and you have seen too much, you say. I am in ignorance, and you, in satiety. "You don't even care about reading now." Is it possible? And I am as "fresh" about reading as ever I was—as long as I keep out of the shadow of the dictionaries and of theological controversies, and the like. Shall I whisper it to you under the memory of the last rose of last summer? I am very fond of romances; yes! and I read them not only as some wise people are known to do, for the sake of the eloquence here and the sentiment there, and the graphic intermixtures here and there, but for the story! just as little children would, sitting on their papa's knee. My childish love of a story never wore out with my love of plum cake, and now there is not a hole in it. I make it a rule, for the most part, to read all the romances that other people are kind enough to write—and woe to the miserable wight who tells me how the third volume endeth. Have you any surviving innocence of this sort? or do you call it idiocy? If you do, I will forgive you, only smiling to myself — I give you notice — with a smile of superior pleasure!

It was done. As much to say as I could say at this moment. And so I bid him adieu.

I had much to say to you, or at least something, of the "blind hopes," etc., but am ashamed to take a step into a new sheet. If you mean "to travel," why, I shall have to miss you. Do you really mean it? How is the play going on? and the poem? May God bless you!

Ever and truly yours,
E.B.B.

I carefully compiled the sheets and folded them just so. And then I did something that had become a habit — unnoticed at first, but now embraced.

I kissed the envelope.

And then I called Wilson to come, to send it on its way.

After giving her instruction, I added one more. "And these," I said, pointing to the two new medicines left by Dr. Chambers. "Dispose of these, if you will."

"But—"

"I wish them gone."

With a curious look she nodded and took them away.

I felt better already.

Cleansed of the past and ready for the future.

Ten

Come then.

I could not believe I actually wrote those words! It was May twentieth, two months to the day since I had written Robert the letter which presented my past upon a platter. That he had not gone running into the night, put off by its depressing and finite nature, was a surprise. And a relief. And yet the transition from letters to the chance of meeting face-to-face did not come easily. There were accusations and miscommunications about our motives and the true meaning of our words. There were assurances towards me that I was the only person he ever wrote letters to, and to him the assurance that I did not write to others as to him. And there were illnesses — on his part, not mine. He was prone to debilitating headaches that lasted for days and days, that even forced him to end his society for the season last.

But as a meeting became nearly inevitable, I realized the more I exhibited wariness and gave excuses, the more import I put on the occasion. Wasn't it unwise to do such a thing? For what if the meeting went badly? Would its outcome seem a matter of life and death because I had elevated it to such a level? It was best to just let it be and keep my continued fears and anxieties to myself.

And so, on May the sixteenth, I had taken a deep breath and penned the words that would bring this event into being: *Come then.*

To my delight, Robert—who had claimed he was not going anywhere for weeks to come because of his headaches—jumped at my words. What I had suggested just last Friday was accepted by return letter later that same evening, and the meeting was arranged for today—Tuesday. Four days from agreement to commencement.

I was in a tizzy for it. Never had my heart beat so wildly as on this day. Never had my mind swam through oceans of what-ifs and could-bes. Would he like me? Would he be appalled by my appearance and the limits of my world? Would we both become tongue-tied when seated within the same time and space?

The last was a very real fear when it was considered that our letters were enjoyed in a delayed manner thus: I wrote him on one day, but he would not read my words until another. And then his response written on that day would not be read by my eyes until yet another day. But to be in the same room, and experience the words in the moment, and be able to respond in kind . . . how heady was the very thought of it!

I looked at the clock. It was nearly three. Nearly time to finally see my Robert.

My Robert?

I shook my head at the audacity. He was a friend, a fellow poet. What-ever feelings I had garnered during our four months of letter writing were based on the mutuality we shared within those identities.

Nothing more.

Then why had I instructed Wilson to purchase new black ribbons for my hair? Why had I felt enormous relief when my sisters had told me they were going out for the afternoon? That Papa was gone at work was a given—although I had not been able to keep the meeting from him. I simply could not bend the trust we shared.

Papa had been agreeable to a visit from a poet. And George was gone to his work as a barrister. The other brothers, though not employed, were rarely home at this time—which, of course, was why I had instructed

Robert to come after two and before six. I had informed him that one of my sisters would bring him up to my room, but now . . . with the house completely mine (ours), I had instructed Wilson to do the honours. She was waiting for him even now. I just hoped her face was not pressed against the window.

I lay upon my sofa and arranged the silk of my black dress around me. I had never before despaired of not having frocks of lighter colors—until now. I had worn black since Bro's death—velvet in winter and silk in summer—and had always been pleased enough with it. But now . . . would the somber colour add to the oppression of my room? I did not think it oppressive, but in the past three days, trying to envision it as seen through Robert's eyes . . .

Flush whimpered and jerked his head. I realized I had been stroking a trough within the fur of his neck. "Sorry, boy." I forced my hand to lie elsewhere.

And then . . .

I heard two voices, one Wilson's and one . . .

I jerked aright, sending Flush to the floor. I did not apologize and urge him back, for all my thoughts and emotions were tuned to another.

I heard his feet upon the stairs!

I reminded myself to breathe.

"Just here, to the right, sir," I heard Wilson say.

"Thank you."

And then . . . he was there. His eyes quickly searched the room until they found mine. He smiled. "Dear Miss Barrett. Finally we meet." He drew front and center a bouquet of flowers. "From my mother's garden to your hands."

"They are beautiful," I said. "Wilson?" She took them away to find a vase.

His hands free, he came to my side and took my hand in his, drawing it to his lips. . . .

The word *swoon* came to mind as I felt myself become heady at his touch. And yet, I was not one to do such a thing. I was not a young girl

NANCY MOSER

aching for the attention of a young beau. I was a woman, nearly forty and far beyond the frivolities of—

I barely felt his lips upon my hand, and yet I wished for them to linger. . . .

He seemed to feel the same, for he held my hand a moment longer, peering into my eyes.

Suddenly, I worried what he would see. I knew I was deathly pale, and when seeing myself in the mirror was struck by the two dark caves that were my eyes. Although I never expected anyone to count me pretty—and had told myself such vanity was absurd—I now wished for some measure of beauty.

If only in Robert's eyes.

He stood above me and I realized I had not offered him a chair. At the moment I began to do so, he fetched one for himself and pulled it close, but not too.

"And so, my dear, dear, Miss Barrett. We are finally met."

Somehow I found my voice—which had been another worry, since I knew it tended towards reediness and softness to the point of non-existence. "I am very glad you have come, Mr. Browning."

He took a large breath and scanned the room. "So this is the chapel."

"It is my room—such as it is."

He rose to stroll about it, and I sensed he was not one to sit still long. He moved to the window. "What an interesting shade." He extended it full down in order to see the castle that was painted upon it. "Your castle in the clouds?"

I had never thought of it as such, but the description was apt. "My father says it makes my room look like a confectioner's shop."

"Light and sweet. I can see that."

He adjusted it to the halfway point where I had placed it to control the afternoon light. "And this ivy," he said, fingering a leaf. "It is quite . . . copious and healthy."

"My cousin, Mr. Kenyon, gave that to me. I am afraid I have let it have full run of the room."

174

"Since you are unable to travel, you have set it free to roam?"

Again, he gave apt words to items that I had long taken for granted. But before I could respond, he said, "How long have you been unable to walk?"

I looked at him agog. "I can walk."

He looked genuinely surprised and returned to his chair. "I had heard you were crippled because of a childhood fall from a horse."

I laughed. "I have heard that too, but I assure you, my legs are quite sufficient." On a whim I felt the need to show him. "Here," I said, extending my hands to him. "Help me up."

Even as he took my hands in his I questioned, *What am I doing?* And yet, looking into his brown eyes, feeling the strength transferring from his hands to mine . . .

I swung my legs to the side and let myself be lifted to my feet. We both peered down, as if my legs were a separate entity to be watched in case of mutiny.

But they did not betray me. I looked up at Robert and he down at me. "See? I am not disabled."

"Indeed, you are not." He pulled my hand into the crook of his arm. "Shall we take a stroll about the room, Miss Barrett?"

Although it was ridiculous—to meander in and around chairs and tables that were barely set wide enough for myself in my crinolines, it was as exhilarating as if we had strolled through Regent's Park itself. Flush danced around us, as excited as I. We paused at my library and chatted over this volume and that, and at the fireplace he commented on the portrait on the mantel of my mother, calling her "as lovely as her daughter." Then we stood at the window discussing the habits of the pigeons that populated the rooftops.

On the way back to the sofa, we passed a mirror, and both, at once, looked into its reflection. "No," he said. "Do not look away." He straightened his back and adjusted my hand upon his arm as if posing. "Behold the poets!" he said.

My thoughts flew faster than my logic and made me consider what a fine-looking pair we made. He was more masculine than his portrait (which I had instructed Wilson to remove from the wall), his head a tad large for his body, which was solid yet slim. He was short for a man — I would guess him to be five and six, and wore fashion with an impeccable flair.

What were his thoughts of me? I didn't wish to know. He must have sensed my dis-ease, for he moved us on our way.

"Here we are," he said as we returned — far too soon — to the sofa. "Safely back home again." He eased me to seating and waited patiently as I moved my legs to their familiar recline. "So. How did you enjoy our journey?"

"It was quite delightful. And just the right length." I felt myself out of breath and my legs weak, but was determined to ignore both symptoms.

Once he was settled across from me, he asked, "If you will pardon my intrusion . . . you wear mourning, or do you simply prefer black for fashion?"

"I . . ." I found I had no explanation that I wished to share — even with Robert. "Both," I said, leaving it at that.

"I am sorry. I shouldn't have asked such a thing. A thousand pardons."

"Granted," I said. But since he had breached the personal subject of looks, I asked a question of my own. "Your appearance does not match your work."

"Match . . . ?"

Could I explain it well? "You do not look the poet. You are not timid or withdrawn, nor do you act pensive or overtly intellectual."

His laugh was boisterous. "Oh no, I try very hard to hide my intellect." He leaned forwards in confidentiality. "You see, London society disdains undue inflections of the mind as much as they disdain a paletot for evening wear. Or if one does possess a mind as well as the coveted wit and fashion, it is best to keep it hidden in a pocket until one is alone."

"Or among true friends," I said.

His smile was genuine. "Or among true friends."

Then, to my dismay, he sat back in his chair, crossed one leg over the other, and began to dissect me with his gaze. "But as to you, Miss Barrett, does your appearance harmonize with the essence of your work?"

I chastised myself for ever initiating the subject of appearances. "I hope not," I said.

He seemed surprised. "Whyever do you say that?"

"Because I am here, like this . . ."

"I find *here* to be an interesting locale, and your *like this* to be completely acceptable, as it is you I have come to see. Extraneous details have no bearing in *you* any more than my coat and walking cane have any bearing on me. We each are as we are."

I knew he was exaggerating for my benefit, and loved him for it. But I had to turn the conversation from our façades. "Speaking of our work . . ."

"Were we speaking of our work?"

He made me smile. "We are as of now. How do you go about the task? Writing is such joy to me and—"

"Joy?" He shook his head. "I take no pleasure in writing—none, in the mere act—though all pleasure in the sense of fulfilling a duty, whence, if I have done my real best . . . judge how heartbreaking a matter it is to be pronounced a poor creature by this critic or that acquaintance. But I think you like the operation of writing as I should like that of painting or making music, do you not?"

"I do. Greatly."

"I thought as much."

"But," I said, "you will never persuade me that I am better at the process, or do as well as you. We look from different points of view. Yours is the point of attainment."

He shrugged. "I know there is a great delight in the heart of the thing; and use and forethought have made me ready at all times to set to work. But I don't know why my heart sinks whenever I open my desk and rises when I shut it."

"I cannot believe that," I said.

He raised a hand to take a vow. "Writing is my life, but it is work." He grinned. "And I have always disdained work."

I remembered Mary Mitford's objection to Robert—that he had never held a job, that his father financed his publishing ventures. But I could not let my thoughts linger there too long. His father loved him and supported him in all ways. That was to be commended.

"And you, Miss Barrett. I suppose you run to your pen each morning as if it were fresh air just waiting to be breathed in and exhaled into beautiful poetry."

"If only it would be created as easily as breathing."

"But you enjoy the process, in spite of the challenge."

"Perhaps because of the challenge."

"Ah, there it is," he said, leaning back in his chair. "The difference between us. You embrace the challenge and I seek an easier way."

"Whether struggle or ease, we both gain results," I said.

"But you to a greater degree. For who knows my name?"

"Plenty, I would think. Your work, your plays—"

He laughed. "Have earned the scorn of many, the praise of few, and too few shillings to repay my father for the process. But you, Miss Barrett, you are heralded as the greatest poetess of the age. All Britain has heard of you—and America besides."

I did not want to compare our successes, for it would cause both of us embarrassment. "I do not care for money or fame," I said, "only for—"

He laughed and slapped a hand upon his thigh. "Oh, to not care for money! I admire you for that, Miss Barrett."

He took me wrongly. "I only meant that I have resigned myself to never gaining good compensation from my writing like Wordsworth or Dickens. If only I can write enough, earn enough, be known enough to be allowed to continue to be published . . ."

"Aha! So your joy in writing *is* connected to being published?"

I felt myself redden. "The Bible says we are not to place our light under a bushel, but place it on a stand for all the world to see."

"On that stand your work is surely a beacon. And mine is a flickering candle, ready to be snuffed into darkness by the faintest breeze."

"No, Mr. Browning. Do not say such a thing."

"I may say it because it is true. But be assured, Miss Barrett, that I hold no jealousy towards your success, only admiration and pleasure. I did not come here to compete with you, but to know you. You, just you, Miss Barrett."

I believed him. And all my fears regarding his motivation, that he might want to see me out of curiosity, or to be able to say that he had attained what no one else ever could, was stifled and extinguished. I felt assured enough—even after this short knowing—that he wished to visit me for me, and me alone.

"I just thought of something," he said. "If you had not mentioned my work in your 'Lady Geraldine,' I would not have written to you and—"

I held up a hand, stopping his words. "You wrote to me because of a mention in one of my poems?"

"Why, yes. I told you as much in my first letter."

"No, you did not," I said.

"Yes, I am quite certain I did."

"No, you did not," I repeated, and I knew I was right, for I had read and reread the letter so many times that I nearly knew it by rote. "You said, 'I love your verses with all my heart, dear Miss Barrett' and—"

"Did I say it so?"

"You did. And you did not mention 'Lady Geraldine.'"

He shrugged. "Well, then, perhaps I didn't. But I did mention your poems, I do remember that distinctly, so whether or not I pointed out your mention of my 'Pomegranate' by name, the effect of my contacting you—and the sentiment within that letter—are the same." He reached across the space between us and touched the edge of the sofa. "I love your verses with all my heart, dear Miss Barrett. And now, having met you, I have even more to love."

He had passed over the point in contention, but it still hung with me. "If not for the mention of your work in mine—" I said again.

"That whim to mention a fellow poet . . ."

"We would not be—"

"Here. Now. Fully met."

Oh yes.

The clock on the mantel struck the half hour. I would not have been surprised if it had struck six, but it was only four-thirty. And yet that was enough. For now. Our first meeting had exceeded all my hopes and expectations. It was best to let it end on this perfection.

As if reading my mind, he stood. "I should go."

"Yes," I said, although reluctance was heavy upon me. "You will come again?"

His eyes sparkled and his face beamed. "Tomorrow?"

My, my! "Next Tuesday, at this same time?"

"So long . . ."

I agreed it would seem a lifetime, and yet I wished a bit of time to fully digest . . .

I thought of something. "Please, Mr. Browning, a favour. Tell no one of our meeting."

He pondered this a moment. "I suppose that means I cannot dance through the streets, shouting your name to the heavens, exuberant with glee?"

"Not today."

He reached down to kiss my hand once more. "As you wish, dear lady. Till Tuesday, then."

I called for Wilson and she showed him the door. I held my breath in order to hear every footfall, every word, wishing to hold on to his presence as long as possible.

And then there was silence. Silence on the outside, but within . . . such a cacophony of noise arose within me, as if every thought, every emotion, every aspiration ever pondered had been awakened and were all talking at once, giving their opinions and offering advice. I pressed my hands against my head, trying to contain—

Wilson rushed into the room, out of breath. I had not even heard her return up the stairs. "How did it—?" Upon seeing me she stopped short. "Miss? Are you all right?"

I lowered my hands, but the inner noise did not dissipate. "I am . . . I am fine."

Wilson gave me one of her appraising looks and put her hands upon her hips. "You don't look fine, not one little bit. In fact, I am thinking you need to get in your bed right this minute. I could make you a draught to help you sleep and—"

Sleep was the last thing I wanted. "Coffee," I said. "I want strong coffee."

"But it will only keep you awake and—"

"Yes."

She eyed me a moment, then smiled. "Mr. Browning riled you up, didn't he?"

"He did no such thing."

Her smiled broadened. "Begging your pardon, but by that blush upon your face, I'd say you were lying to me."

"Just get me the coffee, Wilson. And be quick about it." I added, "Please."

"Yes'm," she said. But she was smiling as she left.

Which caused me to do the same. Although I was not unfamiliar with the facial expression, today, at this moment, it sprang from a deeper place than had heretofore been tapped.

What did it mean? I did not know.

But I liked it. Immensely.

⁓❦⁓

Wilson brought the coffee and I drank two cups, wishing to prolong the swell of my happiness. But my elation was short-lived. In its place came the flood of pent-up feelings that had assailed me upon Robert's departure. The initial delight gave way to second-guessing. What did he truly think of me? Had I made a good impression? Had he enjoyed our encounter as much as I?

I relived every memory, testing each word, each gesture, each expression through the filter of the rationality that came with the passage of time. I expected to find differences between what I had felt within the moment and what I could study from a distance. Yet I was pleasantly surprised to find there was no alteration. The heady euphoria of our conversation held fast—each witty comment, each compliment, each smile, each laugh, each . . . touch.

I singled out touch as the one element, the one singular sensation that was completely new to me. I could not remember ever touching or being touched by a man who was not a relative or a doctor delivering his healing.

And yet, Robert had taken my hand as easily as if such contact were the norm. Which made me . . . Had Robert been close to many women? Surely he had. He was a dynamic, charismatic, handsome man who traveled through society with more ease than I traveled from one side of my room to the other.

The tug in my midsection shocked me. What was this odd sensation? Could it . . . no, certainly it could not be . . . yet it must be . . .

Jealousy?

I gasped at the knowledge.

I had not been immune to this vice—Mrs. Norton, in particular, elicited its fire in me—but I had never experienced its bite in regard to a man. A young man, at least. I held dim memories of feeling jealous of Mr. Boyd's attentions towards others, and yet that was not the same. Mr. Boyd was decades my senior. He had been introduced into our family as a tutor, and had remained a mentor, with me his adoring pupil. There had been no touch of a man, as a *man*. . . .

I had been ill since I was a young teen. My entire womanly years had been spent set apart from the normal places where girls met boys and let nature and romance take their course. I had told myself I did not care, that I—among all females—did not need or desire *amour*.

And this is not that.

"No, it is not," I said aloud. "Stop being the silly schoolgirl. It is utterly inappropriate and unbecom —"

I stopped chastising myself when I heard footsteps upon the stairs. Papa's footsteps! I looked to the clock. It was time for our evening prayers. Normally I looked forward to this time shared, but tonight . . . I had no talent for hiding agitation. Papa had often claimed that my face was as transparent as my heart. I had always taken his assessment as a compliment, but tonight, some guile would have served me well.

As usual, he paused at the door and knocked on the jamb. "Ba?"

Fueled by a new breath, I answered him, "Come in, Papa."

He entered, with his Bible beneath his arm. Then he stopped. "What is wrong? What happened?"

With his question came an answer, spilling from my lips with an abandon that was unfamiliar. "I am all right, Papa. Do not worry about me, but . . . but it is most extraordinary how the meeting of Mr. Browning does beset me — I suppose it is not being used to seeing strangers in some degree — but it haunts me. It is a . . . a persecution."

His eyebrows met at the middle. "He is . . . Mr. Browning is your poet?"

His wording was far too apt. "He is not my poet, Papa, but a fellow poet, a comrade."

"So he did come to call today?"

"Yes."

"And he upset you. And so . . ." He waved a hand between us, as if swatting the very thought of Robert away. "You must not see him again."

"No, no, Papa," I said. "It is not a bad reaction, but simply one unexpected. I am out of practice at such things and —"

"Such things being . . . ?"

"Meeting face-to-face with any visitor outside the family. Other than Miss Mitford, Mrs. Jameson, and a few others, I only converse — in person — with family."

"I should never have given my permission."

I had made a huge blunder telling him about the meeting. So used was I to telling him everything. . . . And yet I had to calm down or all would be lost. With a determination that I rarely tapped, I dug deep within, past the excitement and questions, and found the pool of normalcy that had served me all these years. "I assure you that is not necessary, Papa," I said, trying to sound offhand. "We are both working on projects that need the additional help of a peer's edit, so you see, it would serve us both if our meetings continued. Our work would be served well."

He looked at me askance and I knew he was not convinced.

I stood and extended my hand, inviting him towards me. "Our prayers, Papa?"

We knelt together and prayed as we did every evening.

But not exactly as we did . . . for on this evening my prayers were transformed and expanded to include one other person who deserved God's blessings.

❦

"Miss. Miss?"

I awakened to Wilson nudging my shoulder. She did not usually awaken me.

I opened one eye, then closed it. "Leave me be. It was late before I slept and I wish to—"

"Then I suppose you are not interested in reading a certain letter from a certain gentleman?"

I sprang upwards, letting the bedclothes fall from my shoulders and gather on my lap. "A let—?"

She handed it to me with a dramatic sweep of her arm. "He musta wrote it soon as he got home for you to get it this very morning."

So it would seem. I broke the seal, then thought better of the company. What if he wrote so soon after to tell me that, though he esteemed me as a correspondent, he would not be able to visit me again?

I held the letter to my chest and told Wilson, "Thank you for bringing it so quickly. That will be all."

She gave me a pout but left me to my privacy.

I closed my eyes and uttered a quick prayer. Then I read the letter:

Tuesday evening

I trust to you for a true account of how you are—if tired,
if not tired, if I did wrong in any thing—or, if you please,
right in any thing (only, not one more word about my "kindness," which, to get done with, I will grant is exceptive). But
let us so arrange matters if possible, and why should it not
be that my great happiness, such as it will be if I see you as
this morning from time to time, may be obtained at the cost
of as little inconvenience to you as we can contrive. For an
instance, they all say I speak very loud (a trick caught from
having to talk with a deaf relative of mine). And did I stay
too long?

I will tell you unhesitatingly of any errors I find in the
printing of your books—nay, I will again say, do not humiliate
me by calling me "kind" in that way.

I am proud and happy in your friendship—now and ever.
May God bless you!

R.B.

A laugh escaped my lips and I halted its expansion with a hand. Robert was worried about talking too loudly? Staying too long? Such trifles
compared to the dire alternatives that had wracked my mind! All was well.
There would be more meetings!

I had to respond to him at once, and so scrambled out of bed to
fetch a lap desk and stationery. I returned to the covers and puffed the
pillows just so behind me. I poised the pen above paper, giving myself but
a moment to let my thoughts congeal.

And then, I began. . . .

Indeed there was nothing wrong—how could there be?
And there was everything right—as how should there not
be? And as for the "loud speaking," I did not hear any, and,

instead of being worse, I ought to be better for what was certainly (to speak it, or be silent of it) happiness and honour to me yesterday.

Which reminds me to observe that you are so restricting our vocabulary as to be ominous of silence. First, one word is not to be spoken—and then, another is not. And why? Why deny me the use of such words as have natural feelings belonging to them? And how can the use of such be "humiliating" to you? If my heart were open to you, you could see nothing offensive to you in any thought or trace of thought that has been there.

I teased him, even as I stated my true feelings. I simply had to be allowed the use of such words as *kindness* and *grateful*. Yet I forced myself to be put in his shoes. Was Robert so used to expressing himself freely that perhaps he had accrued an offhandedness in regard to people being deigned kind and grateful? As to myself, who had been an invalid for most of my life, I saw such traits as truly God-sent and did not offer mention of them lightly.

I went back to my response.

It is hard for you to understand what my mental position is after the peculiar experience I have suffered, and what a sort of feeling is irrepressible from me to you, when, from the height of your brilliant happy sphere, you ask for personal intercourse with me. What words but "kindness," but "gratitude"? But I will not in any case be unkind and ungrateful, and do what is displeasing to you. And let us both leave the subject with the words because we perceive it from different points of view; we stand in the black and white sides of the shield; and there is no coming to a conclusion.

Enough of that. I hoped the issue of *kind* and *grateful* was put to rest. Now, I proceeded towards the future, towards our next meeting.

But you will come on Tuesday—and again, when you like—it will not be more "inconvenient" to me to be pleased. It will be delightful to receive you here whenever you like. Believe it of

Your friend,
E.B.B.

And there it was, the complete fruition of our first meeting. The thing was accomplished, acknowledged, and set forward to occur again, and I could not have been happier.

I noticed a flash of movement outside my room. "Wilson?" I asked.

She came fully in, her curiosity unconcealed. *Well?* her expression asked.

I folded the letter in half and placed it in an envelope. "It was a good letter received," I said. "And I have made a good response. Would you see that this gets out, please?"

"Immediately, miss." And she meant it, for I heard her verily gallop down the stairs.

It was none too fast for me.

⁓✥⁓

I lived by the post.

Although I had always enjoyed receiving letters from my various correspondents, waiting for Robert's next letter consumed me. I tried to read books but perused the same page—yea, the same sentence—over and over without gaining comprehension. I passed time in conversation with Arabel and Henrietta, but was very willing to let them hold center court, telling me of their days. Only once, when Henrietta began a discourse regarding Surtees Cook, did I long to burst through and say, "But I too have met a man of interest." But I did not. For though I felt assured that Robert and I would continue our meetings (may there be many, many more!) I was old enough, wise enough, and owned enough of a pragmatic nature to realize that friendship was all I required of him, desired of him, and was all I had to give. To think there could be anything beyond such amity was absurd. I was thirty-nine years old. I was not a giggling girl, seeing romance in every shadow and sunbeam. And Robert was not a boy. Although he was six years my junior, he had shown no evidence that his life required a passion beyond the pen and his poetry. If it *had* required such, would he not have found it by now?

My sisters sat with me on my sofa. Henrietta spread before me samples of fabric for a new dress. I had little interest but for their diversionary nature. In fact, "I see no need for a new dress at all, Henrietta. It is not as though the ones I wear each day are tattered."

"It would take a hundred years for you to tatter them, Ba. But the styles have changed. The bodice is no longer long and pointed, but ends straight across at the waistline."

I smiled at her enthusiasm. "I hardly think I need to worry about styles up here in my room."

"But you do not need to stay up here, Ba. You've been feeling better, yes? I see a new sparkle in your eyes, and your strength is—"

"I have seen it too," Arabel said. "The weather is quite delightful of late. I could ask Stormie or Alfred to take you on a carriage ride."

I could not remember the last time I had been in a carriage. "I am not sure about that."

"We could ask Dr. Chambers," Arabel said. "If he approves, then—"

"Then you would have true need of a new dress," Henrietta said. "And perhaps one in a color beyond this depressing black. Perhaps a pretty pink or a pale yellow."

My head began to shake *no* of its own volition. I could not imagine myself in such colors. Pastels were for young girls, not for spinster poets.

Henrietta popped to her feet. "I have other fabric samples downstairs. Ones that Arabel and I collected for our own dresses. I will go get—"

Wilson came in, breathless. She held a letter in her hand. Her eyes surveyed the situation, and with calm containment, she set the envelope on the table beside the sofa. "A letter for you, Miss Elizabeth," she said.

With a glance I knew it was from Robert. The time for sisterly diversion was over. I needed to be alone. The only way—save being rude and asking them to leave directly—was to . . . "Why don't the two of you go fetch the other samples. And perhaps some drawings of the new styles."

"I have a new *Godey's*," Henrietta said. "There is a dress on the second page I think you would love. It's in a delicate lavender."

Lavender would never do, but I went on, encouraging their exit. "Go now, both of you, and while you are gone, I will read my letter."

Wilson saw them out, did not leave, but rather busied herself arranging items in the bureau. She had been so supportive of me during my correspondence with Robert, and so discreet, I let her stay.

Upon opening the letter and setting my eyes upon the very first words . . .

I recoiled by instinct, and must have gasped, for Wilson came to my side, offering aid.

"No, no," I said, waving her away. "Go, just go. And shut the door behind you!"

I did not watch her go but assumed she did, for my sight was locked upon the awful words from Robert. Upon second reading I grouped them in short snippets that stood out amidst his flowery prose.

I love you.

Marry me.

You, above all women.

Your beauty.

Ecstasy.

Beyond reason.

Passion.

"No! No, no, no, no!"

I threw the pages to the floor. He had been rash, impulsive, impetuous, and imprudent. We had spent four months carefully sowing the seed of our friendship, watching it grow into a seedling that held the promise of a continued acquaintance, a deepening camaraderie, a delicate alliance, a precious companionship, one poet to another.

You are not without blame.

Indeed, I had allowed my femaleness to touch upon the connection of us, man and woman, and had enjoyed the foreign sensation. And yet, I had also contained myself and dispelled such an absurd notion as beyond my wishes, my ability, and all possibilities. For Robert to dive from the precipice of friendship into the well of love and passion . . .

Your beauty . . .

"My beauty?" Flush looked up at me, as if wondering how he could be expected to answer such a question. Indeed. For I knew I was *not* beautiful. I was pale and tiny, with eyes too dark and large for my face. My hair was my one virtue, but I had it styled with curls far forward, to hide the insufficiencies of my countenance. Although the words I placed within my poems and prose had merit, the words that came directly from my mouth seemed laughable as my voice revealed itself to be weak, thin, and without any pleasant tone or tenor. That Robert had kept control of his emotions during the separation created by writing letters, but had flown into such reckless talk upon one visit . . .

His intemperate fancies were unbecoming. And mortifying. We were not lovers, we were comrades, friends, fellow mentors. He mocked me by acting as if there were something more — could be something more. Such wild speaking! It was a mere poet's fancy, a confusion between the woman and the poetry. And above all else, it must be stopped. At once.

I found paper and pen and began a reply:

You do not know what pain you give me in speaking so wildly. And if I disobey you, my dear friend, in speaking of your wild speaking, I do it not to displease you, but to be in my own eyes, and before God, a little more worthy, or less unworthy, of a generosity from which I recoil by instinct and at the first glance. My silence would be the most disloyal of all means of expression. Listen to me then in this. You have said some intemperate things . . . fancies, which you will not say over again, nor unsay, but forget at once, and forever; and so will die out between you and me alone, like a misprint between you and the printer. And this you will do for my sake, I who am your friend (and you have none truer) and this I ask, because it is a condition necessary to our future liberty of intercourse.

I looked up from the page, realizing that I had forgotten to breathe, as all my breath and life had gone into the flush of words upon the pages, chastising him for *his* words upon *his* page. Did he not realize that by saying what he did he may have ruined everything? Tipped the delicate balance?

The question remained: Did I want our friendship to continue? Could it continue with his reckless words hanging between us? A rung bell cannot be unrung. . . . How could we recapture what we had, knowing what we knew, feeling what we felt?

There would have to be rules made and conditions met — stringently adhered to. If he could not agree to these conditions, then what we had would be no more. He had to understand that, he had to realize the delicate conditions upon which I based my life.

You remember — surely you do — that I am in the most exceptional of positions; and that because of it, I am able to receive you as I did on Tuesday; and that, for me to listen to "unconscious exaggerations," is as unbecoming to the humilities of my position, as unpropitious (which is of more consequence) to the prosperities of yours. Now, if there should be one word of answer attempted to this; or of reference; I must not . . . I will not see you again, and you will justify me later in your heart.

So for my sake you will not say it and spare me the sadness of having to break an intercourse just as it is promising pleasure to me. To me who has had so many sadnesses and so few pleasures . . . You will do this! and I shall owe you my tranquillity, as one gift of many. For I have much to receive from you in all the free gifts of thinking, teaching, master-spirits . . . ! I appreciate you, as none can more. Your influence and help in poetry will be full of good and glad-ness to me—for with many to love me in this house, there is no one to judge me. Your friendship and sympathy will be dear and precious to me all my life. The mistakes I have made, that need your forgiveness, I put away gently, and with grateful tears in my eyes. You are not displeased with me? That would be hail and lightning together. I do not write as I might, of some words of yours, but you know that I am not a stone, even if silent like one. And if in the unsilence, I have said one word to vex you, pity me for having had to say it. And for the rest, may God bless you far beyond the reach of vexation from my words or my deeds!

Your friend in grateful regard,
E.B.B.

I sat back and looked at the letter. How would he react to it? I did not wish to upset him and yet with his impulsive . . . He had been far too forward, putting me in the position to rein him in. More than anything I prayed that he would accept the distinctive limits that had to be put around our relationship, for if he did not, then *we* could be no more.

Suddenly, I heard a bump against the door, then a rustling of skirt to skirt, then whispering. Had I alarmed Wilson so greatly that she had run to my sisters?

Tucking the letter into an envelope, I sealed it, addressed it, and set it on the table beside me—facedown. I pressed a hand to my chest and allowed myself fully three breaths in and out. They were accomplished raggedly, but they *were* accomplished. Only then did I say, "Come in."

The door opened slowly and the three women peered in at me as a gaggle, their faces full of questions and concern. I was touched by their caring but wondered how much they knew. So far Wilson had been my confidante. As a result of my outburst, had I forced her to break our bond of privacy?

I could not proceed until I knew what they knew. I looked at my maid. "What did you tell them?"

"That you have received a letter that has upset you horribly." But as soon as she glanced at Arabel, and then at Henrietta, I knew she had told them more.

Henrietta broke from their trio and ran to my side, kneeling beside me. "Why didn't you tell us Mr. Browning had come to call? Or that you . . . you two . . ."

I glared at Wilson, but it was Arabel who came to her defence. "She came to us to tell us you were sorely upset, but would not tell us the reason until we ordered her to."

"They threatened me with dismissal if I didn't tell them, Miss Elizabeth. I tried not to, truly I did."

I believed her. Although I had never heard Arabel talk sternly to any of the servants, Henrietta was not averse to playing the part of mistress to a fuller extent.

Arabel came into the room, and Wilson followed, shutting the door behind her. "What can we do to help?" Arabel asked. "We could send one of the brothers after him, to berate him for breaking your heart."

"We could get Henry to do more than *berate*," Henrietta said.

They obviously had it all wrong, and yet in quick retrospect I could see how my dramatic reaction would elicit such a conclusion. "There will be no need of that," I said. "Mr. Browning has not abandoned me. Quite the opposite." I let those three words imply the full of it.

As if in concert, the eyebrows of all three ladies rose. "He . . . he declared himself?"

"Fully and with flourish," I said.

"After one meeting?" Arabel asked.

I nodded.

Henrietta laughed, and then she began to applaud. "Bravo, Ba! I never would have guessed you were capable . . . that you had that kind of power . . ."

My face grew hot. "I had no such power, I did not try to—"

"All the better," Henrietta said. "And more impressive."

The heat intensified, as did an odd sensation of pleasure. Although

I was still appalled and upset by Robert's wild declarations, it was a compliment to my womanhood. I, who had left my womanhood behind years ago.

"How did you respond?" Arabel asked.

I retrieved the letter. "It is done. Here."

Henrietta gasped. "You told him to never come back?"

"I spelled out to him the boundaries of our friendship. If he abides by them, then we can continue our meetings. If he cannot, then . . ."

Henrietta stood. "What are your boundaries?"

"I wish for him to be my friend, my peer, and my teacher."

Her face looked aghast. "That's all?"

After a moment of silence, we all laughed, and it came as good relief. "That is all," I said. "I am not a woman who seeks love. I seek—"

"You do not seek it, but perhaps it has found you just the same."

"No," I said emphatically. "Most certainly not. I am too old, too ill, too—"

"Nonsense," Henrietta said. "Mr. Browning knows all of these things and yet he still declared himself to you. As such, you cannot use them as excuses against it."

She was right.

Yet the way my stomach tightened and my lungs clenched . . .

"Are you afraid of love?" Arabel asked.

Henrietta let out a sarcastic *harrumph*. "That *is* the way Papa would like it to be." She gently shoved my legs to the side so she could sit on the edge of the sofa beside me. Her voice softened. "But even Papa does not have the power to stop love." She nodded twice.

"So you love Mr. Cook?"

"We love each other."

I knew there had been an infatuation, but I thought Papa's anger against it had quelled its growth into love. "You are not considering marriage, are you?" I asked.

"We would like to marry. . . ."

Ah. So. Wanting to marry and getting Papa to agree to it were two drastically different things. Like wanting the moon to turn green and getting it to do so.

Henrietta changed the direction of our conversation away from herself. "If you, as Papa's favourite, could get him to agree to your marriage—"

"Never!" I said.

Henrietta studied me a moment. "Mr. Browning did not propose?"

I would neither confirm nor deny. The point was that marriage in the Barrett household was not an option. It had always been so. There was no discussion.

Although I appreciated their concern, and loved them for their support, nothing would be gained from further discussion. I extended the letter into the air between us. "Would one of you see that this is posted as soon as possible?"

All three women stared at the letter, none taking it. "You have refused him?" Henrietta asked.

I could not answer directly without saying too much. I repeated myself. "I have set the boundaries. What happens next is up to him."

"I will take it," Wilson said, snatching it away from me.

The sisters readied to leave. Arabel turned at the door. "Does Papa know Mr. Browning came to visit?"

"He does," I said. "He gave his approval, but—" I remembered my blunder in sharing with him my agitation that same evening. "*If* Robert comes again, I would rather Papa did not know."

Both sisters nodded, but Henrietta added, "Papa only knows a small portion of Mr. Cook's visits. How I wish there were no need to deceive him," she said.

Deceive Papa? Was that what I was doing?

My mood—which had been lifted by my sisters' visit—fell into greater depths. A good daughter did not deceive her beloved father. If I wished to be a good daughter, I would revise the letter that Wilson held in her hands and tell Robert it was finished for good. There would be no more visits. His impulsive declarations gave me a good excuse to end it all, right now, right here.

And yet . . .

When Wilson excused herself to do the task which I had requested, I did not call her back.

Indeed, a small hidden part of me beckoned her to go faster.

⁓⁂⁓

I clutched Robert's letter in a hand, stretched my arms above my head, and opened them to the heavens and the dear God who had listened to my prayers. *Thank you, Father. Thank you.*

I had been a fool. Robert had received my letter of admonishment and had replied immediately. There had been a misunderstanding, his dramatic nature taking hold when it should have been held silent.

I lowered the letter to read a portion again:

I wrote to you in an unwise moment, on the spur of being again "thanked," and, unwisely writing as if thinking to myself, said what must have looked absurd enough as seen apart from the horrible counterbalancing never-to-be-written rest of me. If I could rewrite it, if it could be rewritten and put before you, my note would sink to its proper and relative place, and become a mere "thank you" for your good opinion, which I assure you is far too generous.

Will you forgive me on my promise to remember for the future, and be more considerate? I am glad that, since you did misunderstand me, you said so. All I meant to say from the first of the first—I shall be too much punished if, for this piece of mere inconsideration, you deprive me, more or less, or sooner or later, of the pleasure of seeing you—a little over boisterous gratitude which caused all the mischief, pray write me a line to say, "Oh . . . if that's all!" and remember me for what good I have in me (which is very compatible with a moment of stupidity). Let me not for one fault (and that the only one there shall be) lose any pleasure for your friendship. I am sure I have not lost it. . . .

God bless you, my dear friend!

R. Browning

And by the way, will it not be better, and more co-operating in your kind promise to forget the "printer's error" in my blotted proof, to send me back that same "proof," if you have not inflicted proper and summary justice on it? Seriously, I am ashamed.

As was I. And relieved. For in the interim between receiving the letter in question, until the moment when I received his apologetic answer, I had found myself grieving a friendship that was very dear to me.

But now, that friendship could continue.

To put a final period to the exchange, I wrote a response and made all things right. And then, in what perhaps would be considered a fit of enthusiasm, I called Wilson to me and said, "Come, Wilson. Get me ready to go out. For I have a letter to post."

"Out?"

I laughed at her reaction, and the laughter gave me the additional strength I needed. I would most likely pay for the excursion physically, but the emotional release would be worth the price.

My friendship with Robert was worth the price.

Any price.

Eleven

I laughed.

I know that is not an accomplishment for most people, but to me, the sound was nearly foreign—or at the very least, only newly reborn.

My pleasure put the burden upon Arabel to bang a hand upon the wall of the brougham in which we were riding, chastising Stormie and the driver for taking the carriage too fast. "Slow, brother! You are going to topple us!" she shouted.

"Whoa there, slow down" came the driver's voice.

I felt our speed decrease and heard Arabel take a breath of relief. "That brother of ours is positively reckless."

"I don't mind," I said.

I felt Arabel's eyes upon me but did not return their gaze. I was too busy watching the swell of London pass by, seeing the myriad of people going about their lives, hearing the clomping of the hooves upon the cobblestone, and feeling the summer breeze upon my face.

Holding on for support against the jostling, I leaned farther towards the open window. The buildings were too high and the streets too narrow for the sun to kiss my cheek, but I knew it wanted to—and *that* brought me joy. How I wished we were traveling in an open barouche where the sun could reach me. Yet even though I was still *inside*, my soul soared and lifted itself to all that was *outside*.

I felt my sister's hand upon me. "Ba, you really should sit back. We don't want you taxing yourself and—"

I remained where I was, although I did turn to her. Yet as I did, she peered out her own window with fresh interest. "What is he doing?" she said. "I told Stormie to turn round at the gates of Regent's Park, not enter it."

I sat back enough to explain. "And I told him to go further this time. I have seen the extent of Wimpole Street; it is time to ride around the park."

She stared at me, incredulous. "What has gotten into you, Ba? You are different. Cook said you are requesting copious amounts of milk, and Henrietta found you sitting in the sun—on more than one occasion."

"Milk makes me strong," I said—or so Robert had said to *me*. "And I have received many compliments regarding my healthier countenance and the fact I have been walking." I sat up straighter, feeling my pride. "It is well that I no longer wobble like a two-year-old child."

"But we have been giving you such advice for years and you have never once followed it. Why now?"

Although my sisters were well aware of Robert's weekly visits, and had been present when I'd been so upset by his too-forward letter, they took me at my word that I had set proper boundaries between us. They considered him but an acquaintance.

"Why now?" I repeated. I sighed with great extravagance. "Because it is time."

⁓⁂⁓

"I am so proud of you."

Robert's compliment was a balm to my ears, a bouquet to my soul. "The outing through the park was quite wonderful," I said.

"Just as I said it would be."

I nodded once. "Just as you said it would be."

He sat back in the chair nearest the fireplace—the barren fireplace, for it was a hot summer. "Which means I am wise," he said. "A wise man. An incomparable man. A man beyond my peers."

"It was just a ride in a carriage, Robert."

He rose to his feet. "No, Miss Barrett, it was far more than that! It was an excursion from one world to another, a rite of passage, a quest towards your . . . your . . . *raison d'être*."

I easily translated his French. "My reason for being?"

He gave me a gallant bow with arm outstretched. *"Oui, mademoiselle. Absolument."*

I relished his enthusiasm but also the chance to argue. "So riding in a carriage is my reason for living?"

"You mock me."

"Absolument."

His smile was one of purest pleasure. "Towards the furtherance of your quest . . . have you decided how you are going to respond to Mr. Kenyon's invitation?"

Upon hearing that I was getting out of the house, Cousin John had offered me the use of his home as an alternative destination to Regent's Park. "I am considering it," I said. "Strongly."

"Bravo, again, Miss Barrett!"

It was disconcerting to realize how much his praise resounded over the praise of anyone else—not that I could remember any recent familial praise. I had never deserved any. I was a reclusive nonentity with no hope for a future apart from one dark day flowing into the next.

That was then. This was now.

But Robert . . . repeatedly he declared me his superior and lifted me up with zealous commendation. His compliments were hard to embrace. I was superior to nothing, to no one. I was not life and light to another. I was a burden to all.

Yet as Robert doggedly gave evidence of his affection and esteem, I felt the scales of my inbred pessimism begin to fall away. Bit by bit I shook myself free of their shackles. Although I was not ready to invite optimism as my companion, with each of Robert's visits, with each sentence spoken in person or on paper, I found myself closer to dispelling pessimism altogether.

He returned to his chair. "Now that we've taken in fresh air and sunshine, *and* made you consider society . . . if only the incomparable Dr. Browning could get you to cease your association with Madame Opium."

This was not the first time he had brought it up. "It helps me sleep," I said.

"But have you not admitted you use it otherwise?"

I smoothed my skirt—anything to avoid his discerning eyes. "On occasion I use it when I feel irritable, to steady the action of my heart."

"Mmm."

I continued my defence. "It helps my lungs, eases my cough. I see nothing wrong with such positive usage—nor do my doctors."

"Using anything for year upon year is . . . is not right. How many years now?"

"A decade, I suppose."

His eyebrow rose, signaling that he knew I was stretching the truth. I did the math in my head. "Fine. Two decades, then."

"And . . . ?"

"Two decades and four, to be exact."

"Twenty-four years." He rose to pace in front of me, hands clasped behind his back like a confident barrister presenting a case. "Far too long for any medicinal to be a part of one's life."

"But it has helped—"

He turned towards me and stopped. "Has it?"

I felt my anger rise, yet I had no argument for him—no good argument. "Do you think I have wanted to be confined to this room, that my ailments are of my own creation?"

He rushed to my side, knelt, and took my hand in his. "I did not mean to upset you—I would never wish to do that. And I don't mean to put blame or make accusations regarding your condition. I know you are a delicate flower, and yet I have also witnessed a change. I have seen you bloom and grow."

I looked at his eyes, so full of sincere caring for me, and I longed to reach out and touch his hair or cup his face in my hand. But to do so would be the essence of impropriety and would encourage his feelings beyond what I could allow. But I *could* acquiesce to his assessment. "I do feel myself growing. It's miraculous, this feeling of sprouting life in me and out of me. And recently, I have even begun to sleep better, and—as you yourself have said—I look altogether another person."

"I admire you and care for you, in sickness or health."

His words made me think of marriage vows....

He may have realized the train of my thoughts, for he smiled and added, "Though I will say I do enjoy the benefits of the latter—for both of us. Lately, you have had much more energy."

"I have. And I am determined to get on, and hold on, as the summer progresses." But after summer came the autumn, and the winter.... I was reminded of a new twist in my future, one I had been eager to share with Robert. "I may be taking a trip—much further than my cousin's house or Regent's Park."

He pulled the chair close. "Do tell."

"Dr. Chambers has told me—and Papa—that he does *not* wish for me to spend the winter here in London. With all the strides that have been made towards better health, he fears they will be for naught if I remain here."

"Well, well," Robert said. "I think I like this doctor of yours. Where does he wish you to go?"

I tried to hold back a smile but could not. "Pisa."

Robert's mouth gagged open. "Pisa is magic. It's the blush of a bride, the smile of a child, the song of the wind. I just returned from there the weeks before I first wrote to you."

"I know," I said. "It is a city that has always intrigued me." And had so even more since I'd heard of his love for it.

"What does your father say?"

Ah. There was the rub. "He is against it."

"Then you must convince him!"

The exuberance I had experienced in telling him slipped away. "Dr. Chambers has been trying to get me to go away for years."

"Then why have you not gone?"

I wished I could blame it all upon Papa, but I could not. "When I was much younger, Papa sent me to Torquay for my health. For three years I —" Suddenly, as it often did without warning, the grief of Torquay sprang upon me, and tears were released from their tenuous bondage.

Once again, Robert rushed to my side. "Oh my, oh dearest. What's wrong?"

Even amid my angst, I gloried in the term of endearment that had recently been exchanged: *Dearest.* He to me, and I to him . . .

Robert handed me his handkerchief, and even as I dabbed my eyes, I wondered how could I ever . . . should I ever speak of this wound within me?

He took my hand and whispered, "Please, dearest. I wish to help."

With his words and with the strength and compassion in his countenance, I believed him completely and utterly. And so . . . I began.

"I have never said any of this — I never could talk or even write of it. I have asked no question from the moment when my last hope went, and since then . . . it has been impossible for me to speak about what was in me. What remains in me."

"You are obviously wounded."

"Deeply. Irrevocably." I realized if I were to do this, I could not ask him to remain as he was, kneeling in so uncomfortable a position. "Please be seated, Robert. If I am to continue — and I am fairly stunned to think that I am — I must know you to be comfortable."

He sat in the chair but added, "I imagine I will find little comfort in anything that upsets you so keenly."

"Thank you." I looked away from him, towards the window, letting my memories rush southward, to that place, that bay, that city by the sea, that unforgiving and unforgiven sea. . . .

"Due to my illness, and from doctor's orders, I was sent to Torquay with my sister, and he, my brother whom I loved so, was sent also, to take us there and return. Bro—for we always called him so—was the dearest of friends and brothers in one . . . the only one of my family who—" I grasped another breath in order to continue. "Let it be enough to tell you that he was above us all, better than us all, and kindest and noblest and dearest to me, beyond comparison, *any* comparison." I paused, hoping Robert would understand that I had held Bro even above my father. I did not want to state it so plainly—I could never voice it so—but I wished for him to understand.

I continued. "When the time came for him to go back to London, I, weakened by illness, could not master my spirits or drive back my tears. I assured Papa that he would break my heart if he persisted in calling my brother away—as if hearts were broken so."

"I too am close to my sister," Robert said. "I understand the bond between siblings. You wanted him to stay. That is not a bad thing to desire."

A harsh laugh escaped. "Papa's answer was burnt into me, as with fire, that he considered it very wrong for me to exact such a thing. So there was no separation then, and month after month passed—and sometimes I was better and sometimes worse, and the medical men continued to say that they would not answer for my life if I were agitated, and so there was no more talk of a separation."

Robert smiled tentatively. "And so, Bro was with you—with your father's permission."

I raised a hand to stop his encouragement, for what would come next would dispel all happiness and harmony from his opinion. "Once, Bro held my hand—how I remember!—and said that he loved me better than them all and that he would not leave me till I was well."

Robert made effort to speak, but wisely thought better of it, for by the tone of my telling, he could surely sense a *but* suspended in the air between us that would lead from the good thing to something very bad. And so . . . to move along . . .

"But ten days from that day a boat left the shore which never returned, never. And he had . . . left me. Gone. For three days we waited—and I hoped while I could, oh, that awful agony of three days!"

"He was not gone as in a trip away, but . . . he was capsized?"

I looked again to the window, to the sun, the same sun . . . "And the sun shone as it shines today, and there was no more wind than now." I set my hand upon the table nearby. "And the sea under my windows was like this paper for smoothness—and my sisters drew the curtains back that I might see for myself how smooth the sea was, and how it could hurt nobody. And other boats came back one by one."

"Oh dear . . ."

I thought of something else, some bond that could help explain. . . . "Remember how you wrote in your 'Gismond' . . ." I closed my eyes and recited the poem. " 'What says the body when they spring, some monstrous torture-engine's whole strength on it? No more says the soul.' " I opened my eyes to gaze on him. "You never wrote anything which lived with me more than that. It is such a dreadful truth. But you knew it for truth, I hope, by your genius, and not by such proof as mine. I, who could not speak or shed a tear, but lay for weeks and months half conscious, half unconscious, with a wandering mind, and too near to God, under the crushing of His hand, to pray at all. I expiated all my weak tears before, by not being able to shed one tear—and yet my family was forbearing, and no voice declared, 'You have done this.' "

"They would not dare!" he said. "You did not sail the ship, you did not force your brother to go upon it, you did not control the weather or the tide or the captain or whatever caused the tragedy."

But I forced the issue, making him stay. . . .

I could not heap such guilt upon poor Robert. He, who had suffered so little, did not need to descend to the depths of my despair. I offered him a reassuring smile. "I do not now reproach myself with such acrid thoughts as before—I know that I would have died ten times over for him, and that, though it was wrong of me to be weak, I have suffered for it and shall learn by it. Remorse is not precisely the word for me—not in its full sense. Still I hope you will comprehend from what I have told you, how the spring of life seemed to break within me then; and how natural it has been for me to loath the living on—and even without the loathing, to lose faith in myself. This, I have done on some points utterly."

Robert sat close by, his head shaking no, no, and another time no. He had no words for me, and so I offered a few more of my own. "You will comprehend too that I have strong reasons for being grateful for the forbearance of my family. It would have been cruel, you think, to reproach me. Perhaps so. Yet the kindness and patience of the desisting from reproach are positive things."

Robert glanced towards the door, and I feared he wished to rush away from me, my pain and regret too heady for him to bear within our friendship. Yet as soon as he spoke, I knew the reason for his look to the door.

"Is this why your family lives together under one roof? Why your father is so . . . so . . ."

I guessed what he was thinking, and I chastised myself for previously feeding his opinion of a harsher father than dear Papa deserved. "You must *not* make an unjust opinion out of what I said today. Perhaps it would have been better if I had not said it apart from all context in that way. But you could not long be a friend of mine without knowing and seeing what lies upon the surface and hides below."

"And I am truly grateful that you trust me enough to share what sits so heavily upon your heart. But your family should not blame—"

I interrupted, ignored his accusation, and attempted to explain our unique situation. "Living all together as we do . . . every now and then there must of course be a crossing and vexation—but in one's mere pleasures and fantasies, one would rather be crossed and vexed a little than vex a person one loves. And it is possible to get used to the harness and run easily in it." I looked to the books upon the shelves. "There is a side-world to hide one's thoughts in, and the word *literature* has, with me, covered a good deal of liberty which is never inquired about."

"Are you saying they leave you alone?"

"Within my work I am my own mistress."

"But the rest . . . ?"

"It has happened throughout my life by accident—as far as anything is by accident—that my own sense of right and happiness on any important point has never run contrary to the way of obedience required of me. While in things of lesser import, I and all of us are apt to act with shut doors and windows, without waiting for discernment or permission." My thoughts flew upon the times my siblings and I had wanted to ask Papa for something but had chosen not to. And yet sometimes, at rare times, we had continued on within our own will—aside from Papa's knowledge. "And this last is the worst of it all. To be forced into concealments from the heart naturally nearest to us, and forced away from the natural source of counsel and strength is . . ." I could not say more.

"I do not like hiding my presence from your family, your father in particular," Robert said. "I do not wish to be covert or cause you to be."

He still did not understand the necessity of it. The delicate nature of it all, the fragile balance. "All my brothers are constrained bodily into submission—apparent submission at least—by that worst and most dishonouring of necessities, the necessity of living. Every one of them all, except myself, is dependent in money matters on the inflexible will of . . . Do you see?"

"I think I see very clearly. You are beholden. Obligated."

Yes, and yet . . . "But what you do not see, what you cannot see, is the deep tender affection behind and below all those patriarchal ideas of governing grown-up children 'in the way they must go.' There never was—under the strata—a truer affection in a father's heart, nor a worthier heart in itself, a heart loyaler and purer, and more compelling to gratitude and reverence, than his."

Robert looked at me askance, not believing.

"The evil is in the system, and Papa simply takes it to be his duty to rule, and to make us happy according to his own views of the propriety of happiness. He takes it to be his duty to rule like the kings of Christendom, by divine right. But he loves us through and through it—and I, for one . . ." I paused. "I love him."

"That is laudable. You are a good daughter."

I shook my head to negate his compliment. "When, five years ago, I lost what I loved best in the world beyond comparison and rivalship . . . everyone who knew me also knew Bro was my first and chiefest affection. When I lost that, I felt that Papa stood the nearest to me on the closed grave, or by the unclosing sea."

"It is natural to lean on relatives amidst a crisis."

No! Robert still did not understand! "I will tell you that not only has Papa been kind and patient and forbearing to me through the tedious trial of this illness — far more trying to standers-by like you than one can imagine — but that he was generous and forbearing in that hour of bitter trial, and never reproached me as he might have done. My own soul has not spared me as much. Never once has he said to me, then or since, that if it had not been for me, the crown of his house would not have fallen. He never did . . . and he might have said it, and more, and I could not have answered except to say that I had paid my own price, and that the price I paid was greater than his loss."

"Of course he did not condemn you. Your brother's death was not your fault!"

"You must see how it was, Robert. I said horrible things to him that day. I told him I had no need for him. So you see, not with my hand but my heart I *was* the cause of that misery. I am the one who made him flee in anger. And though not with the intention of my heart, but with its weakness . . . I *am* to blame. That no one has accused me face-to-face is their virtue."

Robert stood, his head shaking again. "No, I think — you will pardon me, Miss Barrett — but I think you have it all wrong. That you wished for your brother to stay on with you in Torquay reveals your love for each other, your devotion. I am certain he enjoyed your time together as much as you. That he suffered a horrible fate is neither due to your desire to have him with you, nor his choice to go upon the boat that day — on a lovely, still sea. It just happened. And that your family, knowing of your guilt and pain, has not added to the pain by accusing you directly . . . ?

Do you not realize by their silence they cause pain enough? For if they truly loved you—as I love you—they would not allow your guilt to exist in any form. They would have dispelled it upon the first embrace and tear. And that . . ." He blinked a few times and seemed to come out of his anger and return to me fully. He sat by my side. "I apologize for being so forthright and bold. I have no right. I only do it from a sincere desire to see you happy and free from this burden."

I believed him, and I found myself oddly fortified by his understanding. He was my champion, if only to my ears alone.

I had never had a champion—not since Bro . . .

⁓⁂⁓

I paced my room, the nerves within my stomach making idleness impossible.

For the past month there had been talk of my going abroad for the winter. Papa leaned towards Malta, but Cousin John and I preferred Pisa. Of course, I had not told Papa as much.

I was a coward—or had been until this day. Yet the consequences of being spineless took their toll, preventing me from true rest and erasing any issues but this.

But today . . . I had called in reinforcements. Although I had not needed Dr. Chambers' services for many weeks, today he was visiting at my request, for reasons other than tinctures and elixirs. Today, I needed for him to tell Papa that—

Hearing feet upon the stairs, I swung towards the opened door.

But it was only George.

"Are you ready?" he whispered.

"No."

"You're doing the right thing, Ba, an amazing thing for . . ."

"For me."

"An amazing thing for any of us to do."

I had the sudden image of my siblings gathered on the lower landing, listening intently to every word. "I do not wish to make a spectacle, or to be eavesdropped upon."

"Oh, let them listen if they wish," he said. "Perhaps they can learn a few things about . . ." He shrugged.

"Taking a stand, even though it will surely come to nothing?"

He took my hands in his and looked at me intently. "Taking a stand because it is the right thing to do." He gave my hands an extra squeeze. "I am here to help you, Ba. I will do everything I can for you."

And I knew he would. I also knew that my going abroad for a few months was not the issue. It was a means to a process that could aid all of them in the future. As the oldest child, was it my duty to pave the way for all of them? The pressure to succeed pressed against me with new strength.

I heard men's voices below. Papa and Dr. Chambers came up the stairs. I grabbed George's arm for support, but was determined *not* to meet them in my usual position — reclined upon the sofa or bed. *Heavenly Father, please give me the strength I need. . . .* I did not ask God for specific results for this meeting, feeling that gaining strength to get through it well was enough of a request.

Dr. Chambers was the first to make a greeting. "Well, well, what do we have here? My favourite patient up and about?"

"I have been feeling quite well of late," I said. "And I wish to stay that way through the hard winter." I did *not* risk a look at Papa.

"Indeed," Dr. Chambers said. "And if you had gone to a warm clime during previous winters, I would guess you would be completely well by now." He turned towards my father. "I have prescribed it for years."

Papa indicated we all should sit. Papa and Dr. Chambers took the chairs by the fireplace, and George took the small seat beside my sofa. I sat upon said sofa but kept my feet upon the floor.

"It was always Elizabeth's decision not to go away," Papa said. "Even when Cousin Kenyon and Mrs. Jameson encouraged her to go abroad, she always insisted she was just as well off in her own room here. She indicated it was not worth the trouble."

"A very compliant daughter indeed," Dr. Chambers said. "But I do believe there would be probable benefit for a winter in Pisa, or perhaps Madeira."

"Father had mentioned Malta," George interjected.

Probable benefit? This was not strong language. What happened to Dr. Chambers' past assertions that my life depended on it?

"She seems well enough now," Papa said.

Dr. Chambers smiled at me. "I am very pleased with her progress. What have you been doing to elicit such a change?"

"I—"

Papa interrupted me. "That she is here at home, and in better health, is proof enough that a trip away from the family and her home is not needed."

"But, Papa . . ."

He looked at me—the first time he had acknowledged my presence.

"Yes?" he asked.

A wave of fear sped from my heart to my feet and back again. All my carefully rehearsed statements fled and my mind was vacant.

Papa dismissed me by turning his attention back to Dr. Chambers. "When I allowed her to leave the family and go to Torquay, it was in response to a horrible physical breakdown. There was no recourse but for her to seek relief in warmer climes. But now . . ." He swiped a hand across the air between us as if I were a slightly disgusting specimen. "She is well enough. There is no need to cause another upheaval."

My heart slammed against my chest and I wanted to scream, "*This is reason enough for another upheaval: this awful feeling of confinement, of panic that I will never escape.*"

"See?" Papa said, dismissing my silence as acquiescence. "She is fine here."

I moved forward on the cushion, putting my weight more keenly upon my legs and feet, which had the extra support of the floor beneath them. "Escaping the English winter will be everything to me. It involves the comfort and usefulness of the rest of my life."

Papa's eyebrow rose.

I looked to Dr. Chambers and pressed a hand on my chest. "Is it not true, Doctor, that one lung is very slightly affected, but my nervous system is absolutely shattered?"

"Well, yes. Your lungs are still not strong."

I took further strength from his words. "I must go away because the cold weather acts on the lungs and produces the weakness indirectly, whereas the necessary shutting up indoors acts on the nerves. Italy would be a means of escape from these evils. God has opened the door of escape for me, and I must take it."

I looked at Papa, hoping he would grab on to the chance of helping me regain my health. Then I thought of something else. I reached over and put a hand upon George's knee. "A brother can go with me. Surely one of the younger boys would benefit from the outing."

Papa did not stun me with words but with something more terrible: dead silence.

And then he began to study me as only he was able. I felt he knew my thoughts and feelings through such calculated scrutiny. I had to look away. For if he were successful in discerning my innermost motivation, all would be lost.

Finally he spoke. "You do not wish to leave for the benefit of health alone."

It was a statement—one I wished I had not heard and did not have to answer—one I *could* not answer. I loved Robert and he loved me. And with that love came a desire, yes, even a need, to move beyond the life I had been living into something new. But Papa thought I was beyond such feelings, and if he discovered that they did indeed exist within me, that they had been awakened by a man—a man other than him . . .

The gates of Wimpole Street would do more than close, they would be barred and locked. Forever.

I attempted a smile, yet felt its weak and tenuous state. "I would like to see Italy. My brothers have been abroad and so I—"

Papa sprang from his chair. "So it is not for your health you wish to go."

His eyes flashed with a gravity that scared me, and my greatest desire moved away from Pisa and became more immediate. I desired that he would leave, that all would exit my room and leave me alone in it. My head was hurting and I felt my strength dissipate. I longed to lean back against the sofa, close my eyes, and let the day fall around me as it might.

George spoke up. "I think it would be a good idea for her to go, Papa. She will surely get better there and—"

"She is better here."

"But with the winter comes the cold, and Ba has never handled cold well and—"

"She has survived well enough."

"But even Dr. Chambers has said that a winter in a warm climate will be of benefit."

"Probable benefit," Papa said, with a glance at Dr. Chambers.

The doctor turned red, and I could tell he wished he could take his noncommittal words back and replace them with those of more strength.

George tried again. "Ba has asked for so little of you that I think—"

"You think? You think?" Papa rushed to George's chair and stood over him like a vulture over its prey. "I do not ask my children to think! I ask them to obey and appreciate the sacrifices I make for them." He took a step back to include me in his tirade. "What is this undutifulness and rebellion of everyone in this house?"

I was appalled. I had never been undutiful to him, nor rebellious. I put him above all others and had lived my life to please him. My pride caused me to speak out. "I mean no disrespect, Papa. I merely wish to sit in the Italian sun and find solace there."

"Solace? There? You find no solace here, under my roof? Is your life here so horrific, so intolerable that you would go against my wishes to achieve your escape?"

Yes. No. I . . . I didn't know what to say to him. Never had I meant to hurt him or to disparage the home he provided, nor the love he bestowed upon us.

I stood to go to him and apologize, but he waved me back to my seat. "Fine." He spat the word. "I am done with it. For my part I wash my hands of you altogether. Do as you wish."

He stormed from the room, leaving the rest of us in stunned silence. Dr. Chambers stood and came to my side. He took my hand and looked down at me with apologetic eyes. "I am so sorry. I should have been more forceful."

"No, no," I said. "It is not your fault."

He nodded his good-bye and left me alone with George.

"Well, then," George said.

"There is no *well* to it," I said. "I have wounded him."

"He will recover. You have received permission. Focus on that victory."

I shook my head. "There is no victory. I can never go now."

George knelt before me, placing his hands firmly upon my knees. "This is his way, Ba. You know it. He argues his case, then pretends to give in, knowing that we will never go against his initial wish."

"I know. And so I cannot go."

George rose and peered at the empty doorway. "But perhaps you should go anyway. Whether you stay or go there will be displeasure just the same. And the irritation will exhaust and smooth itself away. It always does. You are his favourite, Ba. This might be the time to capitalize on that."

The slightest hint of hope entered the chaos of my mind. Could I go anyway? Papa *had* given permission. Of a sort.

George leaned down and kissed my forehead. "Think about it. This is your chance, Ba. It might be your only chance."

I finally had the room alone—just as I had wanted. And yet in the silence was confusion. What should I do?

And then I knew. Robert. I had to tell Robert about it. The moments of my life were not complete until he was a part of them. I would write him.

Robert would know what to do.

~*~

"How nice of you to invite me on this outing," I told my brother Stormie.

"The . . . the day is f-f-f-air and I j-j-just thought . . ."

Stormie always stammered, and did so more when under stress. Since the day was overcast and the air carried an autumn nip . . . there had to be a reason beyond fresh air that he wished to take me out — alone.

Although I didn't want to dampen the day, my curiosity forced me to ask, "What bothers you, Stormie?"

"Your trip."

"To Pisa. Yes. I hope to go. You and I and Arabel will have a great time of it. I will make certain of it."

He shook his head.

"What?"

"Papa . . . we cannot g-g-go."

"Who cannot go?"

He pointed to himself, then added, "Ara-b-b-bel t-t-too."

I clamped a hand upon his knee. "Papa forbid you to go?"

He nodded. "N-none of us."

"But if none of my siblings are allowed to accompany me, then what use is my gaining his permission?"

He patted my hand.

~*~

Think for me.

Those were the words that concluded my letter to Robert, that alerted him to this latest, awful predicament. For I did indeed need his advice.

Ever since the confrontation with Papa, confusion reigned in my mind — and even in my heart. Any decision to go abroad involved logic *and* the effect that would befall those I loved. If I stayed, there would be tension because I had even asked, and if I left, there would be tension for those left behind.

One minute I dismissed all thoughts of the trip, yet in the next, I made plans. I found a steamer that left for Malta on October third, and from there, on to Pisa I would go. Both Stormie and Arabel had come to see me. In quiet voices they dubbed me "the bravest person in the house."

But I was not brave, or if I did own that attribute, it was but for a moment here, a minute there, before doubt and fear and guilt and dis-ease filtered through the cracks in my resolve and weakened the small cache of courage hidden there.

Think for me. . . .

Where was Robert's response? He was not coming to visit until Friday and I needed his guidance and support now.

Wilson came into the room, bringing me coffee and scones. "Have my sisters checked the mail?" I asked.

"Your sisters are out and about, miss. No one is home."

Their absence gave me hope that delay was not denial. "Please check the mail for me then," I asked. "Perhaps no one has checked the letter box at all."

She hurried to her task and came back in quick order, a letter in hand.

My relief awakened new hope for answers. I ripped open the letter, praying for resolution, praying for clarity.

You have said to me more than once that you wished I might never know certain feelings you had been forced to endure. I truly wish you may never feel what I have to bear in looking on, quite powerless and silent, while you are subjected to this treatment which I refuse to characterize—so blind is it for blindness. For I wholly sympathize, however it go against me, with the highest, wariest pride and love for you, and the proper jealousy and vigilance they entail. But now, and here, the jewel is not being over guarded, but ruined, cast away.

A jewel overguarded . . . it was an apt description. Although I never considered myself beyond a bland pebble, I understood his theory, and I relished that he understood my situation. This was just what I needed: a caring ear. I continued to read:

Whoever is privileged to interfere should do so in your interest—all rationality against this absolute no-reason at all. And you ask whether you ought to obey this no-reason? I will tell you: all passive obedience and submission of will and intellect is too easy, if well considered, to be the course prescribed by God to Man in this life of trials. Chop off your legs, you will never go astray; stifle your reason altogether and you will find it is difficult to reason ill. You say, "It is hard to make these sacrifices!" Not so hard as to lose the reward or incur the penalty of an Eternity to come.

How wise he was! And how telling his words. Was I taking the easy way out by giving in to Papa? Was the blessing not in the blind obedience, but in the testing of one's legs amid life's trials?

I know very well the indulgence that can occur while exercising one's abilities . . . there are difficulties and problems in coming to a solution, set by that Providence which could have made the laws of religion as certain as those of life, and the elements of believing we are right as certain as that condition by which we breathe so many times in a minute to support life. But there is no reward for the feat of breathing, and a great one for that of believing and trusting ourselves. Consequently there must exist a great deal of voluntary effort in believing and acting than by not trying at all—or adopting the direction of an infallible church or the private opinion of another person. For all our life is some form of religion, and all our action some belief that we can make the right choice. There is but one law, however modified, for all people.

Oh, that God would have made His will ours! Giving us *free* will was not free; there were costs to consider and balance. The reward for our choices, for our belief in ourselves and in our desire to do the right thing, were great. But along the way we had to take risks. We had to try.

> In your case I do think you are called upon to do your duty to yourself; that is, to God in the end. Your own reason should examine the whole matter in dispute by every light which can be put in requisition; and every interest that appears to be affected by your conduct should have its utmost claims considered. And this examination made, with whatever earnestness you will, I do think and am sure that on its conclusion you should act in confidence that a duty has been performed—difficult, or how were it a duty? Will it not be infinitely harder to act so than to blindly adopt his pleasure and die under it? Who can not do that?

Difficult . . . oh yes. And what was my duty to myself? I had been so long under Papa's rule that I found it hard to grasp the concept of a will unto my own and not beholden to his. Difficult? Absolutely. But was it possible? I still was not certain I could go against him.

> I fling these hasty rough words over the paper, fast as they will fall—knowing to whom I cast them, and that any sense they may contain or point to will be caught and understood and presented in a better light. The hard thing . . . this is all I want to say . . . is to act on one's own best conviction—not to renounce it and accept another's will and say "There is my plain duty"!

Duty. I had lived the part of a dutiful daughter my entire life. I knew no other way to live. Although I felt Robert understood a great part of me, I was not certain he understood duty. He lived in a home where his parents bowed to his wishes, where he exerted control. The duty within his home came from mutual respect and an unusual equality between parent and child. He was loved and was therefore dutiful. His duty was easily and rarely tested. But mine . . .

I still could not fully grasp the intricacies of the duty that was sovereign in this home—the only home I knew. And though I admired and even envied Robert's casting off of "there is my plain duty," I knew in my soul that the duty that existed in my family was indeed plain, and was something that was put into play every day. It was as essential in our lives as Robert's mention of the feat of breathing. I believed *that. That* ruled me.

The entire issue of going abroad for the winter grew small and insignificant. The diminishment was shocking and caused me to blurt out an entreaty to God, "Help me! Help me grasp the truth."

A listing of truths appeared. Was it my right to demand to be sent away for my own pleasure—health benefit or no? Was it my right to force Stormie and Arabel this same fate? Would we enjoy Pisa? Most probably. But was my determined act of selfish gain something to be fought for, as a lance hurled against the inalienable duty that glued our family together as one unit?

"No." I said the word aloud, and its presence in the room solidified my decision so that I said it again. "No."

Although cognizant of the flaws and foibles of my family's composition, I could not test its boundaries to breaking. I loved my father, and I would express that love for him by abiding by his true wishes. Although he *had* given me permission to go, his disdain in doing so would result in a lasting breach between us.

"I will show him my love by sacrificing for him, giving up my desires in order to submit to his."

I felt great release in this decision—a relief which I often took as affirmation that I was doing God's bidding.

But then I glanced again to Robert's letter. He had worked so hard, had shared his thoughts and hopes . . . and I was going against him. But . . . I searched back in the letter for the words that would give me solace. There, there they were: *Your own reason should examine the whole matter in dispute by every light which can be put in requisition.* He had given me permission to make it my decision.

The memory of the conversation when I had been given permission to make my own decision intruded. Papa's voice played in my head. *"I am done with it. For my part I wash my hands of you altogether. Do as you wish."*

My mouth turned dry. Such anger and spitefulness . . . did he deserve my sacrifice?

Do you deserve mine?

I drew in a breath at the voice of God within me. Christ had been sacrificed for all, for me. Did I deserve such a sacrifice?

I shook my head no with great adamancy. And with that recognition of my humble place in the world, I tossed all thoughts of whether Papa deserved my compliance to the air. *Honour your Father and Mother.*

I would do that and gain the blessing of knowing I had done the right thing.

As for Robert? He would understand. He may not agree, but he would come to understand. I would make him understand.

Besides, with me still in London, and Robert in London . . . our weekly visits could continue. My life depended on that—as much as it did on breathing.

I closed my eyes and took a few breaths in and out, solidifying the decision made. Only then did I look back to the last paragraph of Robert's letter.

> How all changes! When I first knew you . . . you know what followed. I supposed you to labour under an incurable complaint—and, of course, to be completely dependent on your father for its commonest alleviation. Now again the circumstances shift—and you are in what I should wonder at, as the veriest slavery, and I who could free you from it, I am here scarcely daring to write.

He called my condition slavery! He would never understand my decision. Never!

I forced myself to read the final words.

> What retires so mutely into my heart at your least word,
> what shall not be again written or spoken, if you so will . . .
> that I should be made happy beyond all hope of expression.
> Now while I dream, let me dream! If allowed, I would marry
> you now and thus I would come when you let me, and go
> when you bade me . . .
>
> > God bless my dearest E.B.B.

Marry me? I felt my heart skip a beat in acclamation and pressed a hand against my chest to keep it contained. He loved me enough to want me to be his—forever?

Although he had mentioned marriage in that long-ago letter we never spoke about, to receive such a proof of attachment from Robert now, after our affection had naturally grown, not only overpowered every present evil, but seemed a full and abundant payment for the personal sufferings of my whole life.

I looked about the room and found that the small bitternesses of the last few days were gone. The tear marks vanished in the moisture of new, happy tears. How else could I have felt? How would any woman have felt upon hearing such words said—though "in a dream" indeed—by such a speaker?

I got out paper and pen and with shaking hand responded to this man, this Robert Browning. . . .

> You have touched me more profoundly than I thought
> even you could have touched me. Henceforward I am yours
> for everything but to do you harm. However this may be, a
> promise goes to you in it that none, except God and your
> will, shall interpose between you and me. I mean, that if He
> should free me within a moderate time from the trailing chain
> of this weakness, I will then be to you whatever at that hour
> you shall choose . . . whether friend or more than friend . . .
> a friend to the last in any case. So it rests with God and with

you. May God bless you on this and on those that come after, my dearest friend.

I smiled at the world, for what a glorious world it was! I loved two men in this world above all others — Papa and Robert. And now I knew that my decision to honour one would not lose me the other! Would we ever marry? I had more doubts than certainty, and yet the very thought that a man loved me like that . . .

I looked at the clock wishing evening were upon me. For when Papa came to me this night for our prayers, I would tell him of my decision.

With one letter and one statement, I would please both loves of my life.

∼✦∼

For the first time in weeks, I looked forward to Papa coming for evening prayers. Ever since the idea of Pisa or going abroad had come up, there had been tension between us that prayer had helped, but had not overcome.

But tonight, I would put an end to it. I would honour him and please him and earn his title of favourite. And all would be well, and life could continue as it had before — but better. For I had the love of Robert in my life, and with love, all things were good.

Did not love conquer all?

At the appointed time I heard Papa's footfalls upon the stair. My heart caught in my throat, but with a full breath was put in its proper place. I arranged a smile as his greeting.

He rapped on the doorjamb, then entered. Upon seeing my smile he did a double-take. "Good evening, Ba."

"Good evening, Papa." I was pleased that my voice had achieved true pleasure.

He came in and we moved to take our proper places for prayer. But I stopped him with a hand to his arm. "I wanted to tell you that I have decided to abandon any plans to go abroad for the winter. I wish to stay here with you, as you so wish."

He looked down at me, his face unchanged but for a subtle drawing of his brow. And then he did something that pierced as deeply as a knife, that deadened as fully as a poison.

He shrugged.

And with that shrug I knew my sacrifice was for naught. My obedience was neither appreciated nor noted, but expected in the way we expect the sun to rise and set each day. Should we show appreciation for such constancy? Do we praise the sun?

Neither did Papa praise me.

And yet, his shrug was more than an absence of praise, it was a measure of contempt. Not that he didn't love me, but he did not *revere* me. Respect and compassion were absent in his love. I gave my all — was willing to sacrifice for his pleasure as a sign of my true affection — and his course was otherwise.

I was wounded to the bottom of my heart, cast off when I was ready to cling to him. He would not even grant me the consolation of thinking that I sacrificed what I supposed to be good, to *him*.

"Ba? Shall we proceed?"

We got to our knees and bowed our heads, and as he read from the Bible, my mind was elsewhere, caught in a trap of incredulity that I had been so blind, so stupid, so ignorant. And that he . . . instead of loving me with the unconditional love that had been my offering, loved with a possessive hand that hurt in its clutching, that caused bruises and offered no solace.

Papa did not love me as much as I had thought.

But . . .

Someone else loved me more than I had ever imagined.

I would cling to that.

Cling to Robert.

Twelve

Robert tucked a blanket around my feet, then left me to stoke the fire. "I could move the chair closer," he offered.

I laughed. "Any closer and flames will be my companion."

He wiped his palms against his trousers. "The winter *has* been hard on you. I just want you well, Ba."

I extended a hand and he took it and drew near. "Your presence warms me more than a hundred blankets or a thousand fires."

He leaned down, kissed my hand, and winked. "Flattery will get you anything, dearest."

I raised a finger to make a point. "Aristotle said, 'A flatterer is a friend who is your inferior, or pretends to be so.'"

"I do not pretend to be your inferior, I am so." He bowed low. "Your humble inferior."

I reached out, found his sleeve, and pulled him towards me. "It is I who am inferior. You see from above and I from below. You are too good and too high for me, my love."

"Oooh," he said with a grin. "'Beware the flatterer: He feeds you with an empty spoon.'"

I shoved him away. "My spoon is not empty. I mean every word."

He knelt by my side and kissed my hand. He was always eager to calm me and make amends. I was unused to such treatment, such eagerness and generosity to forgive.

My face must have clouded, because he asked the reason.

I had not wanted to tell him, but as usual, I could not help but share every inkling, every notion, every mood or sensation. "He does not come anymore. . . ." The *he* needed no explanation, and yet the event . . . "He does not come to take evening prayers with me anymore."

Robert's fury propelled him to stand. "That is cruel. Despicable."

Although I still felt the sting of Papa's actions, I understood them. "I cannot blame him for his withdrawal when I have done as much in other, more subtle ways."

"But you are still here. You are *not* in Pisa but still here in this house, in this room instead of abroad these four months. He is the one who has moved away."

"We have both moved away. . . ." It was a distressing truth. Ever since the Pisa incident last autumn and the bitterest fact that I *believed* Papa loved me more than he obviously did, I had found myself in a delicate place. I could fall at Papa's feet, declare my love, and beg for his own. Or I could focus on the love of Robert, who did not require such demonstrations, who gave freely and without condition.

"Does your father suspect the reason for your withdrawal?" he asked. "If so, I should meet with him face-to-face and pronounce my love and intentions and—"

"No!"

Robert was taken aback. "If you say you are estranged, wouldn't it be best to bring our relationship into the open? Surely more damage could not be done."

But it could. The memory of Henrietta's battle with Papa, the shouting, the sound of her knees upon the floor . . . I could not risk such an exchange. Better health or no, I feared I would not live through such a spectacle but faint dead away. "I have no spell for charming the dragons, Robert. I am not a starry-eyed young girl who expects those whom I love to seek or attain a perfect love. I know Papa's limitations and the strength of his foundation—and his will."

"But surely he realizes he is doing wrong? There is nothing right about withholding the precious union of prayer between father and daughter."

I nodded, making my point. "The two of us are imperfect beings, Papa and I. He stands firm and unyielding, and I . . ." Was I taking a stand? Not exactly. But we were moving to different sides of the same life.

"And you . . . ?"

"I have made my choice."

"And?"

I held out my hand. "I choose you."

He kissed my hand—as I expected him to—and the very expectation of such an act swept through me with new pleasure. Me. Having a man kiss my hand with true affection. *Expecting* him to extend the gesture.

Then Robert drew back, his face serious. "I . . . you must understand why I turn my thoughts in this direction. If it is indeed as you fear, and no endeavour or concession on my part will serve under any circumstances— and by endeavour, I mean all that heart and soul could bring the flesh to perform . . ." His brow tightened and I could see he was frustrated with what he wanted to say. But then he made an inner decision and sealed it with a nod. "Let me tell you a story . . . the likelihood is, I overfrighten myself for you, by the involuntary contrast with those here in this house. If I was home and went with a letter downstairs and said simply, 'I want this taken to such and such direction tonight, and am unwell and unable to go; will you take it now?' my father would not say a word, or rather would say a dozen cheerful absurdities about his 'wanting a walk,' 'just having been wishing to go out,' etcetera. Do you know that at night he sits studying my works, illustrating them—I will bring you drawings to make you laugh—and yesterday I picked up a crumpled bit of paper—his notion of what a criticism on my last work ought to be—no criticisms that have appeared satisfy him!" He smiled. "Regarding whatever favour I asked, whatever task I desired, he would be kind—out of love. And my mother, she loves me more than all necessity. How I would love for you to meet them. At least my sister, Sarianna."

He looked up at me, his eyes imploring: *Do you understand what I am trying to say?*

I did. But I could not meet his family—who did know of our love. By meeting them, they would surely be held liable for our future actions. I did not wish them to suffer any slinging of the mud. I was also afraid of not being liked enough. In turn, how could I not like *them?* Everything was at once too near and too far, too much and not enough.

Yet the image of his father, so jovial and supportive, so willing to aid his son in whatever his endeavour might be—from posting a love letter to firmly establishing a place in the literary world. The contrast was severe and unspoken. The subterfuge that was a necessary component of life on Wimpole Street—that I could not even ask Papa to post a letter without fear. To others I painted Papa as eccentric but loving, but to Robert, I gave a darker opinion. Could both papas be a true depiction?

They were. Which confused me even more. Yet I knew that in order to keep Robert from facing him, I had to present Papa as inaccessible and intimidating. I could not risk a confrontation between them, a confrontation where I would be forced to publicly choose.

And it was not just Papa who was kept in the dark. My entire family was ignorant of our relationship—even my sisters. We timed Robert's visits when they were absent, and Wilson had the responsibility of posting my letters and listening for the knock of the postman on the door to retrieve his from the mail slot.

Robert's visits were twice a week now, and our letters a daily—if not more frequent—occurrence. Each letter, each visit, spun another layer around our loving cocoon. And we dared not let anyone else know of it lest they intercede and rip a gaping hole. . . .

We told no friends, not even Cousin John, Anna Jameson, or Mary Mitford. It was not that we distrusted their ability to hold a secret sacred, but the fact that one slip . . . I shuddered to imagine Papa finding out in some innocuous, though disastrous, way. A passing comment from the sweet shop where Robert bought a bit of candy for me, a crony of Cousin John's who had heard slim mention of the liaisons going on at Wimpole Street: *Shhh! Don't say a word.* And what if someone in the press found out that two poets—including the enigmatic, reclusive Elizabeth Barrett— were having clandestine meetings? The "meetings" would quickly turn into "rendezvous" and then into "an affair."

I dismissed the dismal designation. We were not having a love *affair*, we were in love, in its most sacred and pure form: *Love suffereth long, and is kind; love envieth not; love vaunteth not itself, is not puffed up, Doth not behave itself unseemly, seeketh not her own, is not easily provoked, thinketh no evil; Rejoiceth not in iniquity, but rejoiceth in the truth; Beareth all things, believeth all things, hopeth all things, endureth all things. Love never faileth.*

Love was a sacred gift from God. I did not wish for it to fail, and so, I held it close and used the full of my restraint. The only way to keep our secret was to keep our secret. To the world Robert's visits could hold no more import than those of Cousin John's.

I felt Robert's hand upon mine. "Ba? Do you understand what I am trying to say?"

"I do. I celebrate the love you share with your parents. I glory in it—for you. And I . . . I grieve what is lacking . . ."

"I grieve with you."

"Which makes it almost bearable."

"Almost?"

It was far more complicated than I could describe. Yet I had to try. "I am reluctant to say this, but in many ways my prison is of my own making. I made it known that I was content in my room with my books and my writing, I was content to be *in* the house with my family, but apart from them. Papa abided by *my* wishes and found benefit to them. In many ways it was I who assigned him his role—and took up my own."

"Benefit for whom?" Robert asked.

I shook my head, needing to continue. "You own a past full of sun-shine and happiness, Robert, but I . . . my past is a drop of ink in a pool of clear water. It radiates outwards, seeping into every droplet, coloring the clearness with dark. The stain cannot be removed."

"But surely if more clear water is added, the darkness can be diluted."

I smiled and cupped his face with a hand. "You are my clear water, Robert. Refreshing and brilliant."

"I do my very best."

And with a surge of new hope and confidence, I had the feeling his best *would* be enough.

⌘

Robert left me and the echo of his voice hung within the confines of my room. But suddenly, as I settled onto my sofa to suffer the rest of the day without him, its fading tone filled me with panic. That he could come and go, and I . . . could not?

It was not only envy that stepped into my presence but an unworthiness. Through our love, it was I who was pulling him away from the life and world outside these walls and forcing him to enter this meager sanctum. *But I love you anyway, dear Ba, your smile, your soft voice, your* — I shook my head against my imagining of Robert's retort. He had not offered such a listing, but suddenly I feared he might. And though many women might enjoy the offering of such compliments, I did not want him to love me based on temporal things like a smile or voice or presence, things that could vanish through mood or an unexpected cloud. He must love me for the sake of love alone and —

I reached for the notebook which was always close by. All thoughts of composing epic poems of Greek heroes had left me. The words that often burst from my soul onto the paper in recent days would be considered mere nothings to the world, but they were everything to me: sonnets of love and angst and confusion. Sonnets from my heart, not from any knowledge or intellect or desire to create prose or poem deemed worthy of criticism or praise.

No indeed. These were the pourings from my heart *for* my heart, though perhaps they were also an offering to God, for it was His eyes alone who read them. Even I did not dwell upon the words once they moved from mind to pen. They did not invoke the need for edit or change, but fell upon the page complete within that moment, expressing that moment, releasing that moment. . . .

And so, I set the newest words free.

> If thou must love me, let it be for nought
> Except for love's sake only. Do not say
> "I love her for her smile—her look—her way
> Of speaking gently—for a trick of thought
> That falls in well with mine, and certes brought
> A sense of pleasant ease on such a day"—
> For these things in themselves, Beloved, may
> Be changed, or change for thee, and love, so wrought,
> May be unwrought so. Neither love me for
> Thine own dear pity's wiping my cheeks dry,
> A creature might forget to weep, who bore
> Thy comfort long, and lose thy love thereby!
> But love me for love's sake, that evermore
> Thou may'st love on, through love's eternity.

I pulled pen away from paper and allowed myself to breathe. Such was the way while writing these odes, as if a breath of air was needed to fuel the start, and was held until the final word.

I glanced at the door and once again was struck by the alteration in my life when Robert was with me—and when he was not. I was unworthy of such love. Its very presence enlarged my worth.

It enlarged my strength, my determination, my cour—

I heard my brothers and sisters below, and then . . . as if their noise controlled all my other senses, I suddenly noticed how warm it was in this place I called home. I had a thermometer in my room and was astounded to read it at sixty-eight.

"It cannot be January anymore. I deem it to be April and I must leave this room!"

I laughed at my pluck, and before my usual restraint could hold me back, I rose and started for the stairs.

Passing through the doorway into the hall was done with a burst of bravado, and yet, standing on the upper landing I experienced a heady wave of hesitation. I had rarely walked these stairs in six years. During my few ventures beyond my room, one of my brothers had usually carried me. Who was I to think I was strong enough of body or mind or soul or—?

"Stop it!" I whispered to myself. I could not allow mutiny to gain a stronghold. I held the upper banister as if gripping the very axis of the earth. *Robert loves me. Robert loves me. Take my strength from that.*

Robert, a man who was noble as a king. If he were here, he would prevail against my fears and fling his royal cloak around me, conquer all fear, and tease away the last misgiving.

With that image encasing my nerves, I knew that here, in this place, in this moment, with the knowledge of all he was and who *I* was within his love . . . all strife ended. He had invited me to come forth. He had done all *he* could do. It was my choice to take the next step from the past into the future.

I spoke to his mental image as a prayer: *Make thy love larger to enlarge my worth.*

Looking down the expanse of stairs that spanned the distance between me and my family, I felt the void expand. I took a step back, newly afraid. To mark this length of space was more than moving from here to there, it was a moving from then to now—with six years of time between—and then beyond the moment of *now* into the future. And yet, amid my hesitation I knew that I sought no copy of my life's first half. I had to leave those pages with all their long musings curled with age. I was being offered my future's epigraph, which would declare the new theme of my life. Robert was my angel, unhoped for in the world, but . . . mine.

I drew in a breath to strengthen me, and with its release prayed to God for a dose of His strength, which would far surpass my own.

And with another breath, and then another, I nodded my consent, and with hand clutching the railing, with body leaning to its side for support, I descended a step.

And then another.

And another.

My legs rebelled at the effort, having been pampered into weakness by years of unuse. I nearly stumbled, but caught myself from full falling.

I paused to recollect my strength. My heart beat double time from the near fall, as well as the intensity and immensity of my journey. The sound of my siblings grew louder, and my heart beat even faster at the imagined look on their faces when they saw me standing in the doorway. I stifled a laugh and let my joy and anticipation give me confidence to keep going.

I reached the proper landing, and with a sudden fear that one of them would spot me by chance instead of dramatic design, I moved immediately towards the doorway, taking one step inside the drawing room, breaking the barrier of their surroundings.

Stormie saw me first. His eyes widened and — throwing aside his shyness and awkward manner — let the love of his heart have free reign. He ran towards me and proclaimed, "I am *so* glad to see you, Ba! So glad!"

The others gathered round in a swell of hugs and well-wishes. "You act as if I walked through a window," I said.

" 'Twould be no more miraculous," Henrietta said.

Occy brought me a chair. "Sit, sit."

And so I let them fuss over me, and wallowed in the fact they were doing so because of my strength and not my infirmity.

As they talked I became one of them, no longer set apart. I realized how I had lived the entirety of my adult life with visions for my company instead of men and women. I had found the population of books gentle mates but hadn't known there was any sweeter music than what they played to me.

But then Robert had stepped forth and had become more beloved than any book or prose. Robert had overcome my past and filled my soul with a complete satisfaction of all my wants.

I let the life of the room embrace me and felt a divine hand upon my shoulder. *See what I can do for you? See what love can do for you?*

Happy tears welled in my eyes as I realized how God's gifts put man's best dreams to shame.

❧

The world.

How it had gone on without me! I, a woman of forty years, who had spent all but a childhood in confinement, now found herself a visitor in a strange land.

For the visit down the stairs into the arms of my family was only the first of many visits — there, and beyond. I ventured forth slowly and carefully, and suffered a few setbacks as my body rebelled: *But wait! You cannot take me out! Do not strain me so!*

But eventually, the strain lessened and I gained strength in the presence of sun and air and people beyond my kin. And today . . .

Arabel, Flush, and I took a carriage ride to Regent's Park. Had it been a year since we had last ventured here together with Stormie?

The sunlight shone through the trees, casting a green light through the branches, as if the sun carried the very essence of the leaves to the ground.

And suddenly . . . I wished so much to walk through a half-open gate along a shaded path that we stopped the carriage and got out and did just that.

I put both feet on the grass . . . what a strange feeling! So soft and movable, like padding placed there just for me.

"Be careful," Arabel said, taking my arm. "You are uncertain."

She was so wrong. I was very certain — if not physically, by the way my soul soared within the moment. I lifted my face towards the sound of the rustling leaves above and noticed that the tree providing me dear shade was a golden chain tree. "A laburnum," I said aloud.

Arabel looked up, as if she would not have noticed otherwise. "The blossoms are lovely," she said.

And suddenly, I knew I needed one for Robert. I reached upwards, but they were too high. "Help me pick one," I said.

"Don't be silly. You can't reach it."

"But I must." To myself I added: *for Robert.* Robert always brought me flowers to celebrate our various anniversaries, even marking the day he came with Cousin Kenyon and did *not* see me years before. And in nine days we would commemorate our first May meeting—that day which made the world tip in my favour. His offerings were never flowers from a hothouse, but from his mother's lovely garden.

The need to have a flower for Robert when he came to visit next became a quest that had to be fulfilled. "Help me, sister. I must have it!"

She tried to protest, but I gave her no choice as I stood upon my toes and reached out . . . stretched muscles long since stretched, brushed it with my fingers, and then—

"Got it!"

I opened my hand and found a few yellow blossoms pulled from the central pendent stem. Their waxy touch felt beyond this world, beyond real. I put them to my nose and breathed in the luscious vanilla scent.

"You only got a tiny sprig, a few blossoms. You can't reach an entire cluster."

Although I would have loved to take the entire tree as an offering to my dear beau, a few blossoms would be enough. In our situation they would have more effect than an entire bouquet.

"We should get back," she said. "Papa might come home and find us gone and—"

A cloud fell upon the moment, causing my joy to turn gray. And then . . . in the instant it took to draw the bloom to my nose once again, I was shown a truth about love that made my knees wobble.

"Are you all right?" Arabel asked.

"I am fine," I said as I willed my legs to remain strong. I needed a moment to let the truth that had thrown me to sink in. "I need to walk a bit."

"But Papa—"

I ignored her and walked across the grass. I tried to grasp the truth that had rocked me, but it tried to hide just out of reach. . . .

I took another whiff of the flower and was brought to remember. With the simple plucking of the flower with the intent of making Robert happy, I had found happiness. That was the way love should work. Robert's love made me feel happy and emancipated. Here I was, out in the world for the first time in far too long because of Robert's love.

In sharp contrast came the cloud . . . thoughts of Papa's love for me. His love consumed me like a shroud, cloaked me in anxiety, bathed me in fear of an unwitting transgression that would bring his displeasure. Being loved by Papa involved clutching my arms around myself in protection. Being loved by Robert allowed me to open my arms wide in joyful supplication.

Arabel called from the carriage. "Ba, we must not linger."

I glanced back but did not wish to reenter the confines of the carriage. Not when I had entered this Garden of Eden and plucked for my love a token, proving to myself—and to him—that he was never far from my thoughts.

In fact . . . I turned full circle, scanning the park. Surely Robert was *here*, for *he* was always the impetus of joy in my life. When I did not see him . . . It seemed illogical not to see him close by. Robert *was* joy.

As I turned back to the carriage, I took solace in the end of this experience by knowing that Robert was never far away, for my thoughts were always his to own. *Dearest, we shall walk together under the trees someday.*

And so I walked back to the carriage that would return me to my prison, holding Robert's flower against my lips, drawing into my nostrils the flavour of this moment and my offering of love.

∽✤∾

I could not wait for him to come. . . .

I sat at my dressing table, adjusted the ringlets at my face, then let my gaze drop to the laburnum blossoms nearby. They too had been waiting for Robert, drinking in the water I had drawn for them in a teacup. They were holding out with dogged determination.

As was I.

Even though Robert often came to visit twice a week, it was not enough. If only I could hide him behind the chair, or drape a velvet scarf over him, setting a plant upon his head to disguise him from curious eyes and keep him here, always here, all to myself.

I heard Wilson on the stair. "He's here, Miss Elizabeth."

Had I been so entrenched in my reverie that I had not heard the door below?

It didn't matter. He was here and my world was once again complete.

Robert rapped on the doorjamb—as he always did—and entered, his face beaming—as it always was. He carried a bouquet of roses—as he often did.

"For you, dearest Ba," he said with a bow.

"I'll take them, sir," Wilson said. She left to arrange them in a vase.

He came forward and kissed my cheek. "And how are you today?" he asked.

I turned around on the vanity bench, hoping that I blocked the view of the flowers. "I have a gift for you," I said.

"You are my gift."

I pushed past his fervent compliment, needing to complete my offering. I rose, took his hands, and led him to the chair. "You must sit and close your eyes."

"But then I cannot see you and—"

I put my hands upon my hips. "Robert."

He acquiesced, settled into the chair, rested his elbows upon the arms, and clasped his hands between. He leaned his head against the cushion and closed his eyes. "There," he said. "I am ready."

I hurried to the teacup and took the blossoms from their holding place. I wiped their drips upon my skirt and carried them to Robert. I held them beneath his nose. "Inhale," I said.

"In—?"

"Sniff."

He took a breath in through his nose and his eyebrows rose. "Vanilla?"

"Open your eyes."

He opened them and found the yellow flowers within my hands. His face was curious for a moment.

"I picked them for you."

The room was silent as the full implication took hold.

"You? You picked them? Outside?"

I nodded and felt tears intrude. "I . . . I went out and saw them and had to have them—for you. You have brought me so many flowers. It's time I gave a few of my own." I had to explain more, try to explain what I'd felt in the park. "When I picked them I turned around with the feeling that you were there with me, and was rather surprised you were not. For you *are* always with me in thought and . . ." I extended the flowers to him. "For you, dear Robert. A humble offering and small token of my love."

He extended his hands, cupped before me, and I transferred the sprig of blossoms into his care. He held them there a moment, gazing down at them. Then he looked upon my face and I saw tears in his eyes to match mine. "You have entered the world," he said. "You have been set free."

I knelt before him, resting my head upon his knee. "You are my saviour, Robert. You have helped me move from the dark door of death into the bright light of life."

He lifted my head and placed his hands upon my cheeks. "Then let it be finished. Marry me, Elizabeth. We are neither one complete without the other. Let us do what God has ordained through our love."

He had spoken of marriage before—as early as last autumn—but I had not allowed myself to think with full reason, with full heart . . .

He must have seen my hesitation, for he said, "My own Ba! My election is made, or God made it for me, and it's irrevocable. I am wholly yours. I see you have yet to understand what that implies."

As the implication became fully clear I found it hard to swallow.

He laughed and stroked my cheek. "Dearest love of my life, light of my soul, joy of my heart. Marry me."

My heart leapt forward, commanding my mind, prodding my words, determining my fate. "I . . . yes. I say yes."

I watched his face transform as happiness and relief removed all shadow and doubt and replaced it with the smooth glow of contentment. Then he gently put a finger beneath my chin and lifted it just so — just so he could move close and finally touch his lips to mine.

The kiss lasted but a moment, yet in that moment, sealed a lifetime.

⁓✤⁓

"Are you all right, miss?" Wilson asked as she brought my evening coffee.

Had I ever been right before now?

I tried to suppress the smile that had not left my countenance since Robert's proposal, but . . . so pleased with the miracle of such an act, it would not comply. I knew I looked crazed, for I was not — had not previously been — one for expressions of utter joy. My previous life held no comparison to *now*. There was no measuring stick with which to compare it.

"I am quite fine, Wilson. That will be all."

She looked askance at me a moment, and a slight smile seeped onto her face. She was a smart woman. And though she had no way of knowing the content or significance of Robert's last visit — unless she had been listening at the door — she always took pleasure in my happiness after seeing him. That this visit had yielded an extraordinary happiness . . .

To my relief she did not ask more but said, "As you wish, miss," and left me alone.

But not alone. Never again alone. For wherever I was, wherever my heart beat and my thoughts soared, Robert was with me. A year ago he came to me for the first time and the miracle was begun. Did I ever think I should live to thank God that I did not die six years ago?

There was only one truth: My thoughts were of Robert—all the time. No man could mean as much to any woman as he did to me. The fullness was in proportion to the vacancy: the black gaping hole that existed before this silver flooding. Who could blame me for standing—as if in a dream—and disbelieving my own fate? Was ever anyone taken so suddenly from a lampless dungeon and placed upon the pinnacle of a mountain, without their head turning round and their heart turning faint, as mine did? He loved me more and more . . . Should I thank him or God?

Both. And there was no possible return from me to either of them. I thanked Robert as one unworthy . . . and as we all thanked God. How could I ever prove what my heart was to him? How would he ever see it as I felt it?

I took a sip of the coffee and let its warm bite flow through me. Then suddenly, words interrupted my thoughts and formed lines. Stanzas . . .

Knowing that the words would only linger but a moment before dissipating into a mist I could not recapture, I hurried to the desk and drew pen and paper close.

> How do I love thee? Let me count the ways.
> I love thee to the depth and breadth and height
> My soul can reach, when feeling out of sight
> For the ends of Being and ideal Grace.
> I love thee to the level of everyday's
> Most quiet need, by sun and candlelight.
> I love thee freely, as men strive for Right;
> I love thee purely, as they turn from Praise.
> I love thee with the passion put to use
> In my old griefs, and with my childhood's faith.
> I love thee with a love I seemed to lose
> With my lost saints—I love thee with the breath,

Smiles, tears, of all my life!—and, if God choose,
I shall but love thee better after death.

Upon writing that last awful word—a word which had hovered round me for twenty-five years—I found that I could now say it without fear. For God had not let death take me. He had saved me and seen me through my suffering—for this. For Robert. For love.

I pressed a hand to my chest and let the tears flow. Tears of relief, tears of gratitude, and tears of joy.

I was alive and the past was no more. I was Robert's, he was mine, and the future was ours to share. Unto death. Beyond death.

For love never dies. Did I not love Bro as much now as I had when he was with me? And Mother?

Was not God love? Did the Bible not say, *We love Him, because He first loved us?*

And so . . . I would love Robert forever. It was God's command: *These things I command you, that ye love one another.*

I would do my part and accept this wondrous gift.

Praise ye the Lord. O give thanks unto the Lord; for He is good: for His mercy endureth for ever.

Thirteen

"I cannot go on like this!"

I put a quick finger to my lips and glanced at the door. Even though no one was home, the instinct for silence, just in case . . . "Calm yourself, dear Robert. I did not say I would not marry you, only that we need to plan things with great care." I decided to add, "Wanting more than what we have . . . I feel greedy."

Robert pressed a hand against his forehead and grimaced. He fell into the chair with his eyes closed.

"Another headache?" I asked.

"More of the one that never leaves me."

The tacit reason for the headache remained unspoken. Instead I offered him medical advice—how odd that I was now the healthier of us two.

"I still think you should try strong coffee or smoking or putting your feet into a mustard bath. I have heard that—"

He opened one eye. "Can you imagine me? Sitting still with my feet in dingy water?"

Actually . . . no.

"And I've told you I detest coffee. You can extol its benefits from today to Christmas and I will not be compelled to suffer its bitterness. And smoking makes me cough. As for the bulk of your usual advice . . ." He pointed towards my dressing table. "Opium is out of the question."

He was incredibly stubborn. "And so, you suffer."

With a grimace he sat upright. "I suffer because our plans remain indecisive. You said we could marry in the summer, but summer is here and we have no plan. This living without you is a torment."

Although I did want to marry him, the very thought of the logistics were a torment to *me*. How could it be done? Neither one of us were used to making such arrangements, and every time I thought of Papa's certain wrath . . .

I made a concession to ease Robert's present pain. "We've touched on it before, but perhaps we should further . . . How will we live?"

"Ah. Money." Although Robert caressed the word with little enthusiasm, his countenance gained a hint of liveliness—albeit anger. "I have heard Mr. Kenyon speak ill of my earning capabilities, and he has told me of a Mrs. Procter being dismayed that I did not have seven or eight hours a day of an occupation."

Mrs. . . . ? "The wife of the writer—alias of Barry Cornwall?"

"The same."

I felt my ire rise. "I should tell her that you do not require an occupation as a means of living because you have simple habits and desires—nor as an end of living, since you find one in the exercise of your genius. If Mr. Procter had looked as simply to his art as an end, he would have done better things." I raised my chin to add a final snub. "If I am correct, *his* last book was published nearly fifteen years ago."

Robert laughed. "Ba, my champion!"

I regretted bringing up the subject. "Nobody should have the power to count whether the sixpence we live by comes more from you or from me . . . and as it will be as much mine as yours, and yours as mine when we are together . . ." I took a fresh breath to fuel my anger. I had enough money for both of us. "Let us join in throwing a little dust in all the winking eyes, Robert. But I would rather see winking eyes than those that stare."

"Staring eyes? How so?"

I had not meant to say it so. "I . . . I do wonder what people will think."

"They will think we must love each other enormously to undertake such a venture."

That was true, but . . . "I am known to be an invalid, and forty years in age. You are younger, the quintessence of a man, with a world of women to choose from."

He took my hand. "No world of women. Only you."

I had to continue, to make him see our act through larger eyes. " 'Twill be seen as odd. As desperation on my part — to escape my father's house and my spinsterhood — and perhaps as . . . as a . . ." I hesitated to state it so plainly.

"As a what?"

"As a financial decision on your part."

He drew back. "People will say I'm marrying you for your money?"

I shrugged.

"Do you think such a thing? If so, I would ask you to transfer your own money to your brothers and sisters, so that — "

It was my turn to take his hand in mine. "I don't believe that." I took a fresh breath, yet hurried to continue. "You are generous and noble as always — but no, I shall refuse to give away God's gifts, which were perhaps given towards this very end, and apart from which, I should not have seen myself justified to cast the burden of me upon you. I care as little for money as you do — but this thing I will not agree to, because . . . I just shouldn't do it." And that, I hoped, was that.

He stood a moment, looking at me. A year ago I would have looked away, embarrassed or uncertain, but now I held his gaze, for it was important for him to take my words in true sincerity.

As was the norm, the smile that broke across his face raced the room to find me, and was returned. He said, "Do you remember that the first words I ever wrote to you were 'I love you, dear Miss Barrett'? It was so — could not but be so. I have always loved you, as I shall always love you."

It was, most surely, *not* coincidence, but precedence, or even prescience of what God had in store for us.

I gathered a cold compress for his head and urged him to sit back down. "Although I was hesitant about your love at first, Robert—unbelieving that you could ever love someone such as I—now I am fully convinced you do love me, for me, as I am."

He kissed my hand. "I want *you*, dearest Ba. All of you. I have told you—warned you perhaps—that I am supremely passionate."

I felt myself blush and covered his view with the compress. To think of myself as the recipient of passion was still new to me, yet I embraced the notion as another miraculous blessing. "Let this be a point agreed upon by both of us. The peculiarity of our circumstances will enable us to be free of the world . . . of even our friends. We must use any advantage, act for ourselves, and resist the curiosity of the whole race of third persons, even the affectionate interest of such friends as dear Mr. Kenyon."

"And Mrs. Procter."

"Especially her." I left the subject of money behind—for good, I hoped. "We will marry and leave England within the fewest possible half hours afterwards. For I shall not dare breathe in this England and wonder *There is my father* and *There is yours*. Do you imagine that I am *not* afraid of your family? I would be even more so if it were not for the great agony of fear on the side of my own house."

He moved the compress aside. "I know, dearest, and—"

I covered his eyes once more. I had to finish. "I must love you unspeakably even to dare think of a plan such as ours."

Robert set the cloth aside and pulled me close. "Listen to me, Ba. Listen to Scripture: 'If two lie together, then they have heat: but how can one be warm alone? And if one prevail against him, two shall withstand him; and a threefold cord is not quickly broken.' Hmm?"

"But we are not three, only two."

"God is our third. He has brought us together and will help us remain so."

I put my head against his chest. I did not dare argue against my Robert—or against the promises of our God.

❧

Robert had just left when I heard new footsteps on the stairs. I glanced about the room. Had he forgotten something?

"Robert, I—"

Henrietta came in the room, stopping my words.

"Oh. I didn't know you were home."

She shut the door behind her. "I saw him leave."

Before the inane "Who?" escaped, I caught hold of my senses. "Did you say hello?"

She rushed to have a seat beside me on the sofa. "Hello? Good-bye? I knew Mr. Browning occasionally came to visit, but I never thought you took his company when no one else was in the house."

There was so much she didn't know.

Her eyes moved furtively. "He said something to me. . . ."

I imagined an impulsive Robert taking Henrietta's hands and proclaiming, *"I love your sister dearly. Madly. We are betrothed."*

To my relief she said, "He asked after Mr. Cook."

"So?"

Another glance towards the door and a lowering of her voice. "He knew far more than he should about our . . . about my . . ." She shook her head in a short burst. "Why would you tell a mere acquaintance about my private matters, Ba? What if he tells others? What if Papa finds out that Surtees has been visiting me far more often than he realizes, and that we wish to . . ."

"Marry?"

She put a finger to her lips, clearly afraid of the verbalization of that forbidden word.

Feeling emboldened by my own secret, I asked, "Why do you not just do it?"

Her laugh was tinged with bitterness. "Why don't you?"

245

I moved to protest that marriage for me was a ridiculous notion when I felt my face grow red.

Henrietta clutched at my arm. "Ba? Is Mr. Browning more than a mere acquaintance?"

It was my turn to put a finger to my lips.

Happiness washed over her countenance and she faced me, taking my hands in hers. "Do you love him? Does he love you?"

"I will not speak of such things." I looked to my lap, but I felt her eyes upon me.

"You do love him, I can see it! Oh, Ba, isn't love grand? Papa always spoke against it as if it were some forbidden fruit that would do us harm, but I see nothing harmful in my love for Surtees. If I could run off today and be married, I would bolt out the door with my next breath."

"Why do you not do it?" I asked. "In spite of . . ."

"Surtees has no money, and neither do I. You are the only one with funds, Ba. Do you not realize the blessing of your inheritance from Uncle Samuel?"

I understood full well. "I never think of it, of money," I said.

"That is because you do not go out much. You do not need new dresses and bonnets, and so your money grows. I am forced to take Papa's meager allowance and save nothing. It is up to Surtees to support us, and right now . . . he cannot."

I thought back six years to a moment when Bro stood before me, needing money to marry. I had offered some funds to him, but he had declined. And now, although I would have liked to offer my sister the same, I could not. My finances were a blessing that would allow *me* to marry, and though I loved my sister, I loved Robert even more. I would not abandon our dream for anything.

Or anyone.

"So," she said. "Are you and Robert very close?"

"We are dear friends."

"Are you considering marriage?"

"No, no. You know me, Henrietta. I nearly faint at the very thought of confronting Papa. And you also know he would rather see me dead at his foot than yield the point: and he will say so, and mean it, and persist in the meaning."

She nodded, her face forlorn. "He loves us too much. Too hard."

I nodded my assent. Possession was not love. Robert's written words came back to me: *Will it not be infinitely harder to act than to blindly adopt his pleasure, and die under it? Who can not do that?*

I was the eldest. Although long an invalid, my sisters looked to me for wisdom—the wisdom of books and common sense, rather than that of the world, but wisdom still. I could not encourage Henrietta to stand up to Papa and risk all. Not when I was afraid to do as much.

I laid my hand upon hers. "We must accept the blessings we have been given through the friendship of these two wonderful men. We must let it be enough."

She shook my hand away. "I do not want to accept clandestine meetings the rest of my life. I have wasted too many years already."

Henrietta was three years younger than I. If she considered her years wasted, then mine, at age forty . . .

Suddenly, I saw the moment with complete clarity. There we were, two middle-aged spinsters, mourning our dependence, worrying over what our father would say to us like two little girls without confidence or maturity. It was absurd.

Then, just as suddenly I found myself telling Henrietta, "I will talk to Papa."

She gasped. "Oh, would you, Ba? If he would accept Surtees as my husband, then maybe he would help us financially, at least until Surtees is established."

I will talk to Papa about us, about Robert and me. Again, as the eldest, I knew I had to go first, had to take the first fall for the sake of my siblings. Papa had always loved me most. It was time to take measure of that love, to test it for the good of all those living in this house.

I did not tell Henrietta all this. It was best to let her think I was going to address *her* love, *her* wish to marry. If all went well, I would do so, but if not . . . I did not wish for her to know the extent of *our* plans. I had made such a point to Robert about keeping our love a secret. I would do so — until after I had talked to Papa. That one act would allow full truth to be revealed. That one act would allow me to burst through the door onto Wimpole Street and shout to the world, *"I am Elizabeth Barrett, I am alive, and I am in love!"*

"When?" Henrietta asked. "When will you talk to him?"

My heart flipped a double beat. "Today. When he gets home send him up to me. I will speak to him today."

May God help me.

⟿⟿

I heard Papa's footsteps upon the stairs. The sound that used to fill me with joy now caused shivers to course up and down my spine.

He entered my room, his brow stern, his hands behind his back. "Yes, Ba. What is it?"

It was clear he had not had a good day at work. I should have instructed Henrietta to gauge his mood before telling him that I wished to see him. And yet, she was so eager for me to broach the subject of marriage, there would have been no guarantee she would have heeded such instruction.

"I . . . I wish to speak to you about something."

"So I understand. Henrietta seemed quite adamant."

He took out his pocket watch, looked at it, then returned it to his pocket. And I knew — I knew — that I could not speak to him about any of it.

My body responded to my decision and confirmed its wish to refrain from the stress. My breathing came in short bursts, and my heart beat so rapidly I felt light-headed. "I . . . I . . ."

Papa came towards me. "Lie down, dear girl. I will not have you fainting on me." He helped me to the sofa. "Wilson?"

Wilson appeared in the doorway and with a look saw my need. She busied herself with a fan, supplying me a course of air.

Papa headed for the door. "I'll leave you, then."

"But . . ."

"Obviously you are not well enough to have a discussion of any kind. Whatever it is will wait."

As he walked out, he nearly collided with Henrietta, who must have been listening from the stairs.

"Watch yourself, girl," he said gruffly. Then, with a flip of his hand in my direction, he told her, "Make yourself useful."

She rushed to my side. "Enough, Wilson. I'll take over."

Wilson bobbed a curtsy and left us alone.

Henrietta fluttered the fan furiously. "What happened? I tried to hear but—"

I pushed her attention away angrily and sat upright. "Nothing happened. At his mere presence my heart, my lungs, my nerves . . . I thought I was stronger, but with the very inkling of confrontation I resort to the invalid again! I am a pitiful weakling. Where is my resolve, my strength, my determination?"

"Locked away," Henrietta said. "As is mine. Long ago our ability to stand up to Papa was banished to a dark room in our characters. Unavailable. Invisible."

"If it ever existed at all," I said.

She leaned her elbows to her knees and put her head in her hands. "Oh, Ba, whatever are we going to do? Are we truly doomed to remain here our entire lives?"

I had no answers for her. Or for myself.

⁓✥⁓

"I let her down," I told Robert the next day. "I let *us* down."

He comforted me as I had comforted Henrietta. "A lifetime of submission is not easily overridden, nor is a lifetime under tyranny."

I leaned my head against his chest, letting his arms encase me in their strong safety. "You spoke of going to Italy for a few years," I said. "I think we should go. Away. Far away. Where Papa's hands can't reach us."

He pushed back to see my face. "Really? You agree to Italy?"

"I'd agree to anything to be with you," I said.

"Then Italy it shall be."

I returned to his embrace. "You make the arrangements, Robert. You lead and I will follow."

～❦～

Soon after Robert left, I found that the words bursting within me demanded release. And so, I penned another letter, saying more of what was in my heart.

> And now I must say this besides. When grief came upon grief and I lost Bro, I never was tempted to ask "How have I deserved this of God?" as sufferers sometimes do: I always felt that there must be cause enough . . . corruption enough, needing purification . . . weakness enough, the need for strengthening . . . nothing of the chastisement could come to me without cause and need.
>
> But in this different hour, when joy follows joy, and God makes me happy through you . . .
>
> I cannot repress the "How have I deserved this of Him?" I know I have not—I know I do not.
>
> Could it be that heart and life were devastated then to make room for you now? If so, it was well done, dearest! They leave the ground fallow before the wheat.

I paused and thought about Bro, the one other man I had ever loved with pure affection. What would he say about the words I had written? Knowing how much he returned my love, would he accept his sacrifice if it truly was instrumental in opening my heart to Robert's love?

As I would have died for him, Bro would have died for me.

Perhaps did die for me.

I pressed a hand against my chest, the fullness of blessings making my heart beat faster, but with no risk of faintness. For the blessings of love filled me with excitement, anticipation, and pure gratitude, elements abounding in strength.

How odd I had received such a bounty, all at once, in this phase of my life.

More words begged for release, and I took up my pen again.

> Other human creatures have their good things scattered over their lives, sown here and sown there, down the slopes, and by the waysides. But with me . . . I have mine all poured down on one spot in the midst of the sands! If you knew what I feel at certain moments, and at half-hours, when I give myself up to feeling freely and take no thought of red eyes. Knowing myself, I have wondered more than a little how it was that I could bear this strange and unused gladness without sinking as the emotion rose. I was incredulous at first, and the day broke slowly, and the gifts fell like the rain . . . softly; and God gives strength by His providence for sustaining blessings as well as stripes. Dearest . . .

Dearest. Dearest.

⁓⁂⁓

I adored Robert. He adored me. We wanted to marry. But each time I allowed myself to imagine the logistics of our plan, to even think about telling Papa . . . I was a coward. I had to share the gist of my misgivings with Robert. "Might it not be wiser, dearest, more prudent, for us to remain quietly as we are, you at New Cross, and I here, until next year's summer or autumn?"

With much drama he thrust an imaginary dagger into his chest and staggered backwards against the fireplace. "Oh, show me how to get rid of you!"

"It is just a consideration," I said.

He stood straight and strong with the look of a man who had much to say. "Every day that passes before *that* day is one of hardly endurable anxiety and irritation, and the thought of another year of hope deferred—it's altogether intolerable." He put his hands upon his hips, his forehead furrowed. "Ba. No."

He was right. Of course. Again. This was not the first time we had volleyed these views between us. My fear against his determination. And I knew that delay would not ease the furor our marriage would cause within my family.

His face softened. "We have nothing to gain by delay, and much to lose. Every minute that you are not mine, every hour . . ."

I nodded. We had managed to meet for over a year without Papa finding out. And though it was tempting to continue to ply our good fortune, it would be reckless, and more than that, ungrateful to God's protection for blessings already given.

I offered him a smile of reconciliation. "We are standing on hot scythes, you and I, and because we do not burn our feet—by a miracle—we have no right to count on the miracle extending."

I nodded.

He took my hand and pulled me to my feet, causing Flush to tumble to the floor. "Then let us go now! Right this very minute. Your father is out of the house, your sisters occupied. Tell Wilson to pack you a bag—" He rushed to my armoire and yanked the doors open, pulling a winter dress of black velvet into his arms. "Find me a bag and I will do it myself!" Suddenly he dropped the dress to the floor and took a step away from it. "On further thought . . . leave all these behind." He took my hands and led me in a circle. "Come as you are and take me as I am, and together we will start anew."

Feeling slightly dizzy—or was I merely giddy at the thought of it all?—I stopped our circling and pulled him close for a kiss. "You tempt me, Mr. Browning."

"Only towards good things, Miss Barrett. Our love is the quintessence of all that is good." He resumed our circling. "That I wish to rush towards our union is an attribute and far from folly."

Flush barked, confused by our dance. I began to let one of Robert's hands go in order to comfort the pet, but Robert held it fast and drew me close. He turned my arm behind my back, locking us together. He looked into my eyes with the intensity that was yet another facet of his personality. "I adore you, Ba. I have no heart for more nonsense about when I can take your dearest self into my arms. If my love overflows the bounds and needs to prove itself, so be it. I will prove it again and again. I dedicate my lifetime in the proving. But let us move on with our plans. To remain in limbo is inextricable. To survive, we must move forward."

Forward was a fairly new concept for me. But one that continued to satisfy and entice.

～❧～

The house was full of wedding talk.

Not my own.

My aunt Jane Hedley—my mother's sister—came to visit in July with her husband Bernard—my favourite uncle—and their daughter Constance. They lived in Paris but had traveled to London to make plans for Constance's marriage to a rich man named John Johnston Bevin, whose height at over six feet was as massive as his wealth. Although they did not stay with us, they visited daily and used our drawing room as the center of their plans. As they chattered with my family about wedding gowns and flowers and suppers, I marveled that I did not envy any of it.

I, who had never expected to marry, had not grown into adulthood dreaming of satin and walking down the aisle on my father's arm.

Perish the thought.

And so, hearing my cousin discuss her plans did not negate the specialness of my own. To my mind, the wedding ceremony was just that—a ceremony for show. The vows Robert and I would exchange before God and a pastor would be enough. Our shared "I do" would echo through the heavens with as grand a sound as the mightiest church organ. The look upon our faces would make the presence of company unnecessary, and the final pronouncement as man and wife, under God, would own the scent of a thousand roses.

That there would be no lavish wedding meal, no reception line to embrace family and friends, and no gifts (to admire or appall), was of no import. Rich foods would cause me harm, strong hugs would overwhelm, and gifts would make me feel beholden.

I was set to do this thing simply, with honour and full pleasure.

Constance was in the midst of a discourse on lilies of the valley versus lavender. "I do so love the scent of lavender best, but the daintiness of the—"

Papa, who had not been a part of our discussion, entered the room with some papers. Surprisingly, he approached me. "Here," he said. "You need to sign these."

"What are they?" I asked.

Only then did Papa notice the Hedleys were present. "If you'll excuse us a moment."

"Of course," Uncle said.

Papa angled his back to them just a bit and lowered his voice. "You remember that your uncle Samuel gave you an investment in a sailing ship."

I nodded. The income usually amounted to two hundred pounds per year. The other day Stormie had told me I had eight thousand pounds in that fund. Along with the allowance of fifteen pounds a month that Papa gave me . . . I knew I had enough money to support Robert and me upon our marriage.

"I have determined it is time to transfer that investment to the Eastern Railroad."

I had never been on a train—nor a ship for that matter—but trains were far newer and from what I had heard, loud and dirty and . . . .

"The railroad, you say?" Uncle asked.

Papa made a face, showing his regret that the others had heard. He addressed Uncle Bernard. "I believe it to be a wise move. Do you think otherwise?"

Uncle waved his hands. "No, no. I leave such investment in your capable hands. I'm sure the railroad is the way of the future."

Papa did not respond but placed the paper before me. "Sign here." He handed me the pen, dipped in ink.

Aunt Jane looked up from her discourse with Constance and said, "Is that your marriage settlement, my dear?"

What? My hand flinched and I signed my name wrongly. "Oh no, I —"

Papa snatched the paper from me. "Ba! Concentrate. Can you not even write your own name?" He took the pen, scratched out my mistake, blew on the paper, re-dipped the pen, and handed the document back to me. "Now, again. Carefully."

My hand still shook, but I managed to sign the paper.

I was grateful when Papa left. Returning to my seat, Aunt looked concerned. "You're pale, Ba. Are you feeling all right?"

I feigned a smile and masked my frayed nerves by asking after the flowers.

～❦～

"Will they never leave?" Robert asked me. "How long does it take to plan a wedding, anyway?"

I flicked the tip of his nose. "Months — or so it seems."

He glanced towards the open door. "But in our case we have good excuse, for we are not just planning a wedding, but an escape."

I heard voices from below. Ever since the Hedleys had been in town, Robert and I had been forced to curtail our usual meetings, and shorten the few we dared keep.

"I know what I'd like to do," he said, leaning over me, his face inches from mine. "I'd like to rush down the stairs and burst into the drawing room, my arms wide. 'Excuse me? Excuse me, everyone? I have an announcement to make. Ba and I are —'"

I kissed him quickly on the mouth, then pushed him away. "I think not."

"Why not?" he said. "Other people can marry, but we cannot? Where is the sense in —?"

He stopped speaking at the sound of footsteps on the stair. He hurried to the chair near the fireplace and had just crossed his legs to adopt a nonchalant air when Aunt Jane appeared at the door.

Her eyes found mine, and then . . . she saw Robert. "Oh," she said. "I didn't know you had company."

Like a child, I longed to hide behind the sofa and wait until she was gone. The heat rose in my face, and to disguise it, I lowered my head pretending to find some interest in my hands upon my lap. "I . . . I . . ."

My aunt did a quick curtsy, said, "Pardon me," and left us.

"Well, then," Robert said.

I put a hand to my chest and reminded myself to breathe. "I hope she does not tell Papa."

"Why would she?"

"She might suspect something between us."

"Which all the more tends to her *not* saying anything to your father. Didn't you tell me that when she suspected Henrietta's and Mr. Cook's relationship, she applauded it, and was incensed when she was told of your father's view of marriage?"

"Yes, but—"

"Knowing what she knows, she will not risk causing upheaval in this house by prying."

I stroked Flush's head, trying to find calm. "I hope you're right."

⚬≈⚬

The Hedleys stayed for dinner, and though occasionally I did sup with my family, I could not do so on that night with Aunt Jane in attendance. Perhaps with me absent she would not be tempted to mention her jaunt to my room that afternoon.

I could not eat anything from the plate Wilson brought for me and kept glancing towards the door, wondering if I should descend and join the party. With great determination I remained in my room. Curiosity might lure, but its consequences could easily overwhelm its meager benefit.

When I heard footsteps upon the stairs, I was thankful they were of lighter weight than Papa's. And brisk. Someone was coming with haste.

Henrietta burst into the room and quickly closed the door behind. "You will never guess what was said at dinner," she said.

I feared I could guess *too* well.

Luckily, my sister did not rely upon spoken interest and took a seat beside me, shoving my skirts to make us sit in confidence. "We were nearly finished with the soup when Aunt Jane said, 'I had not seen Ba all day, and when I went to her room, to my astonishment a gentleman was sitting there.'"

"No!"

Henrietta nodded affirmation. "Then Papa turned to Arabel, his eyes stern and silently asking, '*Who was that?*'"

Arabel looked at me and I gave her a tiny shrug and she said, "Mr. Browning called here today."

"No!" I could find no other word. All was lost. Completely lost.

"Then Aunt Jane kept speaking and said, 'And when I entered, Ba bowed her head as if she meant to signify to me that I was not to come in—'"

I gasped. What were we going to do?

My sister took my hand in comfort. "But I saved the day. I interrupted and said, 'Pardon me, Aunt, but you must have been mistaken. I suspect Ba meant just the contrary. I'm sure she was pleased to see you.'"

"She startled me," I explained.

"I thought as much."

"What was said next?"

"Then Papa said, 'You should have gone in and seen the poet.' And then Stormie piped up and said, 'Oh, Mr. Browning is a great friend of Ba's. He comes here twice a week—is it twice a week or once, Arabel?'"

I hid my head in my hands.

"I explained that you hardly saw anybody—except Mr. Kenyon—when Aunt said, 'And apparently a few other gentlemen.' Then she laughed."

My torso fell forward against my lap. It was over. All our months of careful action was negated in one moment of familial prying.

"It gets worse, Ba."

I shook my head, not wanting to hear more. But I had to hear it. All of it. I sat upright. "Go on."

"To Aunt Jane's comment, Papa said, 'Only one other gentleman, indeed. Only Mr. Browning, the poet — the man of the pomegranates.'"

Two points assailed me: Papa knew of Robert's regular visits? and knew of his publication *The Pomegranate*? "If Papa knows . . . why has he not said anything to me?"

"You wish him to?"

"No, no, I wish nothing of the sort. But for him to know and pretend he doesn't know . . ."

"It makes one wonder how much he does know. . . ."

I knew Henrietta was referring to her own love with Surtees Cook.

My mind swam with possibilities. It was obvious Stormie thought nothing was amiss — for surely he would not have mentioned Robert's visits if he thought they would offend Papa. But Aunt Jane's laugh, and Papa's knowledge . . .

"I cannot do this," I whispered for my own benefit.

Henrietta rubbed a hand upon my back. "You must. For yourself and for me. For the brothers too."

Her mention of the brothers surprised me. "One of them wishes to marry?"

"Not that I know of, but they might. But until one of us goes first . . . You are the eldest, Ba. You are Papa's favourite."

"With action I would lose that title."

She shrugged. "Then . . . let it be lost."

"You negate his love so quickly?"

"I challenge his love. Surely he would come to accept a marriage. He is an intelligent man. If he truly loves us, then he will forgive us and accept us and . . ." She studied me. "You don't believe it?"

"I long for it, I hope for it, but . . . no, I don't believe it."

She nodded once and stood. "Then we have a choice to make, you and I. Either we choose the men we love — at the risk of losing Papa's love — or we continue as we are, with the one, forfeiting the other."

That *was* our choice.

Our only choice.

Our agonizing choice.

⁂

I had not been to church in . . . years. Decades? To venture out of my own sanctuary had not been possible. But now, with my health improved, and my determination set afire by love and the new maturity forced upon me, I ventured to Westminster Abbey with Henrietta.

We slid into the back row after the service had begun. I wore a black veil to cover my face, and my black dress offered me the privacy of supposed mourning. Henrietta sat at the aisle, offering a buffer between any who would come after.

I lifted my head to the great rafters and the stone arches. Surely God lived in such a place — which was advantageous, for I desperately needed Him. I needed His strength and desired His wisdom.

In that needy condition my thoughts strayed to a conversation between Robert and I where he'd stated that women were as strong as men — disregarding the issue of physical force. I told him he was mistaken. I would rather be kicked with a foot than be overcome by a loud voice speaking cruel words.

By Papa. The anticipation of cruel words by Papa ruled me.

I would not yield before such words — I would not give Robert up if they were said, but, being a woman (and a very weak one in more senses than the bodily) I knew the words would act on me as a dagger. I could not help dropping and dying before them.

Robert had called such fear the result of tyranny.

Perhaps. Yet in that strange, stern nature of my father there was a capacity to love, and be loved. I did love him — and I knew I would suffer in causing him to suffer.

NANCY MOSER

A man and woman joined the congregation later than we, but luckily took seating across the aisle. My thoughts returned to Papa. Recently, on two or three occasions, he had called me "my love," and even "my puss" — his old words of endearment. I quite quailed before the flattery as if it were so many knife strokes. I could bear anything but his kindness now.

I looked to my right, to the enormous stone columns supporting the great cathedral. Stone. Ever strong and immovable.

Stone was the essence of my difficulty. I had tried to make Robert understand the two ends of truth, both that Papa was *not* stone, and that he was as immovable *as* stone. Perhaps only a very peculiar nature such as his could have held his position in our family so long. And he *was* upright, faithful to his conscience. Robert might respect him and love him in the end. For me, he might have been king and father over me to the end, if he had thought it worthwhile to love me openly enough.

And yet . . . if he *had* been open to my needs, he would not have let Robert come so near. He would have had my full confidence from the beginning, and as such, no opportunity would have been availed for Robert to prove his affection for me, and things would have remained as they were at first when we had just met through our letters.

Regarding our marriage . . . we had to be humble and beseeching — afterwards at least — and would try to be forgiven. Poor Papa! I turned it over and over in my mind, whether it would be less offensive, less shocking to him, if an application were made first. If I were strong, I think I should incline to it at all risks, but as it was . . . If he knew of our plans, Robert and I would be separated from that very moment, hindered from writing, hindered from meeting.

I shook my head against the thought of not being *two* together. I threw myself into the pure, sweet, deep thought of Robert. I was his, his own. No more did I doubt being his. I felt too much his. We were might and right together. He was more to me than the whole world.

If Papa knew or didn't know, we would still marry. But knowing would be worse. The direct disobedience would be a greater offence than the unauthorized act.

I shut my eyes in terror.

Suddenly the organ began to play. Its notes entered my ears and sped to my very soul. They were so grand and all-consuming that I stood, needing to flee away from them.

"Ba . . . what . . . ?" Henrietta whispered as I tried to step in front of her.

"Go," I whispered back. "I must go."

And so she rose from her seat and led the way out. We did not stop until we were in the fresh air, out of reach of the noise.

"What made you want to leave like that?" she asked.

It was hard to put into reason. "The organ . . . it frightened me."

She gave me a questioning look. "It was glorious music. I would have liked to hear it."

Only then did I realize she was right. I had transposed Papa's condemnation into the musical tones, and the deep resonance of the pedal notes had become his voice. I had fled *him.*

I would leave him. Leave his house.

I would.

May God direct us towards the best way.

Fourteen

A bolt of lightning scattered the sky and tattered my nerves. I clung to Robert as though he were a piece of dry land beside a rough sea.

"Gracious, Ba. 'Tis only a little thunder."

I shook my head against his chest. "I have seen what lightning can do."

He was silent a moment. "When your brother—"

"No, no. When Bro died the sea seemed calm. It was in my childhood, when my family lived at Hope End."

"The home with the minarets and domes."

"The very one." I sat upright to tell him the tale. "Once a storm of storms happened and the family all thought the house was struck, but it was a tree within two hundred yards of the windows. The bark, rent from the top to the bottom, was torn into long ribbons by dreadful fiery hands, then dashed into the air, over the heads of other trees, or left twisted in their branches, torn into shreds in a moment, as a flower might be torn by a child. Did you ever see a tree after it has been struck by lightning?"

He shook his head no.

"The whole trunk of that tree was bare and peeled, and . . . and up that new whiteness ran the finger mark of the lightning in a bright, beautiful rose colour, the fever-sign of certain death. Yet the branches themselves were for the most part untouched and spread from the peeled trunk in their full summer foliage. And birds sang in them three hours afterwards."

"An incident rife with Christian symbolism, I would think," Robert said. "And Hope End indeed. It must have seemed like the end of hope."

I had never considered symbolism nor the name of our home in that way, yet . . . after Mother died and after I grew ill . . . my happy childhood home *had* embraced its woeful title.

"But, Ba . . . a tree is not a person, so you should not—"

I shook my head vehemently. "In that same storm, two young women were killed on the hills, each one's death sealed in a moment with a sign on the chest. Only, the sign on them was not rose-coloured as on our tree, but black as charred wood." I took a breath, glad to be done with the telling. "So I get possessed sometimes with the effects of these impressions, and so does Arabel to a lesser degree. Papa gets angry at my reaction and calls it disgraceful to anybody who has ever learned the alphabet."

He took my hand and squeezed it tight. "Although you should not fear lightning when you are safe inside, your father should not condemn you for it." He kissed the top of my head and moved to stand. "Speaking of your father, I must go before he gets home. I've already been here far longer than usual because of the storm."

The lightning cracked again and I shook my head. "You can't. I won't let you go out in this."

He smiled and settled back upon the sofa. "Your wish is my command." He lifted his arm to allow me reentry. "I will stay forever; just say the word."

"Soon," I said. "Soon we—"

Suddenly Wilson burst into the room without knocking. She closed the door and stood against it. "Miss. Sir. Pardon me, but your father has come home early! I heard him say the storm is the worst he has seen in his lifetime."

I stood and took two steps away from Robert. "Does he know Mr. Browning is here?"

"He does. He asked where you were, and reluctantly Arabel told him you were in your room, with a visitor, and when pressed, she told him it was Mr. Browning, and when pressed further, had to admit he had been here for many hours."

My legs buckled beneath me and I fell upon the sofa. "You must go," I said.

"But you just told me—"

"Begging your pardon, miss, but no one is going out. Your father said as much. The streets are empty. There's flooding and . . . no one can leave."

"And so I must stay," Robert said.

I looked to him, to the window, then to Wilson. "Thank you for telling us."

With a nod, she was gone, closing the door behind her. I rushed to it and opened it wide. If Papa came up to see me, he must not find the door closed.

"Come here," Robert said to me.

"No! Don't be silly. I cannot."

"You *could*, and if your father came into the room, it would be a chance to tell him our plans to—"

"No!" I whispered the word with the full power of my fear. "I . . . I see Papa's face as if I can see it though the floor."

"I assure you, even he does not have that power."

I wasn't so certain. I ran to the window, looking out upon the storm. "Does the rain appear to be lessening?"

Robert came behind me and nuzzled his face into my hair. "For you, dearest, it lessens. And as such . . ." He sighed. "I will go."

I was suddenly full of panic. "Is the rain truly lessening?" I wished it to be so. . . .

He did not even look to the window but into my eyes. "It is. I know it is." And so he claimed his hat and stick and, with a gentle kiss, left me.

Even before I heard the door closing below, I wished to call him back. How spineless of me! How weak, how deplorable, that I would allow my fear of Papa's displeasure to overshadow common sense and override compassion for the man I loved. Exhaustion overcame me, and I called for Wilson to help me change into my dressing gown. Sleep—if possible—would force this day to end and a new one to begin.

But as we finished, Papa came to my room. With one sweeping look at my attire, he said, "Has this been your attire since the morning?"

"Oh no, only just now, because of the heat."

His eyebrow rose. "It appears that *that man* has spent the whole day with you."

My mouth opened for me to speak, but I could not think of anything to say.

But Papa did. "Considering your fear of lightning, what if you would have become ill of it, ill with only Mr. Browning in the room? Such an indiscretion is not to be permitted."

Finally I managed, "The storm . . . I could not push him out—"

"Hmm." He put his hands behind his back and nodded. "You must watch yourself, Ba. Watch for any hint of impropriety."

"Yes, Papa."

Getting married secretly would do more than hint of impropriety in Papa's eyes.

⁓❦⁓

Cousin John took his usual position standing by the fireplace. "So. Did you see Browning yesterday?"

I tucked away the letter I was writing to Robert. I hoped I would not have another crisis to relate to him before the afternoon was over. Yet I could not deny . . .

"Yes," I said simply.

"I thought so. I intended to come myself, but I thought it probable he would be here, so I stayed away."

I nearly gasped. He knew the frequency of our visits? Did he know the purpose? I took a moment, forcing myself to swallow, hoping the moisture would allow my voice to sound with a modicum of normalcy.

Before I could speak, my cousin took the reins of the conversation away from me. "Is there an attachment between your sister Henrietta and Mr. Cook?"

My heart skipped one beat, then two, and relief allowed me to find my true voice. "Why, Mr. Kenyon! What extraordinary questions, opening into unspeakable secrets."

He looked confused. "I didn't know it was a secret. How was I to know? I have seen him here often, and it's a natural question which I might have put to anybody in the house . . . I thought the affair might be an arranged one by anybody's consent."

I discovered a chance to veil Henrietta's attachment—and even my own. "But you ought to know that such things are never permitted in this house. So much for the consent. As for the matter itself, you are right in your supposition. But it is a great secret, and I entreat you not to put questions about it to anybody in or out of the house."

He nodded, and his face softened with sympathy. "I understand completely, my dear. In this household any act of disobedience might be cast as a crime."

I was shocked. I had never told him details of Papa's demand for obedience, and he was not close to Henrietta. How had he known such a thing?

He must have seen my confusion, for he gave me a knowing nod and placed his forefinger to his temple. "I see things, Ba. I know what's going on."

He knows?

I couldn't talk to him anymore. I had to be alone. I needed to see Robert. I needed . . .

To be gone from this place and free from this intrigue.

❦

Henrietta burst into my room with a face that interrupted my heartbeat.

"What's wrong?" I asked.

She closed the door behind her and came close. "Our brothers, they have been talking about you."

"Me?"

She nodded. "In the middle of simple conversation, Stormie touched me and said, 'Is it true there is an engagement between Mr. Browning and Ba?'"

I pressed a hand to my chest. "What did you say?"

"I said, 'You had better ask them if you want to know. What nonsense, Storm.'"

I breathed again, for the extent of our plans was still a secret—even to my sisters. "Thank you, Hen—"

"That is not all. He said, 'I'll ask Ba when I go upstairs.'"

"Ask—?"

"And George was there too, hearing and looking as grave as a judge."

My head shook no, no, no against them all. "So they are coming up?"

"As they do every Sunday."

"But this will not be like every Sunday. Not if they bring up Mr. Browning and—"

We both turned towards the sound of men's shoes upon the stairs. "Do you wish me to stay?" she asked.

I nodded and tried to collect my thoughts. If asked directly, what would I say? I did not lie to my brothers but through omission. If asked . . .

Occy knocked once, then swept the door wide. "The door closed against us, Ba? Never!"

Occy, Sette, George, Stormie, Alfred, and Henry entered, a mass of oscillating manliness. Arabel brought up the rear, looking as nervous as I felt. The men took their usual places, filling every empty corner of my abode, chatting among themselves.

Before they settled and quieted—and asked the first question—I started my own dialogue. About them. "So, Occy and Sette, tell me about your new jobs. . . ."

And men, being men, were all too eager to speak about themselves. And when it was the normal time for them to leave, they did so, leaving me exhausted from the effort.

Apparently, my "engagement" was a passing fancy, not a valid and pressing thought within their minds. The cloud had passed for the present, and hopefully nothing more would be said of it.

My sisters stayed behind. "That was too close," Henrietta said.

"My heart was in my throat," Arabel added. "One question and all would have been lost, no?"

"No."

Both of them looked at me askance. "No? You would still meet with Mr. Browning?"

More than *meet* . . . I found strength in my own determination. "No, I do not fear offending our brothers. There is no room for fear."

"Then why not tell them that you care for each—"

"No!" I said for the third time. "Their approval or disapproval is equally undesirable, for if they knew of our affection, they would certainly press for me to ask Papa for permission. And in such a storm of opinions and feelings I might actually do such a thing and fail Robert *and* myself, through weakness of the body, though never of the will. Never that."

Arabel set some chairs straight. "You are braver than I could ever be."

"Braver than I," Henrietta said.

It was odd for me to hear them call me brave. Me, the invalid, the weakest link of our family. And yet, they were right. Robert's love had made me strong. My body, my will, my affections, and my conscience untremblingly turned to him.

In so many ways our two had already become one.

❦

Robert and I agreed to meet with less frequency. By insisting on our usual schedule we risked everything. And what would we gain, in the face of that? Robert assured me that he could learn no more about me, be taught no new belief in my absolute peerlessness . . . he had taken a place at my feet forever, so to hazard an entire life of such delight for the want of self-denial during a short time would be horrible.

And so we wrote even more often, allowing the pen and page to do our mingling for us until October, when we would be free. For that was the month of our full bliss.

I dipped my pen in the inkwell and wrote my thoughts on our escape and our income afterwards:

> By living quietly and simply, we shall surely have enough and more than enough. I calculated once that without unpleasant labour, with scarcely an effort, I could make a hundred a year by magazine contributions, and this, without dishonour either. Then you will send the sweepings of your desk to alternate with my sendings. I afraid? No indeed. I think I should never be afraid if you were near enough. Only that you never must go away in boats. . . .
>
> If I am to think and decide . . . I have decided to let us go through France. And let us go quick, quick, and not stop anywhere within hearing of England, not stop at Havre, nor at Rouen, nor at Paris—that is how I decide. May God help us and smooth the way before and behind. May your father indeed be able to love me a little, for my father will never love me again.

I blew gently upon the words, allowing them to dry into an indelible representation of this moment in time, this slice of my thoughts given as an offering to my love.

I had *decided*.

It was a heady accomplishment.

⤙⤚

Our plans progressed. Although both my aunt and uncle Hedley had offered to let me go back to Paris with them this autumn to flee the harsh winter, which would certainly follow last year's mild offering, and though Mrs. Jameson had offered to let me travel to the Continent with her and her niece, I nodded politely but declined. And though they fussed over my health and their fears for me in the upcoming bitter wind of London, I let them do so knowing that our plans were evolving day by day.

Soon. Before the autumn was out, we would be married and gone to Italy. Weather was a constant worry. To cross the Channel . . . I shivered at the thought of being aboard a boat in good weather, much less bad. Robert had said he would wait a year rather than risk my safety.

I could not wait a year. Never. Lately, to hear the voice of my father and meet his eye made me shrink back. To talk to my brothers left my nerves trembling, and even to receive the sympathy of my sisters turned into sorrow and fear, lest they should suffer through their affection for me. How I could look and sleep as well as I did was a miracle—or would have been if the love I felt and received from Robert were not the deepest and strongest thing of all and did not hold and possess me completely.

It was excruciating to have nothing set solidly in place, and yet I suspected it would be just as trying to know exactly when and where and how—

Aunt Jane poured tea for the three of us. She and Uncle had come to visit to bring me up to date with Constance's wedding plans. I listened with a half heart and full nerves. For though I was interested, I was consumed with my own secret plans. My aunt and uncle's presence had made my Friday with Robert perish, and even Saturday, unless there would be a change in their plans. I strove for patience and tried to feel Robert's love through the distance. Yet the truth remained: I could not kiss *mind*.

Aunt Jane sipped her tea, set the cup upon its saucer, and said,

"So. Ba. You have arranged your plans more than you would have us believe."

I bobbled my own cup, nearly sending it to the floor. "I —"

She stopped my words with a hand. "But you are right not to tell us — indeed I would rather not hear. Only don't be rash. That is my only advice to you."

I had no idea what to say. Luckily, Uncle intervened.

"Ba is not a rash person, Jane. She can be trusted with discretion." He leaned towards the two of us in confidence. "We have sensed the difficulties of dealing with love in the midst of your father."

He knew!

My body reacted before my mind had time for restraint. It stood. Tea sloshed over the edge of the cup. "I . . . I can't . . ."

Aunt Jane set her cup down and came to my side, taking my arm. "Now, now, Ba. We didn't mean to upset you. When you go to Italy, we —"

I fell back to the sofa in a near faint, my cup and saucer flying.

"Water, husband," Aunt said.

All is lost, all is lost, all is lost . . .

I felt a damp cloth upon my forehead and allowed my aunt's soft murmurings to soothe me. "There, there. We will not tell your father about your plans to go with Henrietta and Mr. Cook. We would never —"

I opened my eyes. "Henrietta?"

"And Mr. Cook," Aunt said. "When they run off to be married and you travel with them to Italy, we —"

A laugh escaped as I sat erect. "They . . . ?"

Uncle put the basin of water back in its stand. "We won't speak of it any more if it makes you uneasy."

I thought about disclaiming their notion but decided against it. If thinking they held a secret would keep them discreet regarding the relationship my sister and Mr. Cook *did* share, then . . .

"I would rather you didn't speak of it," I said. "Not when Papa —"

Suddenly, Papa came into the room. "Not when Papa what?" he asked.

I resisted the desire to close my eyes and leave this moment. In contrast, I sat upright.

He opened his mouth—most likely to ask the question again—when Aunt Jane intervened. "Ba is looking so well, Edward."

Papa looked confused a moment, then peered at me as if I were a specimen in a cage. "Do you think so?"

"Why, don't you think so?" She moved away from me, and I noticed she slid the damp cloth beneath the folds of her skirt. "Do you pretend to say that you see no surprising difference in her of late?"

His assessment continued and I relished the flush I felt upon my cheeks, for surely the heat would make them appear in rosy health.

"Oh, I don't know," he said. "She is mumpish, I think."

Mumpish? Whatever did that mean?

He continued. "She doesn't talk for herself?"

"Perhaps she is nervous," Uncle offered.

"Humph."

Papa took a seat near Uncle, and they began a private discourse on the politics of the day. Snippets of "Disraeli" and "Corn Law" and "Lord Stanley," which may have caused me interest on another day, did nothing this day but offer relief that Papa was occupied somewhere beyond attention to me.

I made not a sound until they all left me.

Mumpish? The word proved a displeasure. Yet I was sure that I had shown as little sullenness as was possible. But to be very talkative and vivacious under such circumstances . . . I would have surely argued insensibly and caused more harm to our cause than good.

As the air filled in the vacancies of their absence, I pondered *mumpish.* Poor Papa. Presently I shall be worse to him than that. But then, I hope, he will try to forgive me, as I forgave him, long ago.

I hope. I pray.

❦

"Ba!"

As she had done two weeks previous, Henrietta burst into my room, her face flushed with panic.

She did not even wait for a question, nor wait to fully catch her breath from her run up the stairs. "We are moving! Papa says we are moving!"

The words found no meaning to me.

She came closer and said them again. "Papa says we are moving to the country for a month—if not longer—in order that the house may be cleaned and repaired."

Leave? We could not leave—I could not leave! I managed a question. "When?"

"George goes tomorrow to take a house either at Dover, Reigate, or Tunbridge."

I knew Dover—on the coast—to be nearly eighty miles distant, and believed the others to be less, but still at least thirty miles.

Too far for Robert and I to see each other, too distant for me to slip away to be married, and too far for Papa and my brothers to go off to work every day. Whatever house we let would be full of family, all the time, surrounding me, penning me in, keeping me from my love. After the month's absence—which surely could be extended—the weather would be too fierce for Robert and me to leave for Italy.

"I cannot move away," I said.

"I know. That's why I came."

"I must contact Robert immediately."

She gathered my stationery and pen. There was no more time for fear, only time to act.

❦

This is my wedding day.

Although I knew I had not slept fully the entire night, upon seeing it was morning, I opened my eyes fully and let the words linger and take root. Me. Married.

Me. Married. Today. September 12, 1846.

I rang the bell on my bedside table and Wilson rushed in. She had probably been up for hours. When I'd told her our plans, she had been very kind and very affectionate, and never shrank for a moment. I was exceedingly glad that Robert had agreed she could accompany us to Italy. I began to think that none were so bold as the timid when they were fairly roused.

She helped me with the covers. "We must go soon, miss. If you wish to stop at the chemist's for your smelling salts before we go to the church."

Yes, yes, I knew I could not proceed through such a day without them.

For the first time, I wished I had a pretty dress and not my usual black silks and velvets. To be pretty for Robert, to mark the occasion with something special . . .

There had been no time for choosings and fittings, nor could I have risked it. If one brother or Papa had found out their Ba was ordering a new dress in ivory or green . . . As for the expense? Although I could have afforded the dress, it would have been a frivolity. I was far more keen on saving my money to become *our* money. We had no clue as to how much we would need to live in Italy, nor the expense of our travel to get there. So much was unknown.

What *was* known was that my dream was coming true upon this day. My love would be fulfilled — or partly so. For we would not be leaving England today. Nor would we be together this night. Neither were possible. Today we would be married and return to our respective homes to pretend otherwise. I tried not to linger on the pain of it. The joy, and then the bittersweet parting.

But I could not dwell on the imperfections. Today we would be joined, under the blessing of God, who procured it for us, and who would preserve it for us, forever.

❦

To stand next to Robert in public for the first time, in St. Marylebone Church for *our* day, our moment . . . to hold his hand, to feel the brush of his sleeve against mine . . .

The physical aspect of the event faded compared to the bevy of emotions that swirled around and through me.

I listened to the reverend as he spoke of marriage, yet my mind wandered. There was room in me for one thought which was not a feeling: of the many, many women who had stood where I now stood, and to the same end, not one of them, not one since the building was a church, had reasons as strong as mine for an absolute trust and devotion towards the man she married. Not one.

I looked past the reverend to a painting of the holy family behind the altar. A family. Mother, father, son. Would I ever have a son?

My eyes strayed upwards to the half dome that crowned the apse. Jesus sat upon His throne, surrounded by figures in white. I smiled at Him, finding comfort that He—and the Father—were looking down upon our union, blessing it and rejoicing in it. For we were only here now because of that blessing.

I sensed Robert's eyes upon me. I looked at him, smiled, and knew a difference between myself and the women who had married here before. They may have been less happy during *their* marriages here, yet they had the affectionate sympathy, support, and presence of their nearest relations, parent or sibling. I had no one but Wilson to rejoice with me. And Robert only had his cousin, James Silverthorne. Though the absence of my family and his was a disappointment, it did not—could not—quench the swell of happiness that encompassed me.

The words "Robert, will you take Elizabeth to be your wife . . . ?" and "Elizabeth, will you take Robert to be your husband . . . ?" drew my focus back to the moment, to the response that must be made to solidify the vows we had already shared in so many ways, in so many other words exchanged on paper and in person. I was quite willing to repeat them again, in this place, before God and good company.

I will, I will, oh yes, dear Lord, I will.

The room spun with a thousand threads of words and thoughts and senses invisibly interweaving a cloak around us, embracing us with a warmth that surpassed all previous comfort. This was right. It was good. And it was ordained and consecrated by our God.

The reverend raised a hand above our heads. "In the presence of God, and before those gathered here, Elizabeth and Robert have given their consent and made their marriage vows to each other. I therefore proclaim that they are husband and wife." He took our hands and placed them one upon the other. "Those whom God has joined together let no one put asunder."

"Amen," said Robert and I, together, binding the moment in all eternity and with all blessings bestowed.

The moment hung in the air like a breath until Robert said, "May I kiss her now?"

The reverend laughed. "Yes, you may kiss her."

As I turned to my husband and looked up at him, I began to cry. For though we had kissed before, no kiss had been so sweet as this, the delightful first contact of one man and his wife.

⁓⁂⁓

We stood in the back of the church, alone but for the moment when we would exit into the world who might know us, recognize us, and not understand.

"But I don't want to leave you." I drew Robert's hands to my lips. "To go home, to pretend that nothing is different when everything is different . . ."

Robert tucked my head beneath his chin. "We cannot risk it, wife. I will not have your father steal you away to some hiding place where I might never find you. Our plans are nearly in place. Next Saturday, my love. We must hold off until then. One week."

He was so calm about it all, so controlled. So rational. I pulled back in order to see him. "Do you not wish to be with me now, Robert?"

A wry laughed escaped him. He pressed his lips into my hair and whispered his words against it. "Oh, my dearest Ba, my lovely wife, you have no idea how much I want to whisk you away to some private place."

I felt myself blush but shared his desire. I stared down at his silky cravat, and at the pewter buttons upon his burgundy vest, and envied their station, touching him, being so near . . .

Wilson cracked open the church door, and though she did not speak, I saw the furrow of her brow and knew her concern. "I must be getting back," I said. I sighed deeply and looked once more towards Jesus near the altar. *Give me strength, O Lord.* By my very prayer, I found it answered. To Robert I said, "Well, dearest, here we shall go. Necessity makes heroes—and heroines."

And so we left the church. Each one separate. Each one alone.

For a time.

~⋆~

I awakened with a start as my door flung open and my brothers rushed into the room like the sea through a break in a dike.

Sette sat upon the end of my bed and bounced to further wake me. "Why are you not awake yet, Ba? It is afternoon."

"I—"

Occy sat beside Sette. "Since she's such a sleepyhead, we should ignore her opinion about where to live, don't you think, George?"

George was not a kidder and took the question seriously. "No, no. That wouldn't be right. Ba is the eldest. She deserves a say."

Henry perused the bookshelves. "You should get rid of most of these, Ba. Dusty old things. Papa wants the house to be cleaned, and so he should have them start here."

Stormie came to my rescue. "N-n-n-no. Th-those are B-ba's."

Alfred draped himself in an armchair. "She can't take them with her, that's for certain."

It had all happened so fast, with my mind still mired from sleep, that for a moment I thought he was speaking of my not taking all my books with me to Italy.

Then, to add to the commotion, Arabel and Henrietta came in with two female friends from Herefordshire, and also Mary Trepsack, a friend with whom I was to dine the next day.

How I wished I could tell my sisters — and only them — about my marriage. But I dared not, for if I betrayed one pang, I should involve them so deeply in the grief of hurting our father, which otherwise remained mine alone.

And then, as icing to a bitter cake, Mr. Kenyon came in, looked at me, and said, "When did you see Browning?"

I felt my colour change, and I knew it was there for all to see, but I managed, "He was here on Friday." Then quickly, I looked to my sisters and said, "How many trunks are you going to move?"

And so the conversation sped away from dangerous ground.

Yet as my brothers and the girls chattered on, I did not dare to cry out against the noise.

But Arabel . . . she seemed to see through my reticence. She looked at me so intently and so gravely . . .

I could do nothing but look away. And as I sat up and adjusted my bedclothes around me, I had such a morbid fear of exciting a suspicion I was smitten with a pain in my head that seemed to split it in two, one half for each shoulder.

Suddenly some bells began to ring and one girl asked, "What bells are those?"

Henrietta answered. "St. Marylebone Church."

I nearly fainted. But then, as conversation resumed, I found strength in the bells. They were not ringing to ensnare or condemn me, but to remind me of the momentous sacrament that had taken place the day before.

This morning I should have awakened in my husband's arms, to all silence but for the beating of his heart against my ear. It was he alone I wished to see and speak with. All this commotion was of another world, an old world. My past.

My husband was my future.

But to get on with that future, I had to get through the present.

With the bells still ringing in my ears, I sat back and let the cacophony of the others swell around me but not through me. I was not a part of it. I was separate from the rest—as I had always been—yet now my uniqueness stemmed from a new purpose and a new title.

Mrs. Robert Browning.

FIFTEEN

I know the effort you made, the pain you bore for my sake! I tell you, once and forever, your proof of love to me is made. I know your love, my dearest, dearest Ba: my whole life shall be spent in trying to furnish such a proof of my affection, such a perfect proof, and perhaps vainly spent—but I will endeavour with God's help.

I tucked Robert's letter into the satchel I would carry to our escape. In the past six days I had read it a dozen times, letting his declaration of love give me strength.

We had not seen each other the entire week. To do so as man and wife when we were not free to act . . . *that* would have brought the more pain. And so a few letters had sufficed. Not enough, but to some degree.

I had not spent the week lolling in my misery but fighting through it. Robert had written that he had awakened on the morning after our wedding fully free of the headache that had plagued him on and off for two years. *What have you been doing to me, Ba?*

Indeed. Had I been the cause of his pain then, even as now I was its cure?

But alas, what was relinquished from him, came to me. In years past I would have spent the week in bed, nursing the pain in my head, surrendering to it. But now I could do no such thing. There was too much packing and planning.

Not that I was taking much with me. *Do not trouble yourself with more than is strictly necessary, Ba. You can supply all wants at Leghorn or Pisa. Let us be as unencumbered with luggage as possible. The expense (beside the common sense of a little luggage) is considerable; every ounce being paid for . . .*

This necessity for *less* had stung harder than I liked to admit. I always claimed that *things* held little import. But assessing the contents of my room and realizing they represented the contents of my life heretofore . . .

I was attached the least to the clothing. Fashion had never been a burning fire. Since Bro's death, black upon black had been my couture. It was the books that caused me the most consternation, for each one elicited a memory and represented some benchmark in my quest for knowledge. Why the heaviest items in my possession were also the ones I most wished to keep . . .

Yet it was not even the logistics of packing up a life that strained me the most, but fear.

Firstly, I worried that someone from the newspapers would peruse the church registry, find our names there, and fill a column with gossip. Robert tried to assure me: *For the prying penny-a-liners . . . trust to Providence, we must! I do not apprehend much danger.*

Trust in God. Yes, yes, that is what I clung to. That, and the love of Robert's family, who knew the truth. That they could love me when I was taking their son away . . . Robert's mother was not feeling well, and the thought of inflicting more pain on her by having our secret found out before we were safe in Italy made each day excruciating. For even though I had never met any of them, I loved them for their goodness. Dear kind souls.

Such love transfigured me and shamed me for my own father's lack.

What consumed the week were the letters I needed to write to my family, to tell them . . .

I took a moment to look at the letter I had written to George, ready in an envelope but not sealed. There was still time to change it. . . .

I throw myself on your affection for me and beseech God that it may hold under the weight. Dearest George, go to your room and read this letter. After reading it . . . George, dear George, read the enclosed letter for my dearest Papa, and then, gently breaking the news of it, give it to him to read. If you have any affection for me, George, dearest George, let me hear a word—at Orleans—let me hear. I will write. I bless you, I love you.

I am
Your Ba

The letter to Papa . . . I could not read it again. Whatever words I had used would be ineffectual and do nothing to stem his fury. If only I did not love him. He had good and high qualities after all; he was my father *above* all.

He had once called me the purest woman he ever knew, which had made me smile, or laugh, I believe, because I understood perfectly what he meant by that—that I had not troubled him with the iniquity of love affairs, or any impropriety of seeming to think about being married. But now, the whole gender would go down with me to the perdition of faith in any of us. The effect of my wickedness would be, "Those women!"

I had hoped I would have had the courage to address him face-to-face and say, *"With the exception of this act, I have submitted to the least of your wishes all my life long, Papa. Set the life against the act, and forgive me for the sake of the daughter you once loved."* Surely I could have said *that* and then reminded him of the long-suffering I had endured, and entreated him to pardon the happiness which had come at last.

But no. If I had spoken, he would have wished I had died years ago. As for the storm . . . it would come and endure a lengthy time. Eventually, perhaps, he would forgive us. That was my hope.

The family was moving to Little Bookham on Monday next. I had never heard of it, but learned it was six miles from the nearest railroad and a mile and a half from Leatherhead, where a coach ran. Father was successfully moving us to a nether land, which further pressed the necessity of our prompt escape.

That the entire family was packing was another blessing from God, for their actions covered my own.

Robert was taking just a carpetbag and a portmanteau and so I would leave my books behind, leaving room in my own bag and suitcase for the necessities of living. But his letters . . . I took them with me, let the "ounces" cry aloud. I tried to leave them, and could not. They would not be left; it was not my fault. I will not be scolded.

In just a few hours I would be gone. It was dreadful, dreadful, to have to give pain by a voluntary act—for the first time in my life—but so be it. Through God's sacrament my loyalties transferred to my husband, and his to me. *Therefore shall a man leave his father and his mother, and shall cleave unto his wife: and they shall be one flesh.*

Wilson came to the door of my room, her brow moist. "Miss? We must leave. The coast is clear—for now." She snapped her fingers and Flush ran to her. He was ready to go.

As for me . . .

I let necessity dictate the length of my good-bye. With one final glance across the room that I had once called my sanctum, I moved to the stairs and away, keeping my mind focused on the sanctuary I would find within my husband's arms.

❦

We were the perfect pair. I was nervous, frightened, ashamed, agitated, happy, and vulnerable. And Robert was imaginative, captivating, kind, witty, wise (though foolish in just the right places), charming, and giddily happy.

The whirlwind of our travels from London to Paris left us without sleep for the first two days, exhausted either by the sea or the sorrow of what we left behind and how it had to be accomplished. First, there was a stagecoach, then a boat across the Channel to Le Havre, then a coach again to Rouen, arriving at one in the morning. There, we were told our luggage had to continue on to Paris, so we were not even allowed to rest but for a short time in the travelers' room. Robert carried me into the room, eliciting odd glances from the other travelers gathered there. Who was this weakened woman accompanied by a man, a maid, and a dog?

I left their curiosity unfulfilled and took a little coffee as refreshment. I was not able to wallow in the solidity of being inert, because our diligence was leaving . . .

On to Paris. I lost my mind a bit that night, tucked into the carriage, seeing the five horses, then seven, all looking wild and loosely harnessed. Some of them white, some brown, some black, with the manes leaping as they galloped and the white reins dripping down over their heads . . . such a fantastic scene in the moonlight.

I knew I was a little feverish with the fatigue and the violence done to myself in the self-control of the previous few days, and began to see it all as in a vision and to wonder whether I was in or out of the body. But I was adamant to keep moving. I was the surprising force behind our frenetic pace, for I had a feverish desire to go on as if there would be neither peace nor health till we were beyond the Alps. It was as if Papa were after us, trying to catch me to bring me home, where he would shut me in my room and throw away the key forever.

His image, his words of anger, his feeling of betrayal . . .

We finally arrived in Paris on Monday at ten in the morning. Robert found us the first hotel we came upon and we fell into sleep. Upon waking, he sent word to our friend Mrs. Jameson and her niece, Gerardine, who were staying at a hotel nearby. They did not know we were coming, did not know we were married, but Robert and I had discussed the idea of their traveling with us the rest of the way to Italy. Months ago she had offered to take me along with them. . . .

The note gave the hotel's address and was purposely cryptic: *Come to see your friend and my wife EBB . . . RB.*

"Did the note say enough?" I asked him later. "Perhaps she does not know who EBB and RB are. Will she come?"

"She will come. For curiosity's sake, if nothing else," Robert said.

And he was right. She sent word she would come that evening.

I awaited her arrival with great trepidation. Mrs. Jameson—friend or no—would be the first person I would encounter who would judge our marriage. Would she see it as right or wrong? With anger or joy?

At the appointed time there was a knock on the door. My heart tried to break through my chest. Robert answered the door and—

In swept Anna with her hands stretched out and eyes open as wide as Flush's.

"Can it be possible? Is it possible?" she said as her niece watched from the doorway. "You wild, dear creatures."

I received her embrace with an equal dose of surprise and relief.

Never one to remain silent, she said, "Two poets, wed . . . each of you should have married a good provider to keep you reasonable."

Robert opened his mouth to speak, but Anna continued. "But no matter. You are a wise man in doing so, and you are a wise woman, let the world say as it pleases. I shall dance for joy both on earth and in heaven." She looked at me, then at Robert. "My dear, dear friends."

I was taken speechless. For her to be happy for us . . . God was good and abundantly merciful.

She took a seat upon a chair and pointed to the footstool as place for her niece, Gerardine—a girl of thirteen or fourteen—to sit upon. "So then. How long are you in Paris?"

"Not long at all," Robert said. "We travel on towards Italy immediately and—"

Anna shook her head, her finger wagging at him. "No, no, no, Robert. That will never do. Have you not looked upon your new bride?" She laughed. "Looked with the eyes of a stranger, not the eyes of a man in love? For she looks frightfully ill."

Do I? I put my hands to my face, wondering at the paleness of my skin. I was never one to linger in front of a mirror and had only glanced at myself. But as Anna's words fell upon our company, I realized what she said was true. I was nearly spent. I had come this far across sea and land with fear driving me on and on and on.

"Look upon her, Robert," Anna said. "See that I am right in insisting you stay in Paris a short while. Italy will keep."

Robert came to my side. "Would you like to stay here, dearest?"

Anna broke in. "Not *here*, Robert. I will get you a room at the Hotel de la Ville de Paris, where I am staying." She stood. "You simply cannot leave Paris without seeing the sights. The Louvre, my dear," she said to me. "You have not lived until you have seen the divine Raphaels." She fluttered her hands beside her head. "Unspeakable."

I looked up at Robert. "I suppose we could stay a few days."

"Excellent!" Anna crossed to the door, with her niece trailing dutifully after. "Leave the arrangements to me. And you, you concentrate on getting to know one another." With a wink she left us.

We remained silent a moment, stunned at the contrast between Anna's tumultuous presence and her absence. "We never asked them to join us in our travels," Robert said.

"Do we still wish for that?" I asked with a laugh.

He considered a moment. "It *would* be advantageous to have such a well-traveled companion. It might ease . . . It might make things easier, all in all."

I read between the lines. Although Robert and I knew each other well, in the past two days I had seen signs that the reality of my care had been overwhelming to him. If Anna could ease that burden for my husband . . .

And the idea of rest. Just a few days, to regain my strength. If it would keep me from getting ill . . . I did not want *that* burden upon anyone. I had waited too long for this release, this freedom, this joy, to risk losing it but for an act of common sense.

"Let us stay, Robert. And when the time is right, we shall ask Anna to join us as we proceed to Italy."

He nodded with vigor and I knew my acquiescence — my firm decision — was a relief.

The first fatigue has passed and the change and the sense of the Thing Done and the constant love have done me good. I am well, dear sisters, living as in a dream, loving and being loved better every day, seeing near in him all that I seemed to see afar. Thinking with one thought, pulsing with one heart. He says he loves me better than he ever did, and we live such a quiet yet new life, it is like riding an enchanted horse.

"Come, dearest," Robert said from the door to our hotel room. "It is time to go."

Go. Leave our two weeks in Paris and travel on towards Italy. Leave our leisurely walks, dining with friends in restaurants, or just sharing some bread, butter, and coffee in our room. Leave lying alone together each night, watching the stars rise over the high Paris houses, telling each other childish happy things, and making grand schemes for future work.

"Where do we stay next?" I asked my husband.

"Orleans, I think."

I knew his answer before I asked the question, and dreaded hearing it. I had told George to write to me in Orleans. So far, our days had been devoid of consequences. We heard nothing from England and tried to hold our trepidation at bay, finding comfort in our unavailability.

But Orleans . . . would we find letters there? And what would be their content? Acceptance or vilification? Congratulations were not dreamt of. Nor prayed for.

Although I believed God was the maker of miracles, I was not certain even He could change Papa's heart.

⤙❦⤚

Wilson unpacked my suitcase in Orleans. "I heard that Joan of Arc saved this city, that God talked to her and she led an army and—"

"Led an army against Britain. Yes," I said.

"Oh." She changed the subject. "The city is beautiful. The white of the buildings . . . so different from London."

"That it is." I was in no mood for her chatter. Robert had gone out to retrieve any mail we might have and—

He came into the room, a great packet of letters in hand.

"Mail," I said.

"Mail," he said. He nodded to Wilson. "If you please?"

With a quick bow, she left us. But I needed more than just Wilson's absence. "My love . . . if you don't mind, I would prefer to read these alone."

"Don't be silly. I will sit beside you and share with your joy, or your sorrow and—"

"No." I had thought much about this. "Ten minutes. I must meet the agony alone."

"But I will not let—"

I took his hand and squeezed, trying to showcase my strength. "I must."

He searched my eyes for any hint of indecision and, finding none, kissed me once and left me alone.

With the letters. My death warrant.

Flush nuzzled his nose against my skirts, but even he could not be a part of this aftermath. I sat upon a chair with the packet in my lap. I untied the string. . . .

On the top letter I recognized George's handwriting. George, my responsible, logical brother. Surely he would understand why things had to be done as they had been done.

I was mistaken. The salutation was simply *Elizabeth*.

Not *Ba*, not *Sister*, but my given name, which was wholly unused by family as well as friends. As far as *Dear Elizabeth* . . . even that endearment was notably absent.

How could you? I speak for all the brothers in stating that the pain you have inflicted on this family by your elopement is immeasurable. I speak for all our brothers in saying that both you and Robert are without honour. You have exposed our entire family to ridicule and scorn. The slur cannot be withstood. The whole world knows the reason Mr. Browning took you away and such a gold digger should suffer the direst consequences.

You wished for me to intercede with Papa on your behalf? It will not happen. It cannot happen. For we feel the pain that he feels with full power within our own hearts.

We have been insulted and will not forget it. Ever.

I bowed my head, stunned. I had not expected congratulations, but nor had I expected such bitterness, nor to be cut with a sword. And for them to believe Robert had married me for my money? It was preposterous. And we did not elope! For anyone to say as much . . .

And *all* my brothers felt this way? Even dear Sette and Occy, and shy Stormie? I knew they would be hurt that I had not told them in advance, but their response reinforced my decision. Such scorn revealed before our marriage would have been a complication beyond measure.

But not beyond management. We *were* supposed to be married. God ordained our love and blessed it. That we had not had to deal with the complication before the fact was an additional blessing from the Father who *did* love me.

Father. Papa. His letter sat next on the pile. At the sight of his handwriting, my heart fluttered and I felt a faintness I had not experienced in weeks.

I started to put his letter at the back, to be read last, then changed my mind. I had dealt with the effects of my apprehension ever since I'd left Wimpole Street. Although I had been able to shove the fear aside for long moments of joy in Robert's presence, it had doggedly returned to bite me with fresh teeth. I hoped for the best but expected the worst. So what was there to fear beyond my self-inflicted expectations? George's anger had surprised me. Papa's would not.

I slit open the seal of his letter. My eyes scanned the page, looking for key words that would either give me courage to read closer or warn me away.

Disappointed. Betrayed. Pained. Disinherited. Cast from my affection forever.

The words were hard and unsparing, and the last, cruel. I did not want my father's money. But for him to disown me, to declare that I had never existed and he would no longer feel any affection for me . . .

I let the letter float to the floor, not wanting to touch it for a moment more. I waited for the pain to take hold, for a wail to build and demand release.

And waited.

Nothing happened. Although I was hurt to my core, although I suspected the wound inflicted by my father's words would never fully heal, I did not deserve the full cup of vehemence he had served.

I heard the call of a street vendor below our window. *Pommes fraîches! Pommes fraîches!*

Fresh apples, clean air, lovely rivers, lush valleys, and happy people. The life I was living with Robert—even with the travails and trials of travel—far surpassed the life I had left behind on Wimpole Street.

I closed my eyes and let the differences between then and now solidify.

In this life we all get used to the thought of the tomb, but I had been buried in one, buried there in Wimpole Street. That was the whole of it. Just a short time ago everything had been different. For years—after what broke my heart at Torquay—I lived on the outside of my own life, blindly and darkly from day to day, completely dead to hope.

Nobody quite understood this of me, because I was not morally a coward and had a hatred of all forms of audible groaning. But God knew what was within. . . .

Even my poetry was a thing on the outside of me, a thing to be done, and then done. What people said of it did not touch *me*. My old life was a thoroughly morbid and desolate state, which I looked back on with the sort of horror with which one would look to one's graveclothes if one had been clothed in them by mistake during a trance.

I opened my eyes and traded the dark memory for the sunny day. I had survived death and had chosen—of my own free will, and with God's grace—life. That my father and brothers begrudged me the chance was not something I could change. I wanted their acceptance and their forgiveness, but I would not discard or waste the happiness that had been gifted me. To do so would be an affront to God, the giver of the blessings, the guide of my journey.

I looked upon the next letter, from Cousin Kenyon. How we had wanted to tell him our plans. . . .

> Nothing but what is generous in thought and action could come from you and Browning. And the very peculiar circumstances of your case have transmuted what might have been otherwise called "imprudence" into "prudence," and apparent willfulness into real necessity.

I laughed with pure joy. Someone understood our actions.

Heartened, I looked at the last two letters in the pack. One was from Arabel, and one, Henrietta. I opened them freely, and with highest hopes.

I was not disappointed. They were happy for me, elated that I was now with the man I loved, and *away*. . . . Tears appeared and I let them come. Tears of joy were always welcome.

The only hint Henrietta made of repercussions at home was to mention that Papa had declared he could no longer handle my finances—I suppose because I no longer existed—and so had asked Cousin Kenyon to do so. He had also boxed up all my books and put them in storage and was sending me the bill.

That his slight brought me relief was ironic. I would send for my books someday, and I trusted John with the rest.

There was a knock on the door and Robert peeked in. "May I join you now?"

I held out my sisters' letters for him to read. Tears appeared in his eyes, and he kissed the letters and declared, "I love your sisters! It shall be the object of my life to justify the trust shown in these letters. May God bless them."

Although I did not wish to distress him, it was necessary to complete the moment. "There are also letters from Papa and George."

"Are they . . . as expected?"

"Worse. If I had committed a murder and forgery, I don't see how Papa could have shown his sense of it other than he has done for my offence of marrying."

With a sigh, Robert leaned down and swept me up into his arms. He laid me down on the bed and sat beside me. . . .

For hours he poured out floods of tenderness and goodness, and promised to win back for me—with God's help—the affection of those who were angry. It was strange that anyone so brilliant should love *me*, but true and strange it was.

And so, it was impossible for me to doubt it anymore.

Orleans . . . the place where Joan of Arc, while depending on God, had defeated the British in a great battle for freedom.

Joan and I had a lot in common. But there would be no burning at the stake for me.

Robert would not allow it.

Sixteen

"Grazie, Signora."

"Prego." Signora Romano offered a little nod, then took her empty basket away.

Robert rubbed his hands together. "So. What did she bring us today?"

I removed a plate from the top of a deep pottery bowl and let the delightful aroma waft over me. "Mmm. Vermicelli soup." I uncovered more bowls. "We have sturgeon, turkey, stewed beef, mashed potatoes, and . . ." I indicated that Robert should reveal the contents of the last bowl.

"Ah, *delizioso*. Cheesecakes." He put his fingers to his lips and kissed them. *"Squisito."*

I laughed at his enthusiasm and offered him a napkin for his lap. And one for Wilson.

The city of Florence agreed with us. The Arno River rushed through the midst of its palaces like a crystal arrow. It was the most beautiful of the cities devised by man.

The daily meals brought to us by Signora Romano from her nearby *trattoria* were a constant pleasure. We never knew what she would bring, and she seemed to delight in pleasing us. All for the equivalent of two shillings and eightpence a meal. In London we would have paid twenty times as much. And our *donna di servizio* came in every day to clean for a few hours for only six shillings a month. Astounding.

Florence was our second home in Italy. During the months we had stayed in Pisa, the gossip was that we were millionaires, all because we had not haggled with our landlord over the rent. No wonder he'd periodically sent us gifts.

But we had learned much over the following two years. The key word in Italy was *trattare*: bargain. It was a hard concept to embrace, and we were still not skilled at it, not ruthless enough, and yet . . . we were aggressive enough for our tastes and pocketbook.

Robert and I grew up in Italy, in so many ways.

When we were traveling with Mrs. Jameson, she called Robert the most impractical of men, the most uncalculating, rash, and in short, the worst manager she had ever met. And it was true. At first. I know Robert's desire to please me and to ease my journey had led to unnecessary spending. But we soon adapted and found our way. We were told we could live in Italy for £250 a year and it had proved true.

We stayed in Pisa for six months. We did little but recover there, and regroup from our flight from our old life in England to the new one in Italy, which was spread before us like sunshine over a field of sunflowers. We led a quiet life, reading to each other, seeing no one, taking walks to the lovely baptistery. Though I was never strong enough to venture up the stairs in the leaning bell tower, I was much improved over my condition in London. Mrs. Jameson told me, "You are not improved, you are transformed."

And it was true. I was stronger and taking far less opium. By spring of our first year of marriage, I had gradually diminished my intake from twenty-two doses taken in eight days to that amount over seventeen days. And now, two years later, I took far less than even that. And soon . . .

Life was bliss. There was not a shadow between us, nor a word. Only an increase in Robert's affection, and my own.

Sometimes I felt he loved me too much, so much that I felt humiliated, as someone crushed with gifts. Robert's goodness and tenderness were beyond words. He read to me, talked and jested to make me laugh, told me stories, improvised verses in all sorts of languages, sang songs, explained the difference between Mendelssohn and Spohr by playing on the table, and when he had thoroughly amused me, he accepted it as a triumph. I was spoilt to the utmost—who could escape?

Though he was inherently obedient to me, he did not require the same in return. I remembered a day when Flush stole a piece of beef from off a plate and I failed to chastise him. Robert had said, "I do wish, Ba, you wouldn't let him do that with no consequences."

"Well," I said. "I won't do it anymore."

He surprised me by saying, "Don't say such words to me, Ba."

I was confused, for what words were more innocuous than mine? "What ought I to say?"

"Say that you will do as you please as long as you please to do it."

What? What he asked me to do was against my nature.

He observed my puzzlement and said, "Have you not had a lifetime of blind acquiescence? Enough rules and harsh consequences for menial offences?"

My eyes filled with tears. "Why . . . yes. I suppose I have."

"Then I hereby grant you leave from the pressures of all needless compliance—unless, of course, your desire *is* to comply."

His smile . . . it was the light of my life.

But as such, I had eventually seen that Pisa was too serene for him. Robert needed a place teeming with life and laughter and activity. And so we moved to Florence and found an apartment in the Casa Guidi, near the Pitti Palace.

It was situated one story above the street. On the side of the palace was Robert's room and Wilson's bedroom and sitting room. On the other side was a dining room, a drawing room, and my own room with a smaller sitting room. These last three were large in proportion and boasted tall coffered ceilings. There were eight large windows off the drawing room that led to a long balcony. It was not wide, but Robert and I loved to stand upon it and listen to the organ and choir music wafting from the ancient convent church of San Felice across the street. We often stood arm in arm and watched the moon rise over the church.

We took the rooms at Casa Guidi unfurnished for twenty-six pounds a year (furnished would have cost twice that). We enjoyed finding furnishings to fill it, and had created a dreamy look, enhanced by plants at the windows, tapestry-covered walls, and old pictures of saints that looked out sadly from their carved frames of black wood.

What delighted us most about Florence was the innocent gaiety of the people. They were forever at feast day and holiday celebrations, and came and went along the streets, the women in elegant dresses carrying glittering fans, shining away every thought of northern cares and taxes such as make people grave in England. There was little class distinction here. Rich and poor alike listened to the same music, walked in the same gardens, and looked at the same Raphaels. Everyone appeared dressed for a drawing room. They exhibited the most gracious and graceful courtesy and gentleness. The only annoyance was the constant noise of people walking, talking, and singing beneath our windows all night long. I came to believe the people never slept at night except by the merest accident.

"More tea, Mr. Robert?" Wilson asked.

His mouth full of turkey, he put a finger to his lips and nodded. Wilson poured a fresh cup.

Wilson was another blessing. She had proven herself to be far more than a maid. She was a friend, and partook of our outings and even our evening readings to each other.

I slipped a bit of beef to Flush, who wisely sat at my feet and not Robert's.

Our life was full and complete—but for two shadows that hung over us.

Firstly . . . my family. Or rather Papa and my brothers. On countless occasions I had attempted reconciliation through my sisters. But I still had not heard further word from Papa, and had received a few unkind letters from various brothers, reiterating their view that Robert—the real criminal in all this—had overpersuaded me and had married me for my fortune. George had graciously implied he would forgive me, but would never accept "Browning."

I did not reply to his letter. Rather, I supposed they meant to salute me with the point of the sword for the rest of my life.

That London's next winter proved to be as brutal as the previous winter had been mild seemed to have no significance to them. Would I have survived if I had kept to London? Apparently it mattered as little to my brothers as to my father that I was well and happy in my life. I looked back upon the mild winter of our courtship with full gratitude to God. It was His grace that had kept us warm, kept me well, and allowed Robert his frequent visits.

I sighed. If Papa had allowed, I should have loved him out of a heart altogether open to him. It was not my fault he would not let me. Now it was too late. I was not his nor my own, anymore. My love for Papa had always been a peculiar thing. He could have held me by a thread.

Luckily, those friends who knew my father well gave us their blessings. It was some consolation. But upon reflection, I came to realize that what happened to me could not have happened to anyone else in England. The condition of my family's household—the conditions under which it was run—were not the norm. How odd it came to seem, and yet, while living it, how blind we were to the true measure of its idiosyncrasy.

The second shadow that hung over us was twofold. Two miscarriages. In Pisa, I had not believed I was pregnant even when I had felt unwell and had felt pains. Wilson had suggested it was so, and *if* it were so, that the pain was not normal. She had also suggested that the opium I still took at that time could not be good for the baby. But I was so stupid and so enmeshed with the drama of what we had just accomplished with our marriage that I was in denial. Until seven weeks later—five months into a pregnancy—I miscarried. Dr. Cook was blunt in stating that if he had been called six weeks prior, everything would have gone as right as possible.

And then I suffered a second miscarriage last fall, when I was only two months along. I nearly died. I could not help but be bitter to think that if I had died, Robert would not have been able to contact the men of my family.

⁂

"Ba, you're not eating." Robert put a piece of fish on my plate. "Eat it and be strong. I thought we'd go for a walk this afternoon. If you have the time . . ."

Time. Yes. It *was* time. Time for joy.

"I don't feel like eating much right now," I said. "I have been a little queasy of late."

His face instantly mirrored his concern. "You've been without appetite for a good two months. And yet you continue to say you are well? I don't understand."

I looked at Wilson and held her gaze a long moment. Suddenly, her eyebrows lifted. In response I offered her the slightest of nods. She smiled, then rose from the table. "If you'll excuse me?"

Robert called after her, "But, Wilson, you didn't finish your meal." To me he said, "If she doesn't return, I will eat her portion of the cheesecake, I swear I will."

"You may have my portion too, dearest."

He sat back in his chair and tossed his napkin on the table. "Now I know you are not well. Should I call the doctor?"

"Not yet," I said. "But I will let you call him in seven months or so."

"Seven . . . ?" His eyes widened. "No. Really? Are you . . . ?"

"I am."

He nearly knocked his chair over as he rushed to my side, knelt on the floor, and took me into his arms.

I kissed the top of his head. "I will be more careful this time, dearest.

I will even relinquish my opium for the duration. Just in case. I am not a young woman. I am forty-two . . ." I took his face in mine. "I will do anything and everything to have this child—a healthy child."

So help me God.

⤎⁂⤏

The heat was unbearable. Although Florence was our chosen city, and although we called her home, in the summer the Arno nearly steamed with heat. And so we fled to the countryside, searching for relief by heading towards the Adriatic Sea.

Murray's *Handbook for Travellers* suggested Fano, outside of Ancona, would be an acceptable summer residence. . . .

I stood to the side of the window, clad only in my petticoats, fanning myself. "How can there be so much heat? The world will surely turn into a fireball."

Robert was also dressed—or undressed—to his trousers and shirt. "Do come away from the window, Ba. Someone might see you."

I knew he was right, but the need for air . . . I did not much care if the waiter saw me dressed so. The heat had made me demoralized out of all sense of female vanity, not to say decency.

"It is this hotel. Let us go to the church again, where it is cool," he said.

I stopped fanning a moment. "This is the third time you've wanted to go to San Agostino in as many days."

He shrugged, but I saw him gather his notebook and a pencil.

"It's the angel you wish to visit, yes?"

He took a penknife and began to sharpen his pencil over a newspaper. "It is the first time I have felt inspired to write since our marriage, Ba. I cannot waste this muse."

I nodded and reluctantly gathered my dress.

I knew Robert was disappointed in his lack of writing output. When we had first discussed marriage, our desire was to get away, where we could both create new works. And I had succeeded—to a point. I had recently sent a poem called "The Runaway Slave" to America, and had completed a portion of a new poem called "Casa Guidi Windows." I was also working on a new edition of my previous work—as was Robert, to a lesser degree. He had been editing but not creating anything new. His parents had believed in his writing so much that they had never required him to work otherwise. With my brother's mean comments about Robert marrying me for my money . . . I wished for him to feel the fulfillment of fresh creation—and subsequent income.

The painting of the angel, above the altar, that so inspired him was by Guercino. It had enormous outstretched wings and was touching a young child who knelt with prayer-clasped hands. The angel seemed to be teaching him how to pray by looking towards heaven. Perhaps the statue was filling a need in my husband beyond literary inspiration?

Once we were dressed we went to the church. Robert walked faster than usual, and I had trouble keeping up with him, but I did not hold him back. I was pleased at his urgency. I understood it, for when inspired one does not amble, one runs towards the source.

It took a moment for our eyes to adjust from the bright sunshine to the darkness of the church, but I embraced its chill. I let go of Robert's arm, allowing him to step forward towards the altar. His head was high, his eyes straight ahead, focused on the painting.

I also moved forward, taking a place on a chair near a side aisle. Robert stood directly in front of the altar, enrapt. I studied the painting while he did, wanting to see what he saw, feel what he felt.

The child, of about three, on its knees, hands clasped, made me yearn for our own child. Would it be born healthy? Would we have the chance to teach him or her to pray? My arms nearly ached with the thought of holding a child. I bowed my head. *Please, Father. Bring our child safely into this world.*

I heard Robert's feet upon the stone floor. He backed to a chair and placed his notebook on his lap. After only a moment's hesitation, his pencil flew across the page. To witness the full cycle of inspiration, from an ungraspable thought to a formation of words, to their declaration upon a page . . . my heart swelled with gratitude for this man, this vocation we shared, and this moment in this sixteenth-century church. How I wished I could speak with the artist Guercino and let him know that his work had completed its mission of touching another heart and mind. For what more did any mortal want?

How I wished to stand behind Robert and watch the words flow upon the page. But I dared not move and break the tenuous thread that connected my husband and the angel. He was always patient with me and so I would return the favour.

I do not know how much time passed, as my own thoughts traversed from here to there, from prayer to the corporeal. But suddenly, Robert slapped his notebook shut and stood. Only then did he look around for me, as though forgetting I had accompanied him.

"Ba."

"Robert."

He extended his arm to me. "Shall we go?"

"You are finished?"

He patted his notebook, the glow of satisfaction on his face. "I am."

"May I read it?"

He seemed taken aback.

I put a hand upon his. "It's fine. I don't need—"

"No," he said. "I will read it to you. At least in part." He offered me a chair and stood before me. He opened the notebook and held it towards the dimming light:

> "Dear and great Angel, wouldst thou only leave
> That child, when thou hast done with him, for me!
> Let me sit all the day here, that when eve
> Shall find performed thy special ministry,
> And time come for departure, thou, suspending
> Thy flight, mayst see another child for tending,
> Another still, to quiet and retrieve.
>
> "Then I shall feel thee step one step, no more,
> From where thou standest now, to where I gaze,

And suddenly my head is covered o'er
With those wings, white above the child who prays
Now on that tomb—and I shall feel thee guarding
Me, out of all the world; for me, discarding
Yon heaven thy home, that waits and opes its door.

"I would not look up thither past thy head
Because the door opes, like that child, I know,
For I should have thy gracious face instead,
Thou bird of God! And wilt thou bend me low
Like him, and lay, like his, my hands together,
And lift them up to pray, and gently tether
Me, as thy lamb there, with thy garment's spread?

"If this was ever granted, I would rest
My head beneath thine, while thy healing hands
Close-covered both my eyes beside thy breast,
Pressing the brain, which too much thought expands,
Back to its proper size again, and smoothing
Distortion down till every nerve had soothing,
And all lay quiet, happy and suppressed.

"How soon all worldly wrong would be repaired!
I think how I should view the earth and skies
And sea, when once again my brow was bared
After thy healing, with such different eyes.
O world, as God has made it! All is beauty:
And knowing this, is love, and love is duty.
What further may be sought for or declared?"

He closed the book and took it to his chest. I hated to break the moment with a word, but I knew he wished for one. "It is beautiful. I hear your voice in every line. There is such comfort there, with the angel coming down to minister to you, to offer you relief from the burdens of the world." My eyes filled with tears. "I am sorry to have created so many burdens for you. If I could relieve them like this angel, I—"

He sat beside me, his knees touching mine. "Do not say such things, Ba. That our path was hard does not mean it was not also right, nor that it is not paved with blessings. 'For unto whomsoever much is given, of him shall be much required: and to whom men have committed much, of him they will ask the more.' We have been given so much, Ba. And writing again . . . it is the *more* I wish to give back."

As always, our hearts and minds meshed with communal agreement. God was good to send an angel to minister to my husband.

I would seek to add my own comfort to the lot.

If it were possible to *will* oneself to be well, so it was during my confinement. I desired no company besides Robert and Wilson, and ordered white muslin from England to make curtains for my bed. Robert found a lovely chest of drawers to sit nearby made of walnut with ivory inlays. It was indeed a room fit to wait upon a birth.

A box of my belongings arrived from England, including a portrait of my father. I trembled to look at the dear face again, and yet I had it placed so I looked upon him first thing at waking and last thing at night.

"Why do you distress yourself so?" Robert had asked, with Wilson chiming in with similar words.

And though I tried to express why, I found there was no answer— none that could be expressed through logic. Although I was eminently happy in Florence and in my marriage to Robert, the desire to reconcile with Papa was a constant pang within my heart. Did he know I was having his grandchild? Did he care? My sisters had sent me various baby clothes they had made with their loving hands, but they refrained from mentioning Papa, even when I specifically asked. My letters to Papa, my eager hands outstretched across the miles, were never answered. Were they read? Again, such questions asked of my sisters received no response.

I was not certain which alternative suited me better—that Papa read my letters and did not respond, or never read them at all because he had deemed me dead to him. Either way, his silence was a pall upon my happiness.

I sat in my sitting room and hand-stitched a baby gown. I had never considered myself good at needlework, but found a curious talent in it at this late date in my womanhood. When Wilson commented on the excellence of the stitches, I teased that this was my new profession. Poetry would hereby be abandoned.

Actually . . . in my husband's case that was far too accurate. Although I had been encouraged by his poem about the angel at Fano, he had created nothing since. But more worrisome was his acquiescence towards the condition. "I am fine, Ba. When it's time to write, I will write. Have no worries."

But I did have worries. When he had lived at home with his parents, writing had consumed him. His parents had encouraged his focused application, taking care of all the concerns of daily living. But now, living with me . . . Robert was forced to attend to the responsibilities that had heretofore been embraced by others.

It was my fault. Would the literary world blame me for silencing a great poet? When in the mood, Robert could create prodigiously—as could I. But he was so rarely in the mood. . . .

Wilson entered, her face beaming. She carried something pink. "Here it is," she said. "The lining for the cradle. For our darling girl. And in honour of your birthday today."

I ignored the mention of my day. I did not make much of birthdays—unless it was the birth *day* of my child. "Girl?" I asked.

She tucked it into the wicker cradle and added a pink pillow. "Of course."

"How do you know it's a girl?"

"I . . ." She stood upright and cocked her head. "You are such a slight woman I just assumed . . ."

Ah. In truth, I'd also had the notion that I would have a girl because of my small stature. Surely someone like me could not give birth to a robust boy. I was not afraid of the pain—I had suffered pain before, and with birth, knowing the blessing of the outcome . . .

But I did wish for it to begin soon. *That* would be the best birthday greeting.

Hello, dear child, please come and meet us. . . .

⁓❦⁓

Robert sat by my bedside. Another pain began low in my back, and I gripped his hand hard as the pain grabbed me in its vise and squeezed.

"Ba! Cry out! Do not hold yourself in control on my account. I would rather you scream and cry than expend your energy being strong."

I could not answer him, as I had to concentrate on breathing through the agony. I shook my head at his words, and once the pain had released me, I said, "I do not cry out because I feel no need to do so. The pain is intense but does not control me. I am strong enough."

An Italian nurse was getting towels at the ready while Dr. Harding stood on the other side of the bed and nodded. "Indeed you are, Mrs. Browning. In fact, in all my practice I have never seen the functions of nature more healthfully performed."

"See?" I said to Robert.

Robert took out his pocket watch. "But it has been twenty hours. How can anyone endure such—"

Another contraction gripped me, more intense than the last. They were coming more frequently now, and the desire to push was demanding.

Dr. Harding pointed to the door. "Out, Robert. The timing is close now. It will not be long. You must leave us."

I saw the battle in my husband's eyes. He wished to stay by my side, but also, desperately, wished to distance himself from the pain. I gave him leave. "Go. I am in capable hands—both Dr. Harding's and the Almighty's."

Robert kissed me. "I adore you. May God keep you safe, dear Ba."

I closed my eyes and said my own prayer.

And then another pain came upon me and I was forced to trust. Completely.

❦

The baby cried out. A lusty cry, full of life.

"It's a boy!" Dr. Harding proclaimed.

"A boy?" I gave birth to a boy?

I tried to see him, but the doctor and the nurse were busy, with the baby between them.

Sudden fears flooded over me. "Is he all right? Is he healthy?"

A few more moments passed before Dr. Harding turned to face me. He smiled. "He is a fine specimen. Perfect in every way."

I, who was a good deal tired and exhausted, rose up suddenly in my spirits to a sort of ecstasy. I not only forgot the pain but I slapped my hands and clasped them together. "Praise God!"

The tears that had been held at bay during the labour now demanded release. I extended my arms to my child. My hands ached for his touch, my arms trembled with anticipation.

Upon our first touch, I was in love and unspeakable rapture. His face was oval—like mine—and his skin was pink with health. I put my finger against his hand and he took it with strength. He tried to open his eyes and I wondered what he thought about his first glance of his mama.

"Hello, dear one. I have waited a lifetime for you." I gently kissed his head.

Suddenly, Robert burst through the doors. "Ba?"

He ran to my side, his eyes on me, and then . . .

He too saw the child and I saw the love in his eyes.

"It's a boy," I said. "A healthy boy."

"May I hold him?" he asked.

I happily relinquished our son to his father. Robert made soft cooing sounds and rocked him as if he had owned this ability his entire life.

And perhaps he had. For I had just fulfilled the highest natural function of a woman. Was it any less miraculous that my husband — rocking his child and loving him with unconditional love — was fulfilling the highest natural function of a man?

My world was now complete.

SEVENTEEN

⁓

"I do like a man who is not ashamed to be near a cradle."

Robert did not look up to accept my compliment but continued to gaze upon our son: Robert Wiedeman Barrett Browning. Pen for short.

He picked the boy up and settled him into his arms. I could not hear what soft words he said and did not need to. I found myself the opposite of a clinging mother. I was very content to see Pen in the arms of others. Who was I to declare myself a glorious mother, knowing best in all things *baby*? I had never imagined having a child, so had long ago suppressed any inklings of maternal instinct. Not that I was a bad mother. God was good and kind in that regard, and reignited in me that which I had pressed into dormancy.

But I enjoyed seeing others pleasure in our baby. Wilson was a doting auntie, and Signora Bondi, his wet nurse, supplied him with more than enough nourishment. Although I had come through the birth with laudable ease, Dr. Harding had drawn the line at my nursing the babe. Seeing how the stout and rosy Signora accomplished this feat, I did not let disappointment gain a foothold. For my son to be surrounded by four adults who loved him . . . considering the distance between real family, I was happy to provide him with willing substitutes.

Flush was the only one who did not appreciate the boy. Used to getting my full attention, he now barked more often and sulked. I tried to give him his due but found my affections *had* been transferred from dog to son.

Wilson entered. "The post," she said.

My daily hope was that Papa had written to me, but once again I was disappointed. "It's from your sister," I said to my husband.

"Read it aloud." Robert paced with Pen in his arms, rocking as he walked from sofa to window and back.

I cleared my throat. " 'Congratulations on the birth of your son! Nothing can give us more joy. And joy is what we need right now because I am grieved to inform you that—' " I stopped reading aloud as soon as my eyes glanced upon the words *our mother*. But I could not stop reading. Yet as I came to the climax, my legs gave out beneath me.

Wilson was the closest, caught me, and helped me to a chair. "What's wrong?"

"Ba?"

Robert came towards me, the baby well satisfied in his arms. The sight of him now, with his child, after the news I had just read . . .

He handed Pen to Wilson and took the letter from me. I would have done anything to keep its contents from him—to erase the awful reality.

He grazed over the letter, verbalizing a word here and there like stepping-stones taken towards a far shore. " 'Congratulations . . . birth . . . son . . . joy . . . need . . . grieved . . . our mother passed away March the eighteenth. I am so sorry that—' "

Robert looked up and staggered. I helped him to the sofa, sinking beside him. "I am so sorry, dearest. So, so sorry."

He perused the letter again. "She never knew she had a grandson. She never knew!"

I thought about the date of her death. "But surely your family received notice before she died."

Robert slapped the letter against his thigh. "The doctor told them not to tell her. Her heart . . . she did not even get to see the lock of hair we sent to her."

This seemed especially cruel. To have lived to know, and yet to have not been told . . .

Robert rose and began pacing again—solo. "The last time I saw her was the week after our wedding. Two and a half years ago."

His head shook back and forth. "She was the kindest, most noble of women. As a child she knelt every night at my bedside and heard my prayers." He turned to me, his face contorted with grief. "We were going to England to show them our child. To show your sisters . . ."

"We can still go," I said. "Your father and sister would love to see—"

He shook his head vehemently. "It would break my heart to see my mother's roses over the wall, and the place where she used to lay her scissors and gloves."

I went to him and leaned my head against his shoulder. I had no words sufficient—

He broke away from me, his emotions too intense to contain. "We should have been contacted that she was ill! It's not fair to know too late. I would have gone to her and—"

"Sarianna knew that. I am certain she kept the news from us because I was in the last weeks of my confinement. She knew the complications we anticipated over the birth. That Pen and I came through with our health is an unexpected miracle."

He stared at the floor, his hand clutched to his chin. "I have to go. Out. I have to be alone."

He strode to the door, letting it slam. Wilson bounced Pen with soft cooing, but her eyes revealed her panic and distress.

"What should I do?" I asked her. "It is because of me he was away from his mother and his family. Because of me his mother never enjoyed the wedding of her only son, because of me she didn't know of her grandson. I never even got to meet them. How can I make that up to him?"

Wilson had no answers.

There were none.

⁓⋇⋇⋆⋆

As our child grew roly-poly, his father grew pale and wan. He did not eat. He did not sleep. He did not smile.

Robert grieved.

The heat of summer added an oppressive shroud to our home, and I knew that we needed to escape to cooler climes as we had done the previous year.

Robert had handled those preparations, but now he was no more able to plan such an exodus than he was able to plan an outing across the street. The tables had turned. I was the strong one, the one who had to put the needs of my spouse before myself.

And so . . . I found us a place to stay for four months, at Bagni di Lucca, sixty miles northwest of Florence. Its thermal baths brought tourists to the towns nearby, but Bagni di Lucca was the highest town, and as such was fairly free of travelers. It was near the Lima River, at the foot of the Apennines. Our house lay at the heart of a hundred mountains, sung to continually by a rushing mountain stream. Robert took to long walks in the woods, where he could be alone and not meet with a soul.

His soul was the problem.

Although his physical self improved in the lovely surroundings, his inner self was scarred. His mother's death and the guilt that followed made him question his essence, and question the purpose of love. He had been a good son to her—until he had left her. He had loved her as well as any mother could wish. But now that she was gone . . . had his love been worthless? Without her present in the world, the love they had shared seemed meaningless.

But love was eternal. Although I may not have known that before I met Robert, I knew it now. I knew it in his gentle care, his vibrant laughter, and the smile of our son sitting upon our laps. I had been on the edge of death when Robert came into my life, and it was he who had lured me away from the brink and made me see the possibilities in love and in a future where two lives could become one — and create another life in the process. Robert had saved me from death.

Now, it was my turn.

"I am off," he said at the door one morning. He donned a straw hat and gathered his walking stick.

"Would you like me to come with you?" I asked, for I had found strength in this place that had allowed me to wander the woods with Robert, for miles and miles, without feeling the least bit of exhaustion.

"If you'd like," he said.

My stomach clenched at his acquiescence, for this walk would not be like other walks where we said little. I had determined a way to give something to my husband that I had kept secret from him. And today, together in the loveliness of the woods, I would do it. I would share with him . . .

"Just a moment," I said. "I need to get my bonnet." *And the other thing too . . .*

Robert did not notice the small leather notebook as we kissed Pen good-bye and walked into the woods. I kept it at my side, concealed within the folds of my skirt. I slipped my other hand in his arm and we made our way up the path.

My heart beat in my chest with reason beyond exertion. Would Robert like my gift? Or would I find myself wishing I had kept it secret?

Neither one of us spoke, which was fine with me for a while, as I feared if words escaped they would tumble over themselves in a meaningless chatter. This day was not for chatter; it was for communion. And consolation. And compassion.

We came upon a clearing. A meadow of wild flowers lured Robert to pluck some blooms for me.

"For my Ba," he said.

I put my nose to the flowers out of habit rather than the need to enjoy their fragrance. My senses were elsewhere and threatened to expose themselves in odd ways unless I put an end to the waiting and—

"I have something for you too," I said.

"What is that?"

I spotted a fallen log, leaning against a rock. "Sit," I said.

He removed his handkerchief and began to wipe the rock for my own seating. "No," I said. "You sit. I must stand."

His eyebrows rose, but he took a seat upon the log and stuffed his handkerchief into his vest pocket. "So?" he said. "You have piqued my curiosity."

I attempted a deep breath to calm myself but was only partially successful. Would this be a mistake? Once given, I could never take it back. . . .

And yet I sensed it *was* time. I had prayed for my husband for many months, prayed that he would live rightly and turn his face forward, and press forward, and not look back morbidly for the footsteps of those beloved ones who traveled with us only yesterday. They themselves were not *behind* but *before*. . . . It was love that bound us—forever. Yet I doubted that, in his grief, Robert felt that love. He felt alone. Abandoned, and full of regrets.

My hesitation was proving to be onerous, for Robert said, "Ba, you make me worried. What is it?"

It was best just to say it. "Do you know I once wrote some sonnets about you?" My hand removed itself from my side and presented the notebook to him. "Here they are, if you care to see them."

He opened the leather cover where I had kept them. He turned the pages, stopped at a page past the middle, then read aloud:

> "The first time that the sun rose on thine oath
> To love me, I looked forward to the moon
> To slacken all those bonds which seemed too soon
> And quickly tied to make a lasting troth.
> Quick-loving hearts, I thought, may quickly loathe;
> And, looking on myself, I seemed not one

For such man's love!—more like an out-of-tune
Worn viol, a good singer would be wroth
To spoil his song with, and which, snatched in haste,
Is laid down at the first ill-sounding note.
I did not wrong myself so, but I placed
A wrong on thee. For perfect strains may float
'Neath master-hands, from instruments defaced,
And great souls, at one stroke, may do and doat."

"I have not the master's hands," he said. "And you had no need of such a master. You are a priceless instrument."

My throat tightened and I sat beside him. "If I am, it is only because of you, loving me." I had to say more. This was not about me, but about Robert. "And I love you, Robert. During our courtship you drew me away from death and gave me a new life. You loved me, a woman who had resigned herself to never knowing such love, a woman who felt unloved in ways more than she could dare acknowledge."

"You deserved to be loved. It was unconscionable that you were never allowed to be so."

"I thank God I was never allowed to love, nor to dream of it. For when your love came upon me, when my heart was awakened from its sleep, it was a miracle revealed. I would not give up that miracle for a few false loves in my past. Better for my heart to be untested than to experience a counterfeit to this love *we* have between us."

He pulled my face close to be kissed, then closed the sonnets upon themselves. "I wish to read these now. All of them. May I?"

I nodded my encouragement, though my nerves gave testament to my fear that he would not like them, or e'en more, that they would not lift him out of his grief.

He kissed my hand, then shooed me away. "Go on now. Go pick a bouquet and let me read."

I meandered away from him and did my duty picking the wild flowers that carpeted the clearing. But with every bend of waist or knee, I tilted my face to see him. Watch him. Gauge his reaction.

He placed the leather cover on the log beside him and removed one sonnet at a time. He read them aloud—though softly—which I knew would offer them at their best.

Suddenly, I panicked. I had not reread the sonnets for a long time. They had been written during our courtship and revealed both positive and negative emotions that had visited me during those months. Would some of those emotions hurt Robert? Confuse him?

I could not risk it. I approached him. "Robert, I have been thinking and I've changed my mind. I don't think it's a good idea you read those—"

He pulled the current sonnet to his chest and I noticed there were tears in his eyes. "You will not stop me, Ba. These verses . . ." He wiped a tear away. "I thought I knew you, knew all about you, yet these verses show me a new depth of your being."

Probably so, but did he like that depth? "Do they . . ." I hated to ask for affirmation but found I could not resist. "Do they please you?"

He slipped the sonnet in with the others and stood to take my hands. "Dearest Ba, these sonnets are a strange, heavy crown."

I wasn't sure what he meant by that.

He saw my distress. "They are a crown fit for your imperfect king, a wreath of sonnets to crown our love."

I nodded and let relief take its proper place. "I only give them to you now to let you remember the change you made in my life. We were such opposites, Robert. You knew about the outside world but had no struggles within. I suffered within but had little experience with anything beyond the walls of Wimpole Street. But now . . ."

"We complete each other."

"Yes!" My relief was palpable.

He nodded and took me into his arms. "I have been walking blindly in a world of destitution and pain, Ba. But these sonnets have replaced my grief with joy, replaced my depression with hope, and replaced my regrets with acceptance. I cannot change the past and be present with my mother in her last days. But I—"

I thought of a Bible verse that had given me comfort. " 'I will restore to you the years that the locust hath eaten.' "

Robert looked at me, confused. I tried to explain. "Regret is a human condition, but our God is the God of restoration. He urges us to let the past be past. The hole in our hearts carved by sorrow provides us with a larger vessel to be filled with love and happiness. Our pasts made us who we needed to be to love each other, Robert, and that very same love is the balm that leads us towards our future."

He put a hand on my cheek and drew my head to his chest. I thought of one of the last sonnets I had written, soon before our marriage. I quoted to him the first lines . . . " 'How do I love thee? Let me count the ways.' The list is long, Robert. Very long. And will grow longer still."

He smiled. "Then let us begin with number one. . . ."

EPILOGUE

Elizabeth never intended to publish the sonnets, but Robert considered them masterful, at an equal with the sonnets by Shakespeare. At his insistence, they were published in a volume of her poems in 1850 under the odd title *Sonnets From the Portuguese*. It was purposely odd, as the couple wanted to veil the love poems in something ambiguous. In actuality Elizabeth was "the Portuguese." The poem that preceded the sonnets in the volume was called "Catarina to Camoens" and it was a favourite of Robert's, bringing him to tears. And since he likened Catarina to Elizabeth, and Catarina was Portuguese . . . They realized people would think it meant from the Portuguese language, but they didn't care.

Although the Brownings stayed in Casa Guidi for years, they never felt settled there and traveled extensively, often subletting their apartment. They visited Rome, Venice, and Paris, and hoped to travel to Jerusalem and beyond, but Elizabeth's health and their income held them back. Her lungs were still affected by cold weather. And yet, considering the lack of good medical care, they were very adventurous.

After five years away, they also traveled back to England. Robert was hesitant to visit his family's home, so went alone at first. He found his father in love with a much younger cousin, and his sister Sarianna happily running the household. They had moved on with their lives. Robert disapproved of his father's courtship and forced an end to it, which led the elder Browning (and Sarianna) to move to Paris.

Both Elizabeth and Robert continued to send letters to Papa, trying to reconcile. In response they received a packet containing all the letters Elizabeth had ever sent—unopened—along with a scathing letter that astonished both of them in its hatred and vindictiveness. Perhaps Papa had never loved her at all. . . .

Elizabeth's sister Henrietta finally married Surtees Cook on April 6, 1850, and moved to the country in Somerset, where they eventually had three children. They had asked for Papa's approval, but he sent a harsh note condemning her for the insult and threatened to disown her. They eloped. Afterwards, visiting Papa at Wimpole Street, they encountered a "grand battle scene in the drawing room." But in this case, the brothers were on Henrietta's side. Eventually, the brothers came to forgive Elizabeth too.

Elizabeth's other sister, Arabel, never married and continued her charity work while living at home. In her later years, she too came to question her father's love, and his hold over her. . . .

Alfred was also disinherited when he married his cousin Lizzie in Paris, when he was thirty-five. She was twenty-two, and as a child had lived with the Barretts on Wimpole Street because her mother was mentally unbalanced.

The brothers and Arabel continued to live in the family home until their father's death on April 17, 1857, from erysipelas—St. Anthony's fire—a skin disease that could poison the blood. Soon afterwards, with astonishing speed, all the remaining Wimpole children embraced their freedom and moved out of the house.

Elizabeth grieved her father's death deeply, the regret of never being able to reconcile devastating her. She wrote to Arabel: "My soul is bitter even unto death." Papa had died "without a word, without a sign. It is like slamming a door on me as he went out." She hoped "that what he did and the extreme views he took" were the result of "a false theory . . . he did hold by the Lord and walk straight as he saw . . . but as for me, in these days of anguish I have wished—well, there is no use now of writing what—but I did love him. . . . Certainly I would have given my life for his life—yet he went without a word."

Their son, Pen, met his grandfather once by accident. If Papa found out the Brownings were in town, he usually sent the entire family away to prevent contact. But a few times he didn't know, and the Brownings visited Wimpole Street on the sly. On one occasion, Pen was playing boisterously with his uncle George when his grandfather came into the room and "stood looking for two or three minutes."

"Whose child is that?"

"Ba's child."

"What is the child doing here?"

Elizabeth wrote, "Not a word more—not a natural movement or quickening of the breath."

Oddly, as a mother, Elizabeth dressed Pen in elegant, embroidered, and lacy clothes and refused to allow his hair to be cut. He looked like an Italian prince from the past. Photos, even at age twelve, show him looking very girlish. Robert was against this, but bowed to her wishes.

After Papa's death, Occy married and had two children, but his wife, Charlotte, died in the final childbirth.

Sette and Stormie went off to Jamaica to work on the waning Barrett plantations. Stormie had two children (Eva and Arabella) by a woman of color, and ended up marrying their mulatto governess, Anne Margaret Young.

As for the Brownings' writing, over the years, Robert and Elizabeth worked on new projects. Robert had a collection of fifty poems published in 1855: *Men and Women.* He was very proud of this work, but the critics panned it, and the first printing of two hundred copies was sold out, then put out of print. He was very disappointed, as he'd hoped it would be a success and he could provide for his family. "As to my own poems," he said, "they must be left to Providence." They were. This collection is still printed and studied today, but during his lifetime, it was a discouragement.

He did not write another collection of poems until 1864, three years after Elizabeth's death. Instead, he dabbled in painting and sculpting.

In 1850 Elizabeth was in contention to be named England's poet laureate (when Wordsworth died). A supporter wrote, "There is no living poet of either sex who can prefer a higher claim than Mrs. Elizabeth Barrett Browning." However, Tennyson received the honour. In 1856, her novel in verse, *Aurora Leigh*, was published. It was the story of a woman artist who chose her art over a man, and a young, poor girl, who loved her illegitimate child. The theme focused on the difficulties of being a woman—no matter what your class. The story resonated with people, and it was a huge success in England, Italy, and America.

Robert was finally able to become the main provider for his family thanks to Elizabeth's cousin, John Kenyon. When Kenyon died in December 1856, he left the Brownings eleven thousand pounds, with sixty-five hundred going to Robert and forty-five hundred going to Elizabeth. No one could ever again accuse Robert of living off his wife. Henrietta only received one hundred pounds, and Papa refused to give Kenyon's estate her address. Papa received nothing and was incensed. It didn't help that before Kenyon's death Elizabeth had dedicated *Aurora Leigh* to him—a fact that must have infuriated Papa if he had found out, and surely he did. . . .

After her father's death, and then Henrietta's death (probably from a gynecological tumor in 1860), Elizabeth found herself in a state of searching. Unfortunately, she became interested in spiritualism and mediums, and became enamored with one medium in particular, an American, Sophia Eckley. Robert was vehemently against all of it, but Elizabeth desperately needed to reach Bro, Henrietta, Papa, Cousin John, her brother Sam, her mother . . .

This was the one battle between them in an otherwise idyllic marriage. Only when Elizabeth allowed herself to realize the messages from the dead that Sophia conjured up contained Americanisms that would never have been used by her loved ones did she wake up and see the truth.

Elizabeth never fully recovered from the passing of her father and sister. "As for me, I'm made of brown paper and tear at a touch."

She died on June 29, 1861, aged fifty-five, in Robert's arms. Robert lived another twenty-eight years, but never remarried—although there were plenty of women who were interested. One woman broke off their relationship, saying "the spiritual ménage à trois she was having with Robert and the memory of Elizabeth was going to cause her much more pain than pleasure."

Of the Brownings' marriage, author Julia Markus says, "Whatever had altered, trust had not. They breathed with each other's breath. At the beginning they saw the other as a brilliant poet, an amazing intellect, a compassionate and strangely similar heart. They learned their differences through the years. Neither gave over to the other. Each remained a complex and thrilled person. Both believed the years they spent in Italy together, her last years and his middle years, were the only years in which they really lived. Daring to marry secretly and to leave England to fend for themselves, they had actually brought each other to life."

> Let the world's sharpness like a clasping knife
> Shut in upon itself and do no harm
> In this close hand of Love, now soft and warm,
> And let us hear no sound of human strife
> After the click of the shutting. Life to life—
> I lean upon thee, Dear, without alarm,
> And feel as safe as guarded by a charm
> Against the stab of worldlings, who if rife
> Are weak to injure. Very whitely still
> The lilies of our lives may reassure
> Their blossoms from their roots, accessible
> Alone to heavenly dews that drop not fewer;
> Growing straight, out of man's reach, on the hill.
> God only, who made us rich, can make us poor.

Sonnets from the Portuguese (Sonnet 24)

Dear Reader

Truth is stranger than fiction. Actually, in the case of Elizabeth and Robert Browning's love story, it's better than fiction.

You might think the following odd, but when I write these biographical novels I don't get too far ahead of myself with research. I know the basics, then set in from the beginning and research as I write the scenes. The nice thing about this method is that I am often surprised by what I discover. Elizabeth's story has a bevy of plot elements that always make a good story: a shipwreck, an attic retreat, an oppressive father, love letters, clandestine meetings, a secret marriage, an escape to Italy, the birth of a child, and happily ever after. Sigh.

Elizabeth—holed up in her attic sanctum—constantly surprised me by providing real-life incidents that were every bit as interesting as anything I could have made up—or more so.

Here are a few examples of when real life made a good run with my imagination:

- It was ideal that Robert's family dynamics were the opposite of the Barretts'. He had experience in the world but had never been hurt or emotionally challenged, and Ba had little experience with the world but had been emotionally tested. Two opposites, come together to make a whole. I couldn't have cast it better.

- Ba tread carefully with Robert, not wanting to share too soon the grief of Bro's death. Don't we all do this? Wait until we can trust someone before we share the pains from our past?

- Robert moved too fast with his effusive letter after their first meeting, and Ba was frightened by it. The delicate dance of love is the epitome of a good story.

- Ba sacrificed her trip to Pisa for Papa—for nothing. He didn't even acknowledge it. This made me so mad, and yet it was exactly what Ba needed to realize Papa's love *took* far more than it *gave*. What great motivation to move her from the present into a future with Robert.

- It was incredibly poignant when Papa stopped coming up for evening prayers. That man!

- Ba was ignited by spring because she was in love, went on a drive, and picked a flower for Robert as an offering. Where's the violin music swelling in the background?

- The conversations between the Hedleys and Cousin John were perfect examples of misdirection—Ba believes they are on to her plans, while they are actually talking about Henrietta and Surtees. Ooh, the sweet tension.

- The idea of a recluse who lives in silence being overstimulated by music and running from the music of a church organ . . . it's so visual.

- In order to marry Robert (who had little income) and move to Europe, Ba needed money. Their marriage was possible only because she was the one Barrett child to have a sizable inheritance and income. A coincidence? I think not.

- They married and went back to their parents' homes that same day . . . how horrible. The delayed longing. Then the next morning her family commented on the St. Marylebone Church bells ringing. A novelist's ploy? Nope. It really happened.

- Ba's family packed up to move at the same time she needed to pack to run away with Robert. Talk about perfect timing. Also, this is one of those moments when we can see God providing a nudge to get us out of our indecisiveness. If Papa hadn't ordered the move to get the house cleaned (which was odd after living in the house for decades), Ba and Robert wouldn't have been forced to *just do it*!

- When I first started writing the book, I was concerned about what to do regarding Elizabeth's epic poems. I'd read some of them and found them very, very hard to read, much less fathom. When I learned that most nonliterary sorts were only familiar with her love sonnets, I was relieved, for in those sonnets were the words that touched me—they were the story. How ironic that with the depth of her knowledge and expertise in the classics and Greek, the work that has lived on for over 150 years did not come from her head knowledge but from the spillings of her heart.

- And finally, the ending . . . this was my biggest "You're kidding!" moment. When I found out Ba wrote the sonnets privately and only showed them to Robert years later, I thought, "Wouldn't it be wonderful if she gave them to him at a time in his life when he desperately needed to know how much she loved him." Shortly after, I found out that's exactly what happened! His mother died, he was deep in mourning, and she gave him the sonnets. The fact that Robert pulled her from the edge of death with his love and she did the same for him is beyond romantic perfection.

I found much common ground with Elizabeth — a woman with whom I would have thought I shared little. Yet her family loyalty, her work ethic, her health concerns, her quest for knowledge, her desire to avoid confrontation, her longing for praise, her self-doubt, her inner strength, and her utter joy when life gave her more than she ever imagined ... can't we all find parallel threads that traverse these emotions?

And now, for the pièce de résistance. It comes down to this: If Elizabeth had not mentioned Robert's *Pomegranate* work in her "Lady Geraldine's Courtship" poem (which she only finished to make two volumes of her work be of equal length, writing nineteen pages in one day), if Cousin John had not sent a copy to Robert's sister, if Robert had not read that story, if he had not written her a fan letter, if she had not written back, *How do I love thee? Let me count the ways* would not exist.

Nor would this book.

God moves in mysterious ways, His wonders to perform. ...

Nancy Moser

Fact or Fiction in
How Do I Love Thee?

⁓

Chapter 1

- The name of the Barrett home—Hope End—is actually not as menacing as it sounds. "Hope end" means "closed valley." Papa bought it when Ba was three, for £24,000. It consisted of 475 acres near Ledbury. Papa had the huge home rebuilt in a Turkish style, complete with minarets. People came to gawk at it. It was very isolated, which distressed Ba's mother but probably fed her father's motives very well.

- Torquay and the surrounding area are often called the English Riviera because of the beaches and mild climate.

- The "company side of the bed" is Ba's phrase. I love it.

- Balzac's book *Le Père Goriot*, which Ba is reading, is about a father who gives everything to his selfish daughters. The father's last words are: "Don't let your daughters marry if you love them." Ba found it "a very painful book." The comparisons to her own father are obvious. She thought about this book a lot. . . .

- Dr. Barry died of rheumatic fever at the end of October 1839.

- Little is known about Bro's romance. It was mentioned after the fact in a letter from Ba to her brother George, indicating that she had wanted to give Bro money so he could marry.

- No one knows why Ba's mother, Mary Barrett, died on October 7, 1828. After having her twelfth child the previous year, she had been well but for some rheumatoid arthritis. She had gone on a trip to Cheltenham and was a bit ill, but was doing fine enough for her son Sam to attend balls. Then suddenly, she was dead. A heart attack is one theory.

- The descriptions of Ba's room at No. 1 Beacon Street—"In the sea" and "from my sofa"—are hers. The apartment is still there, in the middle of town. It looks out on the harbor and is sheltered by the steep rise of Beacon Hill behind it. It is now the Hotel Regina.

- The scene leading up to Bro's accident . . . It is not known what Ba and Bro argued about the last time they were together, only that they parted with "a pettish word." Considering that Lady Flora died on July 5 and Ba was obsessed with the gossip about it, and Bro's accident was on July 11, it seems possible that his boredom and his penchant for being reckless might have led him to act rashly. This is my supposition, but it seems to make sense connecting the two events.

Chapter 2

- I do not know where the name Flush came from. My description in this chapter is a guess.

- As for the description of Ba's bedroom on Wimpole Street: It *was* on the top floor at the back of the house, faced southwest, overlooked "star-raking chimneys," had a window box, overgrown ivy, a painted shade, bookshelves, an armoire, a dresser, a table for her writing (and the table with a railing Cousin John had made for her), as well as a sofa she often used as a bed. And yet, I also found hints of a real bed, so I put in both a sofa and a bed. Pretty crowded, yet she often had all her family visit. I assume it had a fireplace. I read that Arabel slept in Ba's room, but I couldn't figure out how that would work, so I chose not to mention it.

- Papa took a 24-year lease on Wimpole Street. That's hard to imagine, but he was obviously hunkering down — and was confident his children would remain in the family home forever.

- I have assumed 50 Wimpole Street was a standard London row home; it would have the kitchen in the basement and perhaps a delivery entrance there. The ground floor (the street level) would have a dining room, the first floor (the second floor to Americans) would contain the drawing room, with the bedrooms above that. There would probably not be any running water. Metal pipes did not come into existence in London until after the 1840s. Even then the water system was run by private companies that only turned the water on for a few hours a day until 1871.

- Wimpole Street has many claims to fame. The Barrett home at 50 Wimpole Street is now a hospital run by Britain's National Health Service. Paul McCartney, of Beatles fame, moved into the attic rooms of 57 Wimpole Street, which was opposite the Barrett residence. It was actually the family home of his 18-year-old girlfriend, Jane Asher, and was where he stayed for almost three years. While living there, Paul, with John Lennon, wrote many of the Beatles' most famous songs, including their first American number one hit, "I Want to

Hold Your Hand," which was written in the basement. "Yesterday" was also apparently written there on the family piano. In Jane Austen's *Mansfield Park*, Mr. Rushworth takes a house on Wimpole Street after his marriage. Professor Henry Higgins lived at 27A Wimpole Street in George Bernard Shaw's *Pygmalion*.

- There are two movies made about the Barretts: *The Barretts of Wimpole Street* (1957) starring Jennifer Jones and John Gielgud, and an earlier 1934 version starring Norma Shearer and Charles Laughton. Jennifer Jones dedicated a plaque at 50 Wimpole Street, and a figure of the actress as Elizabeth was unveiled at Madame Tussauds Wax Museum.

- You may be familiar with the famous "Pinkie" painting by Thomas Lawrence, a 1794 painting of a young girl in white with a pink bonnet and sash. This was Papa's sister, Sarah, when she was eleven. It was painted before she and her brothers left Jamaica to finish their schooling in England. She died a year later of TB. Papa owned this painting, but I don't know if it was displayed in the Wimpole Street house.

- The gossip I mention in this book is real. Isolated from the world at large, Ba loved her gossip.

Chapter 3

- Their nicknames: Ba was for baby, Bro for brother. Arabella was called Arabel, and Henrietta was often Addles. Charles was Stormie, Octavius and Septimus were Occy and Sette. Alfred was nicknamed Daisy as a boy. No one knows why. I'm not sure if they called him that as an adult, but it seemed such a silly name that I decided to let Alfred just be Alfred. Daisy for a grown man? I couldn't do it.

- Papa's childhood: Edward Barrett's indulgent mother did him no favors. He was permitted to live in a dream world of his own. He never had to discipline himself by academic studies or learn how to get along with other people. He never had to assume many responsibilities and so became willful, isolated, and insensitive. Papa inherited money from his grandfather, and £30,000 from an uncle—a huge amount. But then... in 1831–32 everything fell apart when there was a slave rebellion in Jamaica and much of the Barrett plantation was destroyed. Papa went from being landed gentry to having to work. Money and an overindulgent mother explain a lot.

Chapter 4

- Her name: Virtually no one called her Elizabeth. She signed her letters to nonfamily members E.B.B., and family and friends called her Ba.

Chapter 5

- Lord Bulwer-Lytton was a popular writer of his day. Some famous phrases of his are "the great unwashed," "pursuit of the almighty dollar," "the pen is mightier than the sword," and "It was a dark and stormy night." Despite his popularity then, today his name is a byword for bad writing. San Jose State University's annual Bulwer-Lytton Fiction Contest for bad writing is named after him.

- Actually, Flush was stolen (this, the first of two times) near their home while Crow was walking him alone on Mortimer Street.

- The guinea did not exist as an actual coin, but prices were still quoted in guineas (got that?). The guinea was a nonexistent denomination worth twenty-one shillings (or one shilling more than a pound). A servant had all living expenses taken care of but earned as little as ten pounds a year. You were considered to be middle class if you had at least one servant. Some vicars earned as little as forty or fifty pounds a year. So five guineas equaled approximately five pounds, which was 10 percent of a vicar's yearly wage! All to ransom a dog.

Chapter 6

- Sette's nearly mortal wound from fencing actually happened in November 1842, but for the story's sake, I placed it in 1844.

- Although Anna Jameson did not have her portrait in Horne's *A New Spirit of the Age*, I fudged to further the story of her meeting with Ba.

- Henry Horne's book *A New Spirit of the Age* bombed. He'd chosen the wrong literary figures and was offensive in his criticism. He got in trouble for not including statesmen, artists, and scientists too. He'd planned to write other volumes encompassing those areas of expertise, but when this book failed, he wisely decided not to. He ran off to Germany instead.

Chapter 7

- Ba's book dedication was very flowery. Papa ate it up. It proved to him that she was dependent, was contrite for her flaws, and loved him to the point where he knew he had no rival. With Bro dead, he *was* her everything. For a while . . .

Chapter 8

- Mary Mitford rides a train to London. Ba can't imagine riding in one. With good cause. In 1845 there were no toilets on trains (not until 1892), no dining cars (1879), no lighting. Yet being able to travel 20 miles per hour was worth the limitations. Originally there were only two classes, first and second, second meaning you traveled in open cars! Ba would *not* have fared well under such conditions.

Chapter 9

- *Le Rouge et le Noir*—*The Red and the Black*—the novel by Stendhal that Ba read . . . Stendhal was considered the father of the psychological novel. Up until this time novelists used dialogue and omniscient narrative. They didn't linger in the heads and hearts of the characters. Ba read this book in its original French.

- Regarding the letters that are quoted in this book: Robert and Ba agreed not to edit their letters, so they were sent to each other as is. I, however, did edit them, as they often were a little stream-of-consciousness in tone, as one thought led to another, and another. I also changed the punctuation to be more easily readable. But the letters in this book *are* based on real letters. I did not change their essence.

- Robert noted the times and dates of his visits with Ba on the back of the envelopes from their letters.

- Surtees Cook and Henrietta were cousins. They shared the same great-grandfather, Roger Altham, whose daughter married John Graham-Clarke, Henrietta's mother's father. My advice? Don't even try to get this straight.

Chapter 10

- Ba's response to Robert's too-forward letter is real. It was written on Friday evening, May 23, 1845. It actually took her a bit of time to get the courage to write back. In fact, her letter starts: "I intended to write to you last night and this morning, and could not." No one knows what Robert's letter said, as it was destroyed at Ba's request—their only letter destroyed. But her "recoiled by instinct" response and a few other phrases are directly from Ba's real reaction. It must have been some letter.

- I don't know if Ba went out to post the letter, but it's a nice thought, yes?

Chapter 11

- Robert hated Ba's opium use, but she saw nothing wrong with it—and never stopped using it. It was not considered a bad drug as it is now. Another word for opium is laudanum. It was taken by drops mixed with alcohol. Ba took forty doses a day, but as biographer Margaret Forster said, "Without knowing the strength of the alcohol with which the grains of opium were mixed it is still impossible to estimate the dosage correctly." Ba did not suffer many of the negative symptoms often associated with opium misuse: a permanent headache, loss of memory, hallucinations. But she was addicted to it.

- The conversation about Bro's death is taken from an August 25, 1845, letter that Ba sent to Robert. It was the first time she ever spoke of it—to anyone.

Chapter 12

- According to Ba's letter of January 19, 1846, the London post did not run on Sundays (to her dismay) but often came more than once a day. The postman knocked on her door—at 8 PM—with a letter! A letter could be sent for a penny for a half ounce, hence the term *penny post*.

- The timing of when Ba wrote the sonnets that were to become her legacy is unknown. She wrote them for her eyes only. Yet the specific

333

emotions expressed in the sonnets seem to fit with some of the incidents mentioned in their letters. Make sure you read the *Sonnets From the Portuguese* offered in the back of this book. They are lovely.

- It is interesting that both Ba and Henrietta loved men who possessed personalities opposite that of their father. Neither Robert nor Surtees were controlling. Both were nurturing. Even Arabel eventually found a nurturing man to have in her life—a pastor friend. But they never married.

- In chapter 12, the verses Elizabeth quotes—1 Corinthians 13:4–7 in the King James Version—oddly use the word *charity* instead of *love*. I assume that eventually proved to be an inaccurate translation, since all versions since have used *love*. I inserted *love* for *charity*.

- I could not find any reference to an actual proposal like this, because Robert was effusive from the beginning about his feelings for Ba, and often talked of their future together. But I thought there needed to be an actual proposal moment, and so . . . here it is.

Chapter 13

- Robert was not experienced with women but tended to like those older than he. His "loves" before Ba had been sisters who were nine and seven years older (Eliza and Sarah Flower) and Euprasia Fanny Haworth, who was eleven years his elder. They were more patrons than girlfriends. In many ways, Robert didn't need the love of a woman. He had his mother and sister to adore him. Biographer Frances Winwar said, "Love itself, however, the great gift of heart, soul, emotion, imagination, of self complete yet yearning for completion, Browning had given to no woman. . . . With Browning love and worship were one."

- The scenes with Ba and Henrietta and then Ba and her father are fictitious. Her brothers never knew about her relationship with Robert (although they probably guessed but were too chicken to ask), but she did tell her sisters, as per an October 11, 1845, letter. I like to imagine her *trying* to confront her father. . . .

- Constance Hedley, Ba's cousin who was getting married, was actually named Arabella. But since Ba had a sister of the same name, I changed her name to be less confusing. The same applies for her uncle Robert, whom I named Bernard. The nerve-wracking conversations with Aunt Jane in chapters 13 and 14 really happened and helped spur Ba toward a quicker marriage.

- Ba lived in a world without music, but when she was exposed, it affected her greatly. The incident of going to church and being frightened by the grand organ is real. Another time her cousin sang a sad song from Bellini's opera *I Puritani* that caused her to leave the room, sobbing. Today it's hard to imagine *not* having music in our lives.

- Ba's prayer, *May God direct us toward the best way*, is real, and is taken from her letter dated July 16, 1846, to Robert.

Chapter 14

- The storm that kept Robert at the Barrett house, the one she finally sent him into, was the worst storm to hit London since 1809.

- The conversation with Cousin John, where Ba thinks he's suspicious about her relationship with Robert, and he's actually talking about Henrietta and Surtees Cook, is real. Things were definitely getting dicey!

- Hearing the St. Marylebone Church bells and the verbal exchange really happened!

Chapter 15

- I find it interesting (and very fortunate) that the Barrett household was packing for a move just when Ba needed to pack for her escape with Robert. God was watching out for her.

- Although Robert and Ba had to travel light when they left England, both of them took their letters with them—and aren't we glad they did! During their courtship they exchanged 573 letters and had 91 meetings. The first time they met outside her room was for their marriage. You can see these letters in a collection at Wellesley College in Massachusetts. They have the mail slot from Wimpole Street too. Another good museum is at Baylor University in Waco, Texas. They have various Barrett-Browning furniture, jewelry, household goods, a lock of Ba's hair . . .

- Papa boxed up Ba's books, and she had to pay five pounds a year for storage until she sent for them two years later.

- Casa Guidi in Florence still exists and is open to the public. It was a suite of eight rooms. The history of the building dates back to the fifteenth century. Robert and Elizabeth Barrett Browning leased one of the apartments in 1847, and it was their home for the remaining fourteen years of their married life. Pen Browning acquired the palazzo in 1893 and initiated efforts to establish Casa Guidi as a memorial to his parents. He died in 1912, with his wish uncompleted. In 1970, Casa Guidi was nearly converted into commercial offices. Through a fund-raising campaign initiated by the New York Browning Society, seven rooms of the original eight were retained. Funding issues led to Eton College taking it over in 1993, when it was restored.

Chapter 16

- Ba did give up morphine/opium while she was pregnant with Pen, and Robert said that by doing so she exhibited an extraordinary strength equal to that of a thousand men.

- The angel portrait that so inspired Robert also inspired the Fano Club, started by William Lyon Phelps, a professor emeritus of English literature at Yale University who was fascinated with the inspiration for Robert's poem. On Easter in 1912, Phelps led a small group to Fano, Italy, where they saw the painting "The Guardian Angel" in San Agostino. Between them, they gathered 75 postcards to mail to America; unfortunately, all of the postcards went down on the *Titanic*. The Fano Club still exists. In order to become a member, you must make a pilgrimage to the church, see the painting, and mail a postcard from Fano to the library at Baylor University stating that you have seen the painting.

Chapter 17

- Sarianna sent three letters to Robert to tell him of their mother's death. The first conveyed congratulations on the birth of Robert's son, the next said their mother was very ill, and then the third told Robert of her death. The second letter was actually written when she was already dead, but Sarianna was trying to lessen the shock. Although Robert's family received word of Pen's birth before Mrs. Browning's death, they did not tell her (on doctor's orders), thinking it would "overexcite the woman who was now dying from a sudden ossification of the heart." As a grandmother myself, I think they should have told her. He turned out to be the only grandchild. Sarianna never married and spent her life committed to her father, her brother, and her nephew.

Discussion Questions for
How Do I Love Thee?

⟨✦⟩

1. In chapter 2, Papa delays bringing Ba back to London from Torquay for a year after Bro's death. What do you think his motives were?

2. In chapter 3, Ba says: "Knowing the foibles and weaknesses of myself and my siblings, I could not consider the gift of more freedom as being a good thing, or wise. Together, we Barretts became strong, each providing some needed aspect of a whole." How could freedom be a bad thing? In your own life, how do members of your family provide "some needed aspect of a whole"?

3. Ba gets frustrated that, as a woman, she can't have a job, and Bro—who can and should work—doesn't want to. Though nowadays we would not want to go back to the way things were, what are the positive and negative aspects of women succeeding outside the home?

4. At first Ba wrote anonymously (as did Jane Austen forty years earlier). Put yourself in their place. How would it make you feel to not be able to put your name on your work? How might *not* taking credit for something be a character builder?

5. Ba is petrified of meeting people, of going out into the world. Does this trait elicit your compassion or your disgust? Why?

6. When Flush is kidnapped in chapter 5, Papa refuses to pay the five-guinea ransom and the thief leaves. Ba wants to confront her father, but Crow says, "You can't do that. You know you can't. Your father . . ." Ba's internal response is, *She was right. If I were to burst into the dining room and demand my father make the ridiculous payment . . . All that I was, all that I tried so hard to be, would be lost.* What do you think she was talking about?

7. In chapter 8, when Ba gets her first letter from Robert, it is very flowery and gushing: *I love your verses with all my heart, dear Miss Barrett . . .* She had no way to know this was his normal tone—extravagant and full of flattery. Yet what might have happened if his letter had been more formal, like the ones she was used to getting from colleagues?

8. In chapter 9, Ba is at a turning point between her old life and the life Robert inspires. What do you think would have happened to Ba if Robert hadn't come along, if he hadn't sent that first letter?

9. After their first meeting, Robert goes overboard and moves the relationship along too fast, too soon. How would you have reacted to his actions?

10. Chapter 11 brings about a huge revelation in Ba's life. She wants to go to Pisa, but Papa is against it. She decides to sacrifice her wants for his. But then, he does not appreciate her sacrifice and she is faced with the limitations of his love for her. Name a time you have sacrificed for a loved one, only to find your act unappreciated. What did you feel? What did you learn?

11. In chapter 12, Ba's world is widening because of loving and being loved. She begins to write her sonnets for her own satisfaction and release. Do you keep a journal or diary? Or poems? What do you gain through this?

12. Do you think Bro's death prepared Ba for the love that was to come—left a hole to be filled? How might things have been different if Bro had lived?

13. As Robert and Ba plan their marriage, how does she begin to exhibit courage?

14. In chapter 14, Ba shares the story about the tree hit by lightning in Hope End. . . . I see a symbolism in regard to Christ, the branches, the bird singing, and even the name of their home. Read the passage aloud. What symbolism can you see?

15. In chapter 14, what do you think about their plans to marry and then return to their homes for a week? Should they have eloped to France or Italy and married there? Why or why not?

16. Traveling in Europe, Ba finally receives letters from Papa and George. Horrible letters. Putting yourself in the men's shoes . . . what fueled their anger? Did they have a right to be angry?

17. Living in Italy was at times idyllic, yet Robert wasn't writing very much and was proving to *not* be a good provider. Should Ba have reacted differently than she did? Were there signs regarding this element of Robert's character that Ba missed?

18. The Brownings' romance and parenthood was especially poignant because it came later in life. How might their relationship have been different if they had met twenty years earlier?

19. It's ironic that Elizabeth is known for the sonnets she wrote for herself. Her other works have fallen into a measure of literary obscurity. What would you like to be known for? What legacy will you leave?

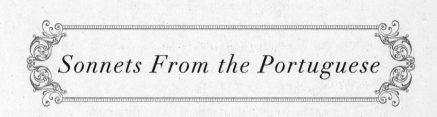

Sonnets From the Portuguese

By Elizabeth Barrett Browning

INDEX OF FIRST LINES

NANCY MOSER

I

I thought once how Theocritus had sung
Of the sweet years, the dear and wished-for years,
Who each one in a gracious hand appears
To bear a gift for mortals, old or young:
And, as I mused it in his antique tongue,
I saw, in gradual vision through my tears,
The sweet, sad years, the melancholy years,
Those of my own life, who by turns had flung
A shadow across me. Straightway I was 'ware,
So weeping, how a mystic Shape did move
Behind me, and drew me backward by the hair;
And a voice said in mastery, while I strove, —
"Guess now who holds thee!" — "Death," I said, But, there,
The silver answer rang, "Not Death, but Love."

II

But only three in all God's universe
Have heard this word thou hast said, — Himself, beside
Thee speaking, and me listening! and replied
One of us . . . that was God, . . . and laid the curse
So darkly on my eyelids, as to amerce
My sight from seeing thee, — that if I had died,
The death-weights, placed there, would have signified
Less absolute exclusion. "Nay" is worse
From God than from all others, O my friend!
Men could not part us with their worldly jars,
Nor the seas change us, nor the tempests bend;
Our hands would touch for all the mountain-bars:
And, heaven being rolled between us at the end,
We should but vow the faster for the stars.

III

Unlike are we, unlike, O princely Heart!
Unlike our uses and our destinies.
Our ministering two angels look surprise
On one another, as they strike athwart
Their wings in passing. Thou, bethink thee, art
A guest for queens to social pageantries,
With gages from a hundred brighter eyes
Than tears even can make mine, to play thy part
Of chief musician. What hast thou to do
With looking from the lattice-lights at me,
A poor, tired, wandering singer, singing through
The dark, and leaning up a cypress tree?
The chrism is on thine head,—on mine, the dew,—
And Death must dig the level where these agree.

IV

Thou hast thy calling to some palace-floor,
Most gracious singer of high poems! where
The dancers will break footing, from the care
Of watching up thy pregnant lips for more.
And dost thou lift this house's latch too poor
For hand of thine? and canst thou think and bear
To let thy music drop here unaware
In folds of golden fulness at my door?
Look up and see the casement broken in,
The bats and owlets builders in the roof!
My cricket chirps against thy mandolin.
Hush, call no echo up in further proof
Of desolation! there's a voice within
That weeps . . . as thou must sing . . . alone, aloof.

V

I lift my heavy heart up solemnly,
As once Electra her sepulchral urn,
And, looking in thine eyes, I over-turn
The ashes at thy feet. Behold and see
What a great heap of grief lay hid in me,
And how the red wild sparkles dimly burn
Through the ashen greyness. If thy foot in scorn
Could tread them out to darkness utterly,
It might be well perhaps. But if instead
Thou wait beside me for the wind to blow
The grey dust up, . . . those laurels on thine head,
O my Belovèd, will not shield thee so,
That none of all the fires shall scorch and shred
The hair beneath. Stand further off then! go!

VI

Go from me. Yet I feel that I shall stand
Henceforward in thy shadow. Nevermore
Alone upon the threshold of my door
Of individual life, I shall command
The uses of my soul, nor lift my hand
Serenely in the sunshine as before,
Without the sense of that which I forbore —
Thy touch upon the palm. The widest land
Doom takes to part us, leaves thy heart in mine
With pulses that beat double. What I do
And what I dream include thee, as the wine
Must taste of its own grapes. And when I sue
God for myself, He hears that name of thine,
And sees within my eyes the tears of two.

VII

The face of all the world is changed, I think,
Since first I heard the footsteps of thy soul
Move still, oh, still, beside me, as they stole
Betwixt me and the dreadful outer brink
Of obvious death, where I, who thought to sink,
Was caught up into love, and taught the whole
Of life in a new rhythm. The cup of dole
God gave for baptism, I am fain to drink,
And praise its sweetness, Sweet, with thee anear.
The names of country, heaven, are changed away
For where thou art or shalt be, there or here;
And this . . . this lute and song . . . loved yesterday,
(The singing angels know) are only dear
Because thy name moves right in what they say.

VIII

What can I give thee back, O liberal
And princely giver, who hast brought the gold
And purple of thine heart, unstained, untold,
And laid them on the outside of the wall
For such as I to take or leave withal,
In unexpected largesse? am I cold,
Ungrateful, that for these most manifold
High gifts, I render nothing back at all?
Not so; not cold,—but very poor instead.
Ask God who knows. For frequent tears have run
The colours from my life, and left so dead
And pale a stuff, it were not fitly done
To give the same as pillow to thy head.
Go farther! let it serve to trample on.

IX

Can it be right to give what I can give?
To let thee sit beneath the fall of tears
As salt as mine, and hear the sighing years
Re-sighing on my lips renunciative
Through those infrequent smiles which fail to live
For all thy adjurations? O my fears,
That this can scarce be right! We are not peers
So to be lovers; and I own, and grieve,
That givers of such gifts as mine are, must
Be counted with the ungenerous. Out, alas!
I will not soil thy purple with my dust,
Nor breathe my poison on thy Venice-glass,
Nor give thee any love—which were unjust.
Beloved, I only love thee! let it pass.

X

Yet, love, mere love, is beautiful indeed
And worthy of acceptation. Fire is bright,
Let temple burn, or flax; an equal light
Leaps in the flame from cedar-plank or weed:
And love is fire. And when I say at need
I love thee . . . mark! . . . I love thee—in thy sight
I stand transfigured, glorified aright,
With conscience of the new rays that proceed
Out of my face toward thine. There's nothing low
In love, when love the lowest: meanest creatures
Who love God, God accepts while loving so.
And what I feel, across the inferior features
Of what I am, doth flash itself, and show
How that great work of Love enhances Nature's.

XI

And therefore if to love can be desert,
I am not all unworthy. Cheeks as pale
As these you see, and trembling knees that fail
To bear the burden of a heavy heart,—
This weary minstrel-life that once was girt
To climb Aornus, and can scarce avail
To pipe now 'gainst the valley nightingale
A melancholy music,—why advert
To these things? O Belovèd, it is plain
I am not of thy worth nor for thy place!
And yet, because I love thee, I obtain
From that same love this vindicating grace
To live on still in love, and yet in vain,—
To bless thee, yet renounce thee to thy face.

XII

Indeed this very love which is my boast,
And which, when rising up from breast to brow,
Doth crown me with a ruby large enow
To draw men's eyes and prove the inner cost,—
This love even, all my worth, to the uttermost,
I should not love withal, unless that thou
Hadst set me an example, shown me how,
When first thine earnest eyes with mine were crossed,
And love called love. And thus, I cannot speak
Of love even, as a good thing of my own:
Thy soul hath snatched up mine all faint and weak,
And placed it by thee on a golden throne,—
And that I love (O soul, we must be meek!)
Is by thee only, whom I love alone.

XIII

And wilt thou have me fashion into speech
The love I bear thee, finding words enough,
And hold the torch out, while the winds are rough,
Between our faces, to cast light on each?—
I drop it at thy feet. I cannot teach
My hand to hold my spirits so far off
From myself—me—that I should bring thee proof
In words, of love hid in me out of reach.
Nay, let the silence of my womanhood
Commend my woman-love to thy belief,—
Seeing that I stand unwon, however wooed,
And rend the garment of my life, in brief,
By a most dauntless, voiceless fortitude,
Lest one touch of this heart convey its grief.

XIV

If thou must love me, let it be for nought
Except for love's sake only. Do not say
"I love her for her smile—her look—her way
Of speaking gently,—for a trick of thought
That falls in well with mine, and certes brought
A sense of pleasant ease on such a day"—
For these things in themselves, Belovèd, may
Be changed, or change for thee,—and love, so wrought,
May be unwrought so. Neither love me for
Thine own dear pity's wiping my cheeks dry,—
A creature might forget to weep, who bore
Thy comfort long, and lose thy love thereby!
But love me for love's sake, that evermore
Thou may'st love on, through love's eternity.

XV

Accuse me not, beseech thee, that I wear
Too calm and sad a face in front of thine;
For we two look two ways, and cannot shine
With the same sunlight on our brow and hair.
On me thou lookest with no doubting care,
As on a bee shut in a crystalline;
Since sorrow hath shut me safe in love's divine,
And to spread wing and fly in the outer air
Were most impossible failure, if I strove
To fail so. But I look on thee—on thee—
Beholding, besides love, the end of love,
Hearing oblivion beyond memory;
As one who sits and gazes from above,
Over the rivers to the bitter sea.

XVI

And yet, because thou overcomest so,
Because thou art more noble and like a king,
Thou canst prevail against my fears and fling
Thy purple round me, till my heart shall grow
Too close against thine heart henceforth to know
How it shook when alone. Why, conquering
May prove as lordly and complete a thing
In lifting upward, as in crushing low!
And as a vanquished soldier yields his sword
To one who lifts him from the bloody earth,
Even so, Belovèd, I at last record,
Here ends my strife. If thou invite me forth,
I rise above abasement at the word.
Make thy love larger to enlarge my worth!

XVII

My poet, thou canst touch on all the notes
God set between His After and Before,
And strike up and strike off the general roar
Of the rushing worlds a melody that floats
In a serene air purely. Antidotes
Of medicated music, answering for
Mankind's forlornest uses, thou canst pour
From thence into their ears. God's will devotes
Thine to such ends, and mine to wait on thine.
How, Dearest, wilt thou have me for most use?
A hope, to sing by gladly? or a fine
Sad memory, with thy songs to interfuse?
A shade, in which to sing—of palm or pine?
A grave, on which to rest from singing? Choose.

XVIII

I never gave a lock of hair away
To a man, Dearest, except this to thee,
Which now upon my fingers thoughtfully
I ring out to the full brown length and say
"Take it." My day of youth went yesterday;
My hair no longer bounds to my foot's glee,
Nor plant I it from rose- or myrtle-tree,
As girls do, any more: it only may
Now shade on two pale cheeks the mark of tears,
Taught drooping from the head that hangs aside
Through sorrow's trick. I thought the funeral-shears
Would take this first, but Love is justified,—
Take it thou,—finding pure, from all those years,
The kiss my mother left here when she died.

XIX

The soul's Rialto hath its merchandize;
I barter curl for curl upon that mart,
And from my poet's forehead to my heart
Receive this lock which outweighs argosies,—
As purply black, as erst to Pindar's eyes
The dim purpureal tresses gloomed athwart
The nine white Muse-brows. For this counterpart, . . .
The bay crown's shade, Belovèd, I surmise,
Still lingers on thy curl, it is so black!
Thus, with a fillet of smooth-kissing breath,
I tie the shadows safe from gliding back,
And lay the gift where nothing hindereth;
Here on my heart, as on thy brow, to lack
No natural heat till mine grows cold in death.

XX

Belovèd, my Belovèd, when I think
That thou wast in the world a year ago,
What time I sat alone here in the snow
And saw no footprint, heard the silence sink
No moment at thy voice, but, link by link,
Went counting all my chains as if that so
They never could fall off at any blow
Struck by thy possible hand,—why, thus I drink
Of life's great cup of wonder! Wonderful,
Never to feel thee thrill the day or night
With personal act or speech,—nor ever cull
Some prescience of thee with the blossoms white
Thou sawest growing! Atheists are as dull,
Who cannot guess God's presence out of sight.

XXI

Say over again, and yet once over again,
That thou dost love me. Though the word repeated
Should seem a "cuckoo-song," as thou dost treat it,
Remember, never to the hill or plain,
Valley and wood, without her cuckoo-strain
Comes the fresh Spring in all her green completed.
Belovèd, I, amid the darkness greeted
By a doubtful spirit-voice, in that doubt's pain
Cry, "Speak once more—thou lovest!" Who can fear
Too many stars, though each in heaven shall roll,
Too many flowers, though each shall crown the year?
Say thou dost love me, love me, love me—toll
The silver iterance!—only minding, Dear,
To love me also in silence with thy soul.

XXII

When our two souls stand up erect and strong,
Face to face, silent, drawing nigh and nigher,
Until the lengthening wings break into fire
At either curvèd point,—what bitter wrong
Can the earth do to us, that we should not long
Be here contented? Think! In mounting higher,
The angels would press on us and aspire
To drop some golden orb of perfect song
Into our deep, dear silence. Let us stay
Rather on earth, Belovèd,—where the unfit
Contrarious moods of men recoil away
And isolate pure spirits, and permit
A place to stand and love in for a day,
With darkness and the death-hour rounding it.

XXIII

Is it indeed so? If I lay here dead,
Wouldst thou miss any life in losing mine?
And would the sun for thee more coldly shine
Because of grave-damps falling round my head?
I marvelled, my Belovèd, when I read
Thy thought so in the letter. I am thine—
But . . . so much to thee? Can I pour thy wine
While my hands tremble? Then my soul, instead
Of dreams of death, resumes life's lower range.
Then, love me, Love! look on me—breathe on me!
As brighter ladies do not count it strange,
For love, to give up acres and degree,
I yield the grave for thy sake, and exchange
My near sweet view of heaven, for earth with thee!

XXIV

Let the world's sharpness like a clasping knife
Shut in upon itself and do no harm
In this close hand of Love, now soft and warm,
And let us hear no sound of human strife
After the click of the shutting. Life to life—
I lean upon thee, Dear, without alarm,
And feel as safe as guarded by a charm
Against the stab of worldlings, who if rife
Are weak to injure. Very whitely still
The lilies of our lives may reassure
Their blossoms from their roots, accessible
Alone to heavenly dews that drop not fewer;
Growing straight, out of man's reach, on the hill.
God only, who made us rich, can make us poor.

XXV

A heavy heart, Belovèd, have I borne
From year to year until I saw thy face,
And sorrow after sorrow took the place
Of all those natural joys as lightly worn
As the stringed pearls, each lifted in its turn
By a beating heart at dance-time. Hopes apace
Were changed to long despairs, till God's own grace
Could scarcely lift above the world forlorn
My heavy heart. Then thou didst bid me bring
And let it drop adown thy calmly great
Deep being! Fast it sinketh, as a thing
Which its own nature does precipitate,
While thine doth close above it, mediating
Betwixt the stars and the unaccomplished fate.

XXVI

I lived with visions for my company
Instead of men and women, years ago,
And found them gentle mates, nor thought to know
A sweeter music than they played to me.
But soon their trailing purple was not free
Of this world's dust, their lutes did silent grow,
And I myself grew faint and blind below
Their vanishing eyes. Then thou didst come—to be,
Belovèd, what they seemed. Their shining fronts,
Their songs, their splendours, (better, yet the same,
As river-water hallowed into fonts)
Met in thee, and from out thee overcame
My soul with satisfaction of all wants:
Because God's gifts put man's best dreams to shame.

XXVII

My own Belovèd, who hast lifted me
From this drear flat of earth where I was thrown,
And, in betwixt the languid ringlets, blown
A life-breath, till the forehead hopefully
Shines out again, as all the angels see,
Before thy saving kiss! My own, my own,
Who camest to me when the world was gone,
And I who looked for only God, found thee!
I find thee; I am safe, and strong, and glad.
As one who stands in dewless asphodel,
Looks backward on the tedious time he had
In the upper life,—so I, with bosom-swell,
Make witness, here, between the good and bad,
That Love, as strong as Death, retrieves as well.

XXVIII

My letters! all dead paper, mute and white!
And yet they seem alive and quivering
Against my tremulous hands which loose the string
And let them drop down on my knee to-night.
This said,—he wished to have me in his sight
Once, as a friend: this fixed a day in spring
To come and touch my hand . . . a simple thing,
Yet I wept for it!—this, . . . the paper's light . . .
Said, Dear, I love thee; and I sank and quailed
As if God's future thundered on my past.
This said, I am thine—and so its ink has paled
With lying at my heart that beat too fast.
And this . . . O Love, thy words have ill availed
If, what this said, I dared repeat at last!

XXIX

I think of thee!—my thoughts do twine and bud
About thee, as wild vines, about a tree,
Put out broad leaves, and soon there's nought to see
Except the straggling green which hides the wood.
Yet, O my palm-tree, be it understood
I will not have my thoughts instead of thee
Who art dearer, better! Rather, instantly
Renew thy presence; as a strong tree should,
Rustle thy boughs and set thy trunk all bare,
And let these bands of greenery which insphere thee,
Drop heavily down,—burst, shattered everywhere!
Because, in this deep joy to see and hear thee
And breathe within thy shadow a new air,
I do not think of thee—I am too near thee.

XXX

I see thine image through my tears to-night,
And yet to-day I saw thee smiling. How
Refer the cause?—Belovèd, is it thou
Or I, who makes me sad? The acolyte
Amid the chanted joy and thankful rite
May so fall flat, with pale insensate brow,
On the altar-stair. I hear thy voice and vow,
Perplexed, uncertain, since thou art out of sight,
As he, in his swooning ears, the choir's amen.
Belovèd, dost thou love? or did I see all
The glory as I dreamed, and fainted when
Too vehement light dilated my ideal,
For my soul's eyes? Will that light come again,
As now these tears come—falling hot and real?

XXXI

Thou comest! all is said without a word.
I sit beneath thy looks, as children do
In the noon-sun, with souls that tremble through
Their happy eyelids from an unaverred
Yet prodigal inward joy. Behold, I erred
In that last doubt! and yet I cannot rue
The sin most, but the occasion—that we two
Should for a moment stand unministered
By a mutual presence. Ah, keep near and close,
Thou dove-like help! and when my fears would rise,
With thy broad heart serenely interpose:
Brood down with thy divine sufficiencies
These thoughts which tremble when bereft of those,
Like callow birds left desert to the skies.

XXXII

The first time that the sun rose on thine oath
To love me, I looked forward to the moon
To slacken all those bonds which seemed too soon
And quickly tied to make a lasting troth.
Quick-loving hearts, I thought, may quickly loathe;
And, looking on myself, I seemed not one
For such man's love!—more like an out-of-tune
Worn viol, a good singer would be wroth
To spoil his song with, and which, snatched in haste,
Is laid down at the first ill-sounding note.
I did not wrong myself so, but I placed
A wrong on thee. For perfect strains may float
'Neath master-hands, from instruments defaced,—
And great souls, at one stroke, may do and doat.

XXXIII

Yes, call me by my pet-name! let me hear
The name I used to run at, when a child,
From innocent play, and leave the cowslips plied,
To glance up in some face that proved me dear
With the look of its eyes. I miss the clear
Fond voices which, being drawn and reconciled
Into the music of Heaven's undefiled,
Call me no longer. Silence on the bier,
While I call God—call God!—so let thy mouth
Be heir to those who are now exanimate.
Gather the north flowers to complete the south,
And catch the early love up in the late.
Yes, call me by that name,—and I, in truth,
With the same heart, will answer and not wait.

XXXIV

With the same heart, I said, I'll answer thee
As those, when thou shalt call me by my name—
Lo, the vain promise! is the same, the same,
Perplexed and ruffled by life's strategy?
When called before, I told how hastily
I dropped my flowers or brake off from a game.
To run and answer with the smile that came
At play last moment, and went on with me
Through my obedience. When I answer now,
I drop a grave thought, break from solitude;
Yet still my heart goes to thee—ponder how—
Not as to a single good, but all my good!
Lay thy hand on it, best one, and allow
That no child's foot could run fast as this blood.

XXXV

If I leave all for thee, wilt thou exchange
And be all to me? Shall I never miss
Home-talk and blessing and the common kiss
That comes to each in turn, nor count it strange,
When I look up, to drop on a new range
Of walls and floors, another home than this?
Nay, wilt thou fill that place by me which is
Filled by dead eyes too tender to know change
That's hardest. If to conquer love, has tried,
To conquer grief, tries more, as all things prove,
For grief indeed is love and grief beside.
Alas, I have grieved so I am hard to love.
Yet love me—wilt thou? Open thy heart wide,
And fold within, the wet wings of thy dove.

XXXVI

When we met first and loved, I did not build
Upon the event with marble. Could it mean
To last, a love set pendulous between
Sorrow and sorrow? Nay, I rather thrilled,
Distrusting every light that seemed to gild
The onward path, and feared to overlean
A finger even. And, though I have grown serene
And strong since then, I think that God has willed
A still renewable fear . . . O love, O troth . . .
Lest these enclaspèd hands should never hold,
This mutual kiss drop down between us both
As an unowned thing, once the lips being cold.
And Love, be false! if he, to keep one oath,
Must lose one joy, by his life's star foretold.

XXXVII

Pardon, oh, pardon, that my soul should make
Of all that strong divineness which I know
For thine and thee, an image only so
Formed of the sand, and fit to shift and break.
It is that distant years which did not take
Thy sovranty, recoiling with a blow,
Have forced my swimming brain to undergo
Their doubt and dread, and blindly to forsake
Thy purity of likeness and distort
Thy worthiest love to a worthless counterfeit.
As if a shipwrecked Pagan, safe in port,
His guardian sea-god to commemorate,
Should set a sculptured porpoise, gills a-snort
And vibrant tail, within the temple-gate.

XXXVIII

First time he kissed me, he but only kissed
The fingers of this hand wherewith I write;
And ever since, it grew more clean and white.
Slow to world-greetings, quick with its "O, list,"
When the angels speak. A ring of amethyst
I could not wear here, plainer to my sight,
Than that first kiss. The second passed in height
The first, and sought the forehead, and half missed,
Half falling on the hair. O beyond meed!
That was the chrism of love, which love's own crown,
With sanctifying sweetness, did precede
The third upon my lips was folded down
In perfect, purple state; since when, indeed,
I have been proud and said, "My love, my own."

XXXIX

Because thou hast the power and own'st the grace
To look through and behind this mask of me,
(Against which, years have beat thus blanchingly,
With their rains,) and behold my soul's true face,
The dim and weary witness of life's race, —
Because thou hast the faith and love to see,
Through that same soul's distracting lethargy,
The patient angel waiting for a place
In the new Heavens, — because nor sin nor woe,
Nor God's infliction, nor death's neighbourhood,
Nor all which others viewing, turn to go,
Nor all which makes me tired of all, self-viewed, —
Nothing repels thee, . . . Dearest, teach me so
To pour out gratitude, as thou dost, good!

XL

Oh, yes! they love through all this world of ours!
I will not gainsay love, called love forsooth:
I have heard love talked in my early youth,
And since, not so long back but that the flowers
Then gathered, smell still. Mussulmans and Giaours
Throw kerchiefs at a smile, and have no ruth
For any weeping. Polypheme's white tooth
Slips on the nut if, after frequent showers,
The shell is over-smooth, — and not so much
Will turn the thing called love, aside to hate
Or else to oblivion. But thou art not such
A lover, my Belovèd! thou canst wait
Through sorrow and sickness, to bring souls to touch,
And think it soon when others cry "Too late."

XLI

I thank all who have loved me in their hearts,
With thanks and love from mine. Deep thanks to all
Who paused a little near the prison-wall
To hear my music in its louder parts
Ere they went onward, each one to the mart's
Or temple's occupation, beyond call.
But thou, who, in my voice's sink and fall
When the sob took it, thy divinest Art's
Own instrument didst drop down at thy foot
To harken what I said between my tears, . . .
Instruct me how to thank thee! Oh, to shoot
My soul's full meaning into future years,
That they should lend it utterance, and salute
Love that endures, from life that disappears!

XLII

My future will not copy fair my past—
I wrote that once; and thinking at my side
My ministering life-angel justified
The word by his appealing look upcast
To the white throne of God, I turned at last,
And there, instead, saw thee, not unallied
To angels in thy soul! Then I, long tried
By natural ills, received the comfort fast,
While budding, at thy sight, my pilgrim's staff
Gave out green leaves with morning dews impearled.
I seek no copy now of life's first half:
Leave here the pages with long musing curled,
And write me new my future's epigraph,
New angel mine, unhoped for in the world!

XLIII

How do I love thee? Let me count the ways.
I love thee to the depth and breadth and height
My soul can reach, when feeling out of sight
For the ends of Being and ideal Grace.
I love thee to the level of everyday's
Most quiet need, by sun and candlelight.
I love thee freely, as men strive for Right;
I love thee purely, as they turn from Praise.
I love thee with the passion put to use
In my old griefs, and with my childhood's faith.
I love thee with a love I seemed to lose
With my lost saints,—I love thee with the breath,
Smiles, tears, of all my life!—and, if God choose,
I shall but love thee better after death.

XLIV

Belovèd, thou hast brought me many flowers
Plucked in the garden, all the summer through,
And winter, and it seemed as if they grew
In this close room, nor missed the sun and showers.
So, in the like name of that love of ours,
Take back these thoughts which here unfolded too,
And which on warm and cold days I withdrew
From my heart's ground. Indeed, those beds and bowers
Be overgrown with bitter weeds and rue,
And wait thy weeding; yet here's eglantine,
Here's ivy!—take them, as I used to do
Thy flowers, and keep them where they shall not pine.
Instruct thine eyes to keep their colours true,
And tell thy soul, their roots are left in mine.